D1111041

The
Clockwork
Three

MATTHEW J. KIRBY

SCHOLASTIC INC.

New York   Toronto   London   Auckland
Sydney   Mexico City   New Delhi   Hong Kong

If you purchased this book without a cover, you should be aware that this book is stolen property. It was reported as "unsold and destroyed" to the publisher, and neither the author nor the publisher has received any payment for this "stripped book."

No part of this publication may be reproduced, stored in a retrieval system, or transmitted in any form or by any means, electronic, mechanical, photocopying, recording, or otherwise, without written permission of the publisher. For information regarding permission, write to Scholastic Inc., Attention: Permissions Department, 557 Broadway, New York, NY 10012.

ISBN 978-0-545-20338-8

Copyright © 2010 by Matthew J. Kirby

All rights reserved. Published by Scholastic Inc. SCHOLASTIC and associated logos are trademarks and/or registered trademarks of Scholastic Inc.

10 9 8 7 6 5   14 15 16/0

Printed in the U.S.A.   40

First Scholastic paperback printing, October 2011
Book design by Elizabeth B. Parisi & Kristina Iulo

For Azure

Table of Contents

CHAPTER 1

The Green Violin

WHEN GIUSEPPE FOUND THE GREEN VIOLIN, HE DID NOT THINK it would help him escape. He did not think it would play at all when he spotted it floating in the harbor. It bobbed and bumped around beneath the pier, still in its case, and a satisfied seagull perched on it. Giuseppe shooed the bird away and fished the case out of the water with a long pole. Inside it, he found the most beautiful, most remarkable violin he had ever seen. The varnished wood rippled deeper than green, like river water. And the instrument was dry, the velvet lining only a little damp around the edges.

A toothless old woman hovered nearby. She smacked her lips and craned her neck to see what Giuseppe had found, but he closed the case and latched it before she could get a look. He pushed through the other scavengers gathered on the wharf, and his boots beat the pier boards like a drum. Moments later, they clicked on wet cobblestones as he sprinted from the shipyards.

He had risked time scrounging the docks because the streets had been generous that day. He had played his old fiddle all morning up at the corner of Dorset Street on the square, and before the sun had even set he had one dollar and twenty-five cents in his pocket for Stephano. He was playing when the first rumors began to flutter around the city like scraps of newspaper. A fine ship loaded with cargo from France had wrecked in that terrible storm the previous night, and the waves had flung the flotsam up and down the New England bay. Giuseppe counted and recounted his money all day, and when he thought he had earned enough, he raced down to comb the beaches and the docks for storm-tossed treasure. He had worried that all the good stuff would be gone.

But now here he was, clutching this green violin, by all appearances an extraordinary instrument and far nicer than the one he usually played. He slipped through the streets, darting between pedestrians and horses and carriages like a sparrow. He found a deserted alleyway and crouched down behind a sour-smelling crate of spoiled cabbages.

There, he felt safe enough to lift the green violin from its case. It was mirror-smooth in his hand, yet soft to the touch. He noticed its delicate inlay, and a scroll carved in the shape of a flower blossom at the head. It truly was a magnificent instrument, but even then, Giuseppe did not think it would help him escape.

He had to pass a few hours yet before he could return to Stephano's lair on Crosby Street. He thought he might as well try to make a few more pennies. The extra money might earn him another crust of bread for supper. Giuseppe took his new violin to one of his favorite corners a few blocks off Gilbert Square, near the Old Rock Church. But before he had even begun to play, one of the older boys sauntered up to him.

"Shove off, runt," the boy said. He smiled, but it was a dirty smile that called nothing but nasty thoughts to mind. "This is my spot."

"I was here, Paolo. I staked it."

The older boy set his hand organ down on the ground and stood up to his full height. He was still smiling. "Boy, you're just dumb, aren't you? Got no sense of survival."

Giuseppe raised his voice. "This is my corner. I was here."

Paolo walked over to a stack of bricks piled against a shabby wall. He picked one up and tossed it back and forth between his hands. "I said, shove off."

The two boys glared at each other. Men and women walked around them, and some strolled right between them as if they were not even there. Giuseppe might have been able to take Paolo if he had Alfeo or stout little Ferro with him. But he was alone and outmatched. He backed away.

"Hang on, what you got there?" Paolo pointed at the violin case.

"Nothing."

"Give it here."

"No."

Paolo cocked his arm back, hefting the brick. "I said give it!"

"No!" Giuseppe ran.

Two paces away, the brick shot past his head, close enough to leave dust in his hair. Giuseppe did not miss a step. He did not slow down, even though he knew that Paolo would not follow him, not when he had that corner. Not so close to nightfall when every single busker out there played for those last few cents before heading back to their padrones. Some nights it was near dawn before Giuseppe had enough money and nerve to head in.

He jogged around and checked a few more corners, all taken. He saw some boys that were littler than him, and he could have driven them off if he wanted to, but he had done that before and he was always ashamed and mad at himself afterward. Gaslights sputtered and hissed up and down the streets as he ran.

He finally settled on a rotten corner at Basket Street and the Old Fort Road, down near the tenements where traffic was slow and poor. But Stephano never came down there to spy on them, so at least it was a chance to try out his new instrument. He tossed his hat on the ground to catch the coins, and raised the violin to his chin. He drew the bow over the strings.

And he stopped.

The clear sound that spilled out of the green violin resonated off the walls. It seemed to penetrate the alleyways and soar up the rickety wooden staircases clinging to the outsides of the buildings. It cut through the street noise, the clopping hooves, the shouts, the factory machinery grinding away around the city. It slid through all of that like a slender hand parting a curtain.

The sidewalk traffic around him had paused midstride. That time of day it was mostly men on their way home, greasy from work. Giuseppe looked in their sooty eyes, and they looked in his, waiting.

He swallowed and chose one of his favorite songs. Many years ago he had heard a woman humming it through an open window as he passed by one of the city's hospitals. The tune made him think of the grassy hills and tree-lined roads back home in Italy. He laid the bow on the strings and played.

As he fiddled that song on the green violin, he felt a new sensation. He played the music. It came from inside him. But once it left his hands through the violin it was as if it turned around and came back to him as something different from what he sent out. The song acquired the autonomy

of a living thing. Giuseppe watched the invisible tune light on each pass-
erby like a cherry blossom carried on a breeze. The tired bodies, stooped
and trod upon, rose up. Their eyes, rimmed with dirt and yellow from
smoke, filled with tears.

The copper and silver coins flashed in Giuseppe's hat. When he finished, the passersby applauded. Applause for him! Applause because of
his new violin.

As the audience broke up and moved on, he counted the money: thirty-
three cents over two dollars, and not in small coins. Most of it was dimes
and quarter-dollars. Giuseppe had never made that much in a day. None
of Stephano's boys had.

And that was when Giuseppe first started to believe the violin could
help him escape, something he had always thought impossible.

He looked at the coins all worn smooth by countless hands, warm from
people's pockets, and the idea came to him of how he might escape. He
felt tears coming, and he pulled his sleeve over his fist to scrub them out.

Giuseppe wondered how much it would cost to buy a boat ticket from
America back to Italy. How much would it cost to see his brother and
sister again? Whatever the price, it seemed to be reachable now, when it
never had before. He had just made two dollars and thirty-three cents
on a single ditty. He would play a thousand just like it if it meant he
could go home. He did not know how he would hide the green violin or
the money from Stephano, but Giuseppe decided he had to try.

He put the violin back in its case, so much more careful with it now.
Some of the onlookers still milled around, perhaps hoping for another
song. Giuseppe bowed his head to them and headed up the street.

He kept off the main thoroughfares to avoid being seen by any of the
other boys. Paolo had noticed the violin, but he was all bluster and lies,

and Stephano knew it. Giuseppe could handle Paolo. But it would be a lot worse for him if someone like Ezio saw him, someone that Stephano trusted.

Giuseppe cut through the back ways and climbed a few low walls and soon arrived at the Old Rock Church. He checked the corner to make sure Paolo was gone before diving into the dark churchyard. He loved how quiet this place had become since they finished the new cathedral on the square. No one came here anymore.

Tonight, the church lights were on and Reverend Grey would be inside, but Giuseppe did not want him to know what he was about to do. Over the last few years the older man had befriended him, even though Giuseppe had never even been inside the chapel. Giuseppe never felt afraid here.

There were monuments and carved crosses and urns and obelisks. Some of the tombstones were etched with the profiled likenesses of the great men buried underneath them, men who had at one time, long past, been important to the city. Giuseppe sometimes talked to them like they were his friends. But in one corner, next to a rosebush, a watchful angel spread its wings over the little tomb of a child. The angel had been carved in the likeness of a young girl, with long hair and a beautiful face, both soft and sad.

Giuseppe walked up to it and whispered, "Hello, Marietta."

Giuseppe did not remember much of his home back in Italy. It was all bits and pieces. He remembered his mother and father, and how one day they were there, and the next day they were gone.

He remembered the funeral in the church full of black veils. He remembered his uncle's smelly cottage, and the man that came jangling a bag of money. He remembered his brother screaming, and his uncle smacking him around, and the man yanking on Giuseppe's arm to pull him away. Giuseppe had gone with him, and the last thing he remembered before the boat and the ocean was his sister, Marietta, crying in the middle of the road.

This statue, the sad angel, reminded him so much of her.

"I'm coming home soon," he said.

Near the angel was another crypt. It belonged to the body and memory of a man named Phineas Stroop, and it had a cracked flagstone on its backside. One day Giuseppe had pulled on that fragment out of curiosity. When it came free, exposing the black insides of the tomb, he gasped and covered his mouth and put the piece right back where it belonged.

No one would think to look in there for a violin.

Giuseppe counted out enough coin to satisfy Stephano for the night, one dollar and ten cents. He grabbed the cold rock with his fingers, begged the pardon of the ghost of Mister Stroop, and held his breath. He pulled the chunk out, and the opening was the deepest, darkest thing he had ever seen. He pinched his eyes shut and set the money and violin inside.

"Now, Mister Stroop." Giuseppe replaced the flagstone. "I've trusted you with something very important. It's going to help me earn enough money to go home and find my brother and sister. So it's important that no one steals it. You understand?"

The stone always understood.

"Good," said Giuseppe. "Don't tell Reverend Grey, either."

He left the churchyard and strolled down the street, as nonchalant as he could manage. His secret thrilled him, but it scared him, too. He did not want to think about what Stephano would do if he ever found out. It would mean the rat cellar for sure, but for how long? Three days? Four?

Giuseppe shuddered. The longest he had ever spent down there was one night.

Several blocks later, he rounded on Crosby Street and shrank to the side of the road. The lamps here drizzled a greenish glow, almost a haze, as if this forsaken part of the city were sickly and frail. At this time of night, bigger boys could be lurking in the shadows. They had jumped Giuseppe before and stolen his money. Sometimes a few of the younger boys waited to band together before going in, but no one had stuck around tonight. Giuseppe reached down a storm drain and pulled out a length of heavy pipe he kept hidden there.

Padrones were not the only criminals taking refuge here. Crosby Street crawled like a warren with pickpockets, streetwalkers, and murderers. They skulked in doorways or gathered in loud, drunken mobs outside the alehouses and gambling halls. Garbage and debris massed and reeked in the street. Empty and broken barrels had been stacked at regular intervals up and down the quarter like defensive barriers. Giuseppe had once overheard a policeman whisper in fear that he would rather take to the open seas in a leaky rowboat during a northern gale than set one foot down Crosby Street.

But the vicious men and brazen women here did not really frighten Giuseppe. Every scoundrel here knew that if they ever touched him or any of the other boys, they would have to answer to Stephano.

Giuseppe darted from one pile of garbage to the next, looking over his shoulder with every other breath. A stray mutt half-bald with mange crossed in front of him. Partway to Stephano's, he caught movement up ahead in an alley. Some careless boy had let an elbow slip into view. Giuseppe twisted his sweaty grip on the pipe. He crept closer and listened. He heard crying.

8

He peered around the corner. One of the newest little boys huddled with his knees tucked up, head down, arms wrapped around his shins. He shook with silent sobs.

Giuseppe stepped into view. "What's the matter?" The boy looked up, panicked as a cornered alley cat. "It's all right." Giuseppe sat down next to him. "I won't hurt you."

Tu sei Giuseppe? The boy sniffed and wiped his nose with the back of his sleeve.

"Yeah. I'm Giuseppe. What's your name?"

"Pietro," he said, and started wailing. *"Che cosa farò?"*

"Shut up, kid." Giuseppe tried to put his hand over Pietro's mouth. "Be quiet. You want the older boys to hear you?"

Pietro fell silent and took a deep breath. "No."

"And talk English, will you?"

"For why?"

"'Cause Stephano will beat you if you don't, that's why."

"I no speak English good."

"You'll pick it up."

"You speak good. How long you here?"

Giuseppe counted back, something he usually tried not to do. "Stephano brought me over when I was five. I'm eleven now, so that makes six years."

"That is long."

"Yes, very long." Giuseppe stood. "You ready to go in? You can come with me."

Pietro stayed on the ground and shook his head.

Giuseppe rolled his eyes. "Look, I don't need this. Why won't you come with me?"

"I no have money."

"How much did you make?"

Pietro shied away from him.

"I'm not going to steal it," said Giuseppe. "I swear. How much?"

"Seventeen cents."

Giuseppe's stomach tightened. "That's all?"

Pietro nodded, head down.

Giuseppe tapped the pipe against his leg. This was bad. The kid would get a beating for sure, and a severe one. Stephano liked to break them early and hard. Giuseppe swore and dug into his pockets.

"Here." He pulled out some of his own money. "Take this. It's seventy cents."

Pietro sagged with relief and looked like he was about to cry again.

Giuseppe scratched his head. "You still don't have much. You might not get supper, but trust me, that's better than the rat cellar."

Pietro closed his small fist around the money. "Thank you."

"Come on." Giuseppe put his arm around the boy and ushered him out of the alley. They trotted the last few yards to Stephano's building. Each story of the wooden structure leaned over farther than the one below it, and its windows stared lightless and hollow into the street below. The exterior of splitting timber slats and flaking shingles appeared benign enough.

A couple of other boys approached the front door, and Giuseppe hung back. He and Pietro waited and watched. No one accosted the newcomers. They made it inside.

"Let's go," said Giuseppe. He still had forty cents. He had brought Stephano less than that before. He could take the punishment, or at least he hoped he could.

Pietro lifted the latch and opened the door. He slipped through and was gone. Giuseppe was about to follow when someone grabbed him from behind. His feet came off the ground, and his assailant dragged him into the street. The pipe flew from his hands.

"You make a lot today, Giuseppe?" The attacker threw him into an oily puddle. "Of course you did."

Giuseppe rolled over and looked up. Ezio towered over him, thin and as cruel as an icy night spent in the gutter. He held a nail-spiked club he had made from the heavy leg of a table. "Give me your money," he said.

"Not tonight, Ezio. I only have forty cents."

"You're lying."

"I'm not."

Ezio appeared confused. "You always bring in more than that." Then he flicked his eyes toward the front door after Pietro. "Oh, I see."

Giuseppe shook his head. "No."

"You know the rules. You can't give another boy your money."

"I didn't."

"Well, if you did, you deserve a whipping just for being stupid. But I think you're in for a painful night, anyway. Now hand over whatever you got left."

Giuseppe scanned the street. He had a clear escape, but running would do no good. Ezio would just wait for him. Stephano let the older boy stay out all night. Giuseppe glowered and pulled out the last of his coins. "Here." He held out his hand.

Ezio snatched the money. Then he grabbed Giuseppe and spun him around. He locked his arm around Giuseppe's neck, choking him, and burrowed through all his pockets. When he found nothing, he slapped Giuseppe across the face and laughed. "Better go inside. Get it over with." He started to walk away, but then he turned back. "Paolo said you had something earlier. He said it looked like a violin."

"You mean this?" Giuseppe held up his well-worn instrument.

Ezio shook his head. "He said you had a new one."

"You deserve a whipping just for believing Paolo."

Ezio grinned. He set off down the street, prowling for the last few stragglers to come in.

Giuseppe hesitated in front of the building. He thought about the whip, the muddy ground in the rat cellar, the nibbling teeth and cold tails. He was tempted to go back to the churchyard for some money. He had enough hidden there.

But then he thought about home, of chasing his brother through the sheep pastures, and Giuseppe stayed where he was. If he let himself, he would use a little of that money every night, and soon it would be gone. He refused to let himself do that, or he would never earn enough for the boat ticket. It was enough that he had the green violin.

He went inside.

CHAPTER 2

Coal Chutes and Clockwork

TODAY FREDERICK SEARCHED FOR THE SCRAP OF METAL THAT would become the chest plate of the clockwork man. He patrolled the factory yards and the dry docks, hands in his pockets, scanning the jagged piles of discarded iron and steel. He had the rough dimensions and measurements in mind but would only know the piece once he found it, and when he did find it, the clockwork man would be nearly complete. Everything except for the head.

He had known from the beginning that the head would be the most challenging obstacle in the construction of his automaton. But he also knew it would be the most impressive and brilliant aspect of his accomplishment. Once it was complete, there would be no denying his freedom from apprenticeship. He would have his own shop. His own designs. Frederick would be the youngest journeyman clockmaker in the city, but also the greatest.

He came to the docks where the wharves sagged under the weight of gaggles of street people. Master Branch had mentioned something about a wrecked ship, with its hull ripped open on the rocks and goods strewn around the harbor. All these people must have descended to see what they could salvage from the disaster. Quite a nuisance, really. But he thought that perhaps there might be something interesting he could use.

Someone bumped him. "Pardon me." A busker boy shoved past Frederick, carrying a violin case.

Frederick opened his mouth to reply, but the boy hurried on without looking back.

The storm had left powdery clouds behind, and a shade of blue in the sky that showed all the other blues what they should look like. Frederick pushed into the crowd and peered down at the debris floating in the water, mostly fragments of wood and broken furniture, and the occasional dress or shirt or bolt of fabric undulating with the waves. Several chests had been hauled up to the pier and opened. People rooted through them like maggots. Nothing of use to him.

Frederick pulled out a handkerchief and held it to his nose against the pervasive smell of the docks: the fish decay, mildew, and seaweed. But these hundreds of working men and women dumped their own overwhelming odors of sweat, filth, and machine oil into the air. They laughed and argued all around him, grease-smeared and vacant-eyed. Their scent and commotion set his head to pounding. He rubbed his temples and closed his eyes. When he opened them, he saw her.

Mrs. Treeless, unmoving and poised like an iron stake driven into the crowd.

Her tiny eyes had found him, too, and she glared. Then she opened her mouth in a toothless grin. The sight of her unlocked doors and threw them wide onto so many memories that Frederick had kept shut away. He froze and began to pant. His stomach ached with remembered hunger. His arms dropped to his sides, exhausted and weak. His back twisted up, anticipating blows that did not fall anymore. She bore a mild and passive smile, lingered for a few moments, and then turned away from him, vanishing into the chaos.

Frederick had to get out of the mob and away from the awful memories pressing in. He forced his way through the crowd of bodies, shaking, with his eyes on the ground. He stumbled from the docks and down the open streets, and he eventually found a quiet spot where he leaned against a coal cart. Frederick breathed through his nose, inhaling slow and deep.

"It's all right," he said to himself. "It's all right." The flutter of panic subsided, and the trembling left his bones.

"You all right there, son?" The coal man looked like a shadow of himself, all dusted black. He held a feed sack up for his mule, and the animal munched away, oblivious to anything else going on.

"I'm fine."

"You sure? You're white as a plucked turkey."

"Thank you, but I'm fine. I just need to catch my breath."

The coal man patted his mule's neck. "Solomon here thinks he's a Thoroughbred, and he eats like one, so it'll be a while yet before we get back on our route. You're welcome to hop up in my cart for a sit."

"Thank you, but I . . ." Frederick looked into the cart. The bed was half filled with coal, with a couple of wide shovels laid on top of the pile. And a chute for pouring the coal down into people's basements from the street. The memories of the workhouse retreated. Frederick measured with his eye. Cut to the right length, a coal chute like that could wrap right around the clockwork man.

Frederick walked up casual-like to the coal man, and rubbed behind one of the mule's long ears. "Is your chute made of tin?"

"Yup. Got to be lightweight so's I can haul it."

"Do all coal men have one?"

"Sure."

Frederick nodded. "I think I'm feeling better now."

"You look better."

"Thanks. You have a nice evening. Solomon, too."

"You do the same, son."

Frederick marched off. He knew of a yard down on the river where barges hauled in coal for the city, and where coal men went to pick up their loads. He was bound to find a spare chute lying around. To get there he followed Basket Street, which cut a broad and angled path through the city. From its crown at Gilbert Square, the busy road ran by the docks and the shipyards, skirted the dense and dangerous tenements, and bottomed out at the Quay on the River Delilah where the tanners and butchers dumped their toxins and offal, and where the seaward current carried the foul sludge into the bay.

The Quay blared with the shouting and cursing of longshoremen, the bleating of farm animals, the clanging of machinery, and the thumping of barrels and crates. Foreign goods entered the city by way of the harbor, but local goods came in from the countryside by river barge at the Quay. Frederick kept his hands and arms in close and tried to be as small as he could. He bolstered himself against the crowd and merged with the swirling traffic of merchants, laborers, cattle, and carts that stretched for a quarter mile along the river.

A cloud of gray dust hung over the coal yard at the far end. Frederick kept his eye on that spot and one hand on his pocket. He had been picked clean in places like this, where people were so unpredictable and out of control. Frederick felt the cool prickle of sweat on his back. Before he reached the coal yard he had been jabbed in the leg by a billy goat's horns, sworn at by multiple men he bumped into, and glared at by a pretty young woman for seemingly no reason at all.

Frederick came to the coal yard's high wooden fence and followed it to the gate. Coal men passed through the entrance with empty carts, and then rolled back out fully laden. Before entering, men had to put out their pipes and cigars so as not to risk igniting the explosive dust in the air. A few of them lingered at the exit gate to relight. Frederick leaned toward them, listening.

"You believe that storm?" one of them asked another.

"It was a bad one. My roof leaked all night. Had to leave my boy home today on account of he got sick from the damp."

"Landlords." He spat.

"It's not so bad. Rent's cheap, so I can't complain too awful much."

"You wouldn't complain if that worthless roof of yours ripped clean off, O'Malley."

Through the entry gate Frederick spotted the huge black mounds of coal bulking under high-roofed structures. He sneaked in alongside a cart, and once through, he dodged behind a nearby shed. He ducked down and surveyed the yard. Coal men backed their carts up to the mounds and then worked to pile them full. Dark rocks rained down, and to a man the workers were blackened. There were shovels every-where, but no coal chutes that Frederick could see. He evaluated his chances of finding an unused chute, and crept forward until he was eye level with a window into the shed.

He peered through the dirty glass. More shovels stacked inside. Some other tools. But in a corner a couple of coal chutes leaned against the wall. Frederick tried the window, and it creaked open. He looked around to make sure no one was watching, then climbed through it.

The dusty air in the shed choked him, and he wiped his eyes. The chutes were old and battered, but he could pound out the dents back at the workshop, so he picked the better of the two, and lifted it. It weighed more than he had expected, but he could manage it. Frederick set it down and opened the shed door. He swung the chute up and over to rest it on his back, his hands over his head to hold it steady. He stepped out pretending he knew exactly where he was going and what he was doing.

No one stopped him as he crossed the yard, until he reached the exit gate where a foreman checked paper receipts to make sure the coal men had paid for their loads. Frederick tried to slip past him.

"Oy, where you going with that?"

Frederick turned his whole body around, swinging the coal chute. "It fell off our cart. I was just coming back for it."

The foreman folded his hairy arms across his chest. "Whose cart?"

"My pa's."

"Who's your pa?"

"O'Malley."

The foreman's eyes narrowed. "O'Malley, huh?"

Frederick bounced a little. "Come on, mister, my pa's waiting for me."

"All right then, go on with you."

Frederick spun around and left the coal yard behind. With the chute on his back, the thick crowds on the Quay would make it difficult to return the way he had come. He cut through an alley, and came out onto an unfamiliar street. He considered asking for directions, but thought that he could certainly find his way well enough on his own. He followed the street, and then followed another, trying to head in the general direction of Master Branch's workshop. He stopped every few blocks to give his back a rest from bending, and to straighten out his neck. He took a few wrong turns, and hit a few dead ends, until he became lost.

Hours passed, and the setting sunlight tipped the tops of the buildings, tossing the narrow streets into shadow. It would be full dark soon. There was no question now. Frederick needed to ask for directions, but he hated doing so. He looked around at the pedestrians sharing the quiet street with him. Three grumpy-looking men milled outside a tobacconist's shop but were not saying much to one another. A washerwoman carrying a heavy bundle of laundry over her head trudged by him with an expression of such exhaustion that Frederick did not feel right asking her for anything.

Then he spotted a young woman wearing a white apron, and a maid's kerchief over chestnut hair. She looked to be about his age.

"Excuse me." Frederick set the coal chute down. "Could I trouble you for directions?"

She smiled. "I haven't seen your cart and donkey, if that's what you're looking for." She had large green eyes.

"What? Oh, the coal chute. No, I'm not a coal man."

"Then why are you carrying that around?"

Frederick shook his head, irritated. "I need the metal. Look, can you give me directions or not?"

She pursed her lips and nodded. "Where do you need to go?"

"Gilbert Square."

"I've just come from there." She turned and pointed up the street. "Follow this road, and you'll come to a synagogue. Take a left there, and then take the second right. Follow that until you hit Basket Street. From there —"

"I know my way from there."

"Good night, then." She turned away, seeming irritated.

"Wait."

She turned back.

"Thank you," Frederick said.

"You're welcome. Travel safely."

Frederick watched her go, and he noticed how long and thick her braids were. They fell like ropes from beneath her kerchief, down her back to her waist. He wished he had asked for her name. He shrugged and hauled the coal chute down the road. The directions she had given him took him past the brightly lit synagogue, around corners, and eventually onto Basket Street, just as she had said.

A short while later he emerged onto Gilbert Square, awash with yellow light and people finely dressed, operagoers and rich folk out dining. The Gilbert Hotel shone with light from every one of its hundred windows. The New Bristol Opera House, bearing its impressive clock face, glittered both from the golden accents on its columned architecture and the jewels in the dresses and hair of the women waiting on its steps. The cathedral loomed over the square, gargoyled and treacherous up high among its dark buttresses and spires, warm and inviting through the wide-open doors at its base.

Frederick gave the spectacle one look and no more. He crossed the square, passing under the ominous dome of the Archer Museum on the opposite side from the hotel. As immense as the building seemed from the outside, the museum had disappointed Frederick his first time through. He had enjoyed wandering among its displays, peering over the objects, artifacts, and curios brought back from distant countries, kingdoms, and empires, but he was dissatisfied with the quantity of what he saw. He felt there should have been much more.

Frederick left the square and entered into the district of the city's craftsmen. Master Branch had his workshop only two streets over from the clockmakers' guildhall. The old man lived above his store, and so had Frederick ever since the old man had rescued him from Mrs. Treeless and the orphanage.

Frederick saw that the lights were out in the shop, but on in the apartment above. He set the coal chute in the alleyway behind their building. The shop bell rang as he let himself in through the front door with his key.

"Master Branch?" he called from the shop's darkened front room. Light tumbled down a narrow staircase to the floor from upstairs. He shut the door behind him and locked it. "It's me, Frederick."

"You're out late tonight," came a voice from above. "Having fun, I hope?"

Frederick clomped up the stairs. "Some. How was your evening?"

"Usual."

Frederick entered the wood-paneled main room of Master Branch's home. It functioned as a kitchen, a living room, a dining room, and a library without any shelves. Stacks and stacks of books lined the walls and stood ready as if they hoped to be on shelves one day. The low ceiling made Frederick feel as though he always had to hunch, but somehow the effect was warm and comforting. Master Branch sat by the fire reading, a cup of coffee on the small table beside him. He looked up with his sharp eyes.

"Is that coal dust, Frederick?"

"Yes. A coal man dumped his load almost on top of me. Nearly choked me to death."

"Hmm. Very inconsiderate." Master Branch returned to his reading, his thin white hair like a fuzz of hoarfrost on his head. "There's some soup if you're hungry. Split pea."

"Thank you." Frederick ladled up a bowl from the cookstove, grabbed what was left of a loaf of crusty bread, and sat down at the table. "A lot of commotion down at the docks today."

"What's that?"

"Commotion. On the docks."

"Oh. So I understand. You went down?"

"Not for long. There wasn't much left."

"Too bad," Master Branch said, but Frederick could see the old man had his eyes and his thoughts in his book. They fell silent, and the only sounds in the room were of the fire settling and popping, and Frederick chewing.

"I saw Mrs. Treeless today," Frederick said.

Master Branch looked up.

"You remember her?" Frederick fidgeted with his spoon. "From the orphanage."

The old man closed his book. "I remember her. A vile woman."

"Yeah."

Master Branch's forehead was creased in worry. "Do you want to talk about it, lad?"

Frederick paused. "No."

"Are you sure?"

"I'm sure." Better to shut tight the doors on those memories.

"All right, then."

More silence, and a short while later, Master Branch stood up. He rubbed his eyes and stretched. "Well, I'm off to bed. Good work today. Very good work."

Frederick did not thank him. "Good night, Master Branch."

"I'll be at the guildhall most of tomorrow. A few apprentices are presenting their works, hoping to make journeyman."

"Can I come?"

"What for?"

Fredrick shrugged. "No reason."

"Lad, you're not fooling anyone. As bright as you are for your age, you are only thirteen. You are not ready, and when you get one chance to present yourself to the guild —"

"That's not a rule."

"Perhaps not, but in all my years I have never seen an apprentice make journeyman after failing his first examination."

Frederick scowled, and his frustration compressed into a chunk of bitterness as gnarled as a peach pit.

"You will make journeyman," Master Branch said. "But not for years. *Scandentes festini casus subitos patiuntur.*"

"What does that mean?"

"It's Latin. It means 'Hasty climbers suffer sudden falls.' Try to be patient, and remember that I'm only looking after your interests."

Frederick nodded without accepting. The fact was, none of Master Branch's previous apprentices had ever made journeyman. Not one.

The old man ducked into his bedroom. "Good night," he said, and shut the door.

Frederick finished eating and cleared his plate. He brushed his crumbs off the table into the palm of his hand, and tossed them in the washbasin. He lit an oil lamp to take downstairs, where he had a bed in a small room behind the counter. Master Branch insisted he sleep down there to make sure no thief broke in and stole the merchandise during the night. Frederick went down and waited a short while until he thought Master Branch would be asleep. When he heard faint snoring coming from the bedroom upstairs, he brought the coal chute in.

Frederick kept the clockwork man in the basement beneath the shop because Master Branch never went down there. The space was small and cramped, but there was a long workbench and an absence of windows so Frederick could spend his late nights there in peace.

He sized up the coal chute, satisfied with how well it fit. He would not be able to cut the metal tonight because of the noise it would make. He would wait until tomorrow when Master Branch was away on guild business, and then he would outfit the clockwork man with a chest. After that he would complete the head, the trickiest, most difficult component of the clockwork. But after that, freedom.

He would not fail as Master Branch feared. He was ready. Once he finished the clockwork man, and they saw how magnificent it was, they would have to let him work. Then he could finally be on his own, independent, self-reliant.

Then he would not have to count on anyone for anything.

CHAPTER 3

A Strange Guest

I N THE EARLY MORNING HOURS, HANNAH READ AT THE TABLE BY the dim light of dawn. She leaned in close to the pages, chin resting on her folded arms, eyes racing over the words, like chasing butterflies over the hills, to catch as many as she could before going to work. She wondered at how such tales of magic could be contained by mere paper and ink for her to read again and again. Which she had.

Hannah kept the wick turned low and had to squint to read until the tender light of the new day filled the one room of her family's shabby tenement apartment. With the dawn came noises from the street, wagon wheels creaking and knocking over the cobblestones as if the waking city were stretching and cracking its joints.

Her two younger sisters, twins, clutched each other in the bed Hannah shared with them. She watched their slow breathing, and then she glanced over at her parents. Her mother slumbered on her side, a slight swell that could almost be mistaken for a wrinkle in the dingy blanket. Her father lay on his back, like a mountain rising up from a plain, and his eyes were open.

That was how it was. Hannah would glance at him from her book, and he would be asleep. The next time she looked, he would be awake, and she would wonder how long he had lain there.

"Papa," she whispered.

She crept away from her stories, tiptoed across the room, and knelt beside the bed. She took his hand.

"Good morning," she said, and kissed the knuckle above his wedding band.

He smiled, his fingers cold and damp, like twigs on the ground in winter. His hands used to be tough and warm and thick-fingered, and she used to feel safe when they held her.

"I was reading the story of a girl," she said. "She traveled east of the sun and west of the moon to save her prince. And before that I read about a cat that wore boots, who . . . Are you hungry, Papa?"

He blinked once to say yes.

Hannah gave his hand a pat and got to her feet. She went to the coal stove, and the heavy iron door groaned as she opened it. She scooped out the previous day's ashes, enveloping herself in a fine gray cloud, and snapped some kindling. Then she arranged the sticks inside the stove and followed that with a few black chunks of coal from a pail that was nearly empty. She struck a match against the iron belly of the stove to light the kindling and left the stove door open to let the fire suck air. Then Hannah set the large copper teakettle to boil, one of the few possessions from their previous life not yet sold to pay for coal or food or rent.

"I'll watch it," her mother said behind her. "You'll be late for work."

"Oh, Mama," Hannah said. "I didn't hear you get up."

Her mother glanced at the book left open on the table.

"I was reading this morning," Hannah said.

"You've been doing that a lot. I'm worried you're not getting enough sleep."

"I'm fine, Mama."

"I know. You always say you are." Creases appeared across her mother's brow. She went to the cupboard and pulled down the coffee tin. It sounded hollow when she shook it and tapped the sides, but she stared into it as if she hoped more grinds might appear.

"I get my wages in a few days," Hannah said.

"Yes. But they're already spent."

The teakettle whistled, and Hannah's sisters stirred.

"It'll be a relief when they're old enough to start school," her mother said. "And I can devote the attention to your father that he needs."

Hannah looked away from her mother, jaw clenched. She snatched up the book from the table and held it to her chest. "I need to leave for work."

"What? Oh, Hannah, I'm sorry. I didn't mean —"

Hannah shook her head. "It's all right."

"No, it isn't. I know how much you loved school, how much you'd love to go back. You're such a smart girl and —"

"Mama. It's fine." Hannah took the book to the small shelf above their bed. There had once been seven other books there. She had kept them in alphabetical order. And then she had sold them off for pennies. She bent and kissed her sisters, each one on the cheek. "If you're up when I get home tonight, I'll read you a story," she whispered.

She went to her father and kissed him on the forehead. "See you tonight, Papa." He smiled, and Hannah tried to imagine him telling her the same. She did not want to forget what his voice sounded like.

Her mother stood by the door with Hannah's lunch pail in her hand, packed the night before. "Have a good day," she said. "Really, I didn't mean . . . You do so much for our family."

"I'd rather not talk about this." Hannah took the pail and gave her mother a kiss that touched more air than cheek. "Don't forget to turn Papa on his side."

"I won't."

Hannah shut the door and climbed down the stairs. She turned up the narrow street and joined the other laborers on their way to work. They filed out from the dense alleys and tumbledown buildings like ants from a hole in the ground, fanning out once they hit Basket Street and the roads opened wide. Hannah nodded to a baker lumbering by, powdered with flour and bent under a hump of baguettes.

She headed up Basket Street, a short while later arriving on the square, where the Gilbert Hotel faced the world like a rich man posturing for a portrait. She stood there a moment, shoring herself up for the long day ahead. Then she sighed and went in through the service entrance.

The hours trampled her on their way through the day. Before the guests had even taken their breakfast, Miss Wool had scolded her something fierce. Then one of the other maids stole a tip left for Hannah. And she burned herself on a clothes iron. But around midday Hannah was in one of the linen closets folding sheets when she heard someone talking in the hallway just outside the door. She heard Mister Grumholdt's rumbling voice, laying down words the way a mason lays bricks. Then she heard the raspy voice of Miss Wool, like feet crunching through dried leaves. Hannah held her breath and put her ear to the door.

"It must be on the top floor," said Mister Grumholdt.

"Then why didn't we find it the first time?" asked Miss Wool.

"We missed it somehow. It's there. I'm sure of it. That's where he had his suite."

"How old are the hotel floor plans for that section?"

"They're recent. The last renovation was only three years ago."

"The treasure would have been hidden long before then."

"Don't you think I know that, woman?"

Hannah cringed and silence followed. Then Miss Wool spoke, her voice low and even. "I don't tolerate that tone from my maids, and I certainly won't tolerate it from you. Mind yourself, Hans."

"My apologies. I suggest we meet in my office and look over the plans in case we missed something. Say, three o'clock?"

"It's three now."

A moment of silence passed, in which Hannah imagined Mister Grumholdt pulling out his gold watch, the one he kept on a heavy chain and checked throughout the day.

"No, it isn't," he said. "Miss Wool, your watch is off. See to that. For now, why don't we just go to my office together. Agreed?"

"Lead the way."

Their voices faded. Hannah let out her breath and resumed folding, spritzing each sheet with rose water.

Treasure. Hidden. Just like the "Tale of the Forty Thieves" from her book.

In her mind she saw chests of gold coins and silver pendants. She saw jewel-encrusted goblets and combs of the most delicate ivory. Lavish silks and heavy brooches. Drooping pearl earrings, and necklaces bearing gems the size of robins' eggs. Diamonds, emeralds, rubies, and carbuncles. Like the treasures that belonged to the wealthy guests who stayed in the hotel.

She had often been tempted to steal from the opulent hotel suites. She would be dusting, or polishing, and there it would be, a ring, a brooch, left so casually on the dresser, almost forgotten. The guests had chests of jewelry; surely they would not miss this one little earring, this one small trinket that would pay a year's rent for Hannah's family.

Hannah shook her head. Those thoughts sent guilt chewing up her insides with cold teeth.

She finished the last of the sheets and started on the pillowcases. The closet door opened and she jumped. Her friend Abigail peeked in.

"Hannah, have you seen Miss Wool?"

Hannah hesitated. "No." She set down the linens. "Why?"

"That new guest on the top floor is asking for her."

"The one with the tiger?"

"Have you seen it?" Abigail slipped into the closet and shut the door. "Does she really have a tiger? Do you think she actually travels with spirits?"

"I don't know. Walter said he saw the tiger."

"Walter." Abigail snorted. "Walter would say anything to impress you."

Hannah blushed. "He is nice, though."

"I suppose." Abigail took the rose water and sprayed some on her neck.

"If Miss Wool smells that on you . . ."

"You worry too much, Hannah." Abigail turned with a little bounce and opened the door. "If you see Miss Wool, tell her the tiger lady is looking for her." She shut the door behind her.

Hannah sighed. Abigail was nice enough, but she did not understand. Abigail's father was a cooper and did all right by his family. They had a small house down on the south side of McCauley Park, and Abigail worked only because she had no interest in school. Hannah finished her folding and put the rose water back on the shelf.

Mister Grumholdt and Miss Wool had seemed to be talking about a treasure hidden somewhere in the east wing of the hotel. But what kind of treasure was it? If it was lost, did it belong to anyone? The hotel was supposed to be full of hidden passageways and secret doors. Hannah imagined herself opening one and finding a shimmering mountain of money. She would take it and buy a home and move her family out of the tenements. She would hire a doctor to look after her father every hour of every day, so her mother could finally have some rest. Hannah would take her younger sisters and go back to school. There would be enough food on the table, and heaps of coal for the stove, and warm clothes and shoes without any holes in them.

Hannah opened the door to the linen closet and bumped right into Miss Wool. It was like running into a thornbush.

"Watch where you're going!"

Hannah curtsied. "I'm so sorry, Miss Wool."

"Stupid, clumsy girl," the woman snapped, but without her usual force behind it. She seemed preoccupied, and kept looking past Hannah down the hall. She patted her gray hair, which was pulled up loose in an elegant swirl on top of her head. But then her eyes went to the closet door. She straightened her apron over her narrow, bony hips. "How long were you in there?"

Hannah swallowed. "Not long."

Miss Wool's face hardened. "Not long?"

"No, only a minute or two."

Miss Wool tapped her toe on the carpet.

31

Hannah cleared her throat. "Ma'am, the new guest on the top floor was looking for you."

"Was she? Well, I can't be bothered with that circus sideshow right now. Go and see what she wants. You may be stupid and clumsy, but surely you can take care of that much."

Hannah dipped another curtsy. "Yes, ma'am." She turned away before Miss Wool could say anything more and hurried down the hallway. She came out on a landing and started up the hotel's main staircase that rose, flight upon flight, around a central gallery, to the uppermost levels.

The staircase was under renovation again. A few months ago masons had broken out the plain white marble and replaced it with a dark stone the brittle color of burnt paper. Hannah thought the new stairs looked beautiful in a stark and dramatic way. But a week ago Mister Twine, the hotel owner, had insisted that they be replaced again, this time with a pink stone veined with ribbons of gold.

She scurried past the masons, careful of her steps around their tools and fresh work, hoping to avoid being noticed. But they looked up at Hannah, and one of them recognized her.

He set down his trowel, and took off his cap. "How's your father, miss?"

She recognized him as well, and shored herself up. "As good as can be expected, Mister Cantwell. He speaks often of coming back to work, once he regains his strength."

Mister Cantwell nodded. "We'd be glad to have him back. Finest stonemason I ever knew, your father. Finest in the whole city."

"Thank you, sir. He says the same of you." Hannah smiled and continued up the steps.

"You tell him there are still plenty of his holly leaves around."

"I will." There were exactly sixty-two holly leaves scattered through the hotel. She had searched them out and counted them many times. Her father loved their scalloped shape, and he had carved them as a motif signature on his work. They were hiding everywhere, like little secrets left just for her.

With each landing the carpet became more luxurious, patterned like the intricate Turkish rugs in the best suites. As she climbed higher, tables cropped up sprouting seasonal flower arrangements that scented the halls with perfume. Alabaster statues rose up in the corners like ghosts, staring at Hannah with blank eyes. From above the gallery a domed-glass ceiling braided sunlight into rainbows, which fell sparkling over the statues and the stairs.

Hannah reached the top floor and dabbed a bit of sweat from her brow with her apron. She had never been up here before. She wondered why the wealthiest guests would choose the highest rooms, which required them to climb so far. But she supposed it was like the mansions up in the Heights where Mister Twine lived. Some people just had to be above everyone else.

From a hallway window, Hannah could look out over the hotel gardens, and there was Alice, working in the flower beds, pointy straw hat wider than her shoulders, seedlings poking out of her apron pockets. Alice was old. Older than Mister Twine. Hannah had never met anyone working in the hotel who could remember a time when Alice was not old. Alice ignored everyone, but she spoke to her plants, and sometimes she even spoke to Hannah.

Hannah paused a moment on the landing before approaching the suite. What if this guest really had a tiger? What if the other rumors were true, that she traveled with the spirits of the dead? And what about the treasure? Mister Grumholdt had said it must be hidden on the top floor. Hannah smoothed her apron and stepped up to the heavy door of the grand suite. She pulled on the doorbell.

No answer.

She pulled harder.

The door opened, and a tall man filled the opening. He wore a gray robe that brushed the floor, and his long black hair fell to his elbows. He stared down at Hannah with eyes so blue they were almost clear. "Yes?" he said.

Hannah took a startled step backward before she remembered her manners. She curtsied. "I was sent to see how I could be of service."

"Where is Miss Wool?"

"She's attending to another matter at the moment and sent me in her stead."

The man frowned. "Come in."

He opened the door wide and ushered Hannah through the entryway into the drawing room. On the far side of the room, beneath a wide window curtained with lace, a large woman reclined on a chaise longue like an Egyptian princess, but not a beautiful one. The woman might have been attractive underneath her roundness, but her girth filled up whatever space her beauty might have occupied. She wore a black dress, brooched at the neck with an agate cameo, and her hair fell loose about her shoulders. She lifted a silver-handled lorgnette to her face, and the spectacles swelled her eyes within the frames.

"Miss Wool sent you?" Her voice chimed like a crystal goblet struck by a spoon.

Hannah curtsied again. "She did, ma'am."

"Well then, come closer."

Hannah glanced around. Not a tiger or spirit in sight. At the moment, it seemed safe. She crossed the room to the couch and bowed her head.

"I need someone," the woman said. "Preferably a young girl on the staff who will be my personal attendant. Can you recommend someone to me?"

"I'm afraid I can't, ma'am."

"Why not?"

"I think that's above my place."

The woman lowered the spectacles to her lap. "And what place would that be?"

"I'm just a maid."

"Just a maid. But you're still a person, aren't you?"

"Of course, ma'am."

"Capable of forming opinions?"

"Yes." Hannah looked up. "But I've learned that in most cases it's best to just keep my opinions to myself."

The woman laughed, a tinkling, trembling laugh. "Would that everyone were as wise as you. What is your name, child?"

"Hannah."

"Hannah, I am Madame Constance Bernadette Pomeroy." She said it as if it were a regal title, not a name at all.

"I'm pleased to make your acquaintance, Madame Pomeroy."

A moment of silence followed, filled with the ticking of a grandfather clock. The woman stared at her. Not intensely, but it made Hannah uncomfortable.

"Sit down next to me, child."

"Ma'am?"

"Sit down. Right there." She pointed as the fellow in the gray robe brought up a chair. "This gentleman is Yakov. He was a Russian soldier." Madame Pomeroy leaned in. "A very dangerous man, mind you. I never really know what he's hiding under that coat. He travels with me as a sort of bodyguard, my own golem."

"A what?"

"A golem, child. A man made of clay and brought to life by the spells of Jewish rabbis and mystics. Marvelous creations. Like a golem, Yakov lives to serve and protect. But unlike a golem, Yakov will talk from time to time. And he can predict the future."

Yakov held the seat for Hannah. "I shouldn't," she said. But she was curious and sat down, anyway. "How does he predict the future?"

"Through dreams and visions. It's his gift. Just as I am given the gift of communion with the dead."

"Oh," was all Hannah could say, wary now. She imagined a tiger behind her, ready to pounce, and ghostly fingers reaching out to her neck. She held still without meaning to.

"There," Madame Pomeroy said. "Now that you're sitting, I want to ask you a few questions, if you don't mind." She pulled out a stack of cards. Not playing cards. These were larger, and Madame Pomeroy shuffled them. "Tell me, child, why are you working in this hotel?"

Hannah looked down at her apron.

"Come, child. What is it?" She began laying cards out on the table and appeared purposeful about where they were supposed to go. She placed four cards in a column. "You can trust Madame Pomeroy."

Hannah knew it was wrong to be so familiar with a guest. She could be punished for it. But something about Madame Pomeroy drew her in. Hannah took a deep breath, and then she told the truth.

"A few years ago my father was struck with apoplexy. He lost his speech and the strength in his legs. He was a stonemason, before. But he couldn't work anymore, so we had to sell our home. My mother can't work, because she has to care for him all the time, and there're my little sisters to look after, too. That left me. Since my father had worked hard for this hotel, I went to the owner, Mister Twine, and I asked him for a job. He took me on as a maid."

Madame Pomeroy had frozen with her hand outstretched, a card quivering between her fingers. "How old are you, child?"

"I'm twelve."

"You carry a heavy weight, for one so young."

"I manage well enough."

Madame Pomeroy set the card in place. She drew another, placed it, and another, and placed it, too, forming a cross of five cards next to the four already on the table. She turned one over, then the next. She studied each, muttered to herself, and said, "Hmm."

Hannah took a few glances around the suite while Madame Pomeroy pored over the cards. The room was finer than any Hannah had been in, with inlaid furniture varnished like a mirror, silver clocks forged into clever animal shapes, fine drawings and paintings hanging on the walls in gilt frames. Hannah's eyes met the blue in Yakov's, and she smiled at him. He smiled in return, but it was more of an attempt at a smile than a smile itself.

"Hmm," Madame Pomeroy said.

Hannah cleared her throat. "I should be getting back, ma'am. Miss Wool will be cross with me."

"Miss Wool." She rolled her eyes. "Let me worry about Miss Wool, dear."

Hannah thought that Madame Pomeroy had no idea what she was asking for.

"Now," Madame Pomeroy said. "You see these cards?"

Hannah looked at them. She saw a man hanging upside down by his foot, a wheel, a tower struck by lightning, and a strange figure that might have been a man, or it might have been a woman. Other cards bore numbered pictures with swords, chalices, coins, and staves.

Madame Pomeroy waved her hands over the table. "These cards hold keys for you, Hannah. Keys to who you have been, who you are, and who you will be, as you experience the journey of your life."

Hannah nodded, skeptical.

"I see you have sacrificed much of yourself, and this has taken its toll. You were once so happy and carefree. Life held such promise. Now you feel trapped. You are full of dark thoughts. Bitterness and sadness devour you like wild beasts."

In her heart, Hannah argued with Madame Pomeroy. What did this woman know of her? Hannah was not sad. She had no right to be. Her father lived when doctors said he should have died, and she had her family. Hannah was not bitter or angry. Who could she be angry with?

She barely heard the knock on the front door of the suite.

Hannah could not be angry with her father or mother. It was not their fault her father had gotten sick. It was not their fault Hannah had been forced to quit her schooling and work at the hotel.

Madame Pomeroy sighed. "Such darkness. You lie all the time, to yourself and to others, and also feel much temptation."

Hannah squirmed in her chair. She did not like this woman.

"You are at a fulcrum, Hannah. A balancing point. There is conflict in your future, a challenge to the old ways by new ideas and a possible reversal in the order of things, the creation of something wholly other. You will meet some who can help you, if you trust and help them. You will have the chance to be happy again."

"I am happy now," Hannah insisted.

Madame Pomeroy smiled. "Hush, child."

"I'm happy!"

"No more lies, Hannah."

Hannah stood up. "I'm not lying! What do you know? You're just a crackpot spiritualist. You don't know me!"

"Hannah!" came a shout from behind her.

Hannah spun around.

Miss Wool stood in the doorway of the parlor. Yakov loomed behind her, his nose wrinkled as if he smelled something foul. Miss Wool charged into the room. "I should have known better than to send you up here. How dare you speak to a guest in this way!"

Hannah panicked. "Miss Wool, I'm so sorry. I don't know what came over me. Please!"

"Silence, girl!" Miss Wool turned to Madame Pomeroy. "I sincerely apologize for this maid's behavior. I assure you she will be dealt with most severely. I can personally guarantee that she will never again show such disrespect to another guest in this hotel."

Hannah nearly collapsed to the floor. Her family would be tossed out on the street. What would they do? How would they care for her father? What about her sisters? She felt like sobbing, begging, screaming.

"It's quite all right, Miss Wool," Madame Pomeroy said, her voice lilting. "I'm afraid that I'm to blame for her outburst. You see, I was doing a reading, and I may have nicked her too close to the bone."

"There is no need to protect her, Madame. I appreciate your forbearance, but let me assure you that this maid will be dismissed immediately." Miss Wool stared down at Hannah.

Madame Pomeroy clicked her tongue. "I think not."

Miss Wool stepped back. "Pardon me?"

"I want to employ her."

"Want to employ who? Hannah?"

"Yes. I am in need of a personal assistant, and I had hoped to ask you for a recommendation. Having met Hannah, I believe she'll do nicely."

"Madame, there are other girls on my staff who would be far superior —"

"No need. I would like to have Hannah assigned to me henceforth. I want her at my disposal at any hour, day or night. This means she will have no time for other duties, I'm afraid. I assume you can spare her, since you were about to dismiss her."

Miss Wool blinked.

"Then it's agreed. Yakov, please show Miss Wool out."

The Russian swept the speechless woman from the room. On her way out the door, Miss Wool whipped a hateful glare at Hannah. Then she was gone. Hannah slumped into the chair, stunned. She heard the front door open, and a moment later, shut.

Yakov reentered the room, a fraction of a grin on his face. "I enjoyed that."

Madame Pomeroy giggled. "So did I. What an odious woman. Now, Hannah?"

Hannah stared.

"Hannah?"

"Yes?"

"You understand what just happened? You will work for me now, at least for the length of my stay."

"Yes, ma'am."

Madame Pomeroy glanced at the cards still spread out. "I don't think we need to go any further with the reading. You got the gist of it, anyway." The woman sat down and scooped up the cards, riffling them back into a deck. She picked up her book and resumed the position of repose in which Hannah had first seen her. "You've had a long day, child. Why don't you go home early this evening. I'm sure your mother could use your help."

"Go home early?"

"You act as though you've never heard the words before. Yes, go home early. But mind you I won't make a habit of this. Far from it. I can be a harsh mistress if your laziness calls for it."

Hannah nodded. "Are you sure I can't be of some help to you now, ma'am?"

"No, Hannah. But I'll see you at sunrise tomorrow."

Hannah remembered to curtsy, in spite of her shock, and left the parlor. Yakov walked her to the door. "Welcome to the movable court of Madame Pomeroy," he said. "May your time with us be pleasant."

"Th-thank you."

He closed the door behind her.

In a daze, Hannah nearly tripped down the stairs. She stumbled down the hallways, tracing the walls with her fingers to keep her balance. She left through the entrance used by the service staff, grateful to have avoided seeing anyone she knew on the way out. Madame Pomeroy may have protected her from punishment for now, but Miss Wool would not let such an affront to her authority go unchallenged. She would find a way to retaliate and Hannah would eventually face her wrath, at the very least when Madame Pomeroy left. She put that thought away for now.

Hannah emerged onto Gilbert Square, breathed deep, and set off for home, down Basket Street and then winding through the side alleys. This early in the evening she crossed streets that were mostly empty, except for the gawkers, gamblers, drinkers, and poor homeless souls who seemed to never leave the streets at all.

She was a block from home when she saw a boy carrying a coal chute on his back. He sweated and huffed and she wondered what he was doing, since he did not look like a coal man at all. He was around her age, with modest clothing and clean, dark hair. And then he stopped her and asked for directions.

She joked with him. He did not laugh. In fact, he did not come across as the kind of boy who liked to laugh at all. He seemed to wear seriousness the way a mason wore calluses. Something in his past had hardened him, Hannah thought. She gave him directions, and he thanked her. She continued on her way, until she came to her building, then mounted the steps to her family's apartment. She reached her landing and opened the tiny door.

Her sisters fought on the floor, crying. They looked up when she came in and called Hannah's name at the same time. Her mother leaned over a steaming pot, forehead glistening with sweat, her hair lank, and the skin around her eyes dark and sunken.

"Hannah!" she said. "You're home early?"

"Yes, Mama."

"Miracles do happen. Come take over supper. I've got to help your father turn over."

Hannah met her father's eyes. "Hello, Papa." She walked over to him and kissed him on the forehead.

"Hannah, please." Her mother held out the ladle.

Hannah sighed. She stirred and cooked. They ate together near her father so he could sit up and join them, something Hannah always came home too late at night to share in.

"One of the guests asked that I be assigned to her," Hannah said between bites.

"What does that mean?" her mother asked.

"I'll be her personal attendant."

"That's wonderful," her mother said. "It sounds like you're certainly securing your position at the hotel."

Hannah looked at the food on her plate. "Uh-huh."

That night, the straw and the fleas in the mattress itched Hannah, and she tossed, fighting for sleep. Street noise kept her awake for hours: the factory men on their way home, shouting and cursing; barking dogs; a baby screeching. She lay there, remembering the whispered conversation she had overheard, and thought about hidden treasure, a room somewhere on the top floor of the hotel that opened with a spoken word or a spell.

But then she heard the pure sound of a violin over the top of it all. One note, as if calling her name, and then it was gone. Hannah sat up, waiting.

The violin returned, birthing a folk song she had heard before, but never like this. It reminded her of walking to school on a fresh spring morning, of playing in the garden outside their old home. But more than a memory, it was as if she were there again. She smelled the lilac growing against the house and felt the warm dirt between her toes. Her mother smiling from the kitchen window, ruddy and plump, and telling her to get back to weeding. The song stopped.

Hannah listened for another tune, but none came. The warmth left behind in her chest reminded her of the hope she had felt earlier. She worked for Madame Pomeroy now. What was it the woman had said? That Hannah stood on a balancing point, a reversal in the order of things.

Hannah glanced across the room and saw that her father was awake. He stared at the ceiling, and she saw glistening tears trail down his temples. He had also heard the violin, and she imagined it had freed him for a few moments from his weakened body. She wondered where the music had taken him, and then felt a pressure building inside, a rising swell of grief. Monstrous in size, it licked her toes and threatened to overwhelm her, drag her down and drown her.

She hit the mattress at her side as if to beat it back.

No. Everything was fine.

CHAPTER 4

A Boat Ticket

GIUSEPPE KNEW THAT STEPHANO WOULD BE WAITING. STEPHANO watched the front door of his den the way a rattlesnake might watch a mouse hole, poised, patient, and cold-eyed. Giuseppe strode through the door with all the boldness he could muster. No sense cowering when he knew what was coming. He shut the door, and before he had even turned around, Stephano was there.

He gripped Giuseppe's shoulder. "Have a good day, did you?"

"No." Giuseppe fought the urge to recoil from the man's touch.

"No?" Stephano bent down to look Giuseppe in the face, his skin as brown and dry as bark beneath a granite-colored beard flecked with food. "And why is that?"

"Ezio took it all."

"So you're a rat." Stephano stood up. He wore a thick vest of woolen lambskin and a wide-brimmed hat stuck with the tattered feathers of a peacock. A huge knife hung from his side on a leather belt. "Rats are vermin, boy. I crush vermin with the heel of my boot. You want to feel the heel of my boot?"

A few of the other boys hung about the room, trying to watch without being noticed. Little Pietro was not among them. Neither were Ferro or Alfeo. They must have already gone into the kitchen for their suppers or upstairs to sleep.

Stephano took off his hat and wiped his forehead with a dirty handkerchief. "How much do you have, Giuseppe?"

Giuseppe laid his old fiddle on the floor. "None. I don't have anything."

A couple of the other boys whispered. Stephano looked around at them. "You hear that, boys?" He hung his hat on a hook near the door. "Nothing."

"I told you, Ezio took —"

Stephano punched him in the gut. Giuseppe doubled over, fell to the ground, and gasped for air.

"Didn't you hear me, boy? I kill rats! If you were careless enough to lose all your money, then you should have gone back out and made more! Get up." He yanked Giuseppe to his feet and breathed alcohol in his face. "And what's this I hear from Paolo? You have something you want to show me?"

Giuseppe could only shake his head.

"You sure about that?" Stephano tossed him to the floor. "'Cause I hear you somehow got yourself a new violin."

Giuseppe tried to speak, choked, and tried again. "Paolo's a liar."

"You're all liars."

He seized Giuseppe by the collar and dragged him down a dim hallway. He wrenched open a small, low door. "You want to be a rat? Fine." Stephano kicked him into the darkness. Giuseppe fell several feet and landed hard on a floor of packed clay. Stephano's silhouette seemed to swell above him, framed by the light coming down from the doorway, as if hanging in the air. "Live with the rats," Stephano said. The door shut, and all the light died.

Giuseppe rolled onto his back and coughed. He rubbed his stomach. That could have been worse. At least he had kept his shirt on and avoided the whip. In his mind he imagined taking that whip to Ezio and Paolo, shredding their clothes and the skin on their backs. He would even let little Pietro take a swing at them.

The daydream lasted only a moment. Giuseppe rolled up to his knees and then to his feet. Lying down was how they got you.

Stephano kept the rats supplied with rags for nesting and just enough food to keep them alive and hungry. Giuseppe had heard the stories. More than one boy had died down here, stripped to the bone. If you stayed on your feet, you could kick them away and keep them at bay. But if you lay down, they would swarm and you would be finished. He did not know whether he believed the stories, but it was better not to take chances. All he could do was stand his ground until Stephano decided to let him out, and hope he lasted that long.

The cellar was rank with the smell of musk and urine and feces. After a few minutes Giuseppe had a headache and felt sick. His eyes adjusted, and he picked his way to the center of the room. The rats scurried and massed in the corners and against the walls all around him. He could hear them clicking and grinding their teeth, like chains through a winch. Hundreds of them. Thousands of them chattering away in the darkness.

He had been much younger the last time he was down here. He had screamed the whole time and flailed wildly whenever he felt something brush his legs. He did not scream this time, but he flinched and kicked at the curious noses, tails, and teeth.

Minutes passed.

Then hours.

Or were those minutes, too, and they only seemed like hours? He tried to hold still and breathe slow. He grew tired and swayed on his feet.

To keep awake and alert he sang to himself. Quiet tunes at first, then riotous songs, and he pantomimed fiddling on a violin. The green violin. He played with a fury, and a madness of music took him. He kicked his feet high and jigged like the piper in the fairy tale, the one who led the rats to the swift river and danced the children into the deep cave. He whooped and spun, the king under the mountain, lord of the rat cellar.

He played and sang until exhaustion brought him down, sweaty and panting. He had fiddled away his fear, and he lay down on the ground. The rats watched him from a safe distance, whiskers twitching. He laughed into their rags. He closed his eyes and he slept.

A hammer of light woke him. He blinked and shielded his eyes. The floating doorway hovered over him, and Stephano's silhouette spoke. "Sleeping? Too old for the rat cellar, I see."

Giuseppe got to his feet.

A rope fell on his head. "Take hold of that, boy."

Giuseppe looped the rope around his hand and walked over to stand beneath the door. A few heaves later and Stephano had lifted him into the hallway.

The building sounded empty. "What time is it?" Giuseppe asked.

Stephano shut the cellar door. "Nearly lunchtime."

That left only half a day to earn a full day's take. Giuseppe would have worried before. Now he had the green violin.

"Grab a crust of bread if you like." Stephano had his hands on his hips.

Giuseppe shrugged. "Not hungry."

Stephano chuckled without smiling. "Liar. But suit yourself. Your fiddle's still on the floor where you left it."

Giuseppe turned to leave.

"Wait a minute, Giuseppe. One more thing."

"What?"

"The rat cellar's lost its hold on you, and that's fine. Happens to all you boys sooner or later. But know this. Now you're too old for it, I got ways to punish you like a man." He raised a fist, sporting knuckle-dusters that could break bones. Giuseppe had seen it happen. "You take my meaning?"

Giuseppe swallowed.

"You're the best musician I got, boy. That don't mean you can get anything past me. You hide something and I'll know it, sure as flies on a dead dog."

Giuseppe grabbed up his old fiddle and opened the front door.

Stephano called after him. "You better make up for last night, boy. I want two dollars!"

Giuseppe slammed the door behind him. He would make Stephano's two dollars with the green violin. He would make more than that.

He retrieved the instrument from the churchyard and found a corner where he could toss his cap. The sky above was overcast, and the mood on the street matched its somber hue. The music of the rat cellar still echoed through his body, so Giuseppe decided to set it free and try to lighten the day for his audience. He struck up the jig, slow and easy at first, tempting as a child calling friends to come play. But then he gave it some musical laughter, and used the notes to hoot and holler. He let the song gather speed, because the violin seemed to want it, too, and the bow leaped against the strings like a pebble skidding across the surface of a pond, carrying all the joy of his remembered summers back home.

Then Giuseppe became aware of another sound, a stomping, and he looked up. His audience, the people in the street, were dancing. Arm in arm or by themselves, they spun and hopped and flew about until the song came to an end. Then they reached into their pockets for money, tossed it into his cap, and wandered away as though their minds did not yet know what their bodies had just been doing.

Giuseppe looked at the violin in his hands, almost frightened of it. But that day, he made four dollars. He could have made more, but he only dared play the green violin twice. When he returned the instrument and deposited his money in Mister Stroop's tomb that evening, he kept one dollar and thirty-eight cents for Stephano, because actually bringing in two dollars for half a day's work would raise suspicions. He also brought along a few extra coins in case Pietro needed help again.

It was well into the night before Giuseppe returned to Crosby Street, and at the entrance he found the little boy waiting for him. Giuseppe smiled and gave him some money, and they went in together, arm in arm, avoiding Ezio.

Pietro took to waiting for him every night, hanging about like a little ghost, and every night Giuseppe had a few coins for him, enough to make up the difference between supper and a beating. Some days Giuseppe even secured a good corner for Pietro to play, and taught him a couple of tunes on the little boy's tin whistle. Two weeks went by like that before Giuseppe felt it would be safe to go down to the harbor and ask about the cost of a steamboat passage to Italy.

He had not been to the docks since the day of the shipwreck, and nothing of the treasures or debris remained. He squinted in the sunlight and felt sweaty at his hairline. Sailors stalked up and down the wharves and scrambled over the rigging out on the ships. Fishermen hawked their morning haul right there on the pier, and cooks and fishmongers hollered their bids for the choicest catch. Brazen gulls hopped around, eyes on the fish, snatching what they could.

Giuseppe strolled on in the direction of the passenger boats and ticket offices. Along the way he saw a group of severe-looking old men in suits, standing close together like a bundle of railroad ties on end, their eyes all trained on a particular ship. They looked out of place here on the docks, and Giuseppe grew curious. He stood back and watched as a wooden crane lifted crates from the deck of the ship, swung them around, and set them on the dock. The sailors checked and rechecked the ropes, and the old men held their breath until each crate touched ground again.

One of them held a stack of papers, and he kept looking back and forth between the papers and each crate as it came down, nodding to himself. Giuseppe drew nearer, and noticed that the crates were stamped with strings of numbers and strange words like KARNAK and UR. Giuseppe had never learned to read well, but these words made no sense at all.

"You there!" The man with the papers pointed a long finger at him.

Giuseppe had not meant to come so close.

"What are you doing?" the man asked, barreling down upon him. He had a sharp, hooked nose and wild hair the color of dust. "Are you spying on me?"

"Spying? No."

"Who sent you? Was it the clockmakers?"

"No one sent me. I wasn't spying."

"Scoundrels! You go back and tell those thieves that these artifacts belong to the Archer Museum!"

Giuseppe did not know what to say.

"Did you hear me?"

"I heard you." Giuseppe spoke the words slow and even. "But I was not spying on you."

One of the man's eyelids fluttered. "The clockmakers didn't send you?"

"No. No one sent me."

An uncomfortable moment passed, in which the man looked him over. Giuseppe noticed that his hair was not the color of dust. It was filled with it. "Hmm," the man said. "Perhaps I was prematurely carried away. Who are you, then?"

"Just a busker." He held up his fiddle. Over the man's shoulder, Giuseppe saw another load of crates rise up from the ship. A sailor shouted something.

"What are you doing down here? Aren't you supposed to be on a corner somewhere?"

Giuseppe shrugged. "I play for the —"

A sharp twang cut him off.

They both looked up. A rope had snapped, and the load of crates careened overhead. One of the smaller boxes toppled off the stack. Giuseppe's eyes traced its fall to the ground where it shattered, scattering straw and splinters of wood. Something round and made of brass clanged and rolled toward them.

The man with the dusty hair screamed as if in pain. He fell toward the brass ball to catch it, while the rest of the men in suits stood completely still, mouths open wide in shock. Giuseppe took a step forward, as if he meant to help. The man scooped up the brass object, and Giuseppe saw that it was not a ball at all.

It was a head. A brass head, with eyes, a nose, ears, and lips, and hair made of wire. The man huddled over it on his knees. He whipped off his coat and wrapped it around the head as if swaddling a baby. He stood up, cradling it in his arms, and when he looked at Giuseppe, there were tears in his eyes.

Giuseppe backed away and ran before anyone could blame him for the broken cargo. He fled down the docks, dodging between wagons and carts loaded with goods, past warehouses and trading companies stacked high with barrels and sacks and boxes. He looked over his shoulder and slowed to a trot when he saw that no one followed him.

Up ahead, almost at the edge of the docks, a large steamship bellied up to a pier. Sometimes, several passenger ships like this one crowded the wharf at once, from all parts of the world, and waterfalls of people came down the gangplanks, flooding the city.

The immigration buildings sat opposite the docks and took up almost a whole city block, like a warehouse for people. Giuseppe entered the main building, lined on either side by walled booths and barred windows through which the shipping agents and the immigration officers conducted their business. The arrangement struck Giuseppe as a mix between a bank and a stable. Hundreds of families massed inside like the cattle and sheep waiting in pens down on the Quay. The shipping companies had offices near the entrance where they sold tickets for passage.

Giuseppe fought his way through the crowd to get there, but before he reached the desk he noticed a little girl waiting in line with her parents. They all looked haggard. The father rubbed his neck while the mother simply stared up into the rafters. The little girl sat on a trunk, and in spite of the dark circles under her eyes and a dirty dress she must have worn the entire voyage, she swung her short legs and smiled.

She did not look timid or scared. She seemed excited to be in a new city, a new country. But she had come over with her family. Giuseppe remembered his own first day, drowning in loneliness like an ant in the ocean. The man who had paid his uncle had led him from the dark bowels of the ship, and they had waited in the pressing crowd. He had held Giuseppe's hand in a painful grip, and never said a single reassuring word.

Then Stephano had come, the man had handed Giuseppe over, and everything had changed. Giuseppe tipped his cap to the girl and kept going.

When he stepped up to the shipping company's window, the man behind the counter looked down at him over half-moon spectacles that rode low on his nose. Small eyes, sharp as needles, peered out from beneath bushy eyebrows.

"What do you want?" His eyes appeared to focus only on Giuseppe's fiddle.

"Uh . . ."

"Speak up, boy. Does your padrone know you're here?"

Giuseppe realized that he had made a mistake. He looked around. He remembered now how Stephano had slipped money into the hands of numerous men that first day, shipping agents and immigration officers alike. The men here were with Stephano and the other padrones.

"Never mind." Giuseppe turned to leave.

"Hold on, I asked you a question. Who's your padrone? Stop!"

But Giuseppe had already started to run, for the second time that day. He burst out of the warehouse. He thundered back down the docks, off into an alley, and soon emerged onto the bustle of Gilbert Square. He cut right across the middle and headed for the Old Rock Church.

After watching the street for a few minutes, he entered the church-yard and smiled at the angel on his way to Stroop's tomb. "Pardon me," he said as he opened the tomb, held his breath, and reached inside, with-drawing the green violin.

A few minutes later, he headed for a block of factories down on the Old Fort Road. He had wasted most of the morning in his failed effort to find out the cost of a steamboat ticket. Soon the factory whistles would blow and the workers would take their noon break. Giuseppe arrived outside the gates and waited amid the vendors setting up their lunch carts. Black kettles bore fried fish, roasted corn, and potatoes boiled with parsley, with fresh milk and cider to drink.

The aromas set his stomach working on the nothing he had eaten for breakfast, but he had no money on him to buy any food. Yet. The ven-dors eyed him sidelong. He ignored their suspicious glares and sat down on a building stoop to wait. He thought about his morning at the docks and cursed his carelessness. Stephano could find out what he was up to if Giuseppe went there himself. He had to figure out another way to learn the price, let alone buy the ticket and board the ship.

Several minutes later, the whistles blared. A few minutes after that, the streets choked up with men from the steelworks, and women from the fabric mills. They formed lines at the food carts, while some sat down with lunches in tin pails they had brought from home. Giuseppe watched them for a few moments, set his hat on the ground, stood up on the stoop, and started to play.

The notes cleared the air, as if peeling away the steam and the smoke and the despair. People stopped chewing their food. They gathered. Even the vendors set down their ladles. Giuseppe played them a country tune about an apple orchard, a silly tune really. But it spirited all the listeners away from where they were, just as Giuseppe had intended it to. He freed them from the city like pigeons from an opened coop, and they took to the sky in droves.

It seemed that everyone there tossed in a coin, and by the time the second whistle blew, calling them all back to the factories, Giuseppe figured he had earned at least three dollars. He stuffed the money into his pockets and put his hat on. He ambled over to a food cart and bought a steaming potato. The vendor, a man by the name of Fleischman, gave him a pinch of coarse salt. Giuseppe took a bite too big for his mouth and cooled it between his teeth. As he chewed, he closed his eyes and sighed. He finished the potato and strolled away just like the satisfied rich folk he had seen walking through the tame side of McCauley Park on Sunday mornings.

A little farther along the road he heard some scuffling and shouting. He peeked around a corner, down a pocket street between factories, and saw a couple of big street kids pounding another boy. The two were gang runners, not buskers, but the boy they had on the ground looked like he came from somewhere up near the Heights. His clothes were nicer, his knuckles were clean, and he looked scared. But he was actually trying to fight them off.

Giuseppe had to do something, but he could not fight them both on his own, and by the looks of it the boy on the ground would be worthless in a scrape. He looked older than Giuseppe by a year or two, but Giuseppe figured even he could take him.

Then Giuseppe caught an idea, and he set his violin safely aside where no one would see it. He stepped around the corner, picked up a small rock, and chucked it. It caught the bigger of the two attackers on the side of the head and bounced hard. They both turned toward him.

"He's mine," Giuseppe said. He leaned up against the alley wall, arms across his chest. "And we're with Stephano."

The one boy rubbed his temple. The other stepped up to Giuseppe. "But he didn't have no instrument."

"He made more than me, so I broke it," Giuseppe said. "I was gonna throttle him, too."

"What about his clothes?"

"That's what he was wearing when we nabbed him a couple weeks ago."

The gang boy made a gesture of stepping aside. "Well, pardon me. Kid didn't have no money, so we was just havin' some fun with him." He held out his hand like an usher. "He's all yours."

Giuseppe hesitated. He stepped around them and walked up to the boy on the ground. The kid looked dazed, like he was lost in a blizzard. Giuseppe balled his fist.

The one with the goose egg on his head called out, "What'cha waiting for?"

He shook his head. "I better not."

"Why?"

"'Cause Ezio wants him."

The two gang runners looked at each other.

"Yeah, Ezio's coming." Giuseppe turned away from them. "He'll be mad enough as it is when he sees what you two did. He wants some for himself." When he turned back, the two were gone, torn off, running down the street.

Giuseppe laughed and held out his hand to the boy on the ground. "I never thought Ezio would save my skin. I wonder what'll happen when this gets back to him. Come on, chap. I'll help you up."

The boy said nothing. He did not move. He just stared at Giuseppe's hand.

"Relax. I wasn't really going to hit you. You all right?"

The boy stiffened. He struggled to his feet like his back was sore. "I'm fine, and I don't need your help up. I didn't need your help at all."

Giuseppe withdrew his hand and lifted both eyebrows. "That's a fine thank-you-kindly. From where I stood, you were getting thumped pretty bad."

The other boy ignored him and brushed off his jacket.

"I'm Giuseppe, by the way. What's your name? What're you doing down here?"

The boy looked at him like it was a riddle. "Frederick," he said. "My name is Frederick." He started gathering up scraps of metal from the ground and said nothing more.

Giuseppe shook his head. "All right, then. I guess you're fine now." He started back down the alley. Over his shoulder he said, "See you around, Frederick."

"Wait."

Giuseppe turned.

The boy hesitated. "That was really something the way you . . . Well, what I mean is . . . thank you."

"You're welcome, Freddy. You should probably clear out of here. Rich chap like you —"

"I'm not rich."

"No?"

"No. I'm only an apprentice clockmaker. What made you think I was rich?"

"You just look taken care of, that's all."

"I take care of myself." He said it as if he was keeping something inside, like a pot simmering with the lid on. "I will be rich one day, though. Soon."

"Is that so?"

"Yes, it is. When I make journeyman, I'll open up my own shop, and make my own clocks."

"You make clocks, huh? I guess that's what this stuff is for." Giuseppe pointed at the pieces of metal in Frederick's hands. "You're pretty smart, aren't you, Frederick? And from what you're wearing, seems your master buys you clothes, so you look respectable."

"I suppose."

"I'm figuring the way I saved you just now, you maybe owe me something."

Frederick clutched the metal tighter. "I suppose that's true as well," he said. "And what would a busker like you be interested in? Do you want food? Money?"

Giuseppe snorted. "Nah. Money's not a problem for me anymore. What I got in mind is a favor."

CHAPTER 5

A Commission

FREDERICK FOUND GIUSEPPE SITTING ON THE STEPS OF THE Gilbert Hotel, right where he had left him. The afternoon glow on the marble stairs lit the pale stone as if from the inside. Giuseppe was leaning forward, elbows on his knees, playing with the sweat-stained rim of his cap. When he looked up at Frederick, he hopped down to him three steps at a time.

"Well?" Giuseppe put his hat on.

"Forty-five dollars."

"That much?"

Frederick nodded.

Giuseppe's shoulders slumped, and he stooped his neck, eyes on the ground. Then he put his hands on his hips. He looked up toward Frederick, but not really at him, like he was working on something in his head. Then his eyes came back into focus, and he smiled.

"Thanks, Freddy. Thanks for the favor." He nodded once and started to leave. "See you around, maybe."

"Why did . . ." Frederick began.

Giuseppe came back.

"Why do you want to go back to Italy?"

60

The busker paused. "That's where my brother and sister are."

"What about your parents?"

"They died."

"Mine too."

"Really?"

"Yeah," Frederick said. "My dad first. Then my mom left me at an orphanage." He was shocked. He had never said that out loud before, to anyone. Not even to Master Branch, who had never pressed him.

"I'm sorry."

The two boys had just shared something. Frederick had not meant to, and he wanted it back. Sharing his memories felt like handing over a sharp knife. A knife that others might handle carelessly. A knife that could be used to hurt him. "It's not a problem," he said. "I do fine on my own."

"Sure. You got out of that orphanage, anyway, right? Now you're a clockmaker."

"An apprentice clockmaker."

"But like you said, not for long."

Frederick smiled. "Hopefully not."

"Where's your place?"

"Master Branch has a shop on Sycamore Street a couple of blocks from the clockmakers' guildhall. I live there in the shop."

"Well, maybe I'll come by and see you sometime."

No one had ever come by to see Frederick before. Everyone who visited the shop was either a customer or a friend of Master Branch. "Please do," Frederick said.

Giuseppe smiled and walked off. His fiddle bounced on his back.

Frederick watched him saunter away and then took in the square. He noted the time on the massive Opera House clock with dismay. It glowered, hoarding counted seconds as if in perpetual irritation at the lack of precision in the world. It was afternoon and Frederick needed to get back to Master Branch's shop. He had spent too much of the day on Giuseppe, time he should have used for his own search.

Several days before, he had fitted his clockwork man with its chest plate. The image of the completed metal body, with its intricacies and subtleties, filled Frederick with a sublime pride that deflated the instant he thought about his creation's missing head. The iron rods and ties, the solid flywheels and delicate gears, the elegant balance and ingenuity amounted to nothing without the engine to drive it. Frederick still had no idea how to resolve this design flaw, and Master Branch's words settled around him like a fog. Frederick leaned into the doubt and pressed forward, his mind engaged in clockwork.

He strode across the square, down streets and lanes, oblivious to the traffic. He filed his vision down to a single point in front of him, and he kept it there as he walked. His automatic steps eventually carried him back to Master Branch's shop. Lost in thought, he went to walk through the front entrance and bumped up against a tall man blocking the door. Frederick looked up, startled. The man wore dark robes, had long black hair, and he eyed Frederick with the suspicion of a guard at his post.

Frederick swallowed. "Excuse me. May I pass?"

"Who are you?" the man asked in a Russian accent.

"Frederick. I'm Master Branch's apprentice."

The man stepped aside without another word, and Frederick skirted past him into the shop. Inside, a very large woman dressed in black tilted halfway over the counter, and Master Branch bent away from her like a reed before a gale.

"Your work is marvelous, Master Clockmaker," she said.

"Thank you, Madame." Master Branch clutched the lapels of his jacket. Frederick knew that such praise made the shy old man uncomfortable.

The woman had a much quieter companion at her side, a young girl with long hair. Both of their backs were to him, but the girl seemed familiar.

"I must commission a piece," the woman said.

Master Branch nodded. "Yes, of course, Madame. In thinking about what you desire, do any of the pieces here inspire you?"

"Let me see." She looked away from Master Branch for a moment to survey the room, and then she spotted Frederick. "And who is this young man?"

The woman's companion turned around then, and Frederick recognized her as the girl from the street. That night her thick hair had been braided, but now it fell loose over her shoulders. She appeared to recognize him, too, because she gave him a curious smile.

Master Branch perked up. "Oh, this is my apprentice, Frederick."

"What a handsome boy," the woman said. "But it looks as though he's been in some sort of row."

Frederick had not thought about how he must look after the alley fight.

Master Branch squinted at him. "Goodness. Are you all right, Frederick?"

"I'm fine."

"Boys. It's just in their nature," the woman said. "Frederick, are any of these your work?" She gestured toward the clocks hanging about the shop, and the watches in the display cases.

"A few," Frederick said.

"Don't be modest, lad," Master Branch said. He appeared relieved at the opportunity to deflect some of the attention, and came out from around the shelter of the counter. "Many of them are his."

The woman turned back to Master Branch. She smiled and began to pace the small shop with her hands behind her back. She leaned her nose toward the clocks and the glass cases, and cooed like a dove. "My, but they are all so wonderful," she said.

"Take your time, Madame." Master Branch rubbed his forehead.

The girl from the street slid over near Frederick, turned to him, and whispered, "Your poor donkey isn't still missing, is he?"

Frederick laughed, but it came out rigid and artificial. He felt a heat like the metal forge on his cheeks. "Thank — thank you again for giving me directions the other night. I was —"

"I believe I have made a selection," the large woman said. She spun on feet that seemed too small for her size. "But I have an unusual request, Master Clockmaker, one that I hope will not offend you."

"At my age I am not easily offended, Madame. Ask of me what you will."

"I would like for Frederick to make my clock."

Frederick felt a thrill that almost lifted him to his toes. He watched Master Branch for the old man's reaction.

"Madame Pomeroy," Master Branch said. "Such a request might very well offend another clockmaker. But I am honest with myself about the degree to which I rely on my apprentice. I will design your clock, and Frederick shall construct it. What would you like us to create for you?"

"There again, my request is unusual. I do not want a clock."

"No?" Master Branch sounded intrigued. "A watch, then?"

"No. Within the courts of the various kings and queens that I've been honored to visit, I have seen many clever little contraptions called automatons."

Frederick studied the woman. There was no way she could know about his clockwork man, but the direction of this discussion still made him uneasy.

Master Branch said, "I have seen many automatons in my day, Madame, and I have made quite a few."

"Wonderful!"

"What type of clockwork would most delight you?"

"There, I trust entirely in your ingenuity."

"Then Frederick and I will strive to satisfy your expectations."

"Thank you, Master Clockmaker, for your modesty and for granting my request. Come, Hannah."

Frederick took note of the girl's name.

He and Master Branch bowed to the two as they left the shop. Through the open door, Frederick saw the tall man withdraw from his post to follow the strange woman and her companion. *Hannah.* The door closed.

Both of them stood there for a moment in a silence that lingered like the traumatized calm after a peal of thunder. Frederick looked at his shoes. "Thank you," he said.

"For what, Frederick?"

"For letting me make the clock."

"But it would have been you."

"But you made sure she knew it."

"Years from now, she'll be wanting your design as well as your work."

Years from now. Frederick looked up at the ceiling, sure that Master Branch had said the same thing to his previous, failed apprentices.

"I'm closing the shop for the rest of the day," Master Branch said. He walked to the door. "I must meet a colleague at the guildhall."

Frederick nodded. "I'll lock up."

Master Branch opened the door. "How would you like to accompany me?"

A pause. "Truly?"

"I have something I'd like to show you."

"Thank you, Master Branch. I'd like to come."

"Let's be off, then."

Master Branch pulled out his keys and locked the door behind them. They crossed a few streets, and Frederick forced a measured pace. He wondered what this meant, that Master Branch was bringing him along. Probably nothing. Master Branch had just said it would be years, after all, but anticipation still tickled him like a gnat in his ear. A couple of blocks from the shop they arrived at the guildhall, and together they entered.

Frederick had been here before on various errands. The building flexed with heavy timbers stained the color of coffee. The columns marched along in regular rows, supporting a lattice of rafters above. Frederick walked among them, admiring the clocks mounted on all four sides of each post. Dozens and dozens of clocks filled the space with so much ticking and chattering that the sound became an excited frenzy in the ear. There were American clocks, German clocks, and French clocks, too. A small group of guild members gathered and leaned in close conversation, tick-tocking in their own way. They murmured a greeting to Master Branch, and Frederick bowed his head to them as he walked by.

Master Branch led him from the main hall and down several dark corridors. They came up to a small door, and Master Branch paused before opening it.

"This is a very special room, Frederick."

"What is it?"

"The guild's private exhibition room." He opened the door. "I thought we might get some inspiration for Madame Pomeroy's commission."

Frederick stepped through and gasped.

Inside were dozens of displays of the most ingenious clockwork he had ever seen. The number and variety of automatons overwhelmed him. He did not know where to focus his attention first.

"Reginald Diamond would eat a mountain of dust the size of his museum to possess this collection." Master Branch motioned for Frederick. "Come look at this, lad."

Frederick stepped up to the first display, a miniature old-style carriage made of wood, with horses and coachmen in replica livery. The wheels appeared to turn once every second.

"What happens on the hour?" Frederick asked.

"The little horses and men come alive. Sometimes the driver raises his whip or waves. Sometimes a horse will stamp its hoof or raise its head. I never know exactly what will happen."

"I want to see the next one." Frederick moved on. "I want to see them all."

"Probably not all today." Master Branch came up beside him, close enough for their shoulders to brush. "I've always loved this next one." He smiled over a life-size clockwork rooster. "Simple elegance."

Frederick shifted a comfortable distance away from the old man. "I like it, too."

The rooster looked real enough to convince a chicken to let it in the henhouse, a squawking barnyard bird bronzed in all its glory. Each unique feather had been stamped from a sheet of metal and shaped. No detail had been overlooked, down to the scales on its feet and the wrinkled skin around its jeweled eyes.

Master Branch said, "Each morning, this clockwork beats its wings and announces the arrival of the sun, just as every rooster has done since the very first rooster on the very first dawn."

Frederick nodded and went on to the next display, a little shepherd boy. It sat on a rock and stared downward, as if resting at the top of a hill, a flock of sheep scattered below it. In its hands it held a flute, and it touched the flute to its lips.

"What does it do?" Frederick asked.

"I'll show you." Master Branch stepped around behind the shepherd and cranked a lever. Clockwork whirred inside. Frederick heard the hiss of air flowing, the sound of the flute, and then the clockwork's delicate wooden fingers flickered over the holes on the instrument. It started playing a song, and not crudely.

"The shepherd can play three tunes," Master Branch said. "It can even change the quality of tone with a velvet tongue. Quite impressive, really."

It was more than impressive. It was a marvel. And Frederick's clockwork man would exceed it once he completed the head.

"How did they do it?" Frederick asked.

"Pardon?"

"How did they build the shepherd? Have you seen inside it?"

"I have."

"What's in the head?"

"Nothing."

"Nothing?"

"It's empty. The movements are in the chest." He chuckled. "Our shepherd is all heart, you see."

"The head is truly empty?"

"Of anything but cobwebs."

Frederick looked back at the shepherd.

"You know, Frederick, there are legends about clockwork heads."

"There are?"

"There was a German friar and magician named Albertus Magnus. Back in the Middle Ages he was said to have made a bronze head that could answer any question asked of it."

Frederick seized on this. "What happened to it?"

"No one knows, really. It's just a story."

"But what do the stories say?"

Master Branch shrugged. "Supposedly it passed from teacher to student down through the ages. Thomas Aquinas received it from Albertus Magnus, and passed it along upon his death."

"But where is it now?"

"The tales give its final resting place as a church somewhere in the Old Country, but others say it was stolen. It has long since vanished from the record. A fairy tale." The old man sighed and walked over to a chair with red velvet cushions. He eased himself into it like a hot bath. "You're awfully inquisitive today, Frederick."

"I'm just curious."

"Better to be curious about legitimate science and keep to Madame Pomeroy's commission."

"Yes, sir." Frederick took a last long look at the shepherd.

"I think I'll wait here for my colleague. You should get back to the shop. I'll show you the rest of them another day."

"Yes, Master Branch." Frederick turned to leave.

"One more thing, lad. *Mortales coelum ipsum petimus stultitia.*"

"Sir?"

"'We mortals storm heaven itself in our folly.' The story goes that when Thomas Aquinas spoke with the bronze head for the first time, he ended up in a rage, beating it with a rod."

"I don't understand."

"Put your trust in people, not in clockwork. The bronze head seldom gave an answer the questioner wanted to hear."

CHAPTER 6

Mister Stroop

H ANNAH SMELLED FLOWERS WHENEVER SHE WALKED BEHIND
Madame Pomeroy, and behind her was the place Hannah liked to
walk the best. When Hannah walked in front of the woman, she always
felt as though Madame Pomeroy was about to run her over and drum
her underfoot. When Hannah walked beside her, she received the same
stares that Madame Pomeroy drew, and that made her blush. So Hannah
walked in a wake of perfume, anonymous as a shadow.

Yakov should have been noticed far more than either of them, but
he could almost disappear into a crowd when he wanted to. He stalked
along just behind them, a constant, watchful eye on the street. Hannah
felt him over her shoulder, like the cougars still said to roam the more
wild places in McCauley Park. She did not know why Madame Pomeroy
had enemies or who they might be. The woman denied any threat of real
harm when Hannah asked about it, but Yakov took no chances. Twice in
the previous weeks he had come in close and whispered a word of warning. Hannah had seen him reach inside his robe for something. She had
grown cold and held her breath, watching Yakov as he watched the
crowd, until the Russian had finally relaxed and withdrawn his empty
hand. "My golem," Madame Pomeroy had said, patting Yakov's arm. With

the Russian, Hannah felt safer on the streets than she ever had before. Except when she used to walk with her father.

Today they were crossing Gilbert Square on their way back from the clockmaker's shop to the hotel. "I am so excited to see what Master Branch will create," Madame Pomeroy said over her shoulder. "Do you know that apprentice boy, Frederick?"

"Pardon me, ma'am?" Hannah said. She had been thinking about the conversation she had overheard between Miss Wool and Mister Grumholdt weeks before. Her duties for Madame Pomeroy had left her little time to even consider the hidden treasure.

"You and Frederick seemed to recognize each other."

"Well, we met briefly on the street a few weeks ago. But I don't know him well."

"I see. I liked him, didn't you? He has a very restless soul, but a kind one deep down."

Hannah said nothing. There was something kind in Frederick, in his eyes when he looked at Master Branch. He cared for the old clock-maker.

They continued walking and passed under the visage of the Opera House. Hannah looked up and sighed. Ahead of her, Madame Pomeroy was looking at the Opera House, also. Then, she gave Hannah one of her mild, knowing smiles. "I think I would like to take in a performance some night."

"Yes, ma'am."

"I keep a box reserved. Plenty of seats."

Did that mean she would be invited? Hannah stopped in the middle of the square, waiting, and then it came.

"You shall accompany me, of course," Madame Pomeroy said, still walking.

Hannah laughed, clapped her hands, and scurried to catch up. "You are too kind, Madame!"

"Don't be silly, child. Ah, here we are. My home away from all my other homes."

They climbed the hotel steps. Hannah could scarcely believe it. She had studied music and the plays of William Shakespeare in school. She used to dream of one day attending a performance, of dressing up in a dazzling gown, hair bejeweled, of seeing the actors rather than imagining them. Her father's illness had stamped out those dreams.

But now, soon, she was going to the opera, and she already felt warmed by gaslight from the stage, a light that was snuffed right out as they entered the hotel's main lobby.

Miss Wool paced the carpet before the grand staircase. The narrow woman looked up as they approached, and it was obvious by her expression that she had been waiting for them. Hannah positioned herself so that Madame Pomeroy stood between her and her boss, like a black lacy shield.

"Madame," Miss Wool said, "the hotel manager, Mister Grumholdt, would like a word with you." She never looked at Hannah.

Madame Pomeroy sighed. "What about?"

"You will have to speak with him to discover that."

"I see. And where is he?"

"I'll escort you to his office."

Miss Wool turned on her heel and marched off. Madame Pomeroy looked at Hannah, shrugged, and followed after. Hannah stood where she was, unsure whether she was expected to go as well. Yakov answered that when he put a hand on her back and gave her a gentle push in the direction his mistress had gone.

They trailed down the hallway. Hannah passed the dining rooms, where her fellow maids were setting places with china and white linen, and then they entered the main ballroom. They crossed the empty floor, footsteps echoing off the polished hardwood. Overhead, the enormous chandelier dripped with crystal and gold, and dust motes floated in and out of the afternoon light. The whole room seemed to glow, as if the walls exuded the joy they had soaked up from countless nights of laughing and dancing.

They reached the ballroom's far side, and down another hallway they came to the office of Mister Grumholdt. Miss Wool rapped with two knuckles.

"Come in," came the reply.

Miss Wool opened the door. "Step inside, please."

Madame Pomeroy turned to her bodyguard. "My, my. It appears as though we're in some sort of trouble, eh, Yakov?"

"No," he said.

"Enter please, Madame," Mister Grumholdt called out to them.

They moved inside, and as Hannah stepped by Miss Wool, the woman smiled at her, a horrible, vicious, satisfied smile, and Hannah shuddered.

Grumholdt stood behind his desk, vest buttons straining over his belly. "Ah, good afternoon, Madame! And this must be your Russian companion. Hello, sir." He turned to Hannah, and his grin fell. He stroked his red mustache. "And this must be Hannah. Hmm. I'm glad you're here, as this largely concerns you."

"Does it?" Madame Pomeroy asked.

"I'm afraid so," Mister Grumholdt said. "You see, Miss Wool has just brought something to my attention. An unfortunate incident that must be dealt with."

"What incident?" Madame Pomeroy put her hands on her hips.

"The incident some weeks ago during which this maid lost the composure we expect of all our staff."

Hannah wanted to flee from the office and looked around for some path of escape. She noticed Miss Wool still bore that wicked grin, and realized that this was it. Weeks later, and here was her revenge. Yakov came up and laid his hand lightly on Hannah's shoulder, as if to steady her.

Grumholdt pulled his pocket watch from his vest, glanced down at it, and put it away. "Surely you understand that I cannot allow the maid's misconduct to go unpunished. We will resolve this here and now."

"I see," Madame Pomeroy said.

"Therefore, I have arranged for you to choose a new attendant from among a selection of better qualified staff."

"I see."

"I apologize for any disruption this may cause."

Madame Pomeroy just stood there. Hannah waited, feeling sick. Grumholdt pulled out his pocket watch.

"Is there someplace you need to be, sir?" Madame Pomeroy asked.

He looked up, red-cheeked. "Not at all, Madame."

"Then listen closely. I have chosen Hannah, and I intend to keep her on. If you remove her from my service, I will leave your hotel."

"Leave?" Grumholdt looked to Miss Wool.

"Yes, leave," Madame Pomeroy said. "I will leave, and take my money with me."

Grumholdt fumbled over his words. "Well, I had no idea . . . That is, I did not suppose . . . If it is that important to you . . ."

"It is that important to me."

"Mister Grumholdt," Miss Wool said. "May I remind you of our discussion."

"I remember it," he said. "But the situation has changed. Madame Pomeroy, please accept my apologies. You are a gracious guest, and although I do not agree with your choice of maid, I will permit Hannah to continue in your service."

"Hans!" Miss Wool shouted.

"Miss Wool, we'll discuss this matter in private. Madame Pomeroy, please enjoy your stay."

"Thank you," Madame Pomeroy said.

Miss Wool puffed her cheeks up, eyes bulging, and then shot from the room like a flare of gunpowder. An awkward moment followed as everyone listened to her curses echo down the hall and avoided looking at one another.

Hannah wiped at a glaze of tears. If it was not certain before, it was now. Once Madame Pomeroy left, she would be fired. She wondered how long Madame Pomeroy would stay. Usually the wealthier hotel guests stayed for weeks or even months, but Madame Pomeroy was not like other guests.

Mister Grumholdt cleared his throat. "I must apologize for Miss Wool." He came out from behind his desk, which was spread with what looked like maps and floor plans to the hotel. "She has been overworked and overwrought of late."

"She was very disrespectful," Madame Pomeroy said.

"I agree."

"Then I have no doubt you will fire her." Madame Pomeroy turned to Hannah, and gave her an almost imperceptible wink.

"Fire Miss Wool?" Mister Grumholdt looked startled. "Why, no. Why would I? Oh, I see." He rocked back on his heels. "Madame, Miss Wool has been supervising my maids for years. I assure you that she has a long history of exemplary service. . . ."

While he blustered, Hannah remembered what Mister Grumholdt had said about floor plans to Miss Wool weeks earlier, and she stole a glance at the desk. The papers were yellow with age, and she struggled to make sense of them. There was a map of McCauley Park, with a circle drawn around an area by Grover's Pond. Then, on a sheet of building plans labeled TOP FLOOR, someone had scrawled the name STROOP over what appeared to be a second suite next to Madame Pomeroy's. But as far as Hannah knew, there had only ever been one suite up there.

"No, Madame," Mister Grumholdt said. "Mister Twine, our owner, would never let Miss Wool go."

"I make it a habit to avoid that word, sir," said Madame Pomeroy.

"What word?"

"Never," said Yakov.

Mister Grumholdt squinted at Yakov as if he had forgotten the Russian was there. "Yes, uh. Well put, sir." He pulled out his pocket watch.

"What time do you have?" Madame Pomeroy asked with an impish smile, and pulled out her own timepiece.

"A quarter to three."

"I think your watch is off."

"Off?" He laughed with condescending tolerance. "I don't think so. Mister Twine gave me this watch upon my appointment as general manager, and I doubt very much that he would bestow a watch that couldn't keep proper time. In fact, Madame, time and again I find this watch to be the only clock in this hotel capable of doing so." He put it away and patted the pocket. Then he returned to his chair behind the desk, looked down, and seemed to notice the maps and plans. "Oh," he said, and hurried to riffle them into a pile. "Pay no mind to all this." And he turned them over as if to hide them.

Madame Pomeroy looked at the hotel manager for a long moment. "Come, Hannah. Yakov."

She spun on her toes and walked out. Yakov waited for Hannah and then followed behind her. They left the hotel manager's office and, as they walked, Hannah threshed thoughts in her head like grain, trying to separate what was important from what was not.

All was not lost yet. If Hannah found the treasure, it would not matter when Madame Pomeroy decided to leave, and Miss Wool could do her worst. And now Hannah had a name by which to pursue the mystery, a name that meant nothing to her. The floor plans she had seen were old and odd. She needed someone she could talk to about all of this, someone who knew the history and workings of the hotel, and no one knew the hotel better than Alice, the gardener.

They reached the main lobby, and Madame Pomeroy was about to mount the marble stairs, which the stonemasons had finished with for now.

"Ma'am?" Hannah said.

"Yes, child?"

"May I go visit with a friend of mine from the staff? I won't be long."

"Well, I suppose. I was going to lie down for a nap, anyway. But mind you, I don't want you getting anyone else in trouble with Miss Wool."

"I won't."

"All right then, run along."

Hannah curtsied. "Thank you, ma'am."

She waited until Madame Pomeroy had ascended the first flight of stairs before heading for the kitchens. She found a tray of almond pastries, grabbed two in each hand, and stuffed them in her apron pockets when Charles, the head chef, was not looking. She left the kitchen and returned to the lobby. She strolled down the wide corridor that divided the east and west wings of the hotel. The hallway ended where two enormous glass doors opened onto the hotel gardens, admitting a breeze scented with grass clippings.

Hannah stepped out onto a gravel path that crunched beneath her feet. The gardens sprouted thick between the hotel wings, like a bouquet in a woman's arms. Hannah walked in the shade of towering oaks, past fragrant rosebushes, and by the hedge maze trimmed square as stacks of bricks. She found her way to a corner of the grounds where Alice had surrounded her small shed with a wall of dense and thorny bushes. Hannah had talked with Alice many times before, but had never been inside. Rumor claimed the old woman slept in there during the summer months, on a bed of pine boughs. Others said she had a cottage somewhere deep in McCauley Park.

Hannah reached the edge of the gardens and came up against the tangled barrier. "Alice?" she called out.

"Go away, please!"

"Alice, it's Hannah. I need to ask you some questions!" She reached into her pockets. "I brought you almond pastries!"

Silence.

"Alice?"

"Hello, dear."

Hannah jumped. The voice came from her left, out of nowhere, and then Alice emerged from the bushes. She was short, but Hannah had never been able to tell if that was simply because her back was so bent. She wore a checkered apron, and had hair that was white and see-through like a dandelion puff.

Hannah pulled out the pastries. "Here you are. Baked fresh today."

Alice's eyes widened. She clapped some of the dirt from her hands in a cloud, but her fingers were still filthy as she reached for the sweets. She took them gingerly, as if they were still hot. As she bit into the first she paused, and then grinned with stuffed cheeks. She swallowed and said, "This tastes like François's handiwork."

"François?"

"The head chef." Another bite, and the pastry was gone.

"The head chef's name is Charles."

"Charles the dishwasher?" She started on the second pastry.

"I heard he used to be a dishwasher. Years ago."

Alice scratched her head, and a few pine needles fell from her hair. "Is that so? Time flies, I must say." And she took another bite.

"Alice?"

"What, dear?" The second pastry vanished, followed by the third. How could such a small woman eat so much so fast?

Hannah tried to sound casual. "Could I ask you a few questions?"

Alice shrugged. She stuck the last pastry in her mouth whole. She chewed, chipmunkish, and swallowed. "Fair is fair," she said. "You brought me four almond pastries, so you may ask me four questions." She turned away and plunged into the shrubs. "Come along, dear!" she called.

Hannah took a breath, wondered what she would see on the other side, and pushed her way into the brush. A branch immediately whipped her in the face, scratching her cheek.

"Ow!" she cried.

"Watch yourself," Alice called over her shoulder. "And go ahead and ask your first question."

Hannah labored to keep up with the old woman, who seemed to know some nature magic that let her slip through the bushes unimpeded.

"Well," Hannah said, grunting. "I was wondering. Were there ever two suites on the top floor of the hotel?"

"Yes," Alice said. "You know how Mister Twine is, always changing things. From boiler room to attic, that hotel's a different building than the one Mister Twine built back when he was a fiery young man."

Mister Twine, a young man?

Alice continued walking. "Not like my garden. The only change I allow is growth, and I forbid anything to be dug up until it dies. Three questions left."

Hannah's skirt snagged and she wrenched it free, tearing it, and then tumbled through the last stretch of bramble into a clearing. There, in a perfect patch of sunlight, Alice's weathered gardener's shed slouched toward several makeshift worktables. Pots of all shapes, sizes, and colors lined the tables, and each pot held a seedling. Beyond them, a wooden trellis arched over a wrought-iron bench, and a hydrangea bloomed behind it, pale blossoms as big as soup tureens. Hannah thought it a charming sitting area, but felt sad when she pictured Alice there alone.

The old woman walked over between two of the tables and motioned for Hannah to join her. "Look at these flowers," she said, clucking and fussing over her plants like a nursemaid. "These are just for me. Aren't they glorious?"

"They are wonderful," Hannah said, although she could not tell one start from another. They all just looked green and tender.

"This one is a snapdragon. Oh, but don't worry, dear, it doesn't really bite. These are pansies, my shy country debutantes come to the big city for the ball. And these are hyacinths. They're haughty with everyone, so don't you pay them any mind."

"Um, I won't." Hannah noticed a table off by itself against the shed, bearing plants that were mature. "What about those?"

Alice looked and then leaned in. "Those are my herbs, dear. They're wise, you know, and they guard their secrets well, but I am clever, too. I'm figuring out their uses. Oh, and don't worry. I won't count that as your second question."

That turned Hannah's thoughts back to the reason she had come. "Alice, why did Mister Twine change the top floor?"

"I can't really say, dear, any more than I can say why he ripped up the carpets time and again, or why he knocked down those columns out front. Oh, but weren't they majestic?"

"I never saw them."

"No? What a pity. Like a pagan temple in Roman times. But I do remember he changed those suites around the time that guest died."

Hannah thought about the floor plans. "A guest named Stroop?"

"Why, yes! How did you know?"

"I've read his name."

"Stroop was a very wealthy man. He had a great big mansion that burned right to the ground up on the Heights." She giggled. "After that, Mister Stroop moved into the hotel so they could rebuild his house. It was only supposed to be temporary, but he never left, and he never rebuilt. He just lived out the rest of his days all alone up there. I'll tell you, he had quite a reputation as a recluse." She shook her head and tsk-tsked. "I just don't understand people like that. He had no wife, nor children. They buried him all by himself in the cemetery of the Old Rock Church. Now that I think about it, I suppose Mister Twine wanted to wall off that room in which poor Mister Stroop expired. Who would want to stay in a room where someone had died? You have one question left."

Hannah paused to consider. A wealthy guest who died in the hotel. A hidden treasure on the top floor. But what about the map of the park? She turned to Alice. "Was there a connection between Mister Stroop and Grover's Pond?"

Alice rubbed her chin, leaving a dirt smear. "Hmm. In McCauley Park? None I can think of, dear. I don't remember him having any degree of fondness for nature. He never even came down to walk in my gardens! He loved only his money. Well, he can keep it. Dirt and manure are my gold, and these flowers are my jewelry. I'm wealthier than all these lords of industry."

Hannah took one last look at the nursery and the gardener's shed. "I'd better be going."

"Oh?"

"Yes. I have work to do."

"Very well. I did enjoy the company. Do bring me some more almond pastries sometime, won't you?"

"I'll try. Good-bye." Hannah turned away, took a step, and then changed her mind. "Alice, could I sit with you for a while under your trellis?"

"That would be lovely, dear. But no more questions. Let's just admire the hydrangeas, shall we?"

"I'd love to," Hannah said.

They sat together for some time, but said very little. Eventually Alice dozed off, and Hannah got up from the bench without waking her. She fought her way back through the bushes and decided she had a little time left before Madame Pomeroy awoke from her nap. So, she left the hotel and walked to the Old Rock Church to have a look at Mister Stroop's grave.

It was a charming place, not so intimidating as the cathedral with its ugly gargoyles and windows like daggers. The Old Rock Church looked humble and solid, the watertight kind of place that offered shelter in a storm. Large trees scattered shade over the building, and a low stone wall surrounded the church's cemetery. Hannah approached, wondering where Mister Stroop might be buried.

She stepped through the gate and then spotted a very small boy nearby. He looked like a street musician, and he hunkered down behind a headstone, peering over it as if spying. Hannah followed his gaze and saw another boy kneeling in the grass before a tomb in a far corner of the churchyard, but she could not tell what he was doing.

She cleared her throat, and the little boy looked up. His eyes went round, he gasped, and then he bolted from the cemetery. Hannah watched him race down the street.

The one he had been spying on did not appear to have noticed any of it. A moment later he stood up and turned away from the tomb. He saw Hannah.

She acknowledged him with a smile.

He came toward her, a fiddle on his back, and tipped his cap. "Afternoon, miss."

"Good afternoon."

He appeared to be a year or two younger than her, and there was some-thing scruffy and wild and restless about him. Even though he was standing still, he had the presence of a hound pup testing the limits of its chain. "Peaceful place, eh?" he said.

"It is."

He nodded. "Come to pay respects?"

"You might say that."

He glanced around, as if he were reluctant to leave. "Yeah, me too. Paying respects."

The two of them stood there. Hannah looked down and smoothed her apron. "Well, have a nice evening."

"Thank you," he said. "You too."

"I will."

He waited a moment longer, and then turned away. He began to whistle a tune that sounded familiar. Before Hannah could place it, he had left through the gate and was gone. She glanced at a few of the gravestones nearby, read over the names and epitaphs but saw no Stroop among them. She surveyed the churchyard trying to figure the most orderly way to check them all, but decided to satisfy her curiosity first. She crossed to the corner where the street musician had been kneeling. Why had he been so reluctant to leave?

The tomb rested over a tranquil spot, tucked away on its own from the others. It was a simple rectangle of weathered marble. There was nothing obvious about it to suggest why the boy was over here. Nothing in the grass around it. She read the inscription and sucked in a sharp breath. Chiseled into the stone were these words:

HERE LIES

PHINEAS STROOP

MCCAULEY HELD THE KEY

TO HIS HAPPINESS

Hannah had found the place where Mister Stroop was buried, and she felt exhilarated at having touched the mystery in some way. She wondered about the words written there, and what they meant. It must have something to do with Grover's Pond. And then she wondered about the street boy's connection to the crypt and the man buried inside it. She was about to sit down in the shade to think on it all when the Opera House clock tolled, resonating over the city, and she jumped.

Madame Pomeroy would be waking up, and she would expect Hannah to be there. The tomb would have to wait for another day. Hannah lifted her skirts and raced from the cemetery, down the streets, across the square, all the way back to the hotel.

CHAPTER 7

Betrayed

GIUSEPPE HID BEHIND THE CHURCHYARD'S ROCK WALL, WATCH-ing the maid. She stood in front of Mister Stroop's tomb, staring at it, and made no sign that she had seen him stash his money and the violin. Then the Opera House clock pealed and the girl nearly leaped in the air. She darted from the cemetery, and before he could move or hide she flew past him not five feet away. But she did not seem to notice him. He watched her run off, and she never looked back.

Giuseppe let out a sigh. His instrument and treasure seemed to be safe. He had nineteen dollars in there now. Almost halfway to a boat ticket. He figured he would have the rest within another two weeks, sooner if Pietro could start paying his own way.

He straightened his jacket and set off to find a corner where he could play for the night's remainder, the more public the better. Maybe on the square. He wanted to be seen playing his old fiddle.

The night came on warm and still. Without a breeze, the city's black breath churned from the smokestacks and settled in drifts, turning everything dark and hazy. Familiar landmarks became indistinct, and the diffused light from the Opera House and the Gilbert Hotel backlit the pedestrians milling across the square.

He took up a spot on a corner and drew his bow over the catgut strings. The old fiddle squealed and yowled. Giuseppe winced at the familiar sound and wondered how he had ever made any money with the thing. But he had made money, and made it even now. Not much, but some. The instrument was like an irritating but endearing friend. For the last several years it had served him as best it could and kept him fed. It was ridiculous, he knew, but there was loyalty there, and affection, and a little bit of guilt over abandoning it for the green violin.

After a few hours, Giuseppe decided he had played for long enough and made enough, too. He headed for Crosby Street, where he met up with Pietro.

"How much did you make?" Giuseppe asked.

Pietro beamed. "I make thirty-seven cents!"

"Still not enough, kid." Giuseppe grumbled a bit and pulled out a few extra coins. "Here you go," he said. "But I can't keep doing this forever. I need my money."

Pietro frowned. "Your money? Is Stephano's money, no?"

"Uh, that's true. But the more I bring in, the better I get treated. So, anyway, you gotta start pulling your own load."

Pietro looked at the money Giuseppe had just given him.

"Come on." Giuseppe put his arm over the boy's shoulder. "You're doing fine."

They penetrated the dank street and came up to Stephano's lair. Inside, the padrone took their money without a word and kicked Pietro's rump on the way back to the kitchen, where a feeble fire glowed in the hearth. On the table there was a bucket next to the usual loaves of bread. Were they getting milk tonight? Giuseppe and Pietro got in line. Behind the table, one of Stephano's girls rationed out portions of food. Every other week the padrone had someone different on his arm, but they always left soon after he put them to work.

She was scowling when Giuseppe came up. She handed him a hunk of hard, dry bread and scooped a ladle into the bucket. It *was* milk. Rich, white, frothy milk that she poured into a tin cup.

"You two share," she said, and nodded toward Pietro. "We're running out."

"Yes, ma'am." Giuseppe took the milk.

Pietro got his bread, and they went to find a spot to eat.

They ended up settled in a corner on the second floor. Giuseppe licked his lips and smelled the milk. He wrinkled his nose. "It's sour," he said. But it was better than nothing. They dipped their bread to soften it, and when the bread was gone Giuseppe gave the last swig of milk, swimming with crumbs, to Pietro. They both wiped their mouths on their sleeves.

"Well, good night, kid." Giuseppe stood up to go find Ferro and Alfeo.

"I come?" Pietro said.

Giuseppe tried to smile. "I think tonight maybe you should go find some friends your own age." The kid needed to start making other allies. Giuseppe did not plan on being around much longer.

Pietro looked up at him. "But you my friend."

"Um . . . yeah, I am. No doubt about it." Giuseppe looked around for someone to pass Pietro off to, but there was no one in the room he trusted. He sighed. "Let's go, then."

They went up another flight of creaking stairs to the floor where

Giuseppe normally slept. He scanned the piles of mildewed straw and threadbare blankets, spotting Ferro near a window. In the summertime, it was best to sleep under the windows, with a cool draft flowing over you on sweltering nights. In the wintertime the best place was in the middle of the room, with lots of bodies around you to keep you warm. Ferro was strong enough to get the best spot any time of year. Giuseppe and Pietro stepped around and over the other boys by the light coming in through the window until they reached him.

Alfeo was lying next to Ferro, his hands behind his head. "I see you brought your pet." He and Ferro laughed.

"Shut up, Alfeo," Giuseppe said. "He's fine. He's just new is all."

"Well, tonight we only saved enough room for you."

Which Giuseppe saw was true. He and Pietro could not both fit there next to them. Giuseppe looked the room over and noticed an open space in a corner on the far side. He pointed toward it. "Why don't you go over there, Pietro?"

The little boy looked like he was about to cry. It seemed like he was always about to cry.

Giuseppe raised his voice. "Just go. You'll be fine, kid." He shooed him off as he would a stray cat.

Pietro turned away without a word, and Giuseppe plopped down on the floor. Alfeo started to tell him about a brawl he had seen between a tinker and a shopkeeper that day. Giuseppe listened, but he followed Pietro with his eyes until the little boy disappeared into the shadows.

"How much you make today?" Ferro asked after Alfeo finished his story.

Giuseppe rolled onto his back. "Not much."

Stephano's voice came thundering up the stairs. "Sleep now, my filthy monkeys! No more talking!"

Ferro lowered his voice to a whisper. "You gave that kid your money again?"

Giuseppe nodded.

"You're too soft, Giu," Alfeo said. "Trust me. You think you're just feeding a puppy, but it could still turn around and bite you."

Stephano roared. "Silence!"

Over the next week Giuseppe's treasure grew. Every day he counted and daydreamed and every night felt closer to home. That maid had never been back to the churchyard as far as he knew, and his money was safe. He had thirty-two dollars in there now. By next week he would have enough, and it would be time to pay a visit to Frederick and see about his help in purchasing the ticket.

He was in high spirits today and whistled as he ambled through the streets, looking for a good corner to play. It was all about timing, really, and a familiarity with the city's habits. It was about knowing when certain people would be in certain places, like the factory workers at lunchtime, or the rich folk on a Saturday night at the opera. The throbbing city woke and slept in parts, like blood pounding to the muscles in heavy use.

Giuseppe knew that right now most of the fishermen, their purses full, having sold their day's catch that morning, had set a course for the Albatross Tavern near the wharves. So he headed that way. He knew some bawdy ballads that could get those sailors jigging and dropping coins.

The gray sky hung low, as if the masts on the tall ships in the harbor could scrape its canopy. Giuseppe passed the docks and took a road that ran along the beach. His steps fell into a slow rhythm with the waves, and he caught the briny scent of seaweed drying in the sun.

Seagulls hovered and dove on the small crabs that scurried over the sand, and Giuseppe saw a small boy chasing the gulls as they touched down. The kid waved his arms, and the birds flapped away screeching. From a distance Giuseppe chuckled, but then he drew closer and got a better look at the boy. It was Pietro. Pietro, who never brought in enough. Pietro, who said he played all day but no one gave him any money. Pietro, who had cost Giuseppe how many dollars and how much time?

Giuseppe stood watching him. Then he shouted, "Hey!"

Pietro skidded to a halt, spraying sand.

"Get over here. Now!"

The little boy's shoulders slumped, and he trudged across the beach.

Giuseppe shook with anger. "You waste a lot of time down here?" He clenched his jaw and wanted to scream. "What are you doing, Pietro?"

The boy kept his eyes down. He shrugged.

Giuseppe lost control. "Look at me, you little runt!" He grabbed Pietro's face and forced it up. "I've been giving you money from my own pocket! I've gone without supper for you! He threw me in the rat cellar! For what? So you can spend your days chasing birds?"

Pietro started to cry.

"Stop that! Stop it right now."

"I sorry, Giuseppe. I sorry."

Giuseppe pushed him to the ground. "No, you're not. I'm finished with you. You hear me? No more money. You get nothing from me."

Pietro burst into a full wail.

"Shut your mouth," Giuseppe said, and walked away.

He did not feel like playing for fishermen anymore. He did not feel like playing at all. He left Pietro sobbing on the beach and could still hear him two streets over. A part of him felt bad for being so harsh, but the other part counted up the money he had wasted on the kid, money that could have gone toward a ticket home. That part of him was not satisfied at all. That part of him wanted to go back and pummel Pietro into the sand.

Giuseppe glowered and paced the city for hours, up and down the streets, ignoring traffic and pedestrians. He finally stormed into the cemetery of the Old Rock Church. He was about to charge over to Mister Stroop's tomb when he noticed Reverend Grey planting a flower over somebody's grave. Giuseppe tried to back away before the old man saw him.

But the reverend looked up. "Ah, Giuseppe!"

"Hello, Reverend."

The old man labored to his feet, his knees and ankles cracking like bending tree branches. "It's so good to see you, my boy. I've been wondering about you. Why haven't you been coming 'round?"

"I have been, Reverend," Giuseppe said in a mumble.

"What's that? Then you must be coming when I'm not looking."

Giuseppe folded his arms.

The reverend pulled out a handkerchief and wiped the sweat off his brow. "Is that brute Stephano treating you any better?"

"Same as always."

The reverend shook his head. "I've said it before, but there should be laws against it. One day, there will be. I promise you."

Stephano ignored laws.

"Well then, how are the other boys? Your friends?"

"They're all right."

"Come," the old man said. "Sit with me. Tell me all about what you've been up to."

Giuseppe paused a moment, and then he realized that he wanted to talk with the reverend. The way they had before. So they sat down together on a shaded bench against the church, and Giuseppe told him all about Pietro and about helping him with his own money. He told of the boy's actions, but he was honest about how he had treated Pietro earlier that day. He left out any mention of the green violin or the money he had saved and hidden in the tomb just a few feet away.

"Well, I'd be angry, too," the reverend concluded. "It sounds like you put yourself at great risk for his sake, and it turned out to be for nothing. And it has cost you."

"That's right," Giuseppe said, and pounded his fist on his leg.

"Of course, if I were this Pietro boy, I'd rather be chasing gulls, too."

"What?"

"Don't mistake my meaning. The boy was in the wrong. But if you think back to your first years here in the city, what was it like for you?"

Giuseppe frowned. In those first years all he had wanted was to have someone rescue him. Back then he thought about his parents all the time and dreamed that they were still alive. It had all been a mistake, and they would come for him and take him home. All he had wanted back then was for everything to be how it had been. Perhaps chasing gulls on the beach was how Pietro had found that comfort, if only for a few short moments.

"When you say it that way, Reverend, I guess I shouldn't be too hard on him."

The old man smiled with such kindness in his eyes. "You're a good boy, Giuseppe. I wish there was something I could do. You deserve a better life."

"I'm going to have a better life. Real soon."

"I pray that you will." The reverend wiped under his eye with one finger. "I'd better be getting inside."

Giuseppe thanked him and they said good-bye. The old man shuffled away, and Giuseppe waited until he had disappeared around a corner of the church. Then he went to Mister Stroop's tomb. He had squandered the day in anger and earned nothing, and he cursed himself for having to dig into his stash, something he had never let himself do. But he needed it for Pietro. He replaced the flagstone and left the churchyard with his old fiddle.

Night fell as Giuseppe crossed town. He lingered at the entrance to Crosby Street, hoping to catch Pietro. The boy never showed. No surprise after the way Giuseppe had yelled at him, but the little boy's absence set him pacing and turned his stomach in shame and worry. He waited an hour, and then Giuseppe went in.

He made it to Stephano's lair without incident. The woman with the milk from the other night stood inside by the door. Her dull blonde hair drooped in front of her eyes. She pushed it back, and held out her hand.

"Give me whatever you made," she said.

He took a step back. In all the years Giuseppe had known him, Stephano had never left the collection at the door to another. The padrone trusted no one with his money.

The woman rolled her eyes, lashes thick with makeup. "Look, kid, you know he'll know. Just give it over."

"Where is he?"

She pursed her lips like a tightened knot, and tapped her toe on the ground.

"You don't know?" Giuseppe asked.

"No, I don't know! He just took off all of a sudden and left me with you brats. 'Just get their money,' he says. Well, I've a mind to just get the money and keep it for myself. I've had enough of this."

"Here," he said, and handed her his take. "Best be long gone before he gets back, though. You know his temper."

Doubt darkened her eyes like a shadow. "Go get some supper."

Giuseppe nodded and left her, but he skipped the kitchen and went to look for Ferro or Alfeo. He wanted to find out what had happened, and along the way he watched for Pietro. He never saw the little boy but found his friends sitting up in their usual spot on the third floor. The other boys in the room talked and laughed as they never could when Stephano lurked on the stairs below them.

But Alfeo was quiet. "Giu, I'm really worried."

Giuseppe set his fiddle on the floor and sat down. "What is it?"

"I think we need to take you to the hospital."

"What happened? Why?"

"Because I've never heard of anyone's shadow falling off before." Alfeo kept a straight face, but Ferro snorted. "And I think you need a doctor to sew your Pietro back on."

Giuseppe punched Alfeo in the face and knocked the boy flat on his back. Alfeo looked up, shocked.

Ferro grabbed Giuseppe's shoulder. "Hey, Giu, he was only joking."

"It wasn't funny."

Alfeo sat up, rubbing his jaw. "Think it'll be funny when I break your nose?"

Ferro turned to him. "Back off, Alfeo."

"But —"

"Back off, or I'll thump you both."

A moment passed. Giuseppe grunted and held out his hand. "I'm sorry."

Alfeo stared at him. Then he took Giuseppe's hand and they shook. "I didn't mean anything by it. Look, we saved enough room for the kid. Where is he?"

Giuseppe looked in the corner. "I don't know," he said. "Either of you know why Stephano's gone?"

"Nope. But Ferro was there when he left. He didn't say anything, did he, Ferro?"

Ferro shook his head. "He was there by the door like always. Then Ezio came in and said something to him. Next thing, Stephano gets this look on his face like he's got murder on his mind. He called Paolo, and the three of them took off."

"What did Ezio say to him?"

"I don't know. Couldn't hear it good. Sounded like something about the Old Rock Church."

Giuseppe went cold. He stopped breathing, and the room noises faded. "The Old Rock Church?" he whispered. Had Ezio found out?

"Yeah. You like that place, don't you, Giu?"

Giuseppe tried to swallow but felt a throat full of gravel. If Stephano knew his secret, if he had found the stash and the violin, it was over. And Giuseppe was dead.

"Giuseppe? You all right?" Alfeo leaned in. "You look like you really do need a doctor."

Giuseppe staggered to his feet. "I gotta get out of here." He snatched up his old fiddle.

Ferro sat back. "What? Why?"

Giuseppe stumbled over a few other boys. "I gotta check on something."

He did not hear their reply. He fled from the room and almost tripped down the stairs, but by the time he reached the front door he felt like he had found his legs. As he approached, the blonde woman stepped in front of him.

"Where do you think you're going?" she asked with a sneer.

"Out," Giuseppe said. He pushed by her and opened the door.

"I'll tell Stephano!" she called after him, but he was already running down Crosby Street.

His rapid footsteps echoed over the cobblestones and bricks, but his racing heart sounded louder in his ears. This could not be happening. How had Ezio found out? He hoped it was not true, that Ferro had misheard, but it was a frail hope. He flew down alleys and streets, the city blocks passing in a blur. He slowed as he approached the Old Rock Church.

A strong wind had whipped up from the east, bearing the tang of seawater through the city. Giuseppe crept up to the churchyard wall and peered over but had difficulty making out anything in the darkness. The trees hissed and rattled overhead, and the cemetery seemed deserted. He felt a swell of relief but decided he had to be certain his treasure was safe. Perhaps it was time to move its hiding place.

He hunched down and ran through the gate, over the grass, to Mister Stroop's tomb.

He froze.

The flagstone lay in the grass, and the crypt gaped open.

"I told you he'd come," said a voice behind him.

Giuseppe spun around. Ezio and Paolo emerged from the shadows. Stephano slid into view behind them like he was rising from a well of black ink. He had one hand on the hilt of his big knife. His other hand held Pietro by the hair. The little boy grasped at Stephano's fist like he was trying to keep him from pulling his hair out.

"You were right, Ezio," Paolo said.

Giuseppe tried to run, but three paces later they were on him. Paolo slammed into his back with his shoulder, and Giuseppe sprawled on the ground gasping for air. He rolled to get up, but Ezio pinned him down and drove his face into the earth.

"Good work, Ezio," Stephano said.

The two boys hauled Giuseppe to his feet. Paolo held one arm and Ezio held the other. Pain flared in both shoulders. He looked at the angel, at Marietta, and saw her crying in the street all over again.

"You can't hide anything from me, Giuseppe." Stephano came up, dragging Pietro with him. "Didn't I tell you that?"

"I don't know what you're talking about," Giuseppe said.

Stephano snarled and punched him in the mouth. Giuseppe's head cocked back from the blow, and he tasted blood.

"Still a liar," the padrone said. He let go of Pietro's hair. "Go fetch it."

Pietro looked at Giuseppe as if he were pleading for something.

"Now!" Stephano shouted.

Pietro squealed and ran off into the darkness. A moment later he came back with Giuseppe's violin case and handed it to Stephano.

"Go back to the house now, Pietro."

The little boy tucked his head. Had Pietro seen him hide the violin? Had the little boy betrayed him? Had they forced him to tell? Giuseppe attempted to meet Pietro's eyes, but the other boy never looked up. He slunk away from them, slipped from the churchyard, and was gone.

Stephano knelt down in the grass before the violin case and snapped the latches open. He lifted the lid and then pulled the green instrument from its velvet bed like he was trying not to wake it.

"Such a pretty thing," he whispered.

"Yes, it is," Giuseppe said. "Where'd you get it?"

Stephano laughed without smiling. "All right. All right, fine. I found it in that crypt over there."

Giuseppe nodded. "I wonder who put it there. Better be careful. You don't want to go angering any ghosts."

"Oh, I don't fear any ghost, boy. You shouldn't, either. I'm the only thing you should fear. You still deny it's yours?"

"Never seen it," Giuseppe said, and spat blood.

"Well then." Stephano turned to Ezio. "You've been hoping for a new fiddle, haven't you?"

Ezio dug his fingers into Giuseppe's arm. "Yes."

Stephano shrugged. "Take this one."

A boiling rage tore through Giuseppe's insides.

"You got him, Paolo?" Ezio asked.

Paolo reached around with his arm and put Giuseppe in a choke hold. "I got him."

Ezio let go and went to Stephano. He took the green violin and held it up to the moonlight. He let out a low, vulgar whistle. Then he bent and withdrew the bow from the violin case. He lifted the instrument to his chin and winked at Giuseppe.

The sight of Ezio about to play his instrument was too much. Giuseppe screamed and thrashed. "Don't you touch it!" But Paolo squeezed off his air, and he sputtered and choked until the night started to vanish into a deeper blackness. He calmed himself to keep from passing out.

Stephano pointed at the green violin. "Don't touch it, you say?"

Giuseppe stared at him with six years of hatred.

"Why should you care?" Stephano asked.

"Because it's mine," Giuseppe said.

Stephano cupped his hand behind his ear. "What's that?"

"It's mine!"

Stephano sighed. "And now it's Ezio's. But I'm keeping the money. I've had quite a windfall."

Giuseppe's eyes welled up. He tried to pinch them shut to keep the tears in, and for a moment he willed the night into unreality. None of this was happening. It could not be. He was too close. Only another week and he would have been on a boat, feeling the rise and fall of ocean swells. After that, home with his brother and sister.

"What should we do with him?" Paolo asked behind him.

Giuseppe opened his eyes. The earlier wind had abated.

Stephano regarded him with the cold indifference of a butcher standing over a carcass, trying to figure the best way to take it apart. "We get rid of him."

Someone shouted nearby. "Hey! What's going on out here?"

Giuseppe recognized the voice of Reverend Grey. They all looked and saw a lantern bobbing toward them from the church. Stephano reached for his knife.

Giuseppe panicked. They would kill the reverend if he got any closer. His mind scrambled, and he looked down. He saw Paolo's foot. He stomped hard on it and wedged his chin under Paolo's arm. He bit down till he felt Paolo's skin tear. The older boy shrieked and Giuseppe sprang from his grasp. He sprinted for the gate and flew into the street. He spared a moment to look back and was relieved to see all three after him.

He barreled down the road, shouts and curses overtaking him, flying like he had wings. He burst onto the square, panting, and darted into the crowd, knowing that would not be enough to slow Stephano. Over his shoulder he saw them charging after him, knocking people aside in their pursuit.

The throng was thickest by the Opera House, and Giuseppe veered that way. Silk and fur and feathers grazed him as he threaded between the rich folk waiting outside. When he came through the crowd, he found himself at the steps leading up to the grand theater entryway. He looked up into the golden light spilling out and thought about fleeing into it, but dove to the left instead. He splashed down the alley between the Opera House and the Archer Museum, hoping he had lost them.

Halfway in he stopped and leaned against a wall next to a small theater door. He had never run so hard in his life, and he felt like someone had stabbed him in his side.

"He's down here!" Ezio stood at the alley entrance, pointing.

Giuseppe looked the other way down the pocket street and then looked at the door.

Stephano and Paolo appeared with Ezio, and they all three bore down on him.

He tried the door, and it opened. Giuseppe stepped through.

CHAPTER 8

The Analytical Engine

FREDERICK LEANED OVER THE DISMEMBERED POCKET WATCH, satisfied. He had laid out all its components on a square of black velvet and found the damaged gear. The owner of the timepiece had dropped it from a moving carriage, and although the blow had temporarily hindered the clock in its function, it would not prove fatal. Frederick replaced the broken part and set about resurrecting the watch.

His motions were practiced and precise. His eyes flitted, and his hands manipulated the pliers, calipers, and other tools like spidery metal extensions of his fingers. While he worked, he thought.

Over the last few weeks he had failed in his efforts to create a head for the clockwork man. Subsequent visits to the automaton exhibition room had yielded nothing of value to him, and he did not know where to turn next for inspiration. He had considered going to the museum, but the collection of clockwork on display there was inferior to anything the guild possessed. He knew a solution to his problem existed, but it eluded him like a pacing figure seen through frosted glass.

Frederick finished the watch and wound it. He set the time and held the piece to his ear, counting along with the gentle beating within. He sighed and took a polishing cloth to it. When he could see himself in the watch's face, he placed the timepiece in a box, ready for the customer to reclaim.

His stomach growled, expressing its emptiness. He left the workroom and climbed the stairs to the apartment. Master Branch sat in his arm-chair before an empty hearth, napping, with an open book in his lap. His feet stuck out wide, and his head had fallen back on the chair, mouth gaping open in a snore. Bread and cheese were laid out on the table next to a pitcher of cider. Frederick lifted the kitchen chair and inched it out so as not to make noise. He sat and ate. The bread was fresh, with a crisp crust and a moist center, and the cheese was nice and sharp.

When he finished, he brushed his hands together and stood. Master Branch still dozed, and Frederick went to him. He grabbed a small pil-low from the other chair and very gently raised the old man's head and set the pillow behind it. He picked up the book Master Branch had been reading, placed the ribbon to mark the page, and set it on a pile of books propped up next to the chair. The old clockmaker had so many volumes Frederick doubted they could all be read in one lifetime.

He looked around, scanning the titles. It occurred to him then that a solution to his problem might be hiding in one of these dusty tomes. It also occurred to him that the idea should have come to him sooner. He started in one corner and looked at the spine of each book. Some had nothing written there and had to be excavated from their piles to glean their topics. There were books of history, books of fiction, travel books, and science books. Of course there were books on clockwork. Frederick paid particular attention to those. Some of the material was interesting, most of it boring and mundane. Frederick read but kept one ear tuned to the chime of the bell on the shop door downstairs. But a lack of customers that afternoon left him able to read for an hour or more.

It was under the window on the south wall where Frederick found a book titled *The Clockmaker's Grimoire*. The words confused him. A grimoire was a book of magic, of arcane knowledge and spells. But there was nothing magical about clockwork. As Frederick opened the cover and read the introduction, he realized the writer had not used the word in its literal sense. It was only that a well-crafted automaton appeared as something wondrous and impossible, something magical to the observer who did not know its inner clockwork secrets. Frederick scanned the contents, and the titles of two chapters froze his eyes on the page.

"'Of Babbage's Difference Engine,'" he read aloud in hushed awe, and then, "'Of Babbage's Analytical Engine.'"

Master Branch twitched and smacked his lips.

If Frederick were seen with the book it might raise questions, so he closed it and put it under his arm. He left the room on his toes, descended the staircase one careful step at a time. He paused when he reached the bottom, looked up and listened, but heard nothing. It was unlikely that Master Branch would notice the missing book right away. Frederick took it down to his secret workroom, where the clockwork man reclined patiently, biding its time, headless and waiting for the spark of life. When he opened the book to continue reading, the bell rang upstairs, and he heard the scuff of the front door.

He set the book down on his worktable with a grunt and trotted up the stairs. He entered the front room and saw Hannah standing in the middle of the floor.

"Hello, Frederick," she said.

"Uh, heh — hello, miss." Frederick stepped behind the counter. "What can I do for you? Are you here about your mistress's commission?"

"Partly. Is it coming along?"

"Quite well, I think." Frederick wiped his forehead. "Master Branch is very pleased. It should be completed within a matter of weeks."

"Excellent. I will convey that to Madame Pomeroy."

Frederick bowed his head.

Hannah glanced around the shop like she was trying to find something else to look at.

Frederick said, "What was the other part?"

"Pardon?"

"You said that was 'partly' the reason for your visit. Is there anything else I can assist you with, miss?"

"Yes," she said, and blushed. "Madame Pomeroy also asked me to see if you would be free to take in an opera this evening."

Frederick cocked his head to one side. "An opera?"

Hannah came up to the counter and laid her hands on the wood. "Yes, an opera. Italian, I think."

"You know about opera?"

Hannah smiled, but there was sadness in it, and she did not meet his eyes. "I used to."

Frederick frowned. "And Madame Pomeroy wants me to attend with her?"

Hannah looked up. "And with me."

The clocks ticking around them suddenly sounded obnoxious and loud. He wanted to wave his arms and shout to quiet them down. "You'll be there?"

"I will."

Frederick took a deep breath. "You may tell Madame Pomeroy that I would be pleased to attend the opera with her this evening."

Hannah curtsied. "She will also be pleased, Frederick." She turned away from the counter and started for the front door.

"Hannah?"

She looked back. "Yes?"

"What should I wear to the opera?"

"Have you never been?"

"No."

Hannah smiled again. "Neither have I." She opened the door. "Just wear your finest. It really doesn't matter. If you're with Madame Pomeroy, people will stare at you, anyway. Be at the Opera House by eight o'clock. We'll meet by the steps."

"I'll be there."

Hannah left, and Frederick let out a long sigh. He was wearing his finest.

Footsteps clomped on the stairs, and Master Branch came down into the shop. "Who was that, Frederick?" he asked through a yawn.

"Madame Pomeroy's attendant." He tried to sound casual. "I think her name is Hannah."

Master Branch looked at him through his white eyebrows. He smiled. "I believe you are correct. She was asking about the commission?"

"She was. I told her when to expect its completion."

"Good."

Frederick cleared his throat, but did not know how to approach the clockmaker about the opera that evening, and then the old man spoke before him.

"Shall we get to work on Mrs. Chatham's mantelpiece?"

"Uh . . . yes, sir."

For a half an hour they puttered around each other in the workroom by their own awkward rhythm. Frederick kept thinking about what Hannah had said, about his clothes. He could not wear what he had on to the opera, but had no money of his own with which to buy a new suit. He hated asking Master Branch for anything, especially money. As they worked he opened his mouth to speak several times but failed to make a sound. When Master Branch announced he would be leaving soon to meet a friend for an early supper, Frederick panicked and just blurted it out.

"Sir, Madame Pomeroy has extended an invitation to me."

Master Branch set down his tools and lifted his glasses. "Has she? And to what have you been invited?"

"The opera. Tonight."

"The opera?" Master Branch stuck out his tongue as if he had tasted something bitter. "I utterly loathe the opera. Perhaps she is unhappy with us."

"I do not think that is the case, sir."

"No? Well, you shall go, of course. I'm sorry to inflict that on you, but she is a customer."

Frederick looked down at his stained shirt, and his pants, worn shiny at the knees. "I don't think my clothes quite suit the occasion."

Master Branch eyed him over. "Nonsense. You look fine."

Frederick nodded. "You do provide well for me, sir. I couldn't be more grateful. But from what I have seen, the opera requires a slightly greater degree of finery."

"Does it, now?"

"Yes. From what I have seen."

"Hmph."

"Perhaps, sir, if you think of it as an investment —"

"How so?"

"Well, Madame Pomeroy is very wealthy and well connected. There will undoubtedly be a number of her acquaintances at the opera this evening."

"Go on."

"We would be wise to keep Madame Pomeroy happy with us, and make a good impression tonight, would we not? For the sake of future customers."

Master Branch raised an eyebrow, like lifting a bank of snow. "Very well. You shall have some new clothes." He pulled out a few dollars from his pocket. "But only as an investment, mind you."

"Yes, sir." Frederick accepted the money.

"Head on down to my tailor, Mister Hamilton. He'll be able to set you up."

"Thank you, sir."

Frederick stepped out of the shop onto the street. He turned to the right down Sycamore Street and followed the lane till he reached the sign over Mister Hamilton's shop, a swinging plank cut to look like a spool of thread. He went inside.

Bolts of fabric lined the walls, and tables bearing different pieces of clothing crowded the small room. The smell of newly woven material stirred unpleasant memories, and something moved in the cellar of his thoughts, bumping the door. Frederick squeezed through the merchandise to the counter on the opposite end of the shop and rang a silver bell.

From a room behind the counter a little voice said, "Coming."

Frederick put his hands behind his back.

Mister Hamilton pushed aside a curtain and stepped into view, a sprite of a man not much taller than his counter. "Yes, young sir, what can I do for you?"

"My name is Frederick. I'm apprenticed to Isaiah Branch."

"Ah, yes, Isaiah. And how is the old clockmaker these days?"

"Quite well, sir."

"Wonderful. You must give him my regards. In the meantime, how may I be of service to you?"

"I need to buy clothes to attend the opera this evening."

He clapped his hands. "Ah, the opera. Very well. How much did you want to spend?"

"I'd like to be as frugal as possible."

"I imagine so, knowing Master Branch. I think I have just the outfit." He skipped over to a table and pulled a pair of trousers from a pile. "I believe these will fit your waist, but we'll have to hem the cuffs." He whipped a fabric tape measure from his pocket and ran it up the length of Frederick's leg. "But only by a few inches. I could take care of it now. Can you wait?"

"Yes, sir."

Mister Hamilton nodded and retreated through the curtains to the back room with the trousers hanging over his shoulder. "How long have you been with Master Branch?" he called out.

"Nearly three years now," Frederick said, raising his voice to be heard.

"And before that? Where do you come from?"

"An orphanage," he said.

The tailor went quiet.

Frederick sniffed and looked around. A bolt of cloth near the counter caught his eye, and the deep cellar memories rumbled again. He reached out to the fabric and took hold of it. The weave felt familiar, and the pattern blazed in his eye. In that moment the cellar door flew open, and like a thunder of footsteps on the stairs, the past rushed up to claim him. . . .

The pattern in the fabric had a flaw. Mrs. Treeless held it up to Frederick's nose. "You see this? I had to shut down the whole loom because of this!"

"I see it," Frederick said, head bowed. "I'm sorry, ma'am."

"Well?" The toothless hag towered over him, smelling of whiskey. "Can you fix it?" The little white dog in her arms, an old, ratty thing, stared at him with vacant, beady eyes.

"I don't know," Frederick whispered. The great machine sprawled out before him, a maze of gears and pulleys, shafts and struts. "I don't think so."

She stamped her foot. "Don't think so?"

"It's beyond my skill."

"Useless boy! I thought you were good with machines." She stormed from the platform. "I'll send someone for the machinist."

Frederick relaxed some and looked down at the other orphans. They waited at their posts on the production line, uncertain of what to do. If they left their places, they might be beaten. If they stood idle, they might be beaten. He leaped down to the factory floor.

A younger boy, a piercer, leaned toward him. "Psst. How long will the loom be down?"

"Hard to say," Frederick said. "A few hours maybe."

The boy coughed. It was the dust from the flax and the cotton. It filled the air and covered every surface, adding grit to the food they ate standing at the loom. Frederick pounded the boy's back to help him choke the dust out.

"Talking, are we?" Roger Tom walked up behind them. The foreman's voice always sounded hoarse, like he had just been screaming at somebody. "Freddy?"

"No, sir."

"How 'bout you, then?" He turned his bulging eyes on the other boy.

"No, sir."

"Really. I distinctly heard talking. Are you suggesting I conjured that out of thin air?"

"No, sir," the boy said.

"So you were talking?"

"No, I —" The boy looked at Frederick, wide-eyed.

In a flash Roger Tom had his belt out. He whipped it around over his head and brought it down on the boy's back with a crack that echoed through the factory. The boy dropped to his knees, but did not scream. All the other orphans stood transfixed, shaking.

Roger Tom coiled the belt around his knuckles. He glared at Frederick, and Frederick dropped his chin to his chest, arms straight at his sides. Roger Tom swung around on the other orphans.

"No talking."

Then the foreman stalked down the line without another word or glance. Frederick turned to the other boy, and without speaking he helped him to his feet. They went back to their positions on the loom, and Frederick held his stomach, relieved that it had been someone else.

A short while later Mrs. Treeless returned. She snatched Frederick by his shirt collar and hauled him with her, the little dog bobbing in the crook of her other arm. "Get up there." She pointed at the machine.

Frederick looked up at the monstrous beast. "I told you, I don't think I can fix it."

Mrs. Treeless stepped in closer. "You're going to try. The machinist will be here soon, but if this loom gets up and running before then I don't have to pay him a cent. You have until he gets here."

"But ma'am, I can't reach the —"

"I don't care if you have to climb all the way inside it! You'll get this loom working. Now, move!"

Inside it. Frederick had seen orphans with missing fingers, even hands. And he had heard of worse happening. Orphans died in horrible accidents working the machines, pulled inside and chewed up, broken bodies scattered over the fabric.

"I can't, ma'am."

She grabbed his ear and hissed into it. "You will, boy, or I'll tear you to pieces faster than any machine." She let go and pushed him toward the loom.

Frederick's stomach felt like he had eaten a bread crust with too many worms. He grabbed up his tools and turned to the beast where its jaws opened. He crouched down and climbed through the teeth, down the throat, to the belly where the air felt heavy and foul with the undigested residue of industry. Frederick closed his eyes for a moment, took a few steady breaths, and then began to work.

He studied the design of the loom, and traced the intended movements of its parts. Machines were the only things that made any kind of sense. Their function followed their design, and he could predict their actions. As he worked, the world outside the machine faded from his mind until the machine was the only thing left. Deep in its bowels he ceased feeling threatened and began to feel comforted and safe.

Time passed and he eventually found the problem. A metal screw had worked itself loose, causing a support arm to wiggle, creating instability in the mechanism and flaws in the fabric's pattern. Predictable. It was a simple repair, and within a few moments he was reluctantly crawling back into the world of the orphanage and fabric mill.

He emerged onto the platform just as Mrs. Treeless greeted the machinist. The lanky worker saw Frederick squirming out from inside the loom and gasped.

"What in blazes were you doing in there?" he said, eyebrows arching.

"I went in to fix it," Frederick said.

The machinist turned to Mrs. Treeless. "You let him?"

She began to pet her dog, plucking at its little curls. "So what if I did? I wouldn't have to if you charged a reasonable fee."

The machinist shook his head. He turned to Frederick. "You all right?"

"I'm fine. I think it'll work now."

At that, Mrs. Treeless, toothless, grinned.

The machinist looked startled at Frederick. "You fixed it?"

Frederick nodded. "I think so."

"I better take a look."

Mrs. Treeless grabbed the machinist's arm. "I won't pay you for it. The boy says it'll run."

He shook her off and went to peer into the loom. "What did you do, lad?"

Frederick described the location and nature of the repair, feeling foolish in the simplicity of it.

"On the contrary," the machinist said. "You've a keen eye. A trained man could've missed it. What's your name?"

"Frederick."

"Well done, Frederick."

"Thank you."

"Yes, yes, yes," said Mrs. Treeless. "Back to work, boy."

It was a few days later that the machinist returned. This time, he brought an old man with him. They came marching down the line with Mrs. Treeless and stopped when they reached Frederick's position on the loom.

The machinist pointed at him. "He's the one, sir."

The old man stepped forward. "You're Frederick?"

"Yes."

"My name is Isaiah Branch. I am a clockmaker."

Frederick bowed his head, puzzled.

Master Branch turned to Mrs. Treeless. "Yes. I will take him."

Mrs. Treeless squinted. "He's worth a lot more to me now. He's got a useful skill."

Master Branch exchanged a look with the machinist. "So he has. Skills wasted in this abomination you call an orphanage."

Mrs. Treeless snickered like she did while she watched Roger Tom at work with his belt. "Say whatever you want, Master Clockmaker. Your scolding don't matter to me any more than a magpie's."

Master Branch stood up straight. "I am prepared to fully compensate you." He looked at Frederick and shifted on his feet. "But I think we should discuss this elsewhere."

Mrs. Treeless shrugged. "If you like."

They turned and walked away.

The machinist walked over and patted Frederick on the back. "You're getting out of this hell on earth, lad."

And that very night, he did.

"Here we are," said Mister Hamilton.

Frederick pulled his eyes away from the fabric, and his mind away from the memories. The past retreated back down the stairs to the cellar, and Frederick shut the door. The tailor came around the counter with the trousers held out across his arms.

"You'll be needing a coat and vest as well?" He stopped. "Are you all right, my boy?"

Frederick swallowed. "Yes, a coat and vest as well."

"Would you like to sit down, you look pale."

"I'm fine. The coat and vest?"

"Yes, um, I believe I have your size." Mister Hamilton hauled a little stool over to Frederick and hopped up on it. He applied the tape measure to Frederick's arms and shoulders. "Yes, I believe I do."

Again he retreated to his back room, and a moment later returned with the matching pieces. "You'll look dashing for the opera. Now, will that be all? Nothing, say, for your master?"

"No."

"Pity. Unless Isaiah Branch has found himself a new tailor, he must be outrageously out of fashion."

Frederick smiled. "That he is, sir. But that's just one of the things people love about him."

He paid the tailor and strolled up the street with his new clothes under his arm, wrapped in a paper parcel with twine. He entered Master Branch's shop and called out. No reply. The old clockmaker must have left for that early supper he had planned. Frederick went upstairs, dangling the parcel on one hooked finger. He unwrapped his new clothes and got out of his old ones. As he dressed, he wondered what the opera would be like.

CHAPTER 9

The Opera

HANNAH SMILED AS SHE LEFT THE CLOCKMAKER'S SHOP. Madame Pomeroy was right. Frederick truly was handsome. She strolled back toward the hotel, and wondered if she would sit next to him at the opera. But she shook her head at the silliness of the thought.

A gilded carriage rolled by, and through the curtains Hannah caught a glimpse of a young, pale woman within. She wore a gorgeous dress of satin dyed the red, almost black color of an overripe cherry. She met Hannah's openmouthed stare with a blank expression, both disdainful and unconcerned. A moment later the carriage had passed, pitching gently on the cobblestones as it lumbered on.

Hannah stood on the sidewalk and sighed after it. That manner of woman could likely attend the opera whenever she fancied. She probably had a new gown made for each occasion, and never wore them afterward, and they gathered dust and moth holes in her armoire.

Hannah looked down and smoothed her apron. Last week Madame Pomeroy had called in a seamstress and ordered a dress made for Hannah. The finished gown was supposed to arrive that afternoon, and Hannah was intended to wear it to the opera that night. Hannah had no notion of what to expect, but felt a thrill of anticipation. However plain, the new dress would have to be prettier than the drab black maid's skirt she wore now.

Hannah pressed on and soon emerged on Gilbert Square. The Opera House sparkled in the afternoon light, and she smiled. She crossed the square and entered the cool hotel foyer. A tall blond porter stood by the entry, his arms folded across his chest, his uniform hat tipped to one side. Hannah cast him a demure smile. He hopped forward and walked up alongside her.

"Hello," he said.

"Hello there, Walter." Hannah kept moving, but slowed her pace.

"I haven't seen you 'round much now you're working for the tiger lady. I've missed you."

"You miss all the girls," she said. "Madame Pomeroy keeps me busy."

He took a few quick steps, almost a skip, and slipped around in front of her. He walked backward for a moment, hands behind his back, grinning at her with his blue eyes.

"So," he said. "Is it true?"

Hannah stopped. "Is what true?"

"That she has a tiger up there."

"You told me you'd seen it."

"Me? Nah. I heard it from somebody, though."

"Well, it's not true. I certainly would have noticed a tiger in her suite."

"What about the ghosts?"

Hannah rolled her eyes. "You know you really shouldn't believe all the rumors you hear, Walter."

"So it is true!"

"I didn't say that." Hannah skirted him and started up the stairs.

"Hey," he called after her. "Some of us are going for a clambake this evening. You want to come?"

Hannah stopped and looked back at him. "I have plans this evening."

"What plans?"

"I'm going to the opera."

"With the tiger lady?"

She ran her fingers over the banister. "And a boy."

"Who?"

"Just a boy. Enjoy your clambake, Walter."

"Come now. Wouldn't you prefer a clambake over some fancy opera?"

Hannah laughed and rose up the flights of stairs. That was Walter. Jovial, and charming, with lips born smiling. Not like Frederick, who seemed to be made of seriousness and nothing else. Where Walter seemed to glide on a boyish and inviting air, Frederick stayed remote and intriguing. Of course, there were those rumors about Walter. Connections and coincidences with several thefts from hotel guests. Hannah chose to ignore such things.

She reached the top floor and used the key she had been given as Madame Pomeroy's attendant to enter the suite. She paused in the entryway.

"Madame?" she called.

No answer.

"Yakov?"

The only sound to reach her was the ticking of the grandfather clock in the drawing room. Hannah had never been alone in the suite before. She wondered if she ought to wait until Madame Pomeroy returned before going in. But then she thought of the treasure. Stroop's suite had been somewhere up here. She tried to recall the image of the floor plans to her mind's eye. The two suites had been arranged next to each other, one on the north end and one on the south. Both looked out over part of the square. Madame Pomeroy's suite took in the view of the Opera House and cathedral, as well as the mansions up on the Heights. What would Mister Stroop have seen out his window?

Hannah left the entryway and opened the door to the southernmost room in the suite, the library. Neither Madame Pomeroy nor Yakov used the room, and Hannah had only peeked in before. Now she crossed to the window and looked out. A buttress of brick blocked her view to the south, but she could see the edge of the Archer Museum.

Hannah heaved the heavy window open, admitting a breeze and noises off the square. She leaned out over the sill, flapped away a few warbling pigeons, and craned her neck to see around the wall. From her stretched vantage point she saw what she had anticipated. There were city blocks and the Old Rock Church's white wooden steeple needling the sky. And the park. *McCauley held the key to his happiness.* Green and billowing, broken only by what looked to be a silver sliver of Grover's Pond.

Hannah leaned back into the room and looked to her left, to the wall of books. Somewhere on the other side was another set of rooms entirely, and the view from that hidden suite would have fallen directly on McCauley Park and on Grover's Pond.

Hannah heard the front door open.

"Hannah? Are you here, child?"

She slid the window shut as quietly as she could.

"Hannah?"

"I'm here!" she called.

"Come to me. I want to show you something."

Hannah closed the door to the library behind her and followed Madame Pomeroy's voice into the drawing room. The woman wore her customary black lace, her hair up in a loose knot at the back of her head. She held in her arms the most beautiful gown Hannah had ever seen.

It was made of pale blue satin that shimmered like the sky reflected in ocean waves. Royal blue applications of panne velvet decorated the dress with iridescent floral shapes, chrysanthemums and flowering vines that grew up from the train to the waist. Embroidered chiffon and lace circled the open neckline and shoulders, and the bodice sparkled with gems of aquamarine. Hannah covered her mouth.

"Come, child," said Madame Pomeroy. "We must get you dressed for the opera."

Hannah took a halting breath, and then began to cry.

"There, there," Madame Pomeroy said. "We must see if it fits, and tears will stain a satin gown."

No one had ever done anything so wonderful for her. Madame Pomeroy's kindness shocked her, and she looked at the older woman as if meeting her for the first time. She wiped her eyes. "It's so beautiful."

Madame Pomeroy looked down at the dress in her arms. "I think so."

"It's for me?"

Madame Pomeroy chortled. "With a waistline this size, you think it's for me?"

A giggle bubbled out of Hannah. "Madame, I don't know what to say."

"You still need to try it on, Hannah."

"Of course." Hannah reached around her back to untie her apron.

Yakov cleared his throat in a corner of the room, and Madame Pomeroy and Hannah looked up at him.

"Come," Madame Pomeroy said. "Let's change you in my room."

Hannah bounced behind the older woman from the drawing room, down the hallway, and into Madame Pomeroy's bedchamber. There her mistress laid the dress out on the four-poster bed and threw the heavy curtains open. Hannah took off her apron, and removed the white blouse and black skirt that all the maids in the hotel wore. She stood, goosebumpy, in her chemise and petticoat and tucked her arms in, hands at her neck. She stared at the gown flowing over the bedspread like a satin waterfall.

Madame Pomeroy lifted the new dress with a flourish. "I dispensed with the corset," she said. "Barbarous devices designed to torture women with suffocation and a bent spine. Besides which, your figure needs no assistance."

Hannah felt her cheeks flush as the older woman unlaced the bodice at the back. A moment later Hannah stepped into the gown, and Madame Pomeroy lifted it up around her. It was like getting wrapped inside a fairy story of dancing princesses. Hannah stood up tall and looked at the ceiling as Madame Pomeroy cinched her in. She felt her mistress's hands working their way up her back, then adjusting the lace around her neck and shoulders.

"There." Madame Pomeroy stepped back and looked Hannah up and down as if she were inspecting a mare at market. "Can you breathe?"

Hannah nodded.

"Well, I must say, you look exquisite, child. Come have a look."

She led Hannah by the hand to a corner of the room with several tall mirrors set at angles to one another. Hannah stepped into their midst and found she could see all of herself, from her head to her bare feet, her front and her backside. She did not look like herself at all, and she felt ridiculous, embarrassed. The girl in the mirror was much too fine. Hannah thought she looked more like a paper doll, not really wearing the gown at all, as if it were only laid over her, fastened with paper tabs.

"Absolutely breathtaking," Madame Pomeroy said.

Hannah did not feel breathtaking.

Madame Pomeroy clapped her hands. "We must do your hair next." She gestured to the ottoman in front of the vanity, and Hannah sat down. She faced an expanse of mirror, and an arsenal of silver pins and combs, powders and creams.

"Now." Madame Pomeroy stepped into the mirror behind her. "I think we shall pull your hair up in a loose twist. Some curls around your face, and some locks looping down in back. Yes, I think so."

Hannah said nothing as Madame Pomeroy fingered out her long braid. Then the older woman pulled out irons for curling and went to work, and within a few moments, Madame Pomeroy started to hum. Hannah closed her eyes at the feeling of someone's hands through her hair, remembering how her mother used to wash and brush and braid. But her mother had not touched her hair in a long time. Hannah felt an urge to turn around and hug Madame Pomeroy, but she kept her eyes closed, held her hands in her lap, and let her mistress take care of her.

Time passed, and every so often Hannah peeked at the transformation taking place in the mirror. It was like being privy to the secrets of some magic being worked. When Madame Pomeroy stood back and said, "There," Hannah opened her eyes fully.

She looked beautiful. Without vanity or shame, she could see that. But would anyone else? "Thank you, Madame," she whispered. She turned her head to see all sides, and the combs and pins glinted in the evening light.

"You are most welcome, child. I quite enjoyed myself."

Neither spoke, but both of them had tears in their eyes.

Madame Pomeroy cleared her throat. "I don't want to sully your face with the vulgarity of makeup. I wear the stuff because I need it. But you certainly do not. Maybe just a little of this." She lifted a bottle of rose water and spritzed Hannah with a floral mist. "Stand up now, child."

Hannah rose, still caught up in the world inside the mirror, and pulled her eyes from her reflection. She did not want to, as if she would cease to be that girl if she looked away. It was still hard to believe it was truly her.

"Here are your shoes and gloves," Madame Pomeroy said, and helped Hannah into them. Then she stepped back and rubbed her chin. "But there's something missing."

A rap at the door.

"Come in, Yakov."

The door opened. "Madame, I . . ." He stopped.

"Yes, Yakov?"

The Russian stared at Hannah. She watched his face, waiting for his reaction. Both corners of his mouth lifted in a grin. "Like a princess," he said.

And Hannah knew the girl from the mirror had come with her. She wanted to rush to him, to hug him in gratitude.

"Very much like a princess," Madame Pomeroy said. "What was it you wanted?"

"It is nearly time," Yakov said.

"So it is." She returned her attention to Hannah. "I know what is missing." She opened one of the dozen small tins on her dresser, one stamped with the shape of a butterfly, and pulled out a key. Then she marched over to a painting and removed it from the wall, revealing a safe. Madame Pomeroy unlocked it and reached inside. She pulled out a box, closed the safe, and replaced the painting.

"I know I'm gilding the lily, as it were, but I cannot resist." She opened the box and presented it to Hannah.

A necklace of diamonds sparkled inside.

Hannah touched her chest. "Madame Pomeroy, I couldn't."

"Nonsense." The older woman set the box down and withdrew the jewelry. She reached around Hannah's neck to clasp it. "It was given to me by one empress or another, but I never wear it. Someone should."

Hannah felt the cold weight of the stones against her skin. All those years admiring the guests' jewelry, and here she was wearing a finer piece than anything she had ever seen.

Madame Pomeroy nodded. "Now you are ready."

As they came down the hotel stairs into the lobby, Hannah glanced at the tiny holly leaf carved near the base of one of the massive marble newel posts. Mister Twine had never desired to replace them, and Hannah smiled at her father's little signature, as if he were whispering to her how beautiful she looked, and wishing her a magical night.

She looked for Walter by the doors, but did not see him. She held the train of her gown up and tried to keep from tripping over the fabric. They reached the marble floor, Hannah in her blue dress, Madame Pomeroy in her customary black, and Yakov in his long gray coat.

"I am so excited," Hannah said, but then Miss Wool appeared in front of her.

The prickly woman raised an eyebrow, and her gaze oozed over Hannah like coal tar, coming to rest on the diamonds around Hannah's neck. "Where are you off to in such a costume?" she asked.

"The opera," Madame Pomeroy said. "I would invite you, but alas I haven't an available seat in my box."

Miss Wool had not taken her eyes from Hannah. "I have no time for such things."

"Well, it appears that time is an enemy to us both," Madame Pomeroy said. "We're running a bit late, I'm afraid. If you'll excuse us."

Miss Wool stepped aside with a curt nod of her head. "Enjoy your time."

Madame Pomeroy blew onward like a billowed pirate sail. Hannah tried to follow after her, but before she could slide past Miss Wool, the woman leaned in toward her.

"You know you're just a toy to her," she said. Then she grabbed Hannah's arm, pulled her close, and hissed in her ear. "Just because you've been to school and wear a fancy dress doesn't make you any better than the rest of us."

Hannah said nothing and kept her head bowed.

Miss Wool released her. "Go."

Hannah curtsied and hurried to catch up with Madame Pomeroy. She did not regain her poise until she passed through the lobby doors. Out on the steps, she took a deep breath, caught sight of the Opera House across the way, and tried her best to ignore the stinging echo of what Miss Wool had said. She and Madame Pomeroy and Yakov traversed the square in silence. Hannah told herself that she was not a toy. The affection Madame Pomeroy had shown her while dressing her felt real. Madame Pomeroy cared for her. They reached the queue of operagoers outside the theater.

Hannah scanned the crowd. "I wonder where Frederick is."

"Oh," Madame Pomeroy said. "With the excitement over your dress I'd forgotten all about him. He said he'd come?"

"He did, ma'am."

"I thought he might. I'm sure he'll be here."

They arrived at the Opera House steps and the setting sun dusted everything with gold. Hannah took note of the women around her. There were so many beautiful faces and gowns, and Hannah's earlier doubt crept back. She worried whether she truly fit in. No one openly stared at her, except a few of the men, which made her blush. But then Yakov came up behind her.

"Like a princess," he said, his hand on her back, and her fears fell away.

As they mounted the first few stairs Hannah heard someone call Madame Pomeroy's name. She turned to see Frederick rushing toward them, waving his arm. "I apologize," he said as he came up, out of breath. "I lost track of time."

"Hmm," Madame Pomeroy said. "Ironic, for a clockmaker."

Frederick grimaced. "Please forgive me, Madame. Your invitation was most gracious."

"Well, I'm glad you could come," Madame Pomeroy said.

"What were you working on?" Hannah asked.

"Reading," he said, and turned to her. His eyes widened. "Oh."

Hannah looked down at her dress, feeling suddenly self-conscious.

Frederick stammered. "I, uh — you look nice this evening, Hannah."

"Thank you," she said. He stood tall and handsome in a suit that looked new, still pressed from the tailor's shop. "You look very fine as well, Frederick."

"Come, you two." Madame Pomeroy winked. "We're going in."

The Opera House blazed inside with gaslight and crystal chandeliers. Enormous vases, larger than any in the hotel, bore explosions of exotic flowers. Gilded cherubs and mermaids and angels leaped halfway from the ornamented walls, like they had been frozen trying to escape into the real world. Their smooth eyes oversaw Hannah's climb with Madame Pomeroy and her party to the second floor.

"It's just what I imagined it would be," Hannah said to Frederick, but found he was still staring at her. She looked down again, but smiled this time, feeling flattered.

He looked around as if noticing their surroundings for the first time. "Oh. Yes, it is impressive."

An usher approached them with a bow, and escorted them to Madame Pomeroy's box. He pulled aside a thick curtain and extended his white-gloved hand to indicate that they should enter. They stepped through the portal into the theater where the view opened wide and fell away.

Hannah gasped and rushed around their seats to the balcony rail. The low murmuring of hundreds of people filled the air like the thrum of cicadas. Hannah looked down a full twenty feet over the opera patrons in the floor seats, and up another two stories at the molded ceiling and massive chandeliers. Frederick appeared beside her. Madame Pomeroy's box nestled right up to the stage, and Hannah had a view into the orchestra pit.

"Shall we take our seats?" Madame Pomeroy asked. Hannah turned and saw that she already had.

Frederick extended the crook of his arm. The seats were only a couple of feet away, and Hannah felt a little silly. But he was obviously trying to play the gallant so she allowed him to escort her. He showed her to a seat beside Madame Pomeroy, and waited until she had adjusted the train of her gown before taking the seat next to her. Yakov stood in the shadows at the back of the box.

Hannah relaxed into the plush seat cushions, contented, waiting for the production to begin. She listened to the cacophony of the orchestra members tuning their instruments. With all the people in the auditorium, the air grew warm, and she touched the back of her hand to her forehead. Across the audience, fans sprouted in women's hands and fluttered like tethered birds. Madame Pomeroy pulled a fan from her handbag and flicked it open. She handed it to Hannah, and then produced one for herself.

Hannah looked at the blue Chinese pattern printed on the corrugated paper: a tall house with a tiered roof, a heron, and a cherry tree in blossom. She batted the air in front of her face, and felt a little cooler.

The lights dimmed, and the audience applauded for several moments before falling, save for a few stray coughs, into quiet anticipation. The orchestra conductor grabbed that silence and held on to it until it seemed ready to break. Then he made a delicate incision in the air with his baton, and the prelude music rose up from below. The melody began as a quiet whisper from the violins, sad and haunted, but soon lightened and expanded in mood until the opera began.

The stage curtain lifted to reveal a French salon full of partygoers in high spirits. The women wore hooped gowns and the men sported top hats and high collars. All of their faces were painted so thick with makeup they looked artificial, made of wax. But the passion in their voices felt utterly real. At the party, a beautiful woman glided through the gathering, and a couple of men approached her.

Madame Pomeroy leaned toward Hannah. "The beautiful one is Violetta," she whispered. "She's been very ill, but that gentleman you see, Alfredo, visited her during the worst of it. He loves her."

"You understand what they're singing?" Hannah asked.

"I speak Italian, yes." She pointed at the stage. "You see, Violetta is refusing Alfredo's advances."

"Who is that other man?"

"That's the baron. He says he loves Violetta as well, but she does not love him."

Soon after, Violetta left the party and withdrew to a quiet room where she sat and looked at her reflection in the mirror. Alfredo entered and sang to her, his voice so sincere and full of longing. Before the curtain came down on the first act, Violetta gave Alfredo a flower, and Hannah could guess what that meant.

The second act opened with Alfredo and Violetta together, in love. They had settled in a quiet house in the country, and it seemed to Hannah a perfect ending. But then Alfredo's father visited Violetta in secret.

Madame Pomeroy whispered, "He's telling her that her relationship with Alfredo is ruining the family's reputation. He's begging her to leave Alfredo, because Alfredo will never leave her."

"Does she?" Hannah asked, breathless.

"She does."

With each note sung Hannah felt the distance collapse between her lofty box and the stage. Alfredo entered and Violetta sang, weeping, of her love for him. She fled from the house, and left a farewell note behind.

"Does it say why she left him?" Hannah asked.

"No. She keeps the reason to herself."

Hannah felt compassion and admiration for Violetta, her strength in bearing her pain in silence. Upon reading the farewell note, Alfredo became angry and rushed after her.

"He believes she has gone to the baron," Madame Pomeroy said.

Then the curtain came down and the lights came up. Hannah became aware that she was leaning forward in her seat, twisting her hands in her lap. She sat back and looked around in confusion.

"Intermission," Madame Pomeroy said.

Hannah blinked and dabbed at her eyes.

"Care for some fresh air?" Frederick asked.

The three of them rose from their seats and left the box, Yakov trailing behind. They filed down to the foyer and then out into the night that had fallen over the square. Charcoal clouds smudged the stars out. Throughout the crowd, men struck matches and touched the licks of flame to cigars and cigarettes. People conversed and laughed.

Madame Pomeroy turned to Hannah. "What do you think of *La Traviata*?"

"I think it's very romantic, but it's also very sad."

"The two feelings are frequent conspirators." She turned to Frederick. "And what do you think?"

He stared at his shoes, which Hannah noticed were not as new as his suit, and he shrugged.

"Please," Madame Pomeroy said. "I want to hear your honest impression."

"Well," Frederick said. "The story doesn't make much sense."

"Hmph," said Yakov with a grin.

Hannah drew herself up. "What do you mean, it doesn't make sense?"

Madame Pomeroy held up her hand. "Please, Hannah. Frederick, what do you find confusing?"

"Well, it seems like everyone's just running around tripping over each other, making mistakes, and then somehow making them even bigger."

Madame Pomeroy nodded. "Go on."

"And why doesn't Violetta just come out and tell Alfredo what's going on? Seems like if she would just be honest with him, there wouldn't be a problem."

"We shall see," Madame Pomeroy said, "what it will cost her to keep her pain a secret."

At that moment a boy flew past them, darting through the opera patrons. Yakov leaped to Madame Pomeroy's side, and reached into his coat. Frederick stood up on his toes, straining to see where the boy had gone.

"I know him," he said. "He's my friend."

Three more figures, one older, two younger, plowed through another group nearby. They nearly knocked over a middle-aged woman, and took off in the direction the boy had run.

"He might be in trouble," Frederick said.

Yakov scowled and withdrew his hand from his coat. Madame Pomeroy crimped her brow in worry and patted his arm. "My golem," she said.

Frederick pointed. "They went down that alley."

An usher rang a hand bell up on the Opera House steps, calling them back from intermission. They moved with the rest of the opera patrons back into the theater, but Frederick kept glancing at the alleyway.

Hannah touched his arm. "I hope your friend is okay."

"Me too," he said.

CHAPTER 10

Escape

GIUSEPPE SPUN AROUND AND SLAMMED THE DOOR SHUT BEHIND him, but had no way of locking it. And here inside the Opera House it was too dark to run. He stumbled forward, kicked an empty pail, and knocked his head on a beam. He put his hands out to feel his way and found a scaffold overhead.

He heard the door open behind him and saw three silhouettes leak in like oil slicks from the alley. The door shut.

"I can't see," one of them whispered.

"Shut your mouth, Paolo." That was Ezio.

"Both of you be quiet, or you'll be running from me." Stephano's voice touched Giuseppe in the darkness like cold fingers through cobwebs.

"Spread out," the padrone said.

Giuseppe dared a silent step forward, and then another. He heard movement behind him and from both sides. Someone kicked the same pail and cursed. They were drawing closer. Giuseppe reached over his head, grabbed a beam, and swung onto it like a monkey. He kept his breathing as low and even as he could, drops of sweat hanging from his eyebrows.

Someone whispered, nearly right below him. "I thought I heard something."

"I'm coming," Stephano said.

Giuseppe's arms and legs quivered. If they reached up, they could touch him. He had to get higher. Very slowly, he slid forward and found a pillar. He held on to it and got his feet under him, and then he stood and found another beam above. He heaved himself up.

"I hear him," Ezio whispered.

Giuseppe heard the scratch of a match. He held still and studied the structure he had scrambled up. It climbed into darkness beyond the reach of the match light, but only a few feet distant a hanging catwalk led deeper into the theater.

"He's up there!"

Giuseppe looked down and saw Paolo pointing at him.

"Get up there!" Stephano shouted.

All three of them reached up and pulled their way toward him.

Giuseppe launched forward, scrambling between beam and post until he reached the narrow catwalk. It swayed under his weight as he ran, and a moment later he felt it lurch. One or all of them were on the gang-plank with him. He saw light up ahead.

He sped along the walkway, his fiddle bouncing on his back. The catwalk ended abruptly at a corner and bent him over the handrail. Giuseppe looked to his left and saw a labyrinthine assembly of planks, staircases, ropes, and pulleys. Curtains and great sheets of painted wood and framed fabric hung high in the air on a system of tracks. Charging footsteps echoed behind him.

He dove for the nearest stairs, and the wood creaked and groaned under him. At the top he spilled onto another catwalk and looked down, the floor some thirty feet below. There were people down there, back-stage, some milling in costumes, others rushing around. A few of them were pointing at Giuseppe, whispering. Stephano hit the bottom of the stairs with a snarl of fury, sweat smearing the dirt on his face. He had his hands on the rails to pull himself faster.

Giuseppe fled along the walkway, up another staircase, along another catwalk, zigzagging through the air. He slowed when he heard no sound of pursuit and eventually ended up perched above the stage. Opera singing rose up around him. A man's voice like the sweet, rich smoke from a pipe, a woman's voice light and clear as sunlight on the ocean. They were singing in Italian, familiar music that reminded Giuseppe of home. He froze for a bare instant and listened.

"Alfredo," she sang. "Little can you fathom the love within my heart for you."

Men worked the ropes and levers from the platform beneath Giuseppe's. He could not see the audience, but he could feel them out there beyond the curtains, all dressed up in their finery, smiling over the performance and basking in the ease of their lives. Not a one of them would help him.

Stephano appeared alone at the edge of the catwalk. Gaslight lit him from below, like hellfire beneath a demon.

Giuseppe ran. The walkway ended at a brick wall, but a ladder climbed from there. It was the only way left for him. He rushed toward it and jumped as high as he could, landing on the fourth rung and scrambling. A hand snatched at the cuff of his pants, and he kicked it off.

At the top of the ladder Giuseppe hit a trapdoor. He felt around, found a latch, and threw the hatch open, emerging into a room of heavy chains and massive gears ten feet across. He kicked the trapdoor shut and ran down a passageway toward another ladder.

He entered into a larger space overwhelmed by an ivory moon, the backside of the Opera House clock. A circle of flaming gas torches burned around its circumference, and the heat washed over Giuseppe's face. He huffed in the heavy air and hurried to the second ladder. He scampered up, through another trapdoor, and climbed out onto the roof. He looked around, spotted a chimney, and hid behind it.

A moment later the trapdoor burst open, and he heard Stephano labor up into the night. The padrone's boots thumped and his breathing was heavy and ragged.

"You think you can hide up here?" he wheezed. "Huh, boy?"

Giuseppe was trapped. The square lay several stories below. Nearby, the dome of the Archer Museum loomed in the night, while across the roof the cathedral's spires stabbed at settling drifts of fog.

Stephano paced the roof, getting closer. "You could have had it good," he said. "If you would have brought me that violin, we could have worked something out, you and me. Your talent and that instrument, we could have gone places." He pulled the big knife from its sheath on his belt.

The alley between the Opera House and the museum opened, a black chasm with a span of five feet, maybe eight. Could he jump it?

"Where are you, Giuseppe?" Stephano's voice came from a few feet away, on the other side of the chimney.

Giuseppe bolted up and sprinted for the edge of the building. He heard Stephano's heavy boots behind him. His legs burned, and the wind blurred his vision with tears. He reached the ledge and launched into the air.

He sailed across the gap and landed in a hard roll onto the roof of the Archer Museum. He shook his head and looked back. Stephano gripped the ledge and stared across the divide. The padrone looked down as if studying the distance, weighing the risks. His body sagged, and Giuseppe could tell he was exhausted. Stephano slammed his fist into the stone and pointed at him.

"You listen to me!" he said. "There's nowhere in this city you can go where I won't find you."

Giuseppe struggled to his feet. He walked right up to the ledge and stood directly opposite Stephano. He had escaped.

"I'll find you and I'll kill you."

Giuseppe tipped his cap to his former padrone. He turned his back on him and walked away, while Stephano screamed threats into the night, his voice breaking over the rooftops.

Giuseppe slipped his old fiddle from his back. He checked inside, relieved that the beat-up case had protected it. He slung it over his shoulder and crossed the roof, an ache collapsing his whole chest. His stomach cramped up. Stephano was right. There was nowhere to hide. He could not trust any of the other boys, not even Ferro or Alfeo. Pietro had shown him that. How long could he move about before one of them spotted him? How long before one of them tried to take him down to please Stephano?

Giuseppe reached the museum's great dome and walked along its base. The charge running through him dissipated, and he deflated like a sail. A quarter of the way around the dome, he found a row of skylights that glowed with the pale yellow of a dying firefly. He crouched and crept up to one and peered down into the museum through sooty glass.

It appeared to be some kind of storage room. Crates like those he had seen unloaded at the docks lined the walls, stacked half a dozen high. Worktables ran up the middle, loaded with lit oil lamps and big magnifying glasses. Here and there were stone objects, carvings and statues, skulls and bones from beasts Giuseppe had never imagined.

A bronze object glinted and Giuseppe recognized the strange head from the docks. Then a man appeared, the man with the dusty hair. He bent over the head and opened a panel in the brass forehead, revealing an intricate nest of gears. The man picked up some instruments and began to probe around inside.

It was too far away to see exactly what he was doing, and Giuseppe did not want to risk being caught up there. He sloped away from the window and around to the far side of the dome, where he found a ladder bolted to the wall. It dropped to a lower roofline, and from there Giuseppe shimmied down the shingles, braced himself against a copper rain gutter, and leaped to a nearby building. He began his passage over the rooftops of the city, traversing an entirely man-made landscape of angles, slate cliffs, and brick precipices, the final boundary before the domain of clouds and birds and aeronauts.

The farther he traveled from the square, the closer the buildings clustered and the easier it was to move between them. After several blocks he used an outside staircase to descend to the street, touching down like a wobbly sailor too long at sea.

He hid in an alley to recover his bearings and to plan his next step and, in the quiet of that moment, thoughts lurking in the background approached. He thought of the green violin and clutched his forehead. He thought of the stolen money, of his brother and sister, and moaned. A tortured moment passed, but he put a stop to it. There would be time to deal with all of that after he had found a place to hide.

He thought about Frederick, but even if he could trust the apprentice he had no sense of the boy's master. No, Frederick's shop would not work.

It had to be somewhere Stephano would never go, even if he thought Giuseppe might be in there. He closed his eyes. In his mind he ran through the city, down familiar streets, into abandoned warehouses and across courtyards. Nothing felt safe. He thought of each of the city's districts. And then the park.

Giuseppe stepped away from the wall. Of course. McCauley Park. It was perfect. But the same things that would keep Stephano out had until now kept Giuseppe out as well. Not too far in, the park turned wild and unmanaged, bristling with fearful tales and frightening legends. But the stories about the rat cellar had been frightening, too.

Giuseppe kept off the main streets, dove from shadow to shadow, hiding even from casual pedestrians out on the street. He took no chances, and managed to reach McCauley Park without being spotted by anyone.

For a while he stood at the edge looking in, listening to the crickets chirp. Gravel paths drifted through the trees like vapor trails left by specters and ghouls. Giuseppe planted his feet on the nearest track and stepped into the woods.

He stumbled often, with the sky blacked out, and chose the trails that led him deeper into the park, until those paths finally dwindled and ended. He told himself that the forest was just a different kind of city, with lanes and byways, and its own citizens. He was a foreigner, but he could learn his way. The farther he went, the older the trees appeared, thicker and grizzled and hard as iron. He heard the sound of water flowing nearby, and picked his way in that direction.

A few moments later he stepped into a muddy streambed. The canopy of leaves parted above it, laying a silver thread of moonlight on the creek. Giuseppe dropped to his knees and scooped up handfuls of cold water. The drink chilled him from the inside and soothed his aching muscles. A boulder jutted out over the riverbank behind him, creating an empty hollow. Giuseppe crawled into it, and curled up like a sleeping pup.

Safe in his cave, he released the thoughts he had kept at bay. *I'll never play the green violin again.* His money was gone, and he had no way of getting home, no way to ever see his brother and sister again. He began to cry and closed his eyes. He hugged his old fiddle until the tears stopped, and he felt better having let them out. Exhausted and shaking, he fell asleep.

A squirrel woke him. He opened his eyes and saw the critter flashing its bushy tail and bawling him out from a nearby tree. He tried to unfold his body and winced, sharp cramps twisting the muscles in his legs. He had a few scrapes and bruises on his arms he had not noticed the night before. He hauled himself out of the cave and stood up, hands on his lower back, arching with his eyes closed.

He yawned and hobbled to the stream for a drink. His stomach grumbled to say that water was not enough. Giuseppe had not eaten anything the previous day, and only a little more than that the day before. The memories of his loss and escape felt distant, as if months or years had already passed. But the pain that hollowed out his gut felt all too recent, and had nothing to do with his hunger.

He climbed up on the boulder he had slept under and looked around. Trees in every direction, and underbrush and bramble hid any paths that might be winding between them. The steadfast squirrel followed him, bounding and hollering from tree to tree.

"All right, all right," Giuseppe said. "I'm going."

He did not know where, but he had no reason to stay where he was. He had made no plan when he decided to hide in the park. He only knew the next step when he took it, and right now the next step was to explore, look for paths, and find some food.

"I might be back, though." Giuseppe wagged his finger. "Come evening, you may look mighty tasty."

He scuttled down the rock and considered his options. If he took off in some random fashion, he was less likely to find a path and more likely to get disoriented. But if he kept to the streambed, he could always come back to the cave for shelter that night.

He looked to both sides, and liked the way the creek widened to the right. He set off, whistling. Last night the forest had seemed haunted, but in the sunshine it felt alive. Not completely safe, but not sinister, either.

Along the way he looked for something edible. He knew almost nothing of wild food, but he doubted he would find a bread crust tree. He did know that certain plants could be poisonous, but without knowing which ones, he felt reluctant to try anything. He stood over some mushrooms, biting his nails. He peered at some tiny red berries, chewing his lower lip. When he found a bush bearing blueberries, he recognized them even though he had never tasted one.

He plucked a handful, and they burst in his mouth, juicy and sweet. He made a breakfast of them, nearly picked the whole bush clean, and patted his full belly with fingers stained purple. He rinsed the stickiness in the creek, and swaggered on. He would be fine out here. He could survive. He had just found his own breakfast.

He had a harder time finding lunch. The berries did not satisfy him for very long, and he scanned the brush for more. He noted several small trails that looked more used by animals than people. Cougars were said to still roam these woods, but he had not seen any sign of one, nor of any bears or deer. He observed plenty of birds, and their song passed among the trees like a rumor.

In the late afternoon, Giuseppe decided to return to his cave. On his way back, he noticed some walnuts hidden in the grass on an embankment. He had missed them on his way through that morning, but gathered them in pocketfuls. He returned to the blueberry bush and snatched the few stragglers left behind.

Back at his cave, he tried to crack the nuts open between two river rocks. When their hard shells finally shattered, they smashed most of the meat inside. The tedious task of picking out the meager bits took most of the evening. And the nuts tasted bitter. He finished his meal with the berries and folded his arms in frustration.

The same squirrel resumed its post as sentry and Giuseppe gritted his teeth at the chattering. His threat that morning had been idle. Even if he could catch the thing, he had no ability to make a fire to cook it.

"You're safe for now," he said.

He curled up under the rock and covered his ears. Before long, he fell asleep.

The squirrel woke him for the second time. Giuseppe leaped from his cave, grabbed a stick, and hurled it. The animal skittered around the tree, and the stick bounced off the bark, harmless.

"Be quiet!" Giuseppe shouted.

He picked up a rock, but the animal climbed higher, out of the reach of anything Giuseppe could throw. It ranted like it was really angry now.

"Suit yourself," Giuseppe grumbled, and dropped the rock.

He turned to the left this time and set off into the day's exploration. There were no berry bushes that morning, and only a few more walnuts by that afternoon. The streambed thinned, and the brush on either side closed in, strung with spiderwebs and studded with thorns. Branches clawed at Giuseppe and scratched him. He pressed as deep as he could, but by evening he gave up and turned back.

He nibbled on what he could get from the nuts and tried to fill up the rest of the room in his belly with water. All that did was wake him up several times during the night with a piercing need to relieve himself.

On the third day he felt weakened, with a tremble in his legs and arms. Stephano kept them all half-starved, and two days of trudging through the woods with even less food had exhausted him. He still resisted the idea of taking off blindly into the forest, but had explored as far as he dared along the creek. So he spent most of the day sulking outside his cave, shouting at that same dogged squirrel. Giuseppe had never encountered a creature more persistent.

He went to bed before the sun had set, with a pain in his stomach that kept him awake. He huddled at the back of the cave, but could not escape the hunger or the reality of his situation. He was in serious trouble. Even if he ventured into the trackless woods in pursuit of food, could he survive on berries and nuts? Giuseppe whimpered. He would starve out here.

For half a breath, he wished he would have thrown that green violin right back into the bay the day he found it. If he had, he would never have played it, and if he had never played it, he would never have gathered up any hope for escape. Everything would be how it was before the shipwreck.

In that moment, the pang of regret passed on like a morning fog swept away by the sun. No. He would never go back to the way it was, not even if it meant his end beneath the trees. He collapsed on the ground. "I'm sorry," he said to his brother and sister. "I tried." His tears fell like glass beads in the dust.

CHAPTER 11

A Whole New Problem

FREDERICK KNEW IT WAS GIUSEPPE. HE CLIMBED THE OPERA House steps and peered at the alley into which the busker had fled, thinking that he should have gone after him to help. That was what a friend would do. Instead he followed Hannah, hoping to see Giuseppe emerge from between the buildings. His friend never appeared.

They reentered the lobby. Hannah took hold of his hand and squeezed it, and that contact forced out all thoughts of Giuseppe. He swallowed.

"What do you think will happen to Violetta and Alfredo?" she asked.

Something implausible, ridiculous, and entirely avoidable, he was sure. "I don't know," he said, and worried about the sweat on his palms soaking into her white gloves. "We'll just have to watch and see."

She let go of his hand, and Madame Pomeroy led the way back to her box. Everyone except the Russian took their seats. Hannah pulled out her fan and waved it in front of her face, sighing like she was trying to blow out a candle. The air from her fan wisped over her, and carried the scent of roses toward him.

"Frederick?" Hannah said.

"Yes?"

"Do you really think Violetta should tell Alfredo why she has to leave?"

"I do."

"But it won't change anything, will it? I mean, she still has to leave him, and telling him would only make it harder. Wouldn't it be better to spare him and suffer in silence?"

Frederick folded his arms. "Maybe. But I suspect not telling him will make it that much worse."

"How so?"

"It just seems that the two are destined for tragedy."

She eased back into her seat and looked down at the stage. "Oh."

The lights dimmed and the curtain rose on another party. Gypsies and bullfighters danced and sang to entertain the party guests. Those scenes were fun. But before long, Violetta entered on the arms of the man Madame Pomeroy had said was the baron, and Frederick rolled his eyes. *Of course.* Alfredo was already there at the party and saw them enter together. He and the baron played against each other at the gambling table. Alfredo finished with a fistful of the baron's money.

After that, Violetta approached Alfredo and sang to him. Frederick did not understand Italian, but he guessed she was asking him to leave the party, which of course he would not.

Frederick heard Madame Pomeroy whisper to Hannah, "She is afraid the baron will challenge Alfredo to a duel and kill him."

"But Alfredo doesn't believe her, does he?" Hannah said. "He thinks she's in love with the baron."

Instead of leaving, Alfredo became enraged and threw the money he had won in Violetta's face. Hannah gasped, and all the party guests onstage became angry at Alfredo and drove him out. Frederick felt for the man. He suffered so much hurt without knowing the reason.

Violetta sang to him as he departed.

Madame Pomeroy translated. "'Alfredo, Alfredo, little can you fathom the love within my heart for you.'"

The act ended.

Hannah cried beside him, both her hands over her face. Her reaction to the story puzzled and annoyed Frederick. They were only actors. Then he felt bad, and reached out his arm to put it around her. But he ended up holding it behind her without touching, like a scarecrow, before pulling it back. Hannah dropped her hands in her lap and turned to him.

"You were right."

He pulled a kerchief from his coat pocket and handed it to her.

"Maybe she should have told him," she said.

"It's his fault, too," Frederick said. "He never really asked her why. It was like he didn't want to know."

She nodded, and the third act began.

Violetta reclined in a bed, with a pale face and shadowed eyes, attended by a doctor. And moments later, alone onstage, she read a letter. Frederick did not need to know what it said. The singer's voice conveyed everything in her heart. Grief and love and weary resignation. In spite of himself, Frederick felt moved, and he wanted to reach out and comfort her, too.

Alfredo arrived but Frederick could see it was too late. Then Alfredo's father entered, bent under a mountain of regret. Alfredo and Violetta sang to each other, and the music seemed to linger in the air long after she died in his arms, like the runnels and fallen leaves after a storm. With that scene, the opera ended. Frederick's chest quivered, and he cleared his throat. He rubbed his eyes.

Hannah clutched Frederick's kerchief. "It was beautiful, Madame," she said.

Madame Pomeroy laid her hand over Hannah's. "A wonderful production."

They rose and shuffled with the crowd through the lobby, out the doors, and down the steps. A few opera patrons spoke in hushed but enthusiastic conversation, extolling one performance or another, but most were silent. Frederick also found it difficult to speak. Words seemed an intrusion.

He decided to walk with them back to the hotel. They ambled across the square and when they reached the entrance Madame Pomeroy turned to him.

"Frederick," she said, and covered a yawn. "Would you mind waiting down here for Hannah? I'd like someone to see her home."

Frederick bowed. "I would be glad to."

Hannah smiled. "I won't be long."

They went inside, and Frederick put his hands in his pockets and looked up at the sky. He paced a little in front of the stairs, casting expectant looks at the hotel entrance. He noticed a blond porter leaning in the doorway, watching him. When they made eye contact, the boy dislodged himself and loped down to Frederick.

"You were at the opera, weren't you?" he said. "With Hannah? I saw you come back with them."

The boy was taller and stronger-looking than Frederick. And he leaned forward with a subtle menace in his posture, as if he was trying to cast Frederick in his shadow.

"I was," Frederick said.

"How do you know Hannah?"

"I am making a clock for Madame Pomeroy."

"Oh," the boy said. He looked Frederick over. "Oh, now it makes sense. So the opera, huh? Isn't that just a bunch of people singing for no reason?"

Frederick smiled. "To you? Most likely."

A grin landed for a moment on the porter's face before confusion set in. And anger. "What is that supposed to mean?"

"Nothing. You should go sometime."

"To the opera?"

"Why not?"

"Maybe I will. Maybe I'll invite Hannah."

Frederick did not like this boy, and did not like the thought of Hannah going to the opera with him. "How good is your Italian?"

"I don't speak Italian. Why . . . ? Wait, you mean they don't sing English?"

"Hello, Walter," Hannah said, gliding down the stairs. "I see you've met Frederick."

"Yeah," he said. "We met."

Hannah had changed out of the blue dress, but Frederick still saw the gown, as if it were hidden beneath her maid's uniform.

"We met," Frederick said. "In fact, I was just telling your porter here that he should attend the opera sometime."

Hannah beamed. "Oh, you should, Walter, you really should. Take Abigail, she would love it."

The porter shifted back and forth on his feet.

Frederick offered Hannah his arm. "Shall we?"

She took it with both hands. "Yes. Good night, Walter."

"Hannah," the porter said. "Grumholdt says I get off in ten minutes."

"But it's after midnight."

"Not by his watch."

The two of them shared a laugh. Frederick watched them and felt like an outsider.

"So if you want to wait," the porter said, "I could walk you home."

Hannah seemed to be thinking about it, and Frederick waited. Then, she reaffirmed her grip on Frederick's arm.

"No, thank you. Frederick will take me."

The porter stopped shifting and fixed them both with a stare.

"Suit yourself, then," he said.

"Good night, Walter," Hannah said as though she were closing a door.

Frederick nodded at the porter, but only got a scowl in return, and Hannah pulled Frederick away. The two of them walked side by side down Basket Street. The sky had cleared, and cold moonlight brushed the streets like whitewash, with splatters of yellow gaslight here and there. They shared the street with a few pedestrians, while stray cats prowled the alleys after rats and mice.

"So where do you live?" Frederick asked.

She looked away. "Near where we met that first time. Down in the tenements. But I haven't always lived there."

He did not know what to say. "Seemed like a better street than some."

She said nothing.

"Better than an orphanage," he said.

"Why do you say that?"

"Because I lived in one."

"You did?"

"Yeah. Since I was six. Then a few years ago Master Branch came for me. He wanted an apprentice." The words surprised Frederick, the second time in the last few weeks he had talked so openly. It scared him, but at the same time it felt good to place his trust in others. In friends.

She leaned in closer. "What happened to your parents?"

"My father died when I was a baby."

Hannah waited. "And your mother?"

Frederick did not answer.

"Did she leave you?"

He shrugged and forced a weak smile. "It's all right."

"But what happened to her?"

"I don't know."

Hannah looked at him with her mouth partway open. Her gaze dropped to the cobblestones. "I can't believe she left you."

"I'm sure she had a reason."

"And you don't know where she is now?"

Frederick wriggled his arm a bit where she held him, and she let go. "No," he said.

"Could you find out somehow?"

Frederick stopped in the middle of the sidewalk. "Look, she had a reason."

Hannah lowered her voice. "I know. I'm sure she did. But have you ever thought of finding out about her?"

Frederick felt the answer in his mouth like a rusted nail he could not spit out. He had reached the limits of what he wanted to share, how much he wanted to trust, and marched forward, staring straight ahead.

"Frederick," Hannah said, behind him. "I didn't — I'm sorry if I've upset you."

"It's fine," he said. "I'm fine."

She sidled up to him as they walked, and from the corner of his eye he could see her taking hesitant glances at his face. They went on in silence until they reached her building.

"Good night," he said, trying to sound friendly. But he did not want any more questions.

H.C. STORM SCHOOL

"I really enjoyed the opera with you, Frederick." Hannah seemed as though she wanted to say something more, but nodded to herself. "So, good night."

Her steps echoed as she climbed the wooden staircase up the side of her building. He waited until she reached her apartment and opened the door. He waved at her, and she waved back before stepping inside.

For a few minutes he stood in the road, looking up at her apartment. Then he turned and strode up Basket Street with his hands clasped behind his back.

Clockwork could not run counter to its nature. The seconds, minutes, and hours moved only forward. Patient, precise, and unstoppable. Memory was an indulgence, an illusion that broke like a wave upon the juggernaut of time. The past remained the past.

Frederick forced his thoughts away from his conversation with Hannah and on to the clockwork man. Babbage's work had been a revelation, but Frederick had not yet finished the chapter on the Analytical Engine. Based on what he had learned thus far, Frederick could not wait to read on. Babbage was a genius. Before the Analytical Engine, he had created the Difference Engine, a device for complex mathematical calculation, and already the implications of that machine had opened up new inroads on Frederick's problem.

Diverted as he was by his thoughts, the journey to Master Branch's shop passed quickly. Frederick arrived, expecting the old man to be asleep. But when he climbed the stairs to the apartment, he found Master Branch awake in his chair, reading before the fire.

He closed his book. "Was it dreadful?"

"At first," Frederick said. "But in the end I actually enjoyed it."

"Opera." Master Branch said it like he was spitting out a piece of gristle. "The important question is whether Madame Pomeroy enjoyed your company."

"I believe she did."

"Did you escort her back to the hotel?"

"I did."

"Excellent. Now I'm off to bed." On the way to his bedroom, Master Branch pointed at the table. "I thought you might enjoy something sweet. I picked up a cake."

Master Branch never bought sweets. Frederick's gaze fell on the table, and his mouth began to water.

"Eat all you like," Master Branch said. "The sugar hurts my teeth."

The old man shut his door, and Frederick scooted up to the table. He cut a wedge of pastry onto a plate and dug into it, wallowing like a bird in a bath. The cake had a dense texture, suffused with butter and lemons, with a crackly icing made of rose sugar over the top. The floral flavor reminded Frederick of Hannah, and he wished he could share some with her. He saved her a piece of the cake, in case he saw her tomorrow or the next day, but ate the rest, pressing the stray crumbs together on the back of his fork.

He brought a candle downstairs to the basement and sat next to the clockwork man with *The Clockmaker's Grimoire*. He flipped the pages in the book until he reached the chapter on the Analytical Engine. He began to read and found a lot of mathematics that were well beyond his abilities, but the idea behind the engine overwhelmed him like a forest fire.

How could he have not thought of it?

How many times had Frederick used Jacquard cards on the looms back at the orphanage? If you could change the pattern of weave by changing the punch cards, why could he not change the behavior of the clockwork man in a similar way? Babbage proposed such a use for differing calculations in his Analytical Engine, but with his experience on the orphanage looms, Frederick was certain he could adapt the concept. There would be a card for walking, and a card for running, a card for writing. A card for anything. And the cards would be inserted and read by the head of the clockwork man.

He lay awake on his back for hours, planning, designing against the dark ceiling. His mind felt as though it smoldered and crackled. It was all coming together now.

Somehow Frederick's past at the orphanage had crept up out of the cellar to help him. Looking back had offered a way to look forward. All the while, Hannah's questions brooded at the edge of his thoughts like a thunderhead out over the sea.

The next morning he went upstairs early to make Master Branch breakfast. He lit the stove and sliced some bread, which he slathered with butter. Then he cracked some eggs in an iron skillet. They sizzled in pork fat and brought Master Branch sniffing from his bedroom.

"Well, this is nice of you, lad," he said, tying on a dressing gown.

"Sit down, sir, eat," Frederick said.

Master Branch pulled out a chair and plopped into it, and Frederick served him a plate of food. Then he cooked himself some eggs and sat down next to the old man.

They chewed and listened to the city waking up, the sounds of rolling commerce out on the street.

"Delicious," Master Branch said, wiping up yolk with his bread. "Thank you."

"You're welcome," Frederick said.

Master Branch rose from his chair.

"Sir?"

"Yes?"

"I was wondering. . . ."

"Yes?"

Frederick put his fork down.

"What is it, lad?"

"Why didn't any of your other apprentices make journeyman?"

"They lacked the necessary talent."

Frederick chewed on that. And on something else.

"Is there another question you'd like to ask?"

"Do you . . . do you know the name of my mother?"

Master Branch lowered himself back into the chair. "I don't. Can you not remember?"

Frederick tried to speak and choked. "No. She was just Ma."

The mantel clock ticked away the seconds of silence.

Frederick stared at the table, studied the wood grain. "Back at the orphanage, would they . . . would Mrs. Treeless know?"

"I imagine she would."

Frederick nodded. "I'll clean up. You can go get dressed."

Master Branch lingered for a moment and then withdrew, while Frederick remained at the table, facing down a whole new problem.

CHAPTER 12

Hannah's Father

IT FELT TO HANNAH THAT THE OPERA SHOULD HAVE CHANGED something in her permanently, but it had not. Madame Pomeroy had kept the dress and locked away the diamonds, and the next day Hannah had put on her maid's uniform as she always did and gone back to work. But something had changed. Something to do with Frederick. She did not know what to make of him. He was like a bird in a turtle shell, fragile and armored at the same time, and after having spent the evening with him, she found that she wanted to pry him out. Over the next few days she hoped for an opportunity to return to his shop to speak with him again, but none came.

Then, on the fourth night since the opera, Madame Pomeroy kept Hannah later than usual. When she reached home and stepped through the door, she knew something was wrong.

Doctor Morse leaned over her father with one hand braced on the headboard, the other touching a stethoscope to her father's chest. Her father's face twisted in a grimace, eyes closed, his clothing soaked with sweat. Hannah's mother stood nearby, plucking at her apron, eyes blank like the broken windows of an abandoned house, while her sisters cried from their bed.

Hannah froze. "What's wrong with Papa?"

Her mother turned. She saw Hannah, and behind her eyes it was like someone had set fire to that empty building.

"Where have you been?" she said.

"At work." Hannah took a step toward her mother. "What's wrong with Papa?"

"I need silence, please," the doctor said without looking up.

Hannah's mother turned her attention back to the bed. Hannah inched up next to her and looked down on her father. His irregular breath seemed to leak from between his lips. The doctor lifted away his stethoscope and pulled out the earpieces, letting the instrument spring loose around his neck.

"His condition is very poor," he said. He spoke low and even, like he was saying a prayer. "I recommend the removal of the leg by tomorrow."

"Remove the leg?" Hannah grabbed her mother's arm. "What's he talking about?"

Her mother shook her head. "It's . . . I . . ." She covered her mouth and began to sob with her eyes open, staring at Hannah's father.

Doctor Morse put his hand on Hannah's back and led her a few feet away. "Your father developed a bedsore that has become gravely infected."

"But how?"

"Your mother believes it to be her fault for not rotating him enough. I have tried to reassure her, but . . ."

"You can't take his leg. He'll need it when he recovers."

The doctor exhaled through his nose. He placed both his hands on Hannah's shoulders and bent to meet her eyes. "Child, your father had a stroke. He will never recover. And now, the wound in his leg is poisoning his blood. We must amputate."

"Hannah," her mother said, "don't make this harder."

Hannah's lip quivered, and she bit down on it. "No. No, you can't." She turned to the doctor. "Isn't there something else we can do?"

Her mother relapsed into tears. The doctor held his chin, tapping his cheek with his index finger.

"Is there something else?" Hannah asked.

"A drug," he said. "It's new, very expensive. It doesn't always work."

"We have to try it," Hannah said.

"Child, in my opinion, there may not be time. And the cost would be —"

"We'll pay for it," Hannah said.

Her mother trembled and said nothing. She just bowed her head and held up her hand as if to stop Hannah's offer from across the room.

"I'll get the money," Hannah said. "Just give him the medicine."

"But the compound takes time," the doctor said. "It won't be ready until tomorrow afternoon, perhaps evening. By then —"

Hannah stamped her foot. "He'll make it!"

The doctor stepped away from her.

Hannah's chest burned, and her voice crumpled to a whimper. "He's strong. He'll make it." Her tears broke free. "Please don't take his leg."

Hannah's sisters had fallen silent on the bed, listening. When they saw Hannah crying, they began to wail.

"I am sorry," the doctor said. "Your mother is the one to make the decision." He turned to Hannah's mother, as if expecting her answer in that moment.

Hannah's mother pressed her palms against her temples. "I don't know what to do."

Hannah pushed the doctor aside and tumbled toward her. She grabbed her mother's hands and held them, their faces inches apart.

"Please, Mama," she said.

"Hannah, I —"

"Papa will make it. I'll get the money."

Her mother stared into Hannah's eyes, as though searching for something.

"I'll get it. You've got to trust me. Just try the drug. Just try . . ." Hannah broke off.

Her mother gave a slight nod. "All right," she said, her voice more of a croak.

"Thank you, Mama." Hannah fell against her mother's chest, and her mother held her there.

"Doctor," her mother said, her voice stronger. "We will try this drug. If it does not work, we will amputate. What must I do in the meantime?"

"Ma'am," the doctor said, "I must advise against taking this risk."

"What must I do?" she asked again.

The doctor came forward, solemn, with his hands clasped before him. "Keep the wound clean, change the bandages frequently. And we must still break the fever. Keep him cool, apply cold water to his forehead and feet. If he begins to shiver, cover him until that subsides and apply the cold water again."

"And the medicine?" her mother said, still holding Hannah.

"If I go straight to the apothecary, he can begin work preparing the drug tonight. As soon as it is ready, I will bring it to you. No earlier than five o'clock tomorrow evening, no later than seven." He cleared his throat.

"I'm afraid the apothecary will expect payment on delivery. The medicine will cost you twenty dollars. Can you have the money by then?"

Twenty dollars? A month of Hannah's wages.

Hannah's mother leaned back and held Hannah at arm's length. Hannah nodded.

"We will have it," her mother said. "Thank you, Doctor."

"I will come back in the morning to see how he is doing."

Hannah clutched the sleeves of her mother's blouse until the doctor had gathered his things and left their apartment. They listened to his steps receding down the stairway. After he was gone, Hannah's mother gathered her back into an angry embrace, and her sisters rushed from the bed.

"Ah-ah!" Her mother pointed at them and they slid in their socks. "Doctor says you two are to stay away from your father. We don't want your grubby little hands making him any worse."

Hannah's sisters pouted and flounced back onto the bed.

Hannah's mother raised her hand to her glistening forehead, as if taking her own temperature. "I hope you know what you're doing, girl."

"I do," Hannah said.

"Where will you get the money?"

"I'm going to ask Madame Pomeroy to loan it to me."

"You think she would do that for you?"

"She seems fond of me."

"But how will we repay it?"

"From my wages, over time." *Or from Mister Stroop's treasure.* "But I have to go see her tonight."

"But it must be nearing midnight."

"I know, but we can't risk any delay."

"All right. But be quick about it. We've got a long night ahead of us."

Hannah leaped to her feet and ran for the door. "I'll hurry back."

"Keep to the well-lit roads!" her mother called after her.

Hannah took the grand staircase two steps at a time, as many as her legs could manage, her black skirt flapping like the wings of a bat. She reached the top floor and paused to catch her breath before pulling the bell on Madame Pomeroy's door.

No one came, and Hannah wondered if her mistress had already gone to bed. Then Yakov answered, still wearing his long gray coat. He opened the door only a few inches, and peered out at her.

"Hannah," he said through the crack.

"I'm sorry for the late hour, but I need to see Madame Pomeroy," Hannah said in a rush.

Yakov glanced back into the suite, darkened behind him. "It will have to wait."

"But it's urgent."

"I am sorry." He moved to close the door.

Out of reflex, Hannah put out her hand and blocked him. The Russian, unperturbed, looked at her hand, fingers splayed against the wood, and then back at Hannah. He said nothing and waited.

"Please," Hannah said. "Is she asleep?"

"No. But she will not see you now." He looked at her hand again.

She pulled it away, and the door closed. Before it latched, she heard Yakov say, "Good night, Hannah."

She stared at the door as if a witch's spell had transformed it into a wall before her eyes. She was like the heroine in a fairy story, on a quest to save her father, and the wall was just an obstacle to be overcome. And Hannah carried the key.

She pulled it out of her pocket and weighed it in her hand. How angry would Madame Pomeroy be if Hannah entered the suite? Surely if her mistress understood, she would not be too wroth with her. But what if she was? What if she dismissed Hannah, stepping out of the way for Miss Wool to devour her?

But she had no other way to get the money for her father's medicine.

Hannah tightened the key in her fist and then slipped it into the lock. She twisted it a hair at a time, hoping to slide the lock quietly. It clicked. She opened the door only as far as she had to and brushed through.

The lights in the entry were off, the hallway to Madame Pomeroy's bedroom a dark tunnel. To her right, a faint, wavering glow emanated from the drawing room, and a low murmuring reached her ears. A moist chill hung in the air like ropes of seaweed dripping from the ceiling, brushing the back of her neck and her wrists. Something in the suite felt very wrong. Hannah crept forward, heart recoiling in her chest, and peered into the room.

Madame Pomeroy sat at a round table opposite from a man and a woman. Yakov hung on nearby with a watchful eye on his mistress. The three at the table had joined hands and had their eyes closed, while the dim gaslight sconces flickered along the walls. Madame Pomeroy spoke, her voice deep and foreign, intoning words as though she were striking a heavy bell.

"I am Evenor," she said. "Father to the great kings of Atlantis. What is it you seek?"

"To converse with the spirit of Phineas Stroop," said the woman at the table.

Hannah covered her mouth to keep her shock inside. It was Miss Wool. And there was Mister Grumholdt at her side. They had their backs to her, but she was sure it was them. His bald head flushed red, and Miss Wool's steely braid coiled like a viper. And they were asking about Mister Stroop.

"Very well," Madame Pomeroy said in the voice of Evenor. "I will reach through the void for the one you seek." Her head slumped forward.

In the minutes of silence that followed, Miss Wool and Mister Grumholdt peeked at each other, and at Madame Pomeroy, but did not speak. Hannah breathed quick and shallow. The rumors were true after all. Madame Pomeroy communed with spirits. Hannah's fingers and toes went numb.

She flinched when Madame Pomeroy lifted her head with a sucking, drowning breath.

"I have found him," she said in the voice of Evenor. "Though I cannot contain his essence for long. Ask of him what you will."

Miss Wool leaned forward. "Where is your treasure hidden, Phineas Stroop?"

Madame Pomeroy's head fell to one side. "What do you mean by treasure?" she asked in a voice that was neither hers, nor Evenor's, but something different, something that sounded weak and old enough to die on the spot.

Miss Wool hit the table with her fist. "Your treasure! The one you hid!"

"For God's sake." Mister Grumholdt reached out and put his arm in front of Miss Wool, as though to restrain her from leaping across the table. "Calm yourself, woman."

Hannah felt hot tears burning her eyes. Why was Madame Pomeroy helping them?

Mister Grumholdt addressed Madame Pomeroy. "You must forgive Miss Wool. She is quite impatient, I'm afraid."

Madame Pomeroy did not reply.

"Um, yes," Mister Grumholdt said. "Well, what Miss Wool meant to ask is where you hid your earthly wealth before you died."

"It is not . . . hidden," Madame Pomeroy said.

Mister Grumholdt turned an ear toward her. "What was that, now?"

"Anyone . . . can find it," Madame Pomeroy said.

"Riddles?" Miss Wool pushed back from the table. "We paid this circus freak for riddles?"

So that was it. They had *paid* her.

"Not . . . a riddle," Madame Pomeroy said.

"Then what do you mean?" Mister Grumholdt asked. "What do you mean, uh, Mister Stroop?"

"McCauley held . . . the . . ." Madame Pomeroy's voice decayed into a wheeze, as if she were moldering and falling apart.

Miss Wool and Mister Grumholdt leaned in.

"McCauley held the . . . key . . . to my . . . happiness. . . ."

Moments passed quietly enough to hear the whisper of the gaslight, and Miss Wool and Mister Grumholdt sat immobile in their chairs as if waiting for the rest of the message.

When none came, Miss Wool bored into Mister Grumholdt. "That's not a riddle?"

"I could hold him no longer." The voice of Evenor sounded, and Miss Wool and Mister Grumholdt jumped. "And now I go as well. Farewell to you, of the lofty branches who so easily forget your roots, and ignore the beckoning of time." Her face fell forward, like the dropping of a curtain.

Hannah rolled back against the wall, away from the scene.

She heard Madame Pomeroy's real voice. "Mister Grumholdt? Miss Wool?" The voice Hannah knew and had trusted. "Did you receive the answers you'd hoped for?"

"No," said Miss Wool.

"Not exactly," said Mister Grumholdt.

"I am sorry to hear that," Madame Pomeroy said. "Bear in mind that spirits see the living world very differently than we do. It is not that they try to confuse us, but rather that we are so confusing to them. Perhaps I can assist you in making sense of the answers you were given."

Hannah shut her eyes. Madame Pomeroy was helping the two most loathsome people in the world to steal the treasure from underneath her.

"Come, come," Madame Pomeroy said. "You can trust me. Let us put aside our previous contentions over Hannah. She is only a maid."

The words burned in Hannah's chest. She thought Madame Pomeroy was fond of her, even cared for her. She had bought her the dress and taken her to the opera. But maybe Miss Wool was right. Maybe Hannah was just a toy to her. *Only a maid?* Hannah could not ask for money from Madame Pomeroy now, not after this. She felt a sob rising and touched her throat.

Where the diamond necklace had rested.

Hannah peered down the nearby hallway. In the drawing room, a muddled discussion had begun, with Mister Grumholdt and Miss Wool attempting to talk over each other. Hannah edged along the wall in the opposite direction, toward Madame Pomeroy's bedroom. She felt her way in the darkness.

It would all be over soon, anyway. Madame Pomeroy would help them find Mister Stroop's treasure, and then she would leave the hotel. Miss Wool would fire Hannah, and her family would lose everything, even the few scraps Hannah had helped them cling to. And if she did not get money for the drug, the doctor would pick up his bone saw and take her father's leg.

She reached the bedroom and found the door open. Inside, a timid ray of moonlight nudged between the curtains, and by its light Hannah crossed the room to the dresser. She avoided looking up at her reflection, and poked around among the tins until she found the one with the butterfly. The key within it looked black in the darkness.

She went to the painting and pulled it down. The tremble in her hands made it difficult to unlock the safe, and she fumbled the key. It fell to the ground and rang out like a dropped coin. Hannah listened to see if the noise had brought anyone from the drawing room, and after that every long shadow caught her breath and reminded her of Yakov.

With both hands on the key she managed to unlock the safe and retrieve the diamond necklace from its wooden box. She returned everything to its place and left the room just as she had found it, tucking the necklace away in her apron. Outside in the entryway, she could hear the conversation still spinning in the next room.

Madame Pomeroy's voice sounded impatient. "Another séance might help, Miss Wool, but there is the matter of price."

Hannah opened the door to the suite, closed it behind her, and raced back down the grand staircase. She did not know what to do with the necklace, but she knew who to ask. She hurried through the lobby and ran a block down Basket Street to the Footstool Tavern.

Men, mostly drivers and servants from around the city, loitered in the street outside. Hannah moved through them with her head down, but felt their gaze land on her like clods of mud. She reached the doorway, but hesitated under the lintel. The alehouse seemed to stretch at the seams, timbers flared outward under the pressure of the crowd packed inside. An old-timer stood on a small stage with an accordion, squeezing out tunes beneath a billowing cloud of tobacco smoke trapped in the rafters.

She scanned the red-nosed faces and saw him, laughing against the bar, shouldered between a few other porters and waiters from the hotel.

"Walter!" she called, but could barely hear herself over the noise. "Walter!" she tried again.

He looked up and squinted, said something to the man next to him, and pointed toward the door. Then he forced his way through the tables full of cardplayers.

He held out his hands as he approached her and mouthed, "What?"

"I need your help," she said.

He cupped his hand behind his ear.

"I need your help!"

He shook his head and gestured out into the street. They walked together a short distance from the tavern, far enough to feel the cool of the night and breathe clean air.

"I need your help, Walter."

He smirked. "Sure you don't want to ask Frederick?"

"Don't be that way."

"I'm sorry." He tipped toward her. "What is it you need?"

"I need to sell something. Jewelry."

"Jewelry, huh? What kind?"

"A necklace. I've heard . . . That is, there are rumors about you. . . . You can sell it for me, can't you?"

"Maybe." He ran his fingers through his blond hair.

"I need the money by tomorrow morning."

He smirked again, like a reflex. "What for?"

"I can't explain right now."

"Fine. You have it with you?"

Hannah looked around to make sure no one was close enough to see. Then she pulled the necklace from her apron pocket. It sparkled with captured flecks of moonlight.

Walter whistled. "Now that's something." He took the necklace from her. "These real?"

"I'm sure they are."

"I don't know if I can fence this," he said. "This pretty item's going to draw a lot of attention."

"I need the money, Walter," Hannah said. "I really need it."

He narrowed his eyes for a moment and seemed to be considering something. Then he dripped the necklace from one hand into the open palm of the other. It disappeared inside his coat.

"All right," he said. "I'll do it."

"Tonight?"

He shook his head. "It'll have to be tomorrow."

Hannah had to accept that. "Thank you." She took his hands. "Thank you."

He waved her off. "Come find me in the morning at the hotel."

"I will."

"Need someone to walk you home?"

"Thank you, but I'll be fine. Good night, Walter."

"Good night, Hannah. Oh, and for you, I won't take a cut." He winked at her.

She went home, and when she arrived she found her sisters asleep in bed, turned away from the oil lamp smoking on the table. Her mother fussed over the blankets around her father's legs. She had changed his shirt and turned him on his side. When she noticed Hannah, she stood up and gave a weak smile, a smile that seemed to be asking for a reason to be there.

"I'll have the money by tomorrow morning," Hannah said.

"Oh, praise the Lord and bless that woman."

"How is he?"

"I think his fever may have come down a little. Maybe." Her mother shook her head. "Blessings by the shovelful. A heap of blessings on her. Perhaps I should go to the hotel tomorrow and —"

"No!" Hannah said in a panic. "That is, I expressed our gratitude, Mama. For both of us."

Her mother accepted this with a nod. She lifted her arms and held them out wide. "Come."

Hannah stepped into her arms and felt them close on her.

"You're a wonderful daughter. I couldn't be more proud of you."

"Thank you."

"No, truly, Hannah. I don't know what we would have done these last few years without you. Some nights I lie awake weeping for what you've sacrificed."

Hannah stiffened. "I'm fine, Mama."

"I know you are. You're so strong, like Hannah from the Bible."

Hannah pulled away.

Her mother was left hugging her chest. She turned and set herself to tidying up the kitchen, wiping a rag over a table that already looked clean. "Strong as you are, it's all right to be sad," she said. "It's all right to be mad. I know I am at times."

"Mad at who?"

"Sometimes I'm mad at your father. Sometimes I'm even mad at you children. Mostly I'm just mad at myself."

"For what?"

"For not taking better care of him so this didn't happen. I knew he worked too hard."

"It's not your fault. And it's not his. It's no one's fault."

"I know. But that doesn't soothe your anger, now does it?"

When her mother said that, Hannah became aware of a burning inside, like a stove in the corner that someone else had crept in to feed and stoke when she was not looking. The embers glowed behind a door of iron.

"I'm fine," she said.

The next morning, Hannah's father felt even hotter to the touch, and his mouth lolled open. He felt distant, as if walled up inside himself. She went to the hotel early to find Walter before reporting to Madame Pomeroy for duty. She wondered if her mistress had noticed the necklace missing. After all, Madame Pomeroy had said she never wore it. In fact, she treated it as though it mattered very little to her. Perhaps its absence would go unnoticed until Hannah could repay her for it.

As she entered the lobby, Hannah found Miss Wool waiting at the foot of the staircase.

"You," she said, pointing a finger at Hannah. "Come with me."

"Begging your pardon, Miss Wool." Hannah curtsied. "But could I come find you later? There's something I have to take care of first thing."

Miss Wool spread her thin lips in a smile. "No. You will come with me now."

Hannah took one last look around the lobby for Walter and did not see him. "Certainly, ma'am."

Miss Wool led her along the same path they had taken earlier to Mister Grumholdt's office. Hannah's heart fluttered in her chest like a dying moth trapped in a streetlamp. Could Miss Wool have learned of her theft? No. How could she?

They reached Mister Grumholdt's office, and Miss Wool did not bother to knock. She opened the door, placed her hand on Hannah's back, and heaved her inside, slamming the door behind them.

Mister Grumholdt sat at his desk, drumming his fingers on the wood next to Madame Pomeroy's diamond necklace. Hannah's heart stopped for the length of a wing beat.

"By the look on your face, I see you recognize this," Mister Grumholdt said.

Hannah realized her mouth was hanging open and closed it, her tongue all dried out.

"Did you actually think you could sell something like that?" Miss Wool said. Her laugh was low and slow, like drips of poison into someone's food. "Walter knew better than to try."

Hannah felt her legs weakening. "Walter gave it to you?"

"Of course he did," Mister Grumholdt said. "The boy's no fool. Got a reward for it, too."

Walter's smirk leered in Hannah's mind. "I . . ." Hannah found a chair by feel and collapsed into it.

"So now," Mister Grumholdt said. He pulled out his watch. "Let's take care of this, shall we? You know, of course, that you are fired. As to criminal charges, against my recommendation Madame Pomeroy has decided not to press them. The necklace was recovered, and she is satisfied."

"Could I speak with her?" Hannah asked, but changed her mind as soon as she had said it. What good would it do? Hannah had stolen from her, and she had been caught. There was nothing Madame Pomeroy could do, even if she wanted to, and Hannah doubted very much that she did.

"Do you suppose that she would want to speak with you?" Miss Wool said, echoing Hannah's thoughts. "She has no desire to see you ever again."

"Your whites, please," Mister Grumholdt said. He held out his fat hand.

Hannah stood and slowly untied her apron. She removed her kerchief. Her father would lose his leg now. Her family would lose their home.

Mister Grumholdt rumpled the uniform into a ball and handed it to Miss Wool. He brushed his hands on his trousers. "That will be all. You may go."

Hannah managed a curtsy and slumped toward the door with ponderous steps. Miss Wool opened it for her and smiled again, wider and thinner. "Good-bye, Hannah."

Hannah held the doorjamb and stumbled through. She drifted down the hallways, through the lobby, and out over the square like a dried leaf tumbled along by a breeze. She had to return home and tell her mother, her sisters, that they could not pay for the medicine. That they had lost everything. She had to stand and feel the hollow space where she had let hope take root. Hope planted by Madame Pomeroy's predictions.

But she could not bring herself to go home yet, and wandered husk-like through the morning streets. She stared at the men and women heading to work, on errands, about their business. How could it be that Hannah's life had come to a wrenching stop and the world took no notice?

But it was not only her life. How could she face her father? She had failed him.

Hannah stopped.

No. It was not all withered away. A tendril of faith remained, a stubborn, woody knot. Miss Wool and Mister Grumholdt had not found Mister Stroop's treasure yet. Otherwise, why seek out a spiritualist like Madame Pomeroy for the answers? She turned around and looked up at the hotel, lording over the lower buildings bowing at its feet.

She realized the treasure was not up there.

If it had been, Miss Wool and Mister Grumholdt would have surely found it by now, with all their knowledge of the hotel and its design. But there had to be a treasure, and a tombstone had told her where she would find the key to this next obstacle. Hannah checked the time on the Opera House clock. Seven in the morning. She had until that afternoon to find the treasure.

She stood up tall and turned in the direction of McCauley Park, walking with the rising sun's rays on her back.

CHAPTER 13

McCauley Park

GIUSEPPE WOKE LATE, THE AIR ALREADY HOT AND HUMID. HE crawled from his den beneath the outcrop, and the squirrel descended. "Shout all you want." He rolled onto his back and looked up at it. "I'm not going anywhere."

He was too hungry. Too weak. Was he dying?

With nothing else to do, Giuseppe pulled out his old fiddle, and never had it sounded so sweet to his ear. The ragged strings sang like the scratchy throat of an old man who had been singing all his life and knew from experience what each song was about. Giuseppe played the tune he had chosen that first night with the green violin, the one that made him think of home. The song sounded different on the fiddle, but not bad. Just closer to the earth.

The squirrel stopped chattering and its tail froze. It seemed to be listening, as if trying to identify this strange birdsong. Giuseppe closed his eyes and played the melody several times over. As soon as he stopped, the squirrel went at him again.

"You still don't trust me?" Giuseppe asked.

"She's probably got a nest with her babies nearby," said a man behind him.

Giuseppe jumped to his feet and spun around.

"Sorry," the man said. "Sorry to startle you." He stood on the boulder, dressed in leather clothing, with a rifle on his back and a gnarled walking stick in his hand. He had a heavy mustache, which drooped down into a beard that ran up his cheeks and left his chin bare.

Giuseppe stepped away from him, up to the edge of the water. "Who're you?"

"My name is Pullman," he said. "I'm the park warden. Who're you?"

"Giuseppe."

The warden hopped down from the boulder. "And what are you doing out here, Giuseppe?"

"Hiding."

"Hiding from what?"

"The city."

Pullman's smile lifted one side of his mustache. "Me too."

The squirrel's cacophony had doubled in force, and it switched back and forth between Giuseppe and the warden.

Pullman looked up. "That's how I found you."

"The squirrel?"

He nodded. "From that racket, I knew something had to be nearby. And then I heard music." Pullman gestured at the cave. "That where you been sleeping?"

"A few nights."

"You have food?"

Giuseppe shook his head.

"I didn't think so. You're thin as a reed." He reached into his satchel and pulled out a handful of nuts and a strip of dried, smoky meat. "Here, eat this while we walk."

Giuseppe took the food and shoved most of it into his mouth in one bite. "Walk?" he said, chewing.

Pullman bounded back up onto the boulder. "I know an old woman who lives in a cabin nearby. Alice. She'll fill you up good."

Giuseppe took a last glance over the shelter by the river and found nothing for him there. He put his old fiddle back in its case and bounded up onto the rock after Pullman. The warden set off, but before Giuseppe followed him he turned back to the squirrel. The animal watched him with its dark eyes.

"Thank you," he said, and added, "You're a good mother." He stepped into the trees.

Giuseppe had a difficult time keeping up. The warden loped along lean trails and through subtle breaks in the foliage, and seemed impervious to the abundant thorns and insects that found Giuseppe's bare spots. After an hour of walking, the warden stopped by a fallen tree, allowing Giuseppe to catch him up. Vibrant moss sprouted over the tree trunk like green hair on a giant's leg, and a blanket of fern spread out around them waist high, bowing in waves with the wind.

"We're almost to Alice's," Pullman said. He sat down on the tree. "Have you ever been in that newfangled cathedral?"

"No," Giuseppe said.

"Well, now you don't need to." He pointed the way they had come. "Look."

Giuseppe turned around, and his eyes opened in awe. Without his realizing it, they had been climbing up a gentle incline and, from their vantage at the top, the forest rolled down in a cascade of leaves. Great trees buttressed a grand woodland hall, and sunlight gleamed through the arching canopy as if through green stained glass. Bashful saplings sprouted at the feet of their parents, hiding among the bushes.

Giuseppe breathed deep. Not a trace of smoke in the air. The park was like a droplet of clear water floating on a sea of machine oil. "Do a lot of people live out here?" he asked.

"It's not allowed."

"Why not?"

"If it were, how long do you think it would stay like this?"

"But what about Alice?"

"Alice." Pullman chuckled. "When she talks about McCauley, I can't tell if she's talking about the park or the man. She's just always been here, like a tree. Since I was a boy following my daddy through the woods."

"Your pa was a warden?"

Pullman nodded. "And his father before him. My great-great-great-grandfather actually knew McCauley."

"I didn't know the park was named after a real somebody."

"Sure it is. Roland McCauley. He and the Gilbert family founded the city. Of course, this was before his mind turned like bad cheese and got real . . . colorful."

"What do you mean?"

"Well, while the Gilberts were cutting down trees and planting fields and building the village, McCauley spent all his time out in the woods like a wild man. He lived with the Indians, and swore he'd leave the land in its natural condition. But as the Gilberts' village became a town, and the town became a city, they drove the Indians deeper into the wilderness and left McCauley's land empty."

"Nobody tried to build on it?"

"Oh, they tried. But McCauley owned the land, and he could do what he wanted with it. It was his own money he was losing." Pullman stood up. "You ready to go on to Alice's place?"

Giuseppe nodded, and Pullman set off. Giuseppe followed him, and as they walked, the warden continued the story.

"When McCauley died, he left a legacy to keep the park safe even after his charter expired."

"Safe from who?"

"Lots of men through the years. That old miser Mister Twine, most recently. He wants to build a hotel up ahead on Grover's Pond. And McCauley's legacy is running out. Soon this will all be up for grabs."

Giuseppe frowned. He had only spent a few days in the park, but already felt a pang of loss when he thought about someone chopping it all down.

A short distance later they reached Grover's Pond, where a muddy bank, overhung with a fringe of grass, encircled the lake. The pond was nearly the size of Gilbert Square, and the water seemed to have swallowed its fill of clouds and sky and trees. Lily pads congregated along the lake edge, and the smell of algae lingered in Giuseppe's nose and mouth like a dead fish.

"Alice lives on the far side," Pullman said. "The water's cleaner over there and you can swim if you want."

"I can't swim," Giuseppe said.

They skirted the pond and reached the opposite shore. The water was clearer there, as Pullman had said, and Giuseppe glimpsed shadows moving under the surface, fat fish gliding through thickets of water weeds on the bottom. A small path led away from the water's edge into the forest.

"I hope she's home," Pullman said. "She usually returns in the afternoon before evening comes on, but sometimes she sleeps in the city."

They rounded a bend, and Giuseppe saw a squat log cabin nestled down among the trees. The small door was painted yellow, and the round timbers had been chinked with white clay. Garden plots surrounded the home with flowers, vegetables, and herbs. Their fragrance overwhelmed Giuseppe as they stepped up to the door, like he was being wrapped in a giant leaf.

The warden knocked.

No answer.

He knocked again. "Alice? It's Pullman."

No answer.

Pullman took a step away from the door. "I guess we'll have to wait. Help yourself to anything from her garden, I know she won't mind. There's carrots and lettuce, some turnips, I think. And behind the house there's a couple of apple trees."

"Are you leaving?"

"I just need to check on a few traps. There's an old snapping turtle in the pond who's been getting too big for his britches, and eating more than his share of fish and frogs . . . birds, even. And I've a hankering for some turtle soup. You wait here, and I'll be back shortly."

Pullman left without waiting for a reply, and Giuseppe shrugged. The sunlight was warm here, without being too hot. The food Pullman had given him earlier had satisfied him for a short time, but Giuseppe's stomach growled, and he could not remember the last time he had tasted an apple. He hardly ever ate fruits and vegetables, let alone something pulled fresh right from the tree or the ground. He decided to try the fruit first and walked around behind the cabin, mouth watering.

The little orchard bore green apples on one tree and red ones on another. Giuseppe pulled down a green apple first, unsure of how to tell its ripeness, but the one he chose looked bigger and deeper in color than the others. When he bit through its crisp skin, sour juice exploded in his mouth and twisted up his cheeks and his tongue. He closed his eyes, chewed with pursed lips, and swallowed. He looked at the apple in his hand and wondered if the red ones were any sweeter.

They were, and just as juicy. He had eaten two of them before Pullman came around the corner.

"Come see," he said, and motioned for Giuseppe to follow him.

The warden led him from the cabin back down to the pond. There on the shore, in the grass, lay a snapping turtle the size of a small barrel. It had a dark shell, fuzzy in places with patches of green water moss, a vicious-looking beak, and two nostrils jutting out square between its glassy eyes. It was dead.

Pullman got down on his haunches and studied the creature. "I had a devil of a time dragging it over here. Thing must weigh near fifty pounds."

"I've never seen one this big." Giuseppe put a hand out and laid it on the cold shell. "The ones in the markets are a quarter this size."

Pullman heaved the animal onto its round back and took hold of the hind legs. "You grab the front. We'll haul it up to Alice's."

Giuseppe stared at the long neck dangling to the ground, the mouth lined with razors.

"It won't bite you," Pullman said.

Giuseppe bent and grabbed the front legs. Together they lifted it and lumbered up the path, the turtle swinging between them as they walked. When they reached Alice's cabin, they set the animal down and took a seat on a wooden bench in one of her flower gardens. Bees hummed around them, lifting from flower to flower as if tied to invisible threads. Pullman took out a rag and wiped his brow.

"So do you meet many people out here?" Giuseppe asked.

"No, not many. Every so often I'll come across a botanist from the city out collecting, maybe a naturalist chasing birds." Pullman stared out over the pond. "So what are you hiding from out here, really?"

Giuseppe paused. Then he told Pullman a little about his life playing on the streets, and a little about Stephano. But he made no mention of the green violin and said that Stephano had just lost his temper on account of Giuseppe not bringing in enough money. That was why he had run away.

"So you don't have anywhere in the city you can go?" Pullman said.

"Not where he won't find me."

Pullman frowned. "I'm sorry. I wish there was something I could do."

It was late in the afternoon when someone called out to them. "Well, hello there!" said an old woman coming up the path. She wore a checkered apron and a pointy straw hat. "What have you caught today, woodsman?"

"Hello, Alice." Pullman stood and Giuseppe did the same. "I brought you a stray to feed. And something to feed him with."

"Oh, I love strays," Alice said. "Of what variety is this one?"

"The scrawny kind. But a good-natured temperament, I would say."

"Well, I must have a look at him." Alice came up and peered at Giuseppe, squinting. "Hello, dear."

Giuseppe swallowed. "Hello, ma'am. I ate a few of your apples. I hope you don't mind."

"Of course not, eat all you like."

Pullman directed her attention to the turtle carcass on her lawn. "Think you could scare up some soup?"

Alice grinned. "I see you finally caught that old geezer. Good for you, woodsman. Yes, some turtle soup would be lovely. Come inside, won't you?"

They followed her through the yellow door, and in her house Giuseppe felt the safest he had ever been since coming to America. There was but one room, with small windows that seemed to trap the sunlight in the cabin and age it to a golden yellow. A low hearth opened onto a wooden floor strewn with dried lavender stems. There was a cupboard lined with bottles of every size and shape. Some jars contained leaves and roots, while others were filled with liquids the color of amber, chalk, and mud. Herbs hung in bunches from every rafter, and a small bed snuggled in the corner under a mound of quilts.

"Sit yourselves at the table there." Alice removed her hat, freeing a tangle of wispy white hair. Giuseppe and Pullman sat down while the old woman stoked the fire back to life. She heaved a kettle up on an iron hook and poured water into it from a large pitcher. After swinging the kettle in over the flames, Alice retrieved a basket hanging from a timber overhead. She handed it to Giuseppe.

"Would you mind getting some vegetables, dear?" she asked. "Some carrots and celery, an onion, and a few ripe tomatoes."

"Certainly, ma'am," Giuseppe said.

"Woodsman, if you would kindly butcher the meat."

"Of course," Pullman said.

Giuseppe took the basket and a knife out into the garden and gathered the vegetables Alice had asked for. It took a little while to realize that the carrots and onions were actually under the ground, but it felt good to move through the cultivated rows and patches, feeling the dirt, helping the old woman. Surely someone who cared as much about growing things as she appeared to was someone he could trust.

He went back inside, the basket full, and watched as Alice chopped and diced the vegetables along with some cloves of garlic. She pulled down herbs from her ceiling, smelled them, and sighed with pleasure. A short time later Pullman entered, carrying a board piled with slabs of pink meat. Alice cut the meat into chunks and tossed it into the kettle now steaming over the fire. She tore the herbs and dropped them in.

"We'll just let that simmer for a spell before I add the vegetables," she said, and took a seat next to them at the table. "In the meantime, why don't you tell me about yourself, dear. I noticed you have a fiddle."

"Yes," Giuseppe said, and he told her the same story he had related to Pullman.

"You poor thing," Alice said. "I wish there was something I could do."

It seemed as though that was just something adults said. Adults like Reverend Grey. But Giuseppe felt that they were saying it more to themselves, so they felt less guilty about doing nothing. But he did not blame them. What they could do for him, they had done.

"The soup smells delicious," Giuseppe said.

"Just wait," Alice said.

She rose from the table and went to the hearth, where she raked a layer of coals under a grill. She set a black iron skillet over the coals to heat through, and spooned in a dollop of butter that sizzled. Next she dumped the vegetables into the skillet and added a scoop of flour. When the mixture had browned, she tipped the contents of the skillet into the kettle and stirred it all together.

"We'll give that another hour or so," she said.

"Would you play for us?" Pullman asked Giuseppe.

The request stopped him. Giuseppe felt something catch inside him like a fish on a hook. Against his will these two had snagged the part of him that darted away from everyone. He realized he wanted to play for them, but not for money. He went for his fiddle.

"What would you like to hear?" he asked as he tuned the instrument.

"Play that song you were playing this morning when I found you," Pullman said.

Giuseppe took the bow and rubbed the first few notes from the strings and felt something different in the music than he had ever felt before. Or perhaps it was not in the music but in him.

Both members of his tiny audience closed their eyes, firelight turning their cheeks red as the cabin dimmed with evening. They listened and he played. The song had the same notes it always had, but they felt more honest in their expression. Giuseppe had always chosen music for how well it would fill his cap with coins. But given as a gift, the song became something even more than if it were played on the green violin.

He finished. He played another. And then a lively jig.

Pullman started tapping his toe to the rhythm. Then he rose from his chair and took Alice's hands. He pulled her up and danced her around the small cabin, kicking his feet high and singing. Alice bobbed along with him, a delighted smile on her face, and watched the warden's bouncing legs as if she had never seen anything like them before. They circled

Giuseppe and he picked up the meter, playing faster. He spun them around like tops, filled the cabin with enough music and joy to blow the roof off.

When the song ended, the dancers hurled apart. Alice slumped into a chair by Giuseppe, and Pullman sprawled wide on the bed, both of them breathing hard and laughing.

"My goodness," Alice said. "You sly woodsman."

Pullman sat up. "I don't know what came over me. Seized by a mood, I guess. I just couldn't stop my legs."

"Well, I thank you. Both of you." Alice dabbed at her brow with her apron and went to the kettle. "I wouldn't care to count the years since I last danced like that." She lifted the lid and peered inside. "It's ready."

She ladled bowls of turtle soup from the kettle, and Pullman brought them to the table one at a time. They all settled into their steaming dishes and ate. The stew was thick and rich, a velvety brown gravy full of vegetables and meat. Giuseppe had never tasted anything like it. The tender chunks of turtle fell apart in his mouth, and he finished the whole bowl before the others had eaten half of theirs.

He wiped his mouth on his sleeve and put his hands in his lap, looking from his empty dish to the kettle by the fire. Alice leaned toward him.

"You are welcome to eat as much as you like, dear."

"Thank you." Giuseppe hopped to the hearth and dished himself up another bowl. When that serving was gone, he had another, and before long, he felt something in his stomach he could not remember feeling for a very long time. He was full, sitting at a table with kind people who looked after him. He leaned back in his chair and let out a long sigh.

After they had all finished, Pullman pushed himself away from the table.

"Well, I'd best be on my way," the warden said.

"It worries me so when you travel in the dark," Alice said.

"Nothing to fret about," Pullman said. "Good night, Giuseppe."

"Where are you going?" Giuseppe asked.

"My cabin. It's not far. But don't worry, Alice will take care of you."

"That's right," Alice said.

Giuseppe bit his lip. "Will you come back?"

"I'll try and stop by tomorrow," Pullman said. "Get some sleep."

They followed the warden outside into the gloaming. The garden had a stronger, sweeter fragrance at night than it did during the day, and fireflies had taken the place of bees among the plants. The moon dangled an image of itself in the pond like a fishing lure, and bullfrogs bellowed from the reeds and mud. Pullman grabbed the empty turtle shell and picked up a heavy bundle from the grass, the rest of the meat he had dressed and wrapped. He nodded and whistled off into the night.

Once he had disappeared from view, Alice sighed. "Come back inside, dear. Let's get your bed made."

Giuseppe followed her back in. She opened a chest at the foot of her bed and pulled out more blankets, which she arranged on the floor near the hearth. Giuseppe sat down among them, cross-legged, and watched Alice tidy up the room.

"Can I help?" he asked.

"Nonsense. You lie down now."

Giuseppe did as he was told and stared into the fire. He watched the flames work over the wood, turning it black and then red before sifting it to ash. He listened to the crickets outside and heard Alice climb into bed behind him. He felt contented and safe for the first time in so long. But that moment did not last. Deep memories rose up strong behind those freshly made that night, old memories of his parents, his brother. Marietta. No matter how wonderful it felt to be there, nestled in his blankets by the fire, this kind old woman was not his family, and her little cabin in the woods was not his home.

CHAPTER 14

The Orphanage

FREDERICK SKETCHED BY THE LIGHT OF A CANDLE NUB, HUD-dled over a desk, the clockwork man stretched out on the worktable behind him. A pile of crumpled paper surrounded him like a snowdrift streaked with inky soot. He gripped the fountain pen hard enough to turn the tips of his fingers white and scratched out a line that ripped right through the paper. He put the pen down and stared at the gash in his design, right at the center of his clockwork head.

He could not make it work.

Babbage had offered him a window that had turned out to be nothing more than a crack in the wall, too small to fit through. Size was the problem. No matter how many designs and iterations, Frederick could not find a way to fit all the necessary clockwork within the nutshell of the head. It was like the automaton shepherd boy back at the guild hall. The movements would have to be relocated to the chest, which would mean tearing the clockwork man apart and starting over. Frederick grieved at that thought. The body was as perfect as he could make it, fluid and elegant and strong, with all the necessary connections converging at the neck.

He sat up straight and rubbed his eyes. Pink sunlight spilled down the stairs from the shop above. He had spent another night awake at his desk, the third in a row. The day after the opera, after talking with Hannah and Master Branch, he had put away thoughts of his mother and gone to work, and every night since then he had been at his desk. He stole naps as he could throughout the day, but felt fatigue sucking at his mind like an undertow.

He palmed the sketch, crumpled it in his hand, and tossed it to the floor, a damaged snowflake. He stood and plodded up the stairs, where he and Master Branch ate breakfast in silence. Afterward, the old man set him a list of tasks to accomplish in the shop that day, and Frederick approached them absently.

He finished the repair of a Black Forest piece whose cuckoo had lost its chirp, and replaced a worn-out balance spring in a silver mantel clock. He then cleaned the dust from a Congreve, allowing the steel ball to roll freely back and forth along its track, measuring time with its tilting. Frederick became lost in the up-and-down rhythm, the ball at play like a lonely boy working a seesaw by himself.

"Are you finished, lad?"

Frederick looked up. Master Branch stood in the doorway.

"What?" Frederick said.

"I asked if you were finished. Three times."

"Oh. Yes, I'm finished."

"Good. Come upstairs for supper."

Supper already? Frederick followed the clockmaker up to the apartment and sat down to a plate of sliced ham and potatoes mashed with butter. Frederick stabbed at the food with his fork, but never lifted any to his mouth. He noticed Master Branch watching him and forced himself to take a bite before the old man could comment.

"Is everything all right, Frederick?" the old man asked, anyway.

Frederick moved his potatoes around. "I'm fine, sir."

"It does not seem that way to me. I don't mean to be harsh with you, but your work has been very slow the past few days. And your eyes are red. Right now you look like you can barely stay upright. Are you sleeping?"

"Not well," Frederick said.

"Why not?"

Frederick put his fork down. "I don't know."

Master Branch opened his mouth, closed it. He opened it again and held it that way as if hoping the words would fly in. "I would point out that these changes began on the very day you asked me about your mother."

"They did?"

"Yes. Which leads me to think they are related."

Frederick said nothing.

"What do you think of that?" Master Branch asked.

What did he think of that? The tiredness was because of his nocturnal work on the clockwork man. Not his mother. But then, he had only begun laboring through the night after the opera, after Hannah had asked him all those questions he could not answer.

"I don't know what to think," Frederick said.

"Well, it's just a thought. I'm just saying that it would be understandable for thoughts of your mother to keep you awake, to distract you."

Frederick knew it was not that. Babbage and the clockwork man had distracted him, and he realized now that was exactly why he had seized on them. It was the avoidance of thoughts about his mother that kept him awake. But how much longer could he avoid them?

"Perhaps," said Master Branch, "it would help to confront whatever it is that's bothering you. Learning her name, for example. If you'd like,

I'll go to the orphanage with you, or even for you, to find out more about her."

"Thank you, sir. But that won't be necessary."

"Are you sure? I truly believe it might help you."

"What I mean is, I think I should go alone."

"Oh." Master Branch seemed to think about it. "If you are sure."

"I am sure."

"Very well." The old man scooped the last bit of food together on his plate, scraping it clean to the last bite. "I believe I could make do without you tomorrow."

Tomorrow. There was weight to the word. It felt too soon. He was not ready. What little food Frederick had eaten turned to a roiling sludge in his belly. He swallowed and nodded.

"Thank you, sir," he said.

Frederick forced himself to consume the rest of his supper, now cold on his plate. He passed another night without sleep, but not down in his workroom. He lay awake on his cot behind the shop, staring at the ceiling, firelight from upstairs leaking between the floorboards like spilled honey.

How could he do this? How could he go back there? The thought of it turned him cold and set him trembling. The orphanage still gaped in his memory, a black sinkhole. If he got too close, he risked falling in, so he had always stayed as far away from it as he could. He could not face that place again, he could not face her. But what would it mean if he did not? His mind tossed back and forth throughout the night, resolved to go one moment, and frightened out of it the next. But his thoughts kept coming back to his mother, and he knew what he had to do.

He had to go back. *Tomorrow*. Right up to the edge of the pit, staring straight into a mouth without any teeth.

Throughout the night he formulated a plan. He thought about what he would ask, and how he would ask it. He would wear his new suit. She would see that he had become something now; he was an apprentice clockmaker deserving of respect. And as furious as he felt at the thought of her, he would have to maintain his composure and treat her with civility. He knew how cruel and vindictive Mrs. Treeless could be.

Frederick stood in the street, hands clenched at his sides, staring at the front door. His legs shook, and he felt his heartbeat up and down his torso, in his throat and ears. The orphanage and factory were smaller than he remembered, and he had expected them to appear sinister somehow. He watched them, paralyzed, for some sign of the old hag living inside, some shadow or mark of cruelty. But the corrugated iron roofs and common redbrick walls matched all the other factories marching down the road.

He gathered himself and looked down at his new clothes, feeling armored in them. He was safe. She could not hurt him now. Frederick lifted his chin and marched into the street, across it, and right up to the door. He placed his hand on the latch and held it there, poised for a moment while he took a deep breath. Then he opened it.

Inside was the dingy entryway through which he remembered leaving with Master Branch years ago. He had no memory of arriving through it with his mother. A faded rug covered a floor that would fill a bare foot with splinters, while a table sat against a wall wearing a coat of dust and an empty vase. A hallway ran off to the right in the direction of the mill and factory floor, while another led toward the dormitory. Next to him, a staircase climbed to the ceiling and through an entry to the second floor. The orphanage office waited directly in front of him, fenced with paneled wood and panes of frosted glass.

Frederick walked up and rapped on the window. "Hello?"

Something creaked inside, the sound of a swivel chair. Then the glass split down the middle and slid open. A pimpled woman peered out at him, a look on her face as though Frederick had carried in a foul odor from the street.

"Can I help you?"

Frederick tried to harden his voice. "I'm here to see Mrs. Treeless."

"She's on the factory floor. State your business with Mrs. Treeless."

"I would like to find out information about the relatives of one of the former children in her . . . care."

The woman's face remained passive. "You look familiar."

He gave her his name. "I left a few years ago. I would like to know about my mother."

The woman grumbled and went to a back corner. She opened a cabinet drawer and riffled through a row of files and papers. "I don't see anything here."

"What do you mean?"

The woman gave the cabinet another glance. "I don't see your file."

"Perhaps if I could speak with Mrs. Treeless —"

"Not without an appointment."

"Please. It will only take a moment of her time."

The woman shook her head.

"Then will you schedule an appointment for me?"

"I'll let her know you stopped by. Come again tomorrow, and I'll tell you if she's agreed to see you."

Frederick ground his teeth. He forced a tight smile and turned away. As he walked toward the front door, he heard the window slide shut behind him.

Outside on the street he walked down the block, peering now and then into the factory yard through gaps in the fence slats. Children scurried from the orphanage to the factory, and Frederick felt their fear of being late, that utter panic when the clock betrayed him by a minute. A cold wave of guilt trickled down his back for being safe on the other side of the fence, where the hours arrived without punishment.

A few steps later he came to a gate in the fence, locked by a loose chain. He tested the opening and thought it barely wide enough to slip through. He looked both ways down the street and squeezed inside. The edges were rough, and he felt a snag and heard a tearing sound behind him. After stumbling into the yard, he checked his new coat and found he had nearly ripped a pocket off.

He ran his fingers through his hair and looked up at the sky, the factory smokestacks spewing poisoned clouds. He could turn back. He could come again tomorrow with Master Branch. But she was in there right now, pacing, spewing, yelling. He squared his shoulders and set a determined course for the large factory doors.

As he drew nearer, the sound of the power looms chewed at his ears. He stepped inside the factory and recoiled from the overwhelming odor of sweat and filth and machine oil. He covered his nose and stared down the rows and rows of machinery on the floor, the struts and ropes and pulleys along the rafters, and the bolts of fabric racing up and down between them. Everything in the factory, every part of it, seemed to be in motion. Wheels spun, shuttles flew, children darted, while steam thunder shook the ground under it all.

How could he ever have been used to this? He looked around and saw a couple of foremen but no Mrs. Treeless. He moved close to the wall, and his eyes ranged down the long factory.

About a third of the way into the building, he saw Roger Tom. It had only been a few years, but the man looked as though something had defeated him. His shoulders sagged, and his neck bent like he had that millstone from the Bible hanging from it. He barked at the children around his feet but did not watch to see what effect his threats had, whether he was heeded or not. He just walked on.

And then Frederick saw her. She came behind Roger Tom, marching between the machinery and children, with eyes like two black wedges, eyes that cracked and broke asunder anything in her path. Frederick cowered in spite of his intent to stand his ground and became furious. At himself, and at her. He lurched forward and landed between Mrs. Treeless and Roger Tom, right in the old crone's path. That brought her up, and it took but a moment for her to recognize him. She clutched her dog, a pathetic little thing now, mostly bald with clouded eyes. It did not move, and Frederick had the morbid thought that it might be dead.

"I saw you down on the pier," she said. "And you saw me, too, didn't you? You had that look. The same one you have now." Her gaze mocked him, and she smiled when her eyes came to the ripped pocket of his coat. "What are you doing here, boy?"

"I came to ask you some questions," Frederick said, his voice sounding weak among the machines.

"Let me guess. Your mother."

Frederick swallowed. How did she know?

"You hear that, Roger Tom?" Mrs. Treeless called over Frederick's shoulder. Frederick looked and saw the foreman standing there, a blank, unreadable expression on his face. "He's come to find out about his dearest mum," she said.

"What was her name?" Frederick asked, his voice getting louder.

Mrs. Treeless smirked. "It's always the mother. You think it'll make you feel better. Well, I can tell you, boy, you were broken when you came to me, and you were broken when you left. All of you brats are damaged, and finding out why your mum left you all those years ago won't mend a thing." She laughed and brushed by him.

"Stop!" Frederick shouted.

Mrs. Treeless halted. Roger Tom glared, and the children nearby stopped to stare.

Frederick had not meant to raise his voice. "You witch," he said, and pointed at her. This was not what he had planned to say. "You will tell me my mother's name."

She narrowed her eyes at him and stroked her dog's remaining fuzz. "I'll do no such thing."

Frederick took a step toward her, and suddenly Roger Tom was there blocking his path.

Mrs. Treeless flapped a hand like she was shaking water off her fingers. "Get out of my factory, boy."

"Tell me her name."

Mrs. Treeless turned to the children nearby. "Back to work," she said, and walked away.

"Tell me!"

She never glanced back.

Roger Tom looked down at Frederick. "I'll show you out," he said.

Frederick thought about pushing past the foreman and chasing after her, but he knew Roger Tom or one of the others would catch him. And probably beat him. And his recklessness had ruined any chance of getting the information he wanted from Mrs. Treeless.

Roger Tom grabbed his arm, but Frederick shook it off.

"I'm leaving," he said.

Moments later Frederick was back out on the street, staring in through the gate as Roger Tom tightened the chain.

"Don't come back," the foreman said.

"Sir," Frederick managed to say. "Do you know who my mother was?"

The foreman frowned. He looked at his boots. "Go back to your home," he said, and then he left.

Frederick lingered for a long time. What had he done? Why had he shouted and made demands? It was like he had slammed the door on himself. He shook his head. He should be glad to be out of that place. He should never have come back. Mrs. Treeless was right. There were no answers that would mend him.

The acid of his rage drained away, and he felt exhausted and limp legged. He slogged to Master Branch's shop as if dragging his feet through a foot of mud. When he arrived he found he had no appetite for the supper the clockmaker had prepared. He had no will to join Master Branch in the workshop. He lay down on the floor by the fireplace and closed his eyes.

When he opened them again it was dark, and there was a pillow under his head. Master Branch sat in his armchair and looked down at him from his book.

"I did not know whether to wake you or not," the old man said. "You were finally sleeping. Are you hungry?"

Frederick sat up and felt a wave rush inside his head. "No."

"Do you want to talk about how today went?"

"No. It was pointless, like I knew it would be." Frederick got to his feet. "I think I'll just go down to bed."

Master Branch nodded. "Very well. I will see you in the morning."

Frederick clomped down the stairs and threw himself onto his cot. He felt as lifeless as the clockwork man in the basement beneath him, and for a moment he envied his creation's handicap. He wanted to empty his head of all its contents, all its memories and questions and doubts. Just spill it all out and crush it under his heel and start from scratch. He had been getting by just fine. He had ordered his world, set its components in motion, and then watched the predictable rhythm unfold.

Frederick could do nothing to rearrange the past. He could not repair it, so he had ignored it, shut the door on a chaos of broken glass, bent gears, and twisted metal. But then Hannah had come and asked him all about it, even though the past should have nothing to do with him now. But it did. And now he could no longer ignore it.

CHAPTER 15

A Memorial Stone

HANNAH LEANED AGAINST A TREE TO CATCH HER BREATH. A single ant crawled from the rough bark onto her hand, and she watched it explore her skin before blowing it off into the dirt. She was sweating in the midmorning heat. She scratched her scalp, wishing in that moment her hair were thinner and shorter. McCauley Park spread away from her in all directions, dense and high. Every branch stretched upward, like hands swaying overhead in slow warning, urging her back.

It helped to pretend the forest was enchanted. Hannah spotted a circle of mushrooms, a fairy ring, and imagined tiny eyes peeking at her through the leaves. Translucent wings fluttering at the edge of her eye. Elves lurking in the shadows beneath the trees. It was more comforting to see these phantasms than to consider what might really be stalking her.

The path she trod had long ago lost its gravel to hard-packed dirt. She had no map, and took those tracks that seemed to lead inward, to Grover's Pond near the center of the wood. She did not feel lost, exactly, but unmoored and alone, and wished for a trail of bread crumbs leading the way back out of the forest. Of course, the birds flapping and calling up in the trees would probably swoop down and gobble them all up, just like in the story.

Her decision to enter the park had been made out of desperation, but now seemed more like stupidity. She had no idea what she was looking for at Grover's Pond. All she knew was that McCauley held the key to Stroop's happiness, Stroop had a clear view of the pond from his suite, and Mister Grumholdt and Miss Wool had circled a part of the pond on a map. With those facts Hannah had decided that Grover's Pond was the next place to search for . . . something.

Back in the city, in her family's apartment, her father lay stricken. If she did not return with money that evening, there would be no medicine, and her father, the strongest man she knew, the finest stonemason in the whole city, would lose his leg.

Time passed, and the sun crossed its halfway peak, sliding down toward afternoon. The dirt trail gave way to matted grass, hard to distinguish from the forest to either side. As she walked along, something faint reached her ear, a slight rushing sound, perhaps a brook. If it was, it might lead her to the pond. She took several steps in the direction it came from, head up, listening. She took a few more steps toward it, and a few more, before deciding it was only the wind through the trees.

She looked down at her feet and found them buried in underbrush. She looked back. More underbrush. Hannah had lost the tiny path she had been clinging to. She rushed to find it, eyes sweeping the green all around her, but saw no sign of the trail. It was as if the forest had just swallowed it up.

Hannah's heart sounded an alarm in her ears, a rapid drumbeat goading her to action. Any action. She ran a short way in the direction she felt that she had come from. No path. She hurried back and chose a different direction. Still no path. After several attempts at this she felt like a mouse that had fallen into a barrel, crisscrossing the bottom in a frantic scramble for a way out. But there was no way out, and running around like a rodent would not solve anything.

Hannah took a few deep breaths, letting them out slowly through pursed lips.

All right.

When she calmed down, closed her eyes, and let the needle of her inner compass point the way, there was one direction that felt more *in*, and one that felt more *out*. If she kept going in she would have to reach the pond soon, and from there perhaps find a different path, or at least orient herself toward the city. And search for the treasure. Out, on the other hand, would certainly be the safer choice. But it also meant failure.

What was she doing? What did she hope to find? A pile of jewels just sitting out here in the middle of the park? Hannah looked over her shoulder and thought about going back. But then what? Where could she go for the money? Who could she turn to?

No. She had to keep going. Deeper.

She reached out and bent off a twig from a nearby branch. She coiled her braid up on the crown of her head and stuck it in place with the stick. She bent and tied up her skirts to keep them from snagging and tripping her. Who was out here to see her ankles, anyway?

She followed the terrain down little draws and back out again, over white and gray boulders splotched with yellow lichen, and through scented pine thickets. A short time later, as she crested a low rise, she caught a glimpse of blue through the trees. She craned her neck and squinted at a patch of smooth water. It had to be Grover's Pond. She wiped her brow and sighed.

She started down the little bluff and strode into a sunny glade, smiling. She caught sight of something large spread out on a rock to one side. It moved as she turned to look at it.

An enormous cougar rose to its feet.

Hannah stared at the beast, feeling as though all her body had stopped working. Her heart. Her breath. All of it frozen. The beast was longer than she was tall, from nose to black-tipped tail, all tawny fur and heavy paws. It stared at her, eyes golden, unblinking.

Hannah lurched backward, arms in front of her like a shield. Her mouth was open, but she was afraid to make a sound. The cougar padded toward her. Its lips rippled and then lifted in a snarl. Hannah stared at its long white teeth.

She heard a sound nearby. What was it? A fiddle? Out here?

"Help!" she shouted.

At her outburst the cougar flinched. Then it roared, a sound to tear the air apart between them. It dipped its shoulders low to the ground, haunches high and taut. It crept toward her, shifting its paws like it was looking for the right footing.

The violin had stopped. She had imagined it.

"Help me!" she shouted.

The cougar roared again and seemed ready to lunge.

Someone appeared out of the trees on Hannah's right. A boy. Familiar.

"Pullman!" he shouted. He bent and scooped up a rock, never taking his eyes from the animal. The cougar had changed its posture, ears back, eyes darting between Hannah and the boy. "Hold still," the boy said to her.

Hannah nodded.

A third figure entered the clearing, a man dressed in leathers. He held a rifle at his shoulder, sighting down its barrel. "Steady, now," he said. "She knows what this is. I'm going to fire a warning shot."

A deafening crack, and Hannah flinched. A plume of smoke, and a spray of dirt kicked up from the ground near the spot where the cougar had been crouching. The animal had already vanished into the trees.

The man lowered the rifle. "Everyone all right?"

"Yes," said the boy.

Hannah took longer to respond. "Yes."

"Good." The man peered into the trees. "Follow me back to Alice's." *Alice?*

Hannah and the boy fell in line behind the man in leathers. She trembled and made fists to tame her hands. Her heart still raced. She reined in her breathing, feeling as if she were stepping down from a knife edge. The attack had happened so fast there had been no time for thought, but now thoughts came in a suffocating rush. *A cougar.* She could have died, been clawed and chewed, eaten, gone. Her mother and father had no idea where she was and never would have known. With the thoughts came tears, and the boy stared at her.

"You all right?" he asked. His eyes fell to her ankles.

She let her skirts back down, embarrassed. "I'm fine." They walked in silence.

A short distance later she saw a small cabin. Gardens surrounded it like a wreath of flowers and vegetables. Hannah smiled. It had to be the same Alice. The sight of the flowers cast off the last edge of panic, and she finally relaxed. A little path led from the cabin door down to the edge of Grover's Pond, a mirror of water in the middle of the park. Hannah wanted to head down to it that moment and start looking for clues. The map in Grumholdt's office had an area circled up on the north side.

"I have a few questions," the man said to her. The muscles on his jaw tightened. "Have a seat, if you please." He motioned toward a bench in the flower garden. "You too, Giuseppe."

Hannah did not have time for questions. But she sat down, and the boy plopped down next to her. He smelled like he had skipped a bath too many weeks in a row, and she realized where she had seen him. The cemetery, at Mister Stroop's tomb. And here he was at Grover's Pond. Had he been carrying a fiddle when she saw him before?

"First," the man said to her, "I'm Pullman. The park warden. What's your name?"

"Hannah." She turned to the boy. "You're Giuseppe?"

He nodded.

"Was it you I heard playing?"

"Yep," he said.

"You heard me call for help?" she asked.

He nodded. "Then I called Pullman."

"Good thing I was here," Pullman said. "Mirabel looked awful agitated."

"Mirabel?" Hannah asked.

Pullman pointed off into the trees. "Mirabel. The cougar."

"You named her?" Giuseppe asked.

"Sure. There's only a few left in these parts. Not hard to keep 'em straight."

"Why didn't you shoot her?" Hannah asked.

"I just said there's only a few left. The park needs her."

Hannah did not understand that.

"How'd you come to be in that clearing with her?" Pullman asked.

"She was lying on a rock in the sun." Hannah shrugged. "I think I startled her."

"Probably did," Pullman said. "But that doesn't answer my question. Just what are you doing out here?"

Why was this park warden being so rude? "Begging your pardon, sir, but that is my business. What matter is it to you?"

He leaned forward, hands on his hips. "It matters to me because it matters to the park. Say I'd come a second later, what then? Mirabel would have been on you, and I would have had to shoot her dead."

Hannah would probably have also died. But it seemed he forgot to mention that.

"So I'll ask again," he said. "What are you doing out here?"

Hannah looked at Giuseppe. "I'm searching for something." The boy showed no sign of recognition or reaction, but he had to know about Stroop's treasure. First, the cemetery, and now all the way out here. Why else would he be in both places?

"What're you looking for?" Pullman asked.

"I'd rather not say." But she had to start looking for it. Now.

Pullman grunted. "Suit yourself. Two kids in as many days." He shook his head. "You'll be all right here till Alice gets back."

"Where are you going?" Giuseppe asked.

"I need to track Mirabel for a bit and make sure she's all right. Don't worry, she's long gone from here."

Hannah was glad to see Pullman go, but the boy looked uncertain. Pullman made it seem like the whole incident was somehow Hannah's fault.

"I'll be fine," she said.

Pullman nodded. He marched away and left Hannah and Giuseppe sitting on the bench. Neither spoke, and Hannah was not about to be the first. She tried to figure out what to do. How much did Giuseppe know about Mister Stroop? How could she look for clues with him around?

"You'll like Alice," Giuseppe finally said.

"I know her," Hannah said.

"You do? How?"

"I work — used to work at the Gilbert Hotel. She's a gardener there."

He tipped his head to one side. "Oh, so that's it."

"That's what?"

"I knew I'd seen you before. You were the maid in the cemetery."

She nodded.

"You were looking at Mister Stroop's tomb," he said.

"So were you."

He dropped his eyes to the ground. "Yeah," he said with sadness in his voice. "Yeah, I was."

Hannah softened inside. "I, um, never said thank you."

"For what?"

"For saving me from the cougar."

"Well, Pullman had the gun. All I had was a lousy rock."

"But you came just the same. Thank you."

"You're welcome." He smiled, and there was an impish charm in it. "So, Hannah, what are you looking for out here?"

Hannah leaned back and considered him. There did not appear to be any guile in his question. He had that same restlessness she had seen in the cemetery, somehow swaggering as he sat there fingering the rim of his cap, but innocent, too, like a hound pup still big-eared and big-pawed.

"You really don't know?" she asked.

"How would I?"

"You were at Mister Stroop's tomb, and now you're here."

"I've been thinking the same thing about you. I still don't have a notion of what you're talking about."

"I'm looking for Mister Stroop's treasure," Hannah said.

Giuseppe blinked. "Mister Stroop had a treasure?"

Hannah nodded. "I was certain you knew."

"Nope." Giuseppe seemed to be thinking things over. "But what would his treasure be doing out here?"

"I don't know. I don't even know what I'm looking for, and this could all just be a waste of time."

Giuseppe hopped to his feet. "Well, whatever it is, maybe I can help you find it."

"Why would you do that?"

"Well, I could use a bit of treasure, if there's enough to go around. Forty-five dollars ought to do it."

Hannah smiled in spite of herself at this scrapper, this wild boy who seemed as much at home in the woods as he did in the streets. She could use the help, and if the treasure lived up to her hopes, then forty-five dollars would be a small price.

"All right, Giuseppe. Here's what I know." She told him all about the legend, the tomb inscription, and the map in Grumholdt's office.

"We better get crackin'," Giuseppe said. "The north side of the pond?"

"According to the map, if I'm remembering it correctly."

They skirted the banks, past clutches of cattails and reeds, startling a frog or two into the water. The sky had become overcast and heavy, and a rain-scented breeze came at them. Thunder clapped and tumbled toward them from the mountains to the north, sounding just like Hudson's ninepins.

"The rain will be here soon," Giuseppe said. "What should I be on the lookout for?"

"Something out of place," Hannah said. "I think we should start searching around here. This seems to be where the circle on the map started. I'll take the bank. You look in the trees."

They parted. Hannah took slow, wide steps, scanning the ground in front of her. Giuseppe picked along the edge of the wood, darting in and out, lifting branches and pushing shrubs aside. They kept pace with each other, glancing up now and again to shrug or shake their heads. Another peal of thunder shook the sky, and the first patter of rain splashed on Hannah's cheeks. The clouds had darkened, thick kohl lines across the sky's face.

Before long they reached the farthest shore and swung around, heading down the other side of the lake. They were leaving the area circled on the map. There was nothing there.

Hannah chewed on her lip. She felt a groan of frustration in her throat, begging to be let out. She could not go back empty-handed. She could not fail her father. She halted her search, afraid to go farther and find nothing. Perhaps she had missed it.

"Hey!" Giuseppe called to her. "Over here."

"What?" Hannah hurried over to him. "What is it?"

"Something out of place." He pointed with his toe at a polished stone laid in the ground at the base of a large oak tree.

It was a flat slab of marble, white as sea foam and ribboned with blue and gray. Someone had carved an inscription into its surface, a beautiful script with organic flourishes, and around the text a border of holly leaves. Their style was unmistakable. She knew her father's work like she knew his face.

"What does it say?" Giuseppe asked.

"Dedicated to Roland McCauley. May his legacy live on in those who share his vision." She paused, then whispered, "It's a memorial stone."

"It looks pretty, doesn't it?"

"Beautiful," Hannah said. But how could it be? Her father's work out here?

The rain began to fall hard, blown sideways in the wind. It wet the stone until the whole surface glistened. Hannah stood there getting soaked, thinking things over. Giuseppe watched her with a puzzled expression, stepping from foot to foot, his hair wet through and stuck to his forehead beneath the rim of his cap.

"So, what next?" he asked.

She lowered to her knees and felt around the edges of the stone. "Maybe it's buried underneath it."

Giuseppe crouched beside her. Together, they wedged their fingers under the heavy slab and tried to lift. It would not budge. Hannah strained, and her throat tightened. The forest around her faded, and she stared at the stone through a blurry tunnel. Her hot tears mixed with the cold rain.

"Hey, it's all right," Giuseppe said. "Maybe we can pry it."

Some of her wet hair had come loose from its braid, and it snaked over her face, across her eyes. She wiped it away with the back of her hand. Giuseppe came with a thick branch and a rock. He set the rock down next to the marble, jammed the stick between them, and threw his weight against it. The marble lifted several inches.

"Get something under it," he said. "Quick."

Hannah snatched another rock and slipped it under the memorial. Giuseppe eased up and let the slab settle on it. Then they took hold of one side and heaved. The slick of rain made it hard to keep their grip, but they inched the stone up until they were able to tip it over. It thumped on the ground, and the underside crawled with centipedes and pill bugs. Worm trails squiggled through the dirt where it had lain.

Hannah dropped to the ground, scooped and dug with her bare hands. Giuseppe said something about a shovel. She ignored him. She clawed at the soil as it turned to mud in the rain, heard herself whimpering and grunting. Her fingertips throbbed, scraped raw. She shivered and sobbed as doubt crept in like a chill, whispering that the treasure was not there.

Then Giuseppe was there next to her. He was using a trowel he had gotten from somewhere, probably Alice's. She snatched it from him and drove it into the ground. She felt him staring at her, but she did not care.

She dug, and dug, and dug. One foot deep, then another, until she was leaning halfway into the hole, and still nothing but more dirt beneath her. She felt a hand on her back.

"Hannah?"

She shook the hand off and stabbed at the earth with the trowel.

"There's nothing down there," Giuseppe said.

"It has to be!" She kept digging.

The hand on her back again. "I don't think so."

Hannah stopped. She pulled up and leaned away from the opening she had made in the earth. "Maybe it's just buried deeper," she said.

Giuseppe looked at the hole. "It's not here."

Hannah dropped the trowel and hugged herself. She started shaking.

"Come on." Giuseppe took her hand. "We need to get you out of this rain."

Hannah nodded and let him lift her to her feet.

It did not seem possible. The treasure was not there. She had come out into the forest seeking a mystery, only to learn that the answer lay in bed back home, unable to speak.

CHAPTER 16

Alice

GIUSEPPE AND HANNAH JOGGED BACK TO THE CABIN TO GET out of the storm. The door was unlocked, and he figured Alice would have insisted they get inside if she were there. He opened the door for Hannah and followed her in. The cabin felt dry and warm but a little dim. Giuseppe ran his hands through his hair and wiped the water from his face.

"Would you like a fire?" he asked.

Hannah sat down at the table, looking exhausted after her frenzy by the stone. She rocked a little back and forth, shivered, and said nothing.

"Hannah?"

"Yes?"

"Would you like a fire?"

She blinked at him. "Yes, please."

Giuseppe threw some kindling on the morning's embers and then a couple of small logs. He crouched in front of the hearth until he felt the heat on his face. "There you are. Come closer."

Hannah scooted her chair nearer to the fireplace. She stared into it, with the same bewildered look in her wide eyes she had when they found that stone, her mouth neither smiling nor frowning, almost as if her lips were waiting to see how she felt. Giuseppe cleared his throat.

"You know something about that carving, don't you?"

She nodded.

"What did it mean?"

She did not answer at first. "I have to get home."

"Well, you should at least wait out the worst of this rainstorm."

She reached up and pulled a stick out of her hair, and her braid slapped her back like a wet rope. "My father made it. That stone out there."

Giuseppe pulled up a chair. "How do you know?"

"I just do." She covered her mouth, still shivering.

Giuseppe squirmed a little next to her. She was older than him by a couple of years and very pretty. Water droplets caught the firelight in her lashes and on her cheeks. Her eyes seemed to glow. Giuseppe got up and went to the floor where he had folded his blankets from the night before.

"Here," he said, and wrapped one over her shoulders.

"Thank you." She pulled it up around her neck. "My father must have known Stroop. But he can't tell me anything."

"Did the stone give you any other clues?"

"No. It's just a memorial. A dead end." She closed her eyes. "I have to get home. The doctor will be there in a few hours."

"Doctor?"

"My father is sick. Very sick. He needs medicine, and we don't have the money to pay for it."

Giuseppe looked away. That was why she had become so insistent out there, so desperate. She needed the treasure. Giuseppe needed it, too, but did not think now was the best time to bring that up.

"Hopefully Pullman will be back soon," he said. "I really think you ought to wait for the storm to pass."

She slumped down into the blanket. "I'm so tired all of a sudden."

Giuseppe realized he felt the same way. The morning had started quiet enough, a breakfast of bread and fresh fruit, a wedge of cheese. Then Pullman had come by and taken him out walking in the forest around Alice's cabin, spotting animals and birds and showing him plants that were edible. After that, Giuseppe had split off on his own a short distance to sit down in the trees and play his fiddle. That was when he had heard the call for help. A girl's voice, terrified, and then a wild roar.

A shiver rattled Giuseppe in his chair when he thought about the beast. Its teeth and claws. He had entered that clearing, seen that cougar, and known it would kill them both. But Pullman had come. Now, sitting in front of the warm fire, the exhaustion of spent fear overwhelmed him.

"I'm tired, too," he said.

The storm pounded the roof and slapped the windows. He listened to it for a long time. His eyes drooped, fragmenting the flames in the hearth.

He heard Hannah's voice but did not catch what she said.

Giuseppe closed his eyes.

The sound of the storm awakened him, loud and raw. He realized someone had opened the door.

"Oh, my," he heard Alice say. "Two visitors?"

Giuseppe got to his feet, blinking. Next to him, Hannah stirred. She stretched, and the blanket fell from her shoulders.

"Hello, Alice," Giuseppe said. "This is Hannah."

"I know, dear," Alice said. "Although I am surprised to see her here. And all covered in mud, too."

Hannah stood up. "Hello, Alice. I came —"

The old woman held up her hand. "I wasn't asking, dear. Not yet." She removed her straw hat and shook the rain from it. She hung it up and stepped between Hannah and Giuseppe to the hearth. "Let's heat up this soup, shall we?" She swung the kettle in over the fire.

Next, Alice gathered up the quilt that had fallen to the floor and folded it, holding it to her chest with her chin. "Are the two of you hungry?" she asked.

Giuseppe was.

Hannah shook her head. "I need to be going, Alice. I'm sorry."

"I don't think you ought to, dear. Not until the storm moves on. The paths are treacherous right now if you don't know your way." She set the quilt with the others by the bed and then lowered herself into a chair. She tapped the table, telling Giuseppe and Hannah to sit.

"Now," she said, and sighed. "Tell me what you were going to say, Hannah. About why you are here."

Hannah scratched her forehead with her index finger. "Never mind."

"Nonsense. You can tell me."

"I . . . was looking for something."

"What was it you were looking for, dear?"

"You remember when we talked in your garden and I asked about Mister Stroop?"

"Of course."

"About his treasure?"

"Yes, dear."

"Well, I'm looking for it. The treasure, I mean, and I thought there would be a clue for it out here."

"Why would you think that?"

Hannah shook her head. "It's a long story."

"I'm listening," Alice said.

"No," Hannah said. "That's all right."

Giuseppe leaned forward and cleared his throat. "She saw a map," he said. "It had the north side of the pond marked. She thought there might be something there."

"Was there?"

Giuseppe looked at Hannah. She seemed so defeated.

"No," she said.

"Just that carved stone," Giuseppe said.

Alice clapped. "Ah, you saw it. Beautiful, isn't it? I remember when that stonemason from the hotel brought it out here. Mister Twine must have paid for it. Or maybe one of the guests. The stonemason had a devil of a time hauling it over the forest trails in his handcart."

Hannah's legs bounced a little, and she kept looking out the window, at the rain streaking the windowpanes.

"While you wait for this storm to let up, you must have some turtle soup," Alice said.

"You'll like it," Giuseppe said, his tongue working in his mouth like he could already taste it.

Hannah nodded. "All right."

"Wonderful." Alice rose and went to the fireplace, her back to them. "Have you seen Pullman today?"

Giuseppe looked at Hannah. She leaned back into her chair, mouth closed. So he told of their encounter with Mirabel, with only a little exaggeration here and there, at which Hannah raised an eyebrow but said nothing. Now that the fear had worn off, there was something exciting about what had happened.

Alice shook her head, wide-eyed. "My goodness. I'm just glad that everyone is unharmed, you both and Pullman, and Mirabel, too."

When steam rose from the kettle, and the aroma of herbs and meat filled the cabin, Alice ladled out three bowls and served them. The soup did not taste as fresh as it had the night before, but was still better by far than anything Giuseppe was used to eating. He watched Hannah, and she seemed to enjoy the few bites she took as well.

"Where do you live?" he asked her.

"Down in the tenements of Basket Street." She dabbed at the soup with her spoon.

"I used to play there. Sometimes."

"Maybe I've heard you."

"Maybe."

"Well," Alice said. "Giuseppe played for Pullman and me last night, and it was simply the most delightful evening I have passed in a very long time." She leaned in to Hannah. "He has a gift, you know."

"It's a talent to play music," Hannah said.

"Oh, not that kind of gift, dear. Not that kind of gift at all."

Giuseppe wondered what she meant by that.

Alice stood. "Would either of you like another helping? There's a little bit left."

Hannah shook her head.

Giuseppe could have eaten another two or three bowls. "Nah. Save it for Pullman."

He watched Hannah finish what was left in her dish. She wiped her mouth. "Thank you, Alice. It was delicious."

"Well, thank you for staying." Alice watched Hannah for several moments. "Whatever has you so worried, dear?"

Hannah said nothing. It seemed that she kept a lot inside, and Giuseppe wondered why.

"Her father is sick," he said.

"Sick?" Alice turned to Hannah. "He's sick, dear?"

She nodded.

Alice grew suddenly serious and returned to her chair. She folded her hands on the table in front of her. "What are his symptoms?"

"He's just sick," Hannah said. "And I need to get back to him."

"Tell me what his symptoms are."

Hannah took a deep breath. "He has a sore, a bedsore that's infected. The doctor said his leg needs to be removed."

"Oh, such barbarians," Alice said. "What does the wound look like?"

"It's red and swollen, and there are dark lines under the skin around it."

"Is it weeping?"

"Yes."

"Fevers?"

"Yes," Hannah said.

Alice tapped her chin and then she stood. "I have something for that." She crossed to the cupboard full of jars and bottles and pulled down a slender vial. She shook it and held it up to the light. "Have him drink this."

"What is it?" Hannah asked.

"A tincture of herbs, dear. And molds gathered around the forest. It will help with the infection."

Hannah reached out and took the vial. She peered at it, brow furrowed.

"Take it to him," Alice said. "You remember what I said about my herbs, that I was finding out their secrets? Well, I have already learned quite a few."

From what Giuseppe had seen of Alice, he believed her. She had a way of wisdom about her that made him trust what she said. Hannah folded her fingers around the vial and slipped it into a pocket in her skirts.

"Thank you, Alice," she said.

"You're welcome. Now, I think the storm has passed."

Giuseppe listened and heard nothing but an afterthought of wind, like a sigh after a good cry.

Hannah looked out the window. "You're right." She got up and went to the old woman. "I wish I could come see you in your hotel garden again."

"But you can, dear. Anytime you want. They ask about you, you know. The pansies, in particular."

Hannah smiled. "I hope they're coming along."

Alice led Hannah to the door and opened it. The smells and sounds of the forest tumbled in as if they had had their ears pressed against the door. Birdcalls and the fragrance of wet soil and pine. Giuseppe walked to the door, his hands in his pockets.

Hannah turned to him. "I guess you're staying here."

"The city isn't safe for me," he said.

She nodded. "Good-bye, then. Thanks for helping me."

"I hope your pa gets better," he said.

"He will," Alice said. "Hurry now."

Hannah stepped through the threshold.

Alice stood in the doorway and pointed. "Do you see that path there by the hawthorn?"

Hannah looked. "Yes."

"Keep to it. It wanders a bit at times, but it leads you right to the Old Fort Road."

Hannah thanked Alice again and walked away, waving from a spot down by the pond before setting off into the trees.

Alice stepped out into her garden and breathed deep. "You're really not going with her?"

"No," Giuseppe said. "Why would I?"

"She needs you."

"Alice, Stephano will kill me."

"I don't think your friends would let that happen."

"I don't have friends," Giuseppe said.

"Hannah is a friend to you now."

Was she? He had thought Pietro was a friend, too.

"You have a gift to share, dear. And apparently there is a treasure hidden somewhere." She fixed her eyes on him firmly.

"You want me to leave?"

"Giuseppe, you may stay with me for as long as you wish to. But I think you know you won't ever make it home to your family if you hide out here in the park."

She was right. As safe as the cabin felt, it was not his home, and as kind as Alice had been, she was not his family. Maybe this was a chance for him to get back what he had lost in the churchyard. Maybe he could still return to his real home and his real family, if he helped Hannah find the treasure. As for him having a gift to share, well, without his green violin Giuseppe was unsure of that.

He went back into the cabin for his old fiddle and then stood in front of Alice. "Thank you for everything."

"Of course, dear." She stepped forward and gathered him in an earthy hug that smelled of mint and lavender. "Hurry now."

Giuseppe nodded and bounced off running, waving one last time over his shoulder before entering the forest. He was pretty sure this was not the smartest thing to do, but it did feel like the right thing. Leaves dripped lazy leftovers from the storm, so that by the time he caught up with Hannah he was wet again.

She smiled as he trotted toward her.

"What are you doing here?" she asked.

"I'm coming with you," he said.

"Where, to my family's apartment?"

He scratched his head. "Is that all right? Don't worry, I'll find somewhere else to stay. I just want to make sure you get there safe."

She relaxed her shoulders. "Thank you. I feel like I've seen Mirabel about a dozen times already."

Giuseppe picked up a stray branch and tucked it under his arm like an aimed rifle. "Don't worry," he said. "She knows what this is." And he prowled ahead like a hunter out for game. Hannah grinned a little at him.

They walked, and evening began to drift among the trees. With the cloud cover lingering after the storm like a threat, it grew dark earlier than it should have. By the time they reached the edge of the park, most of the light in the streets came from gaslight.

"I hope the doctor hasn't come yet," Hannah said.

They hastened down the Old Fort Road, turned on the Cottonway, and followed it to Basket Street. It did not seem to be that late in the evening with all the traffic on the street. A week ago, Giuseppe would have picked a corner to play, but tonight he turned his coat collar up and pulled his cap down low. They jostled along the street with the crowd, and then Hannah led him off into the maze of tenements.

Before long, she stopped at a wooden building and started up the stairs. Giuseppe looked around and realized he had played near here before, that first night he had tried the green violin. The memory stung his eyes, but he shoved it aside and followed Hannah up to her family's apartment.

As soon as they opened the door, a very skinny woman rushed over to them.

"Hannah," she said, her eyes sunken and red.

"Hello, Mama," Hannah said. They embraced.

"I've been so worried," Hannah's mother said. "I expected you back hours ago."

"I know, I'm sorry."

Giuseppe looked past the two of them into the apartment. There were two beds. A large man lay in one of them, pale and sweaty. He was propped up a little, but he seemed to be sleeping, his chest rising and falling unevenly. Two girls played on the floor with straw dolls. They were looking at Giuseppe and whispering.

"How is Papa?" Hannah asked.

"Not well, the fever is back. Do you have the money?"

"No," Hannah said. "I have the medicine."

She pulled the vial from her pocket and crossed to her father. He opened his eyes when she touched his forehead with the back of her fingers.

"Hello, Papa," she whispered.

He gave her a weak smile.

Hannah pulled the stopper from the vial. "Papa, you need to drink this."

Her mother came, and together they hoisted him up a little higher and stuffed another pillow behind his back. Hannah held the vial to his dry, cracked lips and tipped the contents into his mouth. He grimaced, but he swallowed it down.

"Say a prayer it works," Hannah's mother said. "How did you get the medicine from the doctor? And why are you covered in mud?"

"It's a long story," Hannah said.

Giuseppe cleared his throat.

"Oh," Hannah said. She came over, took Giuseppe's hand, and led him into the room. "This is my new friend. Giuseppe."

"*Benvenuto*, Giuseppe," Hannah's mother said.

Giuseppe was surprised. "You know Italian?"

"Not much more than that," her mother said. "Enough to say hello to some of our neighbors. Are either of you hungry?"

They both shook their heads. There did not seem to be much food in the apartment, anyway. "I'm not staying long," he said, still unsure of where he would go when he left. The family had no room for him here. Hannah's sisters got up from the floor and came over to him. Hannah introduced them, and Giuseppe shook their tiny hands.

One of them pointed at his back. "What's that?"

"It's my fiddle," he said.

"Perhaps you could play for us later," Hannah's mother said. She sat down on the edge of the bed, and Hannah's sisters leaned on her, clinging to her skirts. "My husband loves music."

"I'd be honored," Giuseppe said, and meant it. But he was immediately reluctant. Here in this apartment, with this sick man and his lovely family, he felt nervous about playing, something he had not experienced in a very long time. He slipped his old fiddle from his back and set it on the table. He would have felt a lot more confident playing if he had the green violin. This family needed its special kind of music.

"Giuseppe has a gift," Hannah said to her mother.

They all fell into silence after that, watching Hannah's father. A sleep flutter passed over his eyes. Hannah's mother felt his temperature with her palm.

"How long until the medicine works, I wonder."

"I don't know. But it will." Hannah played with the end of her braid. "Mama? Do you know anything about a stone Papa carved out in McCauley Park?"

Hannah's mother nodded. "That was years ago. When he worked for the hotel."

"You never mentioned it before. Do you know why he made it?"

"One of the hotel guests asked him to. Oh, what was his name, Stout? Stoop? Anyway, he called your father up to his suite on the top floor and said Mister Twine had recommended him for a commissioned work. You know how your father was always taking on special projects for Mister Twine. This guest, Stoop, told your father what he wanted and paid him handsomely for it." She reached out and felt his forehead again. "That's how we paid for the new roof . . ." Her voice dropped. "On our old house."

"Did Papa know Mister Stroop well?"

"Yes, that was his name. Stroop. How did you know?"

Hannah shrugged. "I've heard it around the hotel."

"Well, no, your father didn't know him well. Stroop called him up to his suite a few times after that to thank him. He had a telescope up there, and he said he could see the stone from his window. I think he died a very short time later."

"Did Papa ever say anything about Mister Stroop's treasure?"

Her mother frowned. "Not that I can remember. Stroop had a treasure?"

"Some people say he did."

Her mother reached out and felt Hannah's father for the third time. "Oh, my." She adjusted her hand and leaned in closer, like she was listening to him breathe. "I think his fever's come down."

"That quickly?" Hannah touched his forehead, too.

They looked at each other and smiled. They sighed, and in spite of her mother's age, in that moment she and Hannah looked very much alike. Giuseppe felt a jolt of joy flash through the room, like a beam of light off a shiny pot, from person to person. Hannah's little sisters jumped up and danced around, holding hands. Time passed and the fever continued to fall. Color returned to the stonemason's face.

Then his breathing settled, deep and even, and Hannah's mother turned to Giuseppe. "Would you mind playing for us now?"

"Of course," he said, and took a deep breath, nervous again.

"Come, girls." Hannah's mother put her arms around Hannah's sisters. Hannah stood by her father and took his hand in both of hers.

Tonight Giuseppe's music meant something more than it ever had on the street, or even back in Alice's cabin. His legs trembled like he was standing on his very first corner all over again, men and women passing by in such a hurry, so tall and unaware of him. He went to the table and lifted the old fiddle from its case.

But what should he play?

"Do you have a request?" he asked, his throat dry.

Hannah's mother said, "Something to celebrate."

Giuseppe knew immediately which song they needed. He tucked the fiddle under his chin and let the melody glide through his mind for a few moments before letting it go. He eased the notes out quietly at first, unsure of himself. But the old fiddle sang so true, so tender, he gave it more life, and more still, until it did not feel like he was playing it at all. And in that moment, it did not matter which instrument he held in his hands.

"I know that song," Hannah said. "I've heard that song before."

Giuseppe closed his eyes and stood in the high pasture with his father. He looked up, but the sun was over his father's shoulder, and Giuseppe could not see his face in the light. The wind carried the bleating of the sheep they tended, the smell of grass. He ran with the dogs, laughing, chasing his father or being chased. He wanted to get caught and lifted off the ground. In the evening, on their way home, he rode high on his father's shoulders. They sang together and named the colors in the changing sunset.

"Mama."

Giuseppe opened his eyes.

Hannah stood by her father, staring at the foot of the bed.

"What is it?" Her mother looked down and gasped.

Beneath the bedspread, Hannah's father was moving his feet in time with the music.

Giuseppe sensed something happening. He closed his eyes again and gave everything he had to the song.

CHAPTER 17

Her Name

FREDERICK TRIED TO PAY ATTENTION AS MASTER BRANCH explained the clockwork he had designed for Madame Pomeroy. It would be a miniature merry-go-round, encircled with prancing horses in gilded saddles, bejeweled and mirrored. There would be a clock on top, and the merry-go-round would turn with the minutes, but on the hour it would pick up speed, play music, and the horses would rise and fall in mock cantering. Frederick nodded along with the old man's explanation, but he found it hard to concentrate for very long.

"I believe Madame Pomeroy will appreciate the whimsy in this piece," Master Branch said. "Don't you agree, Frederick?"

Frederick nodded. "Uh-huh."

Since the day Frederick had gone back to the orphanage, he had been distracted by thoughts of his mother. He wanted desperately to know about her but was scared to find anything out. It was like waking in the middle of the night to a strange noise out in the shop, when his heart pounded and he stared so long into the darkness it seemed to move; when he held his breath and listened and told himself it was nothing; when his thoughts kept him awake and eventually forced him out of bed, barefoot across the cold floor, to face the unknown that waited for him.

"Would you mind going to the Gilbert Hotel?" Master Branch asked.

"What for?"

"To find out Madame Pomeroy's taste in gemstones. Perhaps her favorite colors. Mind you, don't give out any of our plans. Just ask about her preferences."

"I'd be glad to," Frederick said. Perhaps he would be able to see Hannah while he was there.

"While you do that, I have an errand to run for the guild." Master Branch leveraged himself up from the workbench with both arms. "I'll be back later this afternoon. Please be here so we can begin work on the automaton."

Frederick nodded and the old man left through the front door. Frederick followed him and locked up the shop. Out on the street, clouds massed overhead, and a wind gathered newspaper and garbage from the gutter. Frederick held his jacket close and walked to Gilbert Square.

He saw the Opera House and it reminded him of the evening he had spent with Hannah and Madame Pomeroy at the opera. He smiled when he thought of how involved in the opera Hannah had become. He crossed the square and climbed the hotel steps. The blond porter, Walter, stepped in front of him as he approached the door.

"Seen Hannah lately?" he asked.

Frederick rolled his eyes. "No, not lately."

"Well, if you see her, tell her no hard feelings. All right?"

"No hard feelings?"

"Yeah. Tell her it wasn't personal."

"What wasn't personal?"

"She'll know."

Frederick wondered again how often Walter and Hannah saw each other. How often he offered to walk her home. "Fine. I'll tell her," he said.

Walter stepped back and Frederick entered the lobby. The vaulted room smelled of roses and drying masonry. He inquired at the front desk about Madame Pomeroy, and the attendant told him that she lived in the suite on the top floor. Frederick started up the grand staircase. With each landing the hotel grew more refined and pretentious. Frederick wondered how Hannah felt having to wait on all these rich folk, while her family huddled in their tenement.

He reached the top floor and found the door to Madame Pomeroy's suite. He adjusted his jacket and pulled on the doorbell.

A long moment passed, and then he heard movement inside.

The door opened, and Madame Pomeroy peered out.

"Frederick?"

"Hello, Madame," he said.

"Well, what a pleasant surprise. Do come in." She opened the door wide, but her tone was muted, less buoyant, and her smile appeared forced.

"Thank you." Frederick stepped into the foyer. "Have I come at a bad time?"

"Not at all, child."

"Master Branch sent me to inquire about some of your color and style preferences."

"In regard to my commission?"

"Yes, Madame."

"Then let's sit and talk for a few moments."

She led him into an adjacent drawing room, where she sat and then reclined on a long couch. Frederick sat in a chair near her. He looked around but saw no sign of Hannah or the Russian.

"Now," she said. "Color and style of what, exactly?"

Frederick smiled. "I regret that I am under strict instruction not to give away the nature of the automaton."

"For the better, child," she said, and chuckled. "Oh, but I love surprises."

"But I can tell you that there will be gems."

"What kind of gems?"

"That is what I came to ask you, Madame."

"Ah, I see. Well, I simply adore all precious stones, but I am partial to the darker jewels. Rubies. Carbuncles. Sapphires." She stopped. "But before I go any further, how long until the piece will be completed?"

"A few weeks. But the design is finished."

"A few weeks?" she said. "That may be problematic."

"How so?"

Before she could answer, the front door opened. Frederick turned, hoping to see Hannah, but the Russian stalked into the room. His brow pressed heavy over his eyes, and he frowned when he saw Frederick.

"He's all right, Yakov," Madame Pomeroy said. She held her hand to her chest. "What did you find out?"

The Russian held up a slip of paper, a telegram. "New Orleans," he said.

"How long do we have?" Madame Pomeroy asked.

"Two weeks."

"And a ship?"

"If we go to England or France, four or five days."

Madame Pomeroy shook her head. "Somewhere else."

"A boat leaves for Italy in ten days."

Madame Pomeroy stood. "Italy, then. Make the necessary preparations."

Yakov nodded with a kick of his boot, turned, and marched out. Frederick heard him leave through the front door.

Madame Pomeroy inhaled. "I am afraid my stay has been cut short, child."

"Is everything all right?" Frederick asked.

She smiled. "You are a sweet boy."

Frederick did not know whether it was proper to ask, but he was curious. "What's in New Orleans?"

She sighed and rubbed her temples. "An old enemy. He has arrived in America, and will soon find me here. Unless I leave first. Which brings me to the commission. Now I'm afraid I will have to cancel it. I will, of course, compensate him for the time and resources he has already put into it. I only hope your master will not take offense."

"None at all, Madame. Is there anything we can do?"

"No, child." She held out her hand and gestured him toward the front door. "But I so enjoyed the opera with you."

"I enjoyed it, also," he said. "Madame, where is Hannah?"

"Hannah?" She stopped and Frederick thought he saw her eyes glisten. "Hannah no longer works for the hotel."

"What? Why?"

"It is not my place to say, child. But if you see her, please tell her . . . tell her that I would like to understand. Would you do that for me?"

Frederick was more confused by this than what Walter had said. Something had happened to Hannah.

"Is she all right?" he asked.

"I cannot say. But do give her that message." She opened the door. "And tell her that I am leaving."

"I will," Frederick said.

"Good-bye, child."

Frederick stepped out into the hallway. "Good-bye, Madame," he said.

She closed the door.

Frederick paced the shop, waiting for Master Branch. The old clockmaker had told him to be there that afternoon to work on the automaton, and Frederick had obeyed. But the commission was canceled now, and Frederick wanted to go to Hannah's apartment to try and find out what had happened to her. Master Branch was taking a long time in returning.

Thunderclouds had begun to shower the city, and through the shopwindows Frederick watched pedestrians rushing to get out of the storm. The streets turned to moving sheets of water, gutters full of floating debris. Frederick liked the rain. After a good storm the air felt crisp and light, and the city looked as though it had taken a bath, scrubbed and polished.

Someone flew up against the shop door, holding a newspaper over their head. The door opened, and Master Branch fell into the room. A shiver shook his whole body, and he threw the sodden paper to the floor.

"Dreadful storm," he said. "I've caught my death, I know it." Water hung from the end of his nose, and his thin hair looked glued to his head one strand at a time. "Help me out of this."

Frederick stepped behind him and pulled off the old man's coat. He shook it and hung it on the hat rack by the door. Master Branch sneezed and stooped toward the staircase. "I need a pot of coffee," he said. "Come up with me, lad."

Frederick looked outside. He would have to wait for the storm to let up before going to Hannah's, anyway, so he followed the old man upstairs.

After lighting a fire in the stove and setting the kettle to boil the coffee grinds, Master Branch removed his shoes and dropped into his chair. Frederick blew on the embers in the fireplace and tossed in a couple of logs. Before long, Master Branch had his bare feet propped up, his wet socks hung over the fire screen to dry.

"Come here, lad." Master Branch pointed at the chair opposite him.

Frederick took a seat and folded his hands in his lap.

"I need to tell you of the errand I ran today."

Frederick leaned forward. "Oh?"

"Yes. I told you I went on guild business, but that was not true." He moved his lips as if working them up to say what was waiting in his mouth. "You can probably guess what I'm about to tell you."

"I really can't," Frederick said.

"I went to the orphanage."

Frederick sat back in the chair. "You what?"

"I went back to the orphanage. I thought if I —"

"You had no right," Frederick said.

"I know you told me you wanted to do it on your own, but after you came back that day without any answers I figured I could help."

"Help? How?"

"By finding out what you wanted to know."

Frederick leaped to his feet. "But what if I don't? What if I don't want to know?"

Master Branch let out a low growl that was mostly air. "If you would just be honest, I think that underneath it all you do want to know."

"I don't! I don't want anything. Not from you or anyone else!"

Master Branch pounded the arm of his chair with his fist. "Sit down, boy!" He immediately winced and shook his head. "I'm sorry, Frederick. I'm sorry. Please. Sit."

Frederick had never seen such an outburst from the old man. He slid back into the chair.

"Lad, listen to me. I have given you privacy. I have given you time — years, in fact. Now, I know that I will never be a father to you, or a paternal figure. I know I may never even be your friend. But I hope that one day I can be someone whom you trust."

Frederick felt a warm knot in his stomach. It hurt and soothed at the same time. He did not know what to say. He wanted to tell Master Branch that he did trust him. But the clockwork man in the basement said otherwise.

Master Branch pulled a piece of paper from his pocket. It was damp and the ink had run, but he handed it to Frederick. "Her name was Maggie. Margaret."

The name struck Frederick's memory like a bell. He stared at the paper, read the name again and again, then each blurry letter one at a time as if there were a secret about his mother hiding between them.

"She was ill," Master Branch said. "Consumption. She had nowhere else to turn, and could no longer care for you. She left you and went to a hospital."

"Where?" Frederick asked.

Master Branch shook his head.

The kettle on the stove whistled. The old man let it go for a few minutes, but soon went to pour himself a cup of coffee. Frederick watched him move about the kitchen. He knew he should tell him. Confess his secret ambition and show Master Branch his creation. But Frederick could not make his jaw work. He could not form a single word.

Master Branch came back to his chair. He held the coffee cup in front of his mouth and stared over it into the fireplace. The steam curled around his nose as he sipped his drink, and neither of them spoke for a while.

"I'll need to pick up some more coffee beans tomorrow," the old man said.

A log popped in the hearth.

"Master Branch?"

"Yes?"

"How did you get this?" Frederick held up the piece of paper.

Master Branch hesitated. "I bought it."

Frederick felt guilty. Master Branch lived a comfortable life, but was not wealthy. The old man had already paid Mrs. Treeless once, to take Frederick from the orphanage, and now he had gone back and paid her again. Frederick struggled to understand why.

Master Branch drained the last bit of coffee from his cup. "Ah. I feel much better."

Frederick folded the paper and put it in his pocket. Her name was Maggie. "I feel better, too," he said. But upon learning her name, Frederick found he needed more. Much more. What had happened to her after she left him?

"Hospitals keep records of their patients, right?" Frederick asked.

"I should think so."

Frederick listened for the rain. It had stopped.

"How did it go with Madame Pomeroy?" Master Branch asked.

"Oh. I almost forgot. She's leaving the city in ten days."

"But . . . the automaton will not be completed by then."

"She said she needs to cancel the commission."

"What?" Master Branch scowled and grumbled under his breath.

"She said she would pay you for your work so far."

"It's not that." Master Branch rubbed his chin. "It's just that I was looking forward to making it. I love a challenge."

Frederick got up from the chair and went to the window. A blanket of dark clouds cast the city into an early evening, but it appeared the rain had eased up for the walk to Hannah's apartment. From there, perhaps she would go with him to the hospitals to ask about his mother. He had already wrecked his attempt to learn her name at the orphanage. Maybe Hannah could keep him from tripping all over himself again.

"I think I'll go out for a bit," Frederick said.

"In this weather?"

"It stopped raining."

"Suit yourself, then."

Frederick crossed to the staircase. He started down, but stopped on the third step and looked back. "You know, we could still make it. You and I."

Master Branch looked up. "Make what?"

"The automaton. We could still make it together."

The skin around the old man's eyes crinkled with a grin. "Yes, we could, lad."

Frederick smiled. "I'll try not to be too long."

Outside, Frederick splashed through puddles already draining off the empty streets. Rain gutters gurgled the water running down their throats and spit it out onto the sidewalks. Frederick took the trip across town slowly. This would be the first time he had seen Hannah since the night of the opera, and he felt quite awkward about it. But his awkwardness surprised and puzzled him, and he did not know what to do with it. Perhaps if he practiced what he would say to her . . .

"Greetings, Hannah. It's good to see you."

Frederick passed a lamplighter wearing a long dark coat, a tall dark hat, carrying a pole with the little flame on the end. He marched from lamppost to lamppost, leaving a trail of gaslight behind.

"Hello, Hannah," Frederick said again, a little differently. "How are you this fine evening?"

"On your way to see your gal?"

Frederick stopped. The lamplighter looked at him.

"Excuse me?" Frederick said.

"Sounds like you was working over what you might to say to your gal."

"She's not my gal."

"She pretty?"

"I suppose she is."

"Well, here's some advice." The man poked the lit end of his pole inside the streetlamp, and yellow light poured onto his face. "It only takes a spark to light a bonfire."

"What do you mean?"

"Why use a torch when you can use a flint? No woman likes to hear what ain't sincere. Whatever you say, say it simply and make it count. You'll get your gal."

"She's not my gal," Frederick said.

The lamplighter laughed and tipped his tall hat and moved on to the next lamppost. "Good luck, chap."

Frederick stood in the street for a moment, and then turned around and started back toward Master Branch's shop. Hannah was not his gal, and this was becoming more complicated than he thought it would be. He had no idea what to say to Hannah now. Did *she* think she was his gal? His earlier awkwardness blazed into panic at the thought of seeing her.

He walked back the way he had come, the night almost fully ensconced around him, until he arrived on Sycamore Street. Just because she was a girl, and they had gone to the opera, did not mean there was anything romantic between them.

He stopped in the street again, in front of the clockmaker's shop. She may not have been his gal, but she was still his friend. Why couldn't he just go, say hello, and give her Madame Pomeroy's message? Maybe he would still ask if she would come with him to the hospitals. Maybe. Frederick turned around and headed back toward the tenements for the second time that evening.

Before long he was looking up at Hannah's apartment door from the street, trying to talk himself into climbing the stairs and knocking. As he stood there, the sound of a violin drifted down from one of the apartments, carrying a familiar song. It settled over his head like a heavy blanket, both smothering and safe.

He began to hum along to himself, an echo of something from long before the orphanage. A song his mother used to sing, all the time. Her face emerged from the wreckage of his past, and he remembered her eyes, the rim of green around the blue. He heard her singing, her clear voice, and hummed along with her. But then he stopped. His chest felt like it was about to collapse, and he choked on his tears.

He watched his mother's face as she led him through the orphanage door into the entryway. He saw the old woman missing most of her teeth. He saw his mother coughing and sobbing. And she left him.

He called out to her.

He cried.

Why?

CHAPTER 18

New Clues

HANNAH STARED AT HER FATHER'S FEET. SHE COUNTED FIVE beats, five twitches, five movements of a foot that never moved. That could not move. She did not trust what she was seeing and called to her mother. Everyone in the room turned to stare at her father's foot. Hannah's mother wept and shook her head. Hannah's sisters bobbed up and down at the end of the bed and giggled.

Her father opened his eyes, and Hannah looked right in them. Her father's dry lips cracked into a wide grin, and Hannah smiled back at him. Hannah's mother rushed over and took his hand from Hannah.

"Hello there," she said. She suddenly looked down at her hand, and then turned to Hannah. "He just squeezed me so tight. Could it be that medicine?"

"Maybe." Hannah looked at Giuseppe. "Or the music."

"The music?"

Giuseppe played with his eyes closed, his brow knotted in concentration.

"Don't stop," Hannah said to him. "Please don't stop. Play as long as you can."

Giuseppe dipped his head and fiddle in a bow.

Hannah's sisters held hands and swung each other around the room. "Come dance with us, Hannah!"

Hannah went over to them, and they all three joined together in a circle. The music seemed to throb from the floorboards, setting their legs kicking. Hannah felt completely free. There was no hotel, there was no Miss Wool or Madame Pomeroy. And her father was healthy and tapping his toe to a song. In that moment her family's apartment felt like the entire world, and in that tiny world anything seemed possible. Hannah's sisters broke away like doves taking flight, and Hannah stumbled back to her father's side with a giddy laugh.

She knelt down so her face was right by her father's ear. "I saw your stone today. The one you carved for Mister Stroop. I saw your holly leaves."

His head turned slightly toward her, and she leaned closer. "It's still out there in the park, by Grover's Pond." She touched the whiskers on his cheek. "It's a beautiful stone."

He nodded.

"I count your holly leaves at the hotel, you know. There are sixty-two. Mister Twine changes everything, but he never changes your work. All this time it's like you've been there in the hotel with me." Hannah took a deep breath. "But I don't work there anymore."

"What?" her mother said. Hannah ignored her.

"I lost my job, Papa. So I need to find Mister Stroop's treasure. Did you know he had a treasure?"

He nodded again.

"Do you know where it is?"

Another nod.

"Where is it?" Hannah asked, her heart quickening, but she knew he could not answer.

Her father's eyes looked around the room. Hannah stood and studied his face for some clue, some sign of his thoughts. He let go of her mother's hand and pinched his fingertips together. He stabbed at the blanket with them in time with the music.

"What's he doing?" Hannah's mother said.

"I think he wants to write," Hannah said. But they had no paper in the apartment. She ran to her bed and grabbed her one book from the shelf. Then she sifted through the ash bucket by the stove with her fingers until she found a splinter of charcoal. She opened the book to one of the blank front pages.

"Here, Papa." The charcoal left smudges on his fingers as she wedged it into his grasp. She set the open book on his lap, and held his hand to it. "Here."

He looked down at the page.

Giuseppe fiddled and sweated and grinned. The room sweltered, as though his music had replaced all the air; they inhaled it, suffocated on it. Music filled their lungs and their souls. Her father tapped at the paper with the charcoal, making rhythmic marks. One dashed and squiggly line, then another on top of it. Then several in a row.

"That's a *T*," her mother said, pointing.

"And a *W*," Hannah said.

Her father wrote out another three letters.

"Twine," Hannah whispered.

Her father nodded.

Giuseppe had hunched over his violin, playing close to the ground. His body shook, and Hannah could tell he was nearing the end of the song. The music built in intensity, like a tightening in the room.

"Mister Twine has the treasure?" she asked.

Her father shook his head.

"Does he know where it is?"

Her father nodded.

"He's writing something else," Hannah's mother whispered.

Hannah watched for a moment, and then she looked back at Giuseppe. His fingers flew and his bow became a blur as he rose up on the tips of his toes. Then a last peal of music burst from the fiddle. The final notes lingered in Hannah's ear, like the open silence just after she heard the gate latch in their old garden, and she knew that any minute her father would come through the door, home from work. Giuseppe slumped into a chair, panting. The charcoal ceased scratching. Hannah's father went slack, and his hand fell to his side.

"I can't read what he wrote." Hannah's mother handed the book to her.

Hannah studied it. "It's not a word, Mama. It's a holly leaf."

Her father had lost what strength the music had unlocked in him. The spell had broken. He looked at her, at his family, with tears, but the smile had not left his lips. It had grown even wider. Hannah stared at the page, and then ripped it from the book. She folded it up and tucked it away in a pocket in her skirt. There would be no need to count them anymore. She could carry her father with her.

She bent and hugged him, her arms barely crossing his broad chest. "Thank you," she whispered.

One of Hannah's sisters clapped and pointed at Giuseppe. "Play again!"

He just smiled and shook his head. "That's all I have."

Hannah rushed over to him and hugged him. This strange boy, who smelled of the streets and made magic with his fiddle. "Thank you," she said.

Then Hannah's mother came over and embraced them both, and after that Hannah's sisters came and burrowed in between their legs. They all held on to one another for a long moment, and in that moment the world Hannah had forgotten about, the outside world, seeped back in like a fog under the door. Hannah shivered.

"I have to go," she said, pulling away. "I have to look for the treasure."

Hannah's mother shook her head. "I still don't understand all of this. And Hannah, your job?"

"It's going to be all right, Mama." Hannah believed that, now. "I know what I need to do."

"Hannah, you need to tell me what's going on."

"I'm fine, Mama." Hannah herded Giuseppe to the door. "Look away while I change, please." The sooner they got out on the street, the sooner they could find a place for him to hide and plan how they were going to get the treasure from Mister Twine. Hannah slipped out of the soiled skirt and into her clean one. She handed the dirty one to her mother. "Really, I'm fine."

"Stop saying that. You're not fine," her mother said.

Hannah felt that same fire blaze inside the red-hot stove in her heart. "Yes, I am," she said. She went to the door, opened it, and pushed Giuseppe through. "Good night, Mama. Oh, I forgot. It's after seven o'clock and Doctor Morse will be here any minute. When he comes just tell him Papa started healing on his own."

"I thought you bought the medicine from him."

"I love you, Papa!" Hannah called out. She stepped outside and shut the door.

Out on the landing she smelled coal smoke and felt the cool night. Giuseppe swayed a bit on the stairs as they descended to the street.

"Are you all right?" she asked him.

"I'm tired," he said.

They reached the sidewalk and Hannah held out her hands to steady him. "Lean against me," she said.

"I'm fine," he said. "It was hot up there."

Hannah realized she had no idea where to take him. He probably knew the city better than she did, and McCauley Park was apparently the best hiding place he had come up with. Perhaps it would be better for him to stay here with her family after all.

"Where should we go?" she asked.

"Frederick," he said.

"What?"

He pointed. "Frederick."

Hannah looked. Across the street, next to a boarded-up bakery, Frederick leaned against the wall, watching them. Then he walked across the street toward them, passing from one island of lamplight onto another. His eyes were red, as if he had been crying.

"Hello," he said, his voice flat.

"Hello, Frederick," Hannah said.

"Freddy," Giuseppe said. "What brings you down here?"

"I came to see Hannah."

Giuseppe scratched his head. "You two know each other?"

Hannah turned to Giuseppe. "*You* two know each other?"

"Apparently we *all* know each other," Frederick said. "We just weren't aware of it. Sounds like an opera, eh, Hannah?" He turned to Giuseppe. "So, what brings you down here?"

Giuseppe shrugged. "Playing my fiddle."

"That was you I heard? Playing that song?"

"Yep."

"His music restored some of my father's strength," Hannah said.

"It's a beautiful song," Frederick said.

"Thank you," Giuseppe said with a nod. "Say, Freddy. I need a place to hide out for a few days. Can I stay with you?"

Frederick looked down at the ground, like he was considering it. "Come on, then," he said, and set off after motioning for them to follow.

Giuseppe glanced at Hannah from the side and shrugged again. She smiled and they both followed after Frederick. Giuseppe still appeared a little off balance, but as they crossed the city he seemed to recover. She noticed that he kept his coat collar up around his neck, and kept his face down.

They reached the square. Hannah wanted to talk to Frederick about that night at the opera, but wondered if he was still bothered by the questions she had asked him about his mother. Hannah did not want to hurt him or embarrass him further. Then Giuseppe skipped up alongside Frederick and pointed at the Opera House.

"I've been in there," he said. "I heard them singing about love."

Frederick sniffed. "And what did you think of the opera?"

"It was heart pounding," Giuseppe said, and laughed like he had made a joke.

Hannah hurried up on Frederick's other side. He flicked his eyes toward her, and then back to the street ahead. "And how did you enjoy your night at the opera, Hannah?"

"I had a wonderful time," she said. "I went with the nicest young man."

"Really?" Frederick said.

"Yes," Hannah said. "And afterward we had a wonderful talk."

Frederick said nothing else until they reached Master Branch's shop. All the darkened windows along the ground floor reflected the night back at them. The second-story windows flickered yellow. Frederick held one finger over his lips and went to the front door. He pulled out a key and very quietly unlocked the door. He opened it a few inches, and then reached up inside around the lintel.

"The bell," he whispered. "Go inside."

Giuseppe slipped through, and Hannah followed after him. They stood waiting in the dark as Frederick closed the door and gently released the bell.

"Follow me," he said, and led them behind the counter into the back workroom. There was a cot there, and Hannah wondered if that was where Frederick slept. "Down here," Frederick said. He opened a door and they followed him down a narrow staircase into a room, a cellar judging by the smell of loam, but there was a hint of oil, too. "Hold on."

She heard him strike a match, and his face flared in the darkness, bent over a lamp. Then the light grew like a sigh to the edges of the room, sweeping all the shadows into the corners. They were in another workroom, with a hard clay floor and tools hanging from the foundation beams and ceiling. She turned around, and gasped.

"Who is that?" she said. There was a figure lying on a worktable, covered with a stained white sheet.

Frederick chuckled. "Would you like me to show you?"

"No!" Hannah said. "I don't know. Who is that?"

"It's no one, yet."

Giuseppe cocked his head to one side. "Now what does that mean?"

"I'll show you," Frederick said. His dark mood appeared to have changed almost instantly to excitement. "But first I have to let Master Branch know I'm home. I'll be right back." He bounced up the staircase, but stopped halfway and bent to look at them. "No peeking."

"We won't," Giuseppe said.

"I'll be back in just a few minutes." Frederick's legs disappeared, and they heard his footsteps upstairs. Then the shop bell tinkled and Frederick called out to Master Branch. They heard a muffled voice, and then Frederick said he was coming. Silence after that.

"I'm peeking," Giuseppe said.

"No," Hannah said.

"Why not?"

"He asked us not to."

Giuseppe looked at the sheet. "Don't you want to see him?"

"See who?"

"Whoever's under there."

"No," Hannah said.

Giuseppe bit his lip. "I'm peeking."

But before he could lift the sheet they heard Frederick coming back down the stairs. Giuseppe hopped away from the worktable and grinned at Hannah.

Frederick stepped around to the head of the table and took hold of the sheet. "I've been working on this for some time," he said, and looked at Hannah. "I think it will impress you." Then he took a deep breath and whipped the sheet off the table.

CHAPTER 19

The Archer Museum

GIUSEPPE STUDIED THE METAL FIGURE. IT WAS A MAN, ASSEM-
bled from mismatched metal parts. Some pieces were recognizable,
like the tin coal chute shaped to form a barreled chest, but Giuseppe
could not even guess where many of the other components came from.
The figure's shiny brass arms and legs were jointed and looked heavily
layered with metal muscles, while the hands appeared delicate, capable
of refined movement. The figure looked to be about five feet tall, but
ended at the neck.

"Where's the head?" Giuseppe asked.

Frederick scowled. Then he balled the sheet up tight and threw it on
the floor. "It doesn't have one. Yet."

"You made this?" Hannah asked.

Frederick stuck his chest out. "I did."

"What does it do?" Giuseppe asked.

"When it's finished it will do anything I want it to."

"When will it be finished?" Giuseppe asked.

Frederick ignored Giuseppe's question and beckoned to Hannah. He
guided her to a place at the table near one of the arms. The metal clinked
as he lifted the arm several inches. "Here, hold it," he said.

Hannah put her hands under it, flat like she was about to receive a tray, and Frederick lowered the arm onto them. "Oh," she said. "It's heavy."

"And strong," Frederick said.

"When will it be finished?" Giuseppe asked again.

"I don't know," Frederick said to him. "The head is proving difficult. I think I may be the first clockmaker to ever attempt something like this."

"Really?" Hannah said.

"I don't think so," Giuseppe said.

Frederick narrowed his eyes. "What?"

"I've seen a clockwork head before."

Frederick's eyes grew large. His mouth hung open. "Where?"

"In the Archer Museum," Giuseppe said.

"Impossible," Frederick said. "I've studied every display."

Giuseppe shook his head. "It's not on display. It's in a storeroom."

"How do you know that?" Frederick asked.

"I saw it from a window. On the roof."

"What were you doing on the roof?" Frederick asked.

"That's a long story."

Frederick drummed his fingers on the worktable. "Could you show me?"

"What, tonight?" Giuseppe said.

"Of course."

"Uh-uh." This time of evening Giuseppe risked being spotted, and he had already taken his chances walking from Hannah's apartment across town to Frederick's shop. "Not for a few hours, anyway."

"Why not?"

"Look, Freddy, I shouldn't be here with you. I shouldn't even be in this city. I'm dead if Stephano catches me."

"Who?"

Hannah stepped forward. "Giuseppe, tell him."

So he did. First, he talked about his life in the lair on Crosby Street, the green violin and the theft from the cemetery, and then he told of his skyline escape from Stephano into the park. Gradually, the three of them settled on the cellar floor, and Giuseppe talked about Pullman and Alice.

"Alice is so wonderful," Hannah said. "Pullman was rude."

"He wasn't rude," Giuseppe said.

Frederick turned to Hannah. "You were there?"

Hannah smiled. "Yes, I was."

"I was staying with Alice," Giuseppe said, "and Hannah came out looking for clues. We met by accident."

"Clues for what?" Frederick asked.

Giuseppe figured he would have to tell Hannah's story, too, but she spoke up. She told Frederick all about Mister Stroop and his treasure, and about the memorial stone. She talked about her father, and the message he had written. She told him about how she had been fired from the hotel for stealing from Madame Pomeroy.

"But I had to," she said. "I had no choice."

Frederick leaned forward. "Is your father all right now?"

"He is," she said. "Thanks to Alice's medicine. She's one of the only things I'll miss about the hotel."

Frederick sat up. "That reminds me. Madame Pomeroy gave me a message for you."

"What message?" Hannah said.

"She's leaving the city on a boat for Italy in ten days."

Giuseppe caught his breath. A boat headed *home*.

Hannah held her stomach. "She's leaving?"

Frederick nodded. "And she said she wants to understand."

"Understand what?" Giuseppe asked.

"Why I stole from her," Hannah said, eyes downcast. "I thought she didn't want to speak to me." She went quiet after that.

Giuseppe and Frederick looked at each other, then around the room, and no one spoke. A faint ticking drifted down from the shop upstairs. They all three sat there in the cellar, and Giuseppe thought about how they all three wanted something. Frederick wanted the clockwork head, Hannah wanted the treasure, and he wanted a boat ticket home. And Giuseppe realized that he needed Hannah and Frederick to get what he wanted, and they needed him to get what they wanted.

He cleared his throat. "Listen, you two. I'll help you if you help me."

"What do you mean?" Frederick asked.

"Well," Giuseppe said, "I'll help you get a look at that clockwork head, and I'll help Hannah find her treasure. If you two help me get on that boat going to Italy."

Hannah looked up. "It's like the cards."

"What cards?" Frederick asked.

"Madame Pomeroy's cards. She read my future, and she told me that I would have to trust and help other people, for them to help me."

"It's settled, then," Giuseppe said. "We'll all help each other. Agreed?"

"Agreed," Hannah said.

"Agreed," Frederick said.

"But I can't go anywhere until the streets are quiet," Giuseppe said. "We'll have to lie low for a few hours."

Frederick got to his feet. "Then let me show you some more of my automaton," he said. He helped Hannah up and the trio walked around the worktable. Frederick pointed at particular parts, and explained where they came from and how they worked. He showed them a panel that opened in the chest, revealing the clockwork innards at the contraption's heart.

Giuseppe wondered if making a clockwork man was such a good idea. What would happen if it disobeyed what it was told to do? If Frederick lost control of it?

After a few minutes, the threesome sat back down. Frederick and Hannah huddled together. Giuseppe thought he might steal a moment or two of sleep and leaned back against the wall with his eyes closed. Then Frederick whispered something, and Giuseppe listened.

"Her name was Maggie," he said. "Margaret. She had consumption."

"She was sick," Hannah said. "That's why she left you."

Silence.

"How did you find out?" Hannah asked.

"I went back to the orphanage. But Master Branch helped me. He said she went to a hospital after she left me."

"Do you know which one?"

Silence.

"I'm going to find out, though," Frederick said.

"I'm happy for you."

"Hannah? Would you — would you help me?"

Silence.

"Of course," Hannah said.

After that, Giuseppe dozed off.

◎ ◎ ◎

He awoke to Hannah laughing. Frederick stood at the head of the work-table talking into the metal man's neck, his voice echoing around inside its chest.

"What time is it?" Giuseppe asked.

Frederick looked over at him. "Oh, you're up. It's after midnight."

Giuseppe blinked and yawned. "What should we do first?"

Hannah rubbed her hands together. "The museum. It's too late to go see Mister Twine."

"The museum, then," Giuseppe said.

Frederick picked up the stained white sheet from the floor and shook it out. He flipped it up into the air and it settled down over the clock-work man like a thin frosting of snow. "Let's go," he said.

They tiptoed up the stairs into the workroom, across the shop, and through the front door. Frederick held the bell again, and locked the door behind them. The streets were mostly empty. A dog barked some-where on the next block, and a fine mist glittered under the streetlamps. The storm had left the air cold and wet, and Giuseppe shivered.

Frederick started to lead the way down Sycamore Street, but Giuseppe whistled and pointed down an alley. He knew the back ways to reach the square, the safer ways to avoid being seen. Hannah and Frederick fol-lowed him through the narrow passages, climbing over broken crates and ducking under clotheslines strung between windows.

He guided them to a building a few streets off the square, with a stairway to the roof.

"What are we doing here?" Frederick asked.

"This is the way I came down," Giuseppe said. "There's no way up from the square."

So they ascended single file. Giuseppe in front, then Hannah, and

Frederick at the rear, climbing higher and higher into the night, from one rooftop to another, up ladders and shingled slopes, until they reached the roof of the Archer Museum where the massive dome arched into the sky.

"The windows are over here," Giuseppe said, and they followed him around. When they reached the opposite side of the dome, they found the skylights dark.

Frederick shielded his eyes and peered into the room below. "I can't see anything."

"There was a man down there last time," Giuseppe said.

Hannah walked to the roof ledge and looked out over the city. "It's so beautiful up here." She pointed at the Gilbert Hotel. "I think that window would have been Mister Stroop's."

Frederick stood up and turned to Giuseppe. "How can we get inside?"

Hannah turned around. "You're not serious."

"I need to get a look at that head," Frederick said.

"But what if you get caught?" Hannah said.

"Let's look around," Giuseppe said. He scanned the roof, and spotted a small hatch near a corner on the other side of the skylights. He crossed to it, and Frederick followed him.

"Is it locked?" Frederick asked.

Giuseppe pulled on the trapdoor and it opened. A ladder fell away from them, down into the museum.

"I'm not sure about this," Hannah said.

But Frederick had already disappeared down the hatch.

"Are you coming?" Giuseppe asked her.

Hannah twisted her hands together. "I don't know."

"You can wait here if you want. We'll be back soon."

"No." Hannah stared at the opening. "No, I'm coming."

"Let me help you."

He held one of her hands until she got both her feet on the ladder.

"I'm all right now," she said, and started down.

Giuseppe followed after her and descended into an immense room full of an emptiness that seemed to whisper. Columns of moonlight joined the floor to the ceiling, and the smell of dust stuck to the inside of Giuseppe's nose. The climb down took longer than he had expected, but he eventually reached the bottom of the ladder where Frederick and Hannah waited.

He looked around and took a moment to get his bearings. Stacks of crates fifteen or twenty feet high leaned over them on either side. There was the long row of tables he had seen. The man with the dusty hair had been working on the bronze head about halfway down their length.

"I think it was over there," Giuseppe whispered. Their footsteps echoed off the floor, making it sound as though a ghostly, moonlit army was closing in on all sides.

"Look at these crates," Hannah whispered as they walked. "They're stamped with the names of cities from all over the world. This one is from Prague."

She stopped at an open box and peered into it.

"I think I see the head," Frederick said, and raced ahead of them.

Hannah reached inside the box and pulled out a dried lump of clay. It had strange markings carved into it, and a paper tag tied to it with string. Hannah read the label. "It's a piece of a golem."

"A what?" Giuseppe asked.

"Madame Pomeroy told me about them. They're —"

Before she could finish, Frederick called out. "I found it! Giuseppe, come here."

Giuseppe left Hannah and wandered down the tables. He found Frederick holding the bronze head between both hands. Then Frederick lifted it up, arms outstretched, and peered at its closed eyes.

"I need light," he said, his voice loud with excitement.

"Too risky," Giuseppe said. He looked over his shoulder. "And keep quiet."

Hannah walked up to them, still holding the lump of clay.

"So that's the head?" she asked.

Giuseppe nodded.

Frederick set it back down amid the orderly stacks of papers and maps and strange objects that lined the table. There were statues and figures, some dressed and some naked enough to make Giuseppe blush. A black skull the shape of an anvil bore teeth as long as Giuseppe's fingers. There were rust-colored pots painted with the black silhouettes of soldiers carrying spears and swords, and wearing fringed helmets.

Frederick held his chin and furrowed his brow. "How does it open?" he said to himself. He ran his fingers over the forehead, and then probed the wire hair. "There must be a latch."

A moment later, there was a click, and the forehead fell open. "Aha," Frederick said with a smile of triumph.

Giuseppe heard a scuff off in the darkness at the far end of the room, and all three of them looked in that direction.

"What was that?" Hannah whispered. "Giuseppe?"

He listened. "I don't know."

"It was nothing," Frederick said. He bent down close to the bronze head, squinting into the clockwork brains. "I can't see a thing, I need light." He reached for one of the oil lamps on the table and a box of matches near it.

"Frederick," Hannah said.

"It's fine," he said, and struck a match. He lit the oil lamp, which smoked and cast a pale light over the table. "There, that's better."

Giuseppe stepped out of the lamp's reach and stared off in the direction of the noise.

"This is incredible," Frederick said. "It'll take weeks to sort this out. The level of complexity is beyond anything I've seen."

Giuseppe noticed that Hannah was watching him with a concerned look on her face. "I think we should go, Frederick," she said.

"I'm not ready," he said.

There was another noise, a cough. This time it was much closer. They all froze and listened.

"I think Hannah's right," Giuseppe whispered. "We should go."

But none of them moved.

Someone shouted from the shadows, "Take them, now!"

Then the sound of a stampede rushed toward them.

"Go!" Giuseppe shouted. He grabbed Hannah and pushed her toward the ladder.

"You two run!" Frederick snatched the bronze head. He tucked it under his arm and dove away in the opposite direction.

Giuseppe watched him go for half a breath. What was that fool doing? He ran after Hannah and caught up with her just as she reached the ladder. "Climb," he said.

"Where's Frederick?"

"Just climb!"

Moments later a boulder of a man rolled out of the darkness at the foot of the ladder and grabbed it like he was about to rip it from the wall. Then the thug heaved himself up to the first rung.

"Faster!" Giuseppe shouted, Hannah's skirts in his face.

They reached the top, and Hannah pushed the trapdoor open. She scrambled through, and Giuseppe followed her up onto the roof.

"What about Frederick?" she said again.

Giuseppe looked down the ladder into the boulder's face. His square jaw was clenched tight, his nostrils flared. And he climbed faster than anyone his size should have been able to.

"He's not even breathing hard," Giuseppe said. They had to run. Fast. "Come on!"

He seized her hand and yanked her away from the trapdoor. They fled across the roof, past the skylights, and around the museum dome.

"But Frederick!" Hannah shouted.

"He knows what he's doing." Giuseppe hoped that was true.

CHAPTER 20

The Bronze Head

FREDERICK CROUCHED IN THE GAP BETWEEN TWO CRATES, watching. The huge man chasing Hannah and Giuseppe reached the top of the ladder and squeezed through the hatch. Frederick wiped sweat from his brow and waited, the sound of heavy boots and whispered voices reaching him in his hiding space. More than one of them still prowled the museum floor. A moment later, the huge man poked his head through the trapdoor and shook it.

They had escaped.

"Then get back down here!" someone shouted nearby. A man's voice, sharp and nasal. "There were three of them. And the one that's left has the head."

Frederick slunk back farther into the nook.

"You hear me, whoever you are?" the sharp voice said. "I know you're in here. And I've got two brutes who'll tear you apart without flinching if I order them to."

The huge man climbed down the ladder halfway and then simply slid the rest of the distance to the floor, landing with a boom that shook the air.

"Stay there by the ladder, Mister Clod," the voice said. "Make sure he doesn't try to escape the way his friends did. Mister Slag, stay with me."

262

Frederick looked behind him. The crates came together at an angle, but he thought he might be able to slip between them out the back.

"So the guild thought they could steal from me, eh?" the voice said. Frederick could tell the man was moving, searching, trailed by heavy footfalls. "You took the Magnus head, so I assume the clockmakers sent you."

Frederick swallowed. The man had figured him out.

"So which one are you? Frederick or Giuseppe?"

Frederick covered his mouth.

"I listened in the darkness till I learned your names. Any sign of him, Mister Clod?"

Frederick heard a distant grunt, a deep rumble, as if the building were shifting in that corner.

"Well, keep your eyes open." The voice was closer now. "Frederick, Giuseppe, whoever you are, I am Reginald Diamond. The Archer Museum is mine to care for, as sacred to me as my own flesh, and I treat your thievery as an assault on my person. But if you give yourself up, and restore the Magnus head to me, you will leave this room intact. If not, then Mister Clod and Mister Slag will have their way with you. And they so enjoy having their way."

Frederick scooted backward as silently as he could, on his fingertips and the balls of his feet like a crab. He reached the gap in the crates, and had to turn sideways to slip through. The space behind the row of crates was only a couple of feet wide, running the length of a wall that kept Frederick from retreating any farther.

"I heard something, Mister Slag," the voice said. He seemed to be standing just on the other side of the wall of crates.

Frederick had to move. He turned to the right, away from the ladder, and crept along the wall, putting distance between himself and the voice.

"You don't even know what you have stolen," the voice said, and then broke off in a fit of coughing.

Frederick pressed on, leaving the voice behind. He reached the end of the crates, the end of the wall, and could go no farther. Around the last stack he spied a door, leading who knew where. But it was the only way out. He would have only one chance, but if his pursuers had locked the door on their way in, he had no chance.

Frederick hunkered down, ready to spring.

"Leave the Magnus head here, where it will be safe," the voice said.

Frederick leaped from behind the crates, his feet pounding. He reached the door.

"There!" shouted the voice.

Frederick heard an instant thunder, like trees falling toward him.

He grabbed the doorknob. It turned. Frederick shouldered the door open and ran.

There was a long hallway, and then another door, and then Frederick burst into the museum. It was as quiet and dark as the storeroom had been. High windows admitted failing moonlight, and the glass cases all around him caught slivers of it. Frederick took a few steps around the nearest display, unable to see what it was. He had been to the museum several times and knew the layout, and if he could identify a display he could orient himself and try to escape through the front entrance.

The door flew open behind him, and Frederick bolted, bumping into panes of glass and ropes in the darkness. He heard something shatter over his shoulder, and a curse from the nasal voice.

"You imbecile! That urn was Mayan! Irreplaceable!"

Clod and Slag were having trouble, too.

As he moved, Frederick kept one hand out in front of him, with his body turned sideways to protect the bronze head in his other arm. The museum wings all pointed at the central rotunda under the dome, and Frederick ran in the direction he guessed it to be.

Then he tripped into a roped-off display. The impact knocked his breath from him, but he ducked and kept the bronze head safe at the expense of his shoulder. He jumped to his feet, gasping, and banged his head on something metal. Above him, an empty suit of armor charged on an invisible horse, arm outstretched. Frederick knew right where he was.

"He's up there!" the voice shouted.

Frederick hopped over the rope and sprinted for the rotunda. Moments later he raced into its open space, feet clacking on the stone floor. He slowed as he approached the front doors. Bolts at the top and bottom locked them fast from the inside. Frederick hopped up and stooped down to pull them open, and then threw himself out onto the square.

The door banged shut behind him, and then open again. Frederick took the museum steps four and five at a time, landing on the cobblestones in a stumble that almost sent him sprawling. He sprinted over the square, the bronze head under his arm. A quick backward glance and he slowed down. His pursuers had stopped chasing him.

Clod and Slag hulked at the top of the museum steps, expressionless mountains, and in the valley between them Mister Diamond shook his fist. He had wild gray hair, and a face red from running.

"Believe me, you will regret this!" Mister Diamond shouted.

He motioned with his hands, and Clod and Slag turned away from the square. They lumbered back inside the museum, and after a final sneer Mister Diamond followed them, slamming the door behind him.

Frederick wiped sweat from his forehead with his sleeve. Why had they stopped? They could have overtaken him in the open square.

He felt his heartbeat slow from a gallop to a trot. He looked down at the bronze head and wondered what he was doing with it. What had possessed him? He should have left it and followed Giuseppe and Hannah up the ladder. They could have all escaped together. But instead he had reacted on impulse, without forethought, and now Mister Diamond knew his name and where to find him. He had to return the bronze head.

But not tonight. It would have to be done in a way that would avoid coming into contact with Clod and Slag, or Mister Diamond. Frederick dropped to his knee and set the bronze head on the ground. He removed his coat, and bundled the head inside it.

On his way back to Master Branch's shop he saw a little street musician playing the flute. Trying to play the flute. And it looked like the people out at that time of night were not the sort that spared a coin. The boy's cap was nearly empty. Frederick thought of Giuseppe and felt bad for this tiny busker. He wished he had money to give him, or some way to help, but could only smile and nod.

"You're out pretty late," Frederick said.

The boy stopped. "I no can go back." He looked down at his cap. "I no have money."

"Maybe it's the song you're playing."

The boy looked at his flute.

"Try this one." Frederick hummed the melody his mother used to sing to him, the melody Giuseppe had played earlier that night. "It's pretty simple, isn't it? Can you play that?"

The little boy pinched his brow and closed his eyes. He lifted the flute to his lips, and played the song with several missteps the first time through, but he corrected them and got through the tune. When he opened his eyes, he smiled.

"That a good song," he said.

"My mother used to sing it to me. And I heard it from . . . another busker who played it."

"Who play it?"

"Uh . . ." Was there harm in telling him a name? "A chap by the name of Giuseppe."

The little boy looked suddenly stricken. His shoulders fell and his eyes welled up.

"Hey," Frederick said. "Hey there, it's all right. What's wrong?"

The little boy shook his head and started to pack up his things.

"Do you know Giuseppe?" Frederick asked.

The busker nodded. "He dead."

Frederick wondered if he should say anything, but the boy looked so despondent. "No, he isn't."

The boy's eyes opened wide.

"He's alive and well." But Frederick thought better of telling the boy that Giuseppe was hiding in Master Branch's cellar. "What's your name?"

"Pietro."

"Pietro, play that song I taught you, Giuseppe's song, and I bet you get money by the fistful."

"Thank you," Pietro said. "Thank you." He turned and ran off.

Frederick walked the rest of the way to Master Branch's shop. He hoped that Hannah and Giuseppe would be there waiting for him, and they were, in the alley behind the shop. Both of them seemed relieved when they saw him, but then they became angry. Giuseppe just stood there with his arms folded, and Hannah came up and hit Frederick on his shoulder.

"What were you thinking?" she said.

"I'm sorry," Frederick said.

Then she noticed the bundle under his arm. "You didn't!"

Frederick averted his eyes. "I didn't have a choice."

"You didn't have a choice about whether you stole that creepy head from the museum? Whether you almost got us caught?"

It was *not* stolen. "I'm borrowing it. And no, I didn't really have a choice. I'll return it when I'm done studying it. Besides, you stole Madame Pomeroy's necklace."

Hannah snorted, and threw up her hands.

"Look, I'm sorry," Frederick said. "I didn't mean to get you into trouble."

"It's fine, Freddy." Giuseppe stepped toward him. "But next time we stick together. Got it?"

Frederick nodded.

Giuseppe pointed at the shop door. "I need to get inside off the street."

"Of course," Frederick said, and reached into his pocket for the key.

"I'm going home," Hannah said. "It's late."

"You don't want to come inside?" Frederick asked. "To see the head?"

She raised an eyebrow. "No, Frederick. Good night."

"Good night," Giuseppe said.

Frederick watched her stalk off down the street, feeling a little embarrassed, but the moment did not last long. He looked at Giuseppe and shrugged.

"I can't wait to get inside. Would you mind holding this?" He handed Giuseppe the bundle and unlocked the door. A few moments later they were standing in the cellar, the bronze head propped on the workbench next to the clockwork man.

"Hannah seemed mad," Giuseppe said.

"She'll be fine."

"So what are you going to do now?" Giuseppe asked.

Frederick flexed his fingers. "I'm going to figure out how it works. What it does."

"Will that take a long time?"

"Undoubtedly."

"Then I'm going to sleep." Giuseppe swiped the sheet from the clockwork man and bunched it up. He lay down on the floor with the sheet under his head for a pillow. "Wake me up when you've got it all sorted out."

Frederick ignored him. The clockwork head, the Magnus head, rested peacefully. Whether the name was accurate, and this was indeed the lost bronze head created by Albertus Magnus, was irrelevant. The clockwork inside was all that mattered. Frederick pressed on the button at the back of the head, and the forehead opened up.

Even though he had already seen it once before, the staggering workmanship drew a sigh out of Frederick. He took several minutes, and just admired it without touching, without sticking his fingers in it. The skills required to create such a clockwork were beyond any that Frederick possessed, or had read about, or heard of, even in the most grandiose boasting at the guildhall.

The Magnus head showed its age. Inside it, tiny dings and dents, speckled tarnish, and a buildup of black grime in the cracks and corners all spoke to its origins in antiquity. Frederick assessed the tools and materials he would need to disassemble and restore it, and retrieved them from the workshop upstairs. By the time he returned to the cellar, Giuseppe's chest was rising and falling in the slow rhythm of sleep.

Frederick went to work with deliberate reverence, refusing to allow his excitement to rush him. The entire skull came off in sections, which Frederick polished inside and out, restoring shine to the wire hair. The density of the exposed mass of cogs and gears brought a shiver of fear and awe. Frederick studied every piece before he removed and cleaned it, until he was sure he could replace it when he went to reconstruct the head. A sheaf of loose pages bore his scribbled notes and a few sketches in case he forgot some of the more intricate connections.

After some hours he was able to deduce how small regions of the bronze head worked, but regions only. The jaw, lips, and leather tongue, the ridged bells in the throat. The delicate filaments attached to a vellum drum in the ear. In isolation each area seemed to perform an obvious if limited function, but how all the different parts worked together eluded him.

There was a larger pattern he was missing, like a painting that was too big to see all at once. He could observe isolated figures and brush-strokes, but not the work as a whole. The farther he stepped away from it, the larger the painting grew, as though this genius assembly of clock-work combined to become something greater than a simple combination of the parts would suggest. An alchemy of arithmetic where two plus two equaled ten.

But then Frederick noticed something. A portion of the head appeared damaged. He could not say exactly how he knew that. After hours of dissection this clockwork's small movement simply felt wrong, and more than that, Frederick had a sense of how it should be. Guided by instinct, he set about restoring the gears and levers, rasping off a little burr here, and bending a cog there, shifting a few gears slightly, until it seemed that the movement fit with the surrounding mechanisms.

After that, it was with a feeling of satisfaction that Frederick began to piece the Magnus head back together, a process that took much less time than it had to take it apart.

"Have you figured out how it works?"

Frederick turned and saw that Giuseppe had awoken. The busker knelt on the floor with his hands on his knees, sheet wrinkles imprinted on one side of his face.

"No," Frederick said into the gears.

"What time is it?"

"I have no idea."

"I'll go check." Giuseppe climbed the stairs, and a moment later came back down. "The sun's not up yet, but there's light out there."

Frederick replaced the skull plates, locking them together like puzzle pieces.

Giuseppe came and watched over Frederick's shoulder. "What if you stuck that head on the body you made?"

Frederick looked up at the ceiling. "I can't do that."

"Why not?"

"Because this head was not designed for that body. And it needs to be my original work for the guild examination." But Giuseppe's question raised a possibility in Frederick's mind he had not considered. He had assumed the head was a self-contained automaton. The legend Master Branch had told him mentioned only a head, and that was how he had tried to understand its design. But what if there had once been a body?

There was a flash in his mind, and pieces began to make sense to him. A tiny gyroscope near the middle of the head, which had perplexed

Frederick, might have been a balancing mechanism for an upright clock-work man. And the action and movements that appeared without purpose might have instead been incomplete. Perhaps that was why Frederick could not see how the Magnus head worked. He only had a portion of the painting.

"Frederick," Giuseppe said. "I'm kind of hungry."

"In a moment." What could the rest of the body have been like? He picked up the last plate.

"Do you have some food to spare?"

"I'm sure we do." Frederick locked the plate in place. He felt a subtle stirring under his fingertips.

"Maybe some bread?"

"Shh." Frederick cocked his head. "Do you hear that?"

"What?"

Frederick leaned his ear in close to the Magnus head. "That whirring."

"Let me see." Giuseppe brought his head in close.

In that moment, there was a sound like two coins being rubbed together, and the Magnus head opened its eyes. Giuseppe jumped back, and Frederick stood up straight. Then the bronze jaw slid open, then it closed, then it opened again, accompanied by a wheezing of air.

"Freddy?"

"I don't know," Frederick whispered.

A sound emerged from the Magnus head, a metallic thrumming, like a low bell struck continuously. Then the mouth moved, shaping the sound. *"Cuuuurrrr . . . ?"* The sound stopped.

"Did it just —?" For the first time since Frederick had known him, Giuseppe looked frightened.

"Yes. It spoke."

The sound came again, resonant and stronger. *"Cuurr?"*

"What is it saying?" Giuseppe said.

"I don't know."

Frederick bent down and looked into the clockwork eyes, two spinning discs with slits all the way around, flickering like a magic lantern show. Were they seeing him? How could something be so terrifying and so exhilarating at the same time?

"Cur?" the Magnus head asked.

"I think it's broken," Giuseppe said, frustration and fear in his voice.

Frederick reached around the head, afraid to touch it, repulsed by the living vibration, and pressed the button. As the forehead panel fell open, the motions ground to a halt, the mouth closed, the eyes dimmed, and the turning of clockwork ceased.

"I need to think," Frederick said, staring at it.

Giuseppe inched closer. "About?"

"What to say to it."

"I think maybe it's broken," Giuseppe said.

Frederick rolled his eyes. "It's not broken."

"How do you know?" Giuseppe asked.

"The same way I knew how to fix it."

"Well, I'm not so sure." Giuseppe came around to the head and stooped down. He stared into the clockwork so close his eyes crossed. "It doesn't sound like it's working right."

That was true. "Let's consider all the possibilities." Frederick held up his finger. "One. It's broken."

Giuseppe nodded as if he had already made up his mind about that one.

Frederick held up a second finger. "Two. It is not broken, and is saying a word we don't know."

Giuseppe shrugged.

"Wait a minute." Frederick dropped his hand to his side. An idea seemed ready to light on his head, and he froze where he stood, afraid he would scare it away if he moved. "Why would it be an English word?"

"What do you mean?"

"Master Branch said Albertus Magnus was German."

"So you think that's a German word?"

"Maybe. Unless . . ."

Giuseppe frowned. "Unless what?"

"Master Branch also said that Albertus Magnus was a magician *and* a friar."

"So?" Giuseppe said.

Frederick grinned. "I think it's Latin."

"What's Latin?" Giuseppe asked.

Frederick looked up at the ceiling. "Of course."

"What's Latin?" Giuseppe asked again.

Frederick explained, "It's an ancient language. All the priests and monks in the Old Country spoke and wrote in Latin because they thought it was holy. A friar wouldn't have made the head talk in German, or English, or any common tongue."

"So, who knows Latin?" Giuseppe asked.

"Master Branch does," Frederick said.

"But I'm guessing," Giuseppe said, "that you won't be asking him to translate for a metal head you stole — sorry, *borrowed* from the Archer Museum."

"He has books, dictionaries." Frederick slapped the table. "Wait here."

He raced out of the cellar, but slowed when he reached the stairs to Master Branch's apartment. The rest of the way up, the floorboards seemed to crack and squeal as if they were trying to get him caught. At the top of the staircase he paused and listened to the faint snoring coming from the old man's bedroom before searching the books. He had an idea of where the Latin books were, having seen them on his way to finding *The Clockmaker's Grimoire*. He grabbed one and returned to the cellar.

"I've got it." Frederick held the book at a distance as if it were hot. He set it on the table and started thumbing through the pages. "*Cur.* We'll start with the *c*'s before the *k*'s," he said, passing over the *a*'s and *b*'s. "*Cur.*" He landed on the page, and traced the columns of words with his finger.

"You find it?" Giuseppe asked.

"Here it is." He leaned in to read and then leaned back out. "Why?"

"Why what?" Giuseppe asked.

"No, that's what it means. *Why.*"

"It asked why?"

Frederick leaned in again. "Yes. *Why.*"

"Why what?" Giuseppe asked.

"I have no idea," Frederick said, but that was a good question. He scanned back up the same page and nodded. "I'm going to try something."

He reached over and pushed the bronze forehead closed with two fingers, leaving two moist dots that faded away almost instantly. The same gentle whir emanated from the head, and then the eyes opened back up.

Its mouth moved and intoned the question, "*Cur?*"

"*Quid cur,*" Frederick said.

A moment passed in which the bronze head seemed to be grinding away on the words. "*Cur?*" it said.

"Hmm. That didn't work," Frederick said.

"What did you say?" Giuseppe asked.

Frederick looked down at the book. "Why what."

Giuseppe tugged on his sleeve. "How about this? Because."

Frederick looked at him for a moment. "Let me see," he said, turning pages.

"*Cur?*" the clockwork head said.

"*Quia,*" Frederick said.

"*Cur?*" it said.

Frederick slammed the book shut. "I don't know what it's asking." But it was obvious to him the Magnus head expected an answer.

CHAPTER 21

The Hidden Suite

TOO ANXIOUS TO GO BACK TO SLEEP, HANNAH LAY AWAKE IN the predawn having only dozed for a few hours. Her father's mighty snores across the room rattled the floorboards and brought a smile to her face. Hannah owed Alice a great deal. But even though her father's health had improved, her family's situation had not. Without Hannah's job, there would be no money for rent, and no apartment. No poorhouse would take them once they learned of her father's condition.

She had to find the treasure.

The night in the museum felt like it had been a dream. A dark tale of golden heads and ogres, in a cavern lined with moonlight. But her anger at Frederick felt very real. What if they had been caught? What if he had been caught?

By now Hannah had figured out how single-minded Frederick could be, and determined, and she admired that about him. But not when it caused recklessness. She felt a little guilty for storming off the night before, but she had been so scared for him. When Giuseppe had pulled her away from the rooftop, she felt like they had abandoned him. But then Giuseppe had told her that Frederick had grabbed the head and run off deliberately.

That thought made her want to punch her pillow. Well, at least he was safe.

Her sisters curled up next to her in the bed, and Hannah kissed each of them. She slipped from under the blankets as smoothly as she could, and dressed for the day. In her pocket she felt for the chunk of clay she had accidentally taken from the museum the night before.

She felt guilty for stealing it, but she had not meant to. Those men had come in so fast, and she was so scared. She had put the piece of clay in her pocket without thinking as she ran from them. The words on the tag identified it as a fragment from the forehead of a golem in Prague, reminding her of the way Madame Pomeroy referred to Yakov. The way Hannah thought of him, too. Their protector.

She would return the fragment to the museum if she could think of a way to do it without getting into further trouble. But that did not seem likely, and it was only a silly little piece of clay, after all. Frederick had stolen a whole head, and he had no doubt been up all night with it.

Well, now it was her turn. Today they would search for the treasure, and she drew comfort from the certainty that Mister Grumholdt and Miss Wool had not found the next clue. That was in her pocket, a gift from her father that he would share with no one else.

She left the apartment and descended to the road. The gaslights were still lit along the streets, but tired and weak-looking after their night vigil. Hannah reached Frederick's shop without seeing another soul about and stood at his door, afraid to knock and wake Master Branch. She finally settled on a gentle rap, and a long wait, before Frederick came to the door.

He flashed an openmouthed grin. "Hello. Would you like to come in?"

She looked to the right and left as though deciding whether she preferred to remain in the street. "I suppose."

Frederick opened the door wider. "You're still mad."

"Of course I'm still mad," she whispered as she stepped into the shop. "Think about what could have happened."

"I have thought about it. I'm sorry. I won't do that again."

"Won't do what again?"

"Steal."

"That's not what I'm really mad about, Frederick."

"I was reckless, too. I'll be more careful."

"I hope so."

"There's still that treasure to find."

Hannah nodded. "Yes, there is."

"Hannah, you came back," Giuseppe whispered. He was poking his head out from the back room. "Did you tell her, Freddy?"

Hannah turned to Frederick. "Tell me what?"

"I got the clockwork head to talk."

"It talked?"

Frederick rocked back on his heels. "Yes, it did."

"What did it say?"

"*Cur,*" Frederick said.

"What does that mean?"

"That's what I wanted to know," Giuseppe said.

"Do you want to see it?" Frederick asked.

She was still angry with him, but she was also very curious. "Fine," she said, and followed the two boys downstairs.

The tarnished metal had been polished to a golden gleam, the face just realistic enough to cause disquiet. A cold energy seemed to radiate from it, and Hannah stood away from the table a few feet, her hands in front of her. When she noticed the eyes, spinning like platters, she stepped off to the side where they could not look at her.

"*Cur?*" it said with a voice like two of the hotel's silver pitchers clanged together.

"How did you make it speak?" she asked.

"All I did was clean it and restore a section of gears. When I closed it all back up it just started talking."

"*Cur?*" it said.

"I still haven't figured out how to answer it," Frederick said.

"What does that word mean?"

"Why."

"Why?"

"It's Latin," Giuseppe said. "We think."

Frederick pointed at the ceiling. "I'm going up to get another book. Maybe it will give me some more ideas."

He plodded up the stairs, and after he was gone Hannah turned to Giuseppe. "Do you think he's going to want to leave to come help me search for the treasure?"

"Not likely. Until I said something this morning I think he'd forgotten I was even here."

Hannah sighed. Single-minded and determined.

"*Cur?*" the head asked.

"Will you come with me?"

"Of course," Giuseppe said. "I said I'd help you, and I will. But I can't go out again until later tonight."

Hannah nodded in disappointment. But maybe it was for the better. It would have been difficult to take the two boys into the hotel with her;

they did not know their way around, and would only have drawn attention to Hannah. She needed to get in without Miss Wool or Mister Grumholdt knowing she was there.

"This one has phrases in it." Frederick came back down holding up a book. He set it on the table and opened it.

"Frederick?" Hannah said.

"There must be something in here," he said. "What's it really asking?"

"Cur?" it said.

Hannah could think of several questions, questions she would want the answer to if she were a bronze head. Why was it here in the cellar of a clockmaker's apprentice? Why had Magnus, or whoever he was, made it without a body? Why had he made it at all?

Hannah thought about her sisters. They were always asking why. Why did the coal man forget to come so often? Why did Hannah have to go to work instead of playing with them at home? Why did their mother always have red eyes?

Hannah had different why questions of her own, but already knew there were no answers for them. Why had her father had a stroke? Why him and not someone else? But then, that someone else would have asked the very same thing. The more she thought about it, what other question could the bronze head have asked? Everyone had why questions, but no one had all the answers.

"Cur?" it said.

"Frederick," Hannah said. "Translate this: I don't know."

"I don't know?"

Hannah nodded.

Apparent doubt raised one of his eyebrows. "That's not an answer. I think it wants an answer."

"Just try it, please."

Frederick scratched his head. He flipped back and forth several times in one of his books.

"Cur?" it said.

Frederick took a deep breath. *"Ego non scio."*

As soon as he said it Hannah heard a very subtle click inside the bronze head. *"Nescio quoque,"* it said.

Hannah turned to Frederick. He was already digging through the book.

A moment later, he translated: "I don't know, either."

After the exchange, the bronze head closed its mouth, but its eyes remained open and the clockwork continued to churn inside it.

"Ask it something," Hannah whispered.

Frederick took a few moments to search through the books. "I'm going to ask who created it." He turned to the head. *"Qui te fecit?"*

"Albertus Magnus," said the clockwork head.

Hannah smiled.

Frederick set the book down. "The words were a key. You unlocked it."

"But you didn't answer the question," Giuseppe said.

"That's true," Hannah said. "And I'm leaving now."

Frederick looked up, confused. "Where are you going?"

"To find the treasure," she said. "Remember?"

"Oh. Well, of course I remember. It's just ——" He looked at the bronze head.

"Stay here, Frederick." Hannah turned toward the stairs. "I wouldn't have been able to sneak you two into the hotel, anyway. But I'll come back later, and you can tell me all about your clockwork conversations."

◎ ◎ ◎

"She's leaving the hotel in a few days, so I assumed even you could handle her."

That was Miss Wool. Hannah backed away from the door without looking behind her. She bumped into a table, tipping over a vase with a hollow thunk. It nearly rolled to the floor before she stopped it.

"Did you hear that?" Miss Wool asked.

"Hear what?"

"A noise. In Mister Twine's suite."

"One of the staff?"

"Not this early. I unlocked it for the electricians, but they're not supposed to be here for another hour."

"Electricians?"

"Mister Twine is bringing Edison's electricity into the hotel. He's starting with his own suite."

"Electricity?"

"Are you an idiot? Just get back to work. I will see to it."

The doorknob rattled.

Hannah's heart lurched. Hallways on either side led into adjacent rooms. She bolted to the right and found herself in a library with wide windows and a broad wooden desk. Behind her, the front door opened. Hannah dove behind the desk and scrambled under it.

"Is anyone here?" Miss Wool called out.

Hannah held her breath and listened. Miss Wool seemed to be doing the same. Then Hannah heard the light sweep of the woman's feet over the rugs. She was probably looking at the vase right then, wondering who had tipped it over. Hannah heard her set it upright.

Then Miss Wool began to move through the other rooms. Hannah heard doors opening and closing in an endless hunt that finally brought the woman into the library with her. Hannah closed her eyes tight, waiting and hoping with clenched teeth.

Several moments passed, slow and tortured, like sliding down a rasp. Then Hannah heard Miss Wool leave through the front door. It took another moment or two before she dared poke her head out. The library was empty. The suite seemed empty.

She let out a long, even breath.

So Mister Twine was not here, after all. Hannah would have to call on him at his mansion, if he would see her. It had been terrifying the first time she met him, back when she asked him for a job at the hotel.

Hannah took a last look around the library, and then went back out into the foyer. There was the vase, and the table. The sharp light of morning fell in parallel strips against the floor and walls from two tall, narrow windows. The floors were marble beneath the Oriental rugs, and the stone continued up one of the walls, forming an arched alcove. Hannah looked closer, and noticed a tiny holly leaf carved at the back.

That made sixty-three. She pulled out the scrap of paper on which her father had drawn. *Drawn.* With his own hands. Were it not for the charcoal lines in front of her, Hannah would never have believed it, would have doubted her own memory as a dream. But even with the holly leaf in her hand, Hannah still felt gratitude that in all his renovations Mister Twine had never changed her father's work. Mister Twine even had her father's work right here in his own suite.

She stepped into the alcove and reached out to her father's carving. At her touch, the stone inside the holly leaf gave a little, like a button. She pressed harder. The stone clicked.

A grating sound surrounded her, like a boulder clearing its throat, and the back of the alcove slid away. Hannah stared into a dark passage, cool air pouring over her. The rumors were true. Mister Twine had secret passages for moving around the hotel. And then the puzzle pieces fell into place.

Hannah's mother had said that Mister Twine was always asking Hannah's father for special projects. Projects Mister Twine never changed afterward, despite his willingness to rip out even the most beautiful craftsmanship. What if her father had drawn the holly leaf not simply as a gift to Hannah, but a message? A clue.

The passage entrance yawned like a cave, the cave of the forty thieves. There was a lamp just inside on the ground, and Hannah went to look for matches. Once lit, the kerosene flame revealed the corridor not as an earthen cave, but a clean and narrow hallway. Hannah looked over her shoulder, then entered, and a few feet inside spotted another holly leaf. She pressed it, and the door in the alcove closed, sealing her in.

Echoes of her footsteps seemed to swarm around her, racing ahead and doubling back. At times it even seemed there were footsteps behind her. The corridor ran straight for several yards, and then it branched. Hannah thought about where she was in relation to the hallways and rooms she knew, and turned to the right, wanting to explore.

Periodically, voices penetrated the passage, and Hannah could stop and listen to guests conversing over their morning coffee, or maids cleaning a recently vacated room. It was no mystery now how Mister Twine seemed to know everything that happened in his hotel.

After a short time spent wandering, she came upon a staircase. Hannah climbed up to the third story and found another staircase leading to the fourth. She grew excited. Perhaps these passages offered a way into Mister Stroop's suite. She raced up to the topmost floor, and paused a moment to catch her breath. Up here the corridors felt hot and stifling. Hannah gathered her bearings. She was standing on the border between the two suites. Stroop on one side, Madame Pomeroy on the other.

She took a step toward Madame Pomeroy's side and listened. In the silence, she heard her former mistress's familiar voice on the other side of the wall. The sound brought an ache to Hannah's chest.

"Yes, Yakov," Madame Pomeroy said. "Pack that, but leave that one. I wish to unburden myself of some of these belongings. To travel more lightly than I have in the past."

"And Hannah's dress?" Yakov asked.

It pained Hannah to think back on the night at the opera now. Madame Pomeroy's words to Miss Wool had tainted the memory with bitterness, and the loss grieved her.

"I don't know what to do with that," Madame Pomeroy said. "For now, we leave it."

"As you wish, Madame," Yakov said. "I will miss her. Very much."

Hannah shook her head and fled back along the passage. There was no way to make amends for what she had done. In helping Miss Wool and Mister Grumholdt, Madame Pomeroy had betrayed Hannah, but she had done so without knowing it. Hannah had betrayed Madame Pomeroy's trust knowingly and intentionally, but for her father she would do it all over again. She could not make amends, because she could not bring herself to apologize.

Hannah wiped her eyes and tried to wipe Madame Pomeroy from her mind. She crossed the border into where she thought Stroop's suite had been, and started looking for holly leaves.

Several moments later she found one, and after a moment's pause, she pressed it.

A doorway opened on a forgotten room. Hannah blew out the lamp and felt a chill as she stepped over the threshold into Mister Stroop's suite. The room she entered was a library, much like Madame Pomeroy's. A growth of dust coated every surface, and cobwebs stretched over the bookshelves and fluttered in the corners. Sunlight had faded the curtains next to a telescope. Hannah crossed to it, and looked out the window.

There was McCauley Park, as she had imagined it to be. The place where Alice lived, and where cougars sunned themselves in clearings. Where Pullman wandered, and where wondrous plants grew, herbs and molds that had been made into medicine that saved her father's leg. In that moment Hannah thought she knew the wonder and joy Stroop felt when he looked out his window.

She bent her eye to the telescope, and the lens brought Grover's Pond up close. And at the upper edge of the water, Hannah saw her father's memorial stone. She heard a noise behind her.

"How a fool like you found this, I'll never know."

Hannah spun around.

Miss Wool stood in the doorway. Her eyes swept the room. "Hans and I have been searching for months, and here a stupid maid comes along and manages to lead me to it."

Hannah was trapped. Miss Wool blocked the only exit.

"Yes, I followed you. I almost confronted you back in Twine's office, but I wanted to see what you would do." The woman folded her arms. "So, here we are. I assume you're looking for the treasure."

Hannah swallowed and nodded.

"How?"

"From you," Hannah whispered.

"Speak up!"

"I heard about it from you."

"A thief and a spy." Miss Wool stepped into the room. Could Hannah run past her?

"You can leave, if you like," Miss Wool said. "But the police will be at your door before the day is out. It's prison for you, on my word."

Hannah felt the blood drain from her face. "For what?"

"Theft. Burglary. You're not an employee anymore, and look where I found you. Oh, what will your family do when you're gone?"

Hannah curled her fingers into claws. She wanted to leap on Miss Wool and tear her to pieces, like a cougar in the city.

"Unless," Miss Wool said, and sneered.

Hannah kept her voice even. "Unless what?"

"You help me find the treasure, and say nothing to anyone about it."

"What about Mister Grumholdt?"

Miss Wool laughed. "What about that imbecile?"

"I thought you were working together."

"So did he. But after he ruined our chance to get rid of Madame Pomeroy, I decided to cut him out."

"What chance?"

"When she was threatening to leave if we sacked you. Oh, my. Did you think that was really about you? I wanted her out so we could do a proper search of this floor. But the fool Grumholdt kept you on and kept her happy. Since then I haven't been able to do anything up here without that Russian watching my every move. Especially after that so-called séance. But you found another way."

Miss Wool lifted her chin and continued. "So that is my offer. Help me, and I shall reward you by not calling the police. Say a word to anyone, and your family will visit you in prison. Except your father, of course."

Each of Miss Wool's words flew like a piece of coal into the stove burning up Hannah's insides. Her rage blazed white-hot under a mountain of fuel. She had been building it up all this time, ever since her father's stroke, and now it was primed to explode. Her fury felt like fire in her mouth, in her nostrils. She was not a cougar. She was a dragon.

But in the stories, dragons could be clever and treacherous.

"I'll help you," Hannah said.

"I knew you were capable of some thought. Come then, search these rooms. You can dirty yourself with all this dust. Look sharp, the treasure could be small, a box of precious gems. You know about those, don't you?"

It took every shred of restraint Hannah possessed to curtsy, but she managed a dip and did what she was told. She pulled the books down from their shelves. She dumped the dresser drawers, felt under the furniture, looked behind picture frames, and tossed the bedsheets. Nothing.

Miss Wool marched her from one room to the next, until they ended up in the drawing room and found it had been emptied. The wallpaper peeled up at the corners, and the slackened carpet puckered in the middle of the floor. There was nothing in there to search except a fireplace with a pile of half-burned papers in it. Hannah riffled through them, and found a few pages that still bore legible writing.

"What does it say?" Miss Wool asked.

"Would you like to read it?"

"Make that schooling of yours worth something and tell me what it says!"

"Can you not read, ma'am?"

"Of course I can read." Miss Wool sniffed. "But lately my eyes have been failing."

Hannah coughed in the ash and dust she had stirred up. "A lot of it is all black, burned up. It says 'last will and testament' at the top."

"It does?" Miss Wool's eyes bulged. "Read it, you stupid girl."

"It says, all monies to be deposited in . . . a bank, I can't read the name. And here it says, total value to the sum of one hundred twenty-three dollars."

Miss Wool blinked. "Repeat that amount."

"One hundred twenty-three dollars."

"That's it? That's his treasure?"

Hannah looked the paper over again. "I think that's what it means."

"That's what I've been searching for all these months? A measly one hundred twenty-three dollars! And it's in a bank?"

"Yes, ma'am."

Miss Wool's face turned so red she looked hot to the touch. "Get out."

"What, ma'am?"

"Get out!"

"Yes, ma'am." Hannah shoved the paper back into the fireplace, in among the other fragments. She got up to leave, curtsied, and went to the door. "Can I be of any more help, ma'am?"

Miss Wool whipped her eyes toward Hannah like a rattlesnake. "You may not think I will keep my end of our bargain, but I will. But don't you ever come back to this hotel."

"No, ma'am."

Hannah returned to the secret doorway, lit her lantern, and descended the stairs. She trembled through the corridors with the anger and fear she had kept bound up inside, and prayed that Miss Wool would not take the pages to anyone else to read. After some time Hannah exited the secret network of passages into Mister Twine's suite, and hastened out into the hall, down the grand staircase into the lobby. On her way through the front doors she heard Walter's voice calling her name. She ignored him and barreled down to the square.

Hannah had lied to Miss Wool and made up the message, although the first part was true. At the top it did read "last will and testament of Phineas Stroop," and his signature curled across the bottom of the page. All the writing in between was unreadable. But below Stroop's signature was the name of the document's witness.

Signed by Mister Twine.

It was midday by the time she reached Master Branch's shop, but upon entering found it empty. She called out. No noises from upstairs, but a moment later Frederick burst from the back room.

"Hannah," he said. "Master Branch has been gone all day, and I've been working. Come see!" And he disappeared.

Hannah sighed and followed after him.

In the cellar, Giuseppe stood against a wall with a look on his face that said he was ready to throttle Frederick.

"You would not believe the day we've had," Frederick said, circling his worktable.

"You really wouldn't," Giuseppe said.

"Well, I've had quite a day, too."

"Look at this," Frederick said. He pointed at the clockwork head, which was now attached to the body Frederick had made. The forehead panel was open, exposing its snarl of gears.

"How did you do that?" Hannah asked.

"It told me how." Frederick gestured over a pile of books on the floor. "It took time to translate, but the Magnus head knows a lot about itself. Do you know that it originally had a body? It was made of metal, wax, leather, and glass. All I had to do was figure out how to connect my body to the head. At first I didn't think it would be possible."

"But it helped you?" Hannah asked.

"Yes." Frederick's hair looked unkempt, and his eyes were red.

"I think you need some sleep."

"I will, soon. There's still a problem."

"Frederick, where is Master Branch?"

"Guild business. They summoned him early this morning. I've got it all attached correctly, but the head still can't animate the body."

"Why?" Hannah said.

"That's the one thing I can't ask it. If you ask it when, or what, or how, it can answer. But it can't answer why questions."

Hannah smiled. "Why?"

Frederick cast her an impatient frown.

"I've been telling Freddy that it needs a spell," Giuseppe said. "Magnus was a magician, after all."

"He was a scientist," Frederick said. "For the last time, you don't make automatons with spells."

But you could. Golems were automatons of a sort, and Madame Pomeroy said they were made with spells. Hannah felt for the lump of clay in her pocket, with its strange inscription. It felt warm in her hand, full of portent and potential.

"How did your morning go, Hannah?" Giuseppe asked.

"I didn't find the treasure," she said. It felt too exhausting right now to talk about the secret passages and Miss Wool. "But I found another clue. This evening I'm going up to the Heights to Mister Twine's mansion. But I want you both to come with me this time."

"We will," Giuseppe said. When Frederick said nothing, Giuseppe hit him on the arm.

"Huh? Oh, yes. Of course we will." Frederick scratched his head. "I'm hungry. I think I forgot to eat breakfast. Would either of you like some lunch?"

"I would," Giuseppe said.

"Me too," Hannah said.

"Wait here." Frederick went upstairs.

"He keeps leaving us down here," Giuseppe said.

Hannah looked at the clockwork man, the tin barrel chest and the heavy arms and legs. It all fit together so nicely, except for the bronze head, which seemed foreign and of an altogether different quality. It came from another place and distant time, fashioned by means Hannah could not even guess at. Spells might have been involved for all she knew. Like the spells that may have once brought the piece of clay in her pocket to life. She pulled it out, an idea forming.

"I saw you holding that in the museum," Giuseppe said. "You took it?"

"Shh." Hannah opened the panel door on the chest plate and stared at the gears, avoiding Giuseppe's eyes out of shame. "It was an accident."

"What are you looking for?"

What *was* she looking for? What did she know about clockwork? Nothing. But she knew about people. It was the heart that made people live, and hurt, and love. And this clockwork man did not have one.

She thought of Yakov, her golem, and how he had said he would miss her. She would miss him, too. She kissed the piece of clay, leaving a wet spot, and wedged it inside the chest, away from anything that looked like it might turn or spin or move.

"What are you doing?" Giuseppe asked.

"I'm giving his clockwork man a heart," she said. "Don't tell Frederick."

"I won't," Giuseppe said with a sly smile.

Hannah closed up the door and stepped away from the worktable.

Frederick returned minutes later with a platter of bread and cheese, some fruit preserves, and butter. The three of them finished off every last crumb, and Giuseppe looked like he could still have eaten more.

"Could I talk to the head, Frederick?" Hannah asked.

He got to his feet and brushed his hands off. "Of course."

Hannah rose and followed him to the table. Frederick pressed the forehead panel closed, and the clockwork started turning. The eyes opened, and then the mouth, but instead of saying *"Cur,"* the head made a kind of groaning noise.

Frederick looked alarmed. "What's going on?"

One of the arms lifted, and Hannah jumped back. It shot straight up, pointing at the ceiling. Then it dropped with a thud on the wooden table, and then both arms moved.

Giuseppe backed up against the wall. "I think you two should watch out."

Hannah nodded, but had to pull Frederick away. The look on his face had become one of sheer excitement.

In the next moment the clockwork man sat up. It turned its head from side to side, and gradually the groaning subsided, turning into something that sounded more like a laugh. Then, without warning, it leaped from the table and vaulted up the cellar stairs in two leaps. A second or two of shock passed before the three of them ran after it.

"No!" Frederick shouted. "Come back!"

They tumbled over each other into the shop's front room and found the door still swinging open. Frederick hurried out into the street.

"Oh, no," Hannah said, hanging back. "No, no, no."

Giuseppe came up beside her. "Don't worry. I won't tell. But you know this means we have to help him get it back."

"But you can't go outside right now."

He pulled up his coat collar. "Right now, I'm more worried about what that thing might do."

Hannah nodded. She had not expected this, had not really expected anything to come of it when she put that piece of golem inside the chest, but it was still her fault. Together, she and Giuseppe left the shop and followed Frederick.

CHAPTER 22

Captured

WHEN GIUSEPPE AND HANNAH STEPPED OUT INTO THE STREET, they found Frederick already trudging back. Then Giuseppe saw Master Branch walking behind him, accompanied by the man from the museum with the dusty hair. Giuseppe scanned for the two thugs, but did not see them. He thought about running right then, but could not leave Frederick alone.

"These two were with him," the man with the dusty hair said when they all met in the street. "This girl and this boy. They are all of them thieves."

Master Branch held up his hand. "There is still no proof of that, Mister Diamond."

"There will be once we search your shop, Clockmaker."

Master Branch sighed. He took in Giuseppe, Frederick, and Hannah with weary, worried eyes. "Inside, please. All of you."

Frederick's head swung low, and Hannah was shaking hers. They reentered the shop and assembled in a circle around Master Branch.

"Children," he said, "Mister Diamond came to the guildhall this morning with an accusation of theft. This is a serious business, and we took most of the morning deliberating what to do with it. He named

Frederick as the thief, and said that there were another boy and a girl with him."

Hannah stiffened next to Giuseppe.

Master Branch continued. "Now, I have tried to reassure Mister Diamond that there must be some mistake. Surely no apprentice would endanger the guild's reputation with an act of burglary. But neither can we be seen to condone or ignore criminal acts. As a courtesy, I offered to let Mister Diamond search my shop. I know that his search will be fruitless." With that, Master Branch looked straight at his apprentice.

Frederick would not lift his eyes.

"I think the three of them should remain here with you, Master Clockmaker, while I conduct my search."

"They will remain here, but I will accompany you. You do not have to worry about them fleeing the premises."

Mister Diamond held his hands together, in front of his chest, agitated fingers wriggling like spider legs. "Very well."

Master Branch gestured toward the stairs. "Shall we start with my quarters?" The two of them left, and Giuseppe listened to them moving about overhead. No one said anything, and Frederick did not meet Giuseppe's or Hannah's eyes, either.

Some time later, they came back downstairs, and made a search of the shop. Mister Diamond appeared to be growing increasingly frustrated, and began to curse each time he opened a cupboard or a drawer and found it empty. They moved into the back workroom.

"Where does that door go?" they heard him ask.

"The cellar," Master Branch said. "But we never go down there. The stairs are too difficult for me."

"Then don't you mean *you* never go down there?" Mister Diamond said. They heard the cellar door open, and then footsteps descending. Giuseppe found his heart was pounding even though he knew there was nothing down there.

Mister Diamond seemed to take longer than needed and, when he returned, announced, "Well, someone's been working in your cellar, Master Branch."

"I have used it in the past," Master Branch said.

They came out into the front room, and Master Branch cast a suspicious glance at Frederick as he showed Mister Diamond to the door. "I trust we can put this matter behind us?"

"Hardly." Mister Diamond snorted. "This matter is anything but settled."

"The guild has cooperated with you," Master Branch said. "And even after this search you have produced no evidence. Perhaps if you could put forward any witnesses to corroborate your account —?"

"I already told you, there were no other witnesses."

A shared look flashed between Giuseppe, Frederick, and Hannah. Why would he lie about the other two men who were there?

"Then I believe we are done," Master Branch said. "Whether you choose to let the matter rest or not."

Mister Diamond screwed up his mouth in a frown. "We shall see," he said, and stormed from the shop, slamming the door behind him.

After he left, the four of them stood for a moment before Frederick spoke.

"Thank you for standing up for me, sir."

Master Branch did not look kindly on his apprentice. "Think nothing of it. Any theft by an apprentice would, of course, bar him for life from joining the guild, and I know you would never jeopardize that for yourself." He turned to Hannah and Giuseppe. "I trust neither of you would do anything that might imperil Frederick's standing, either, would you?"

Hannah shook her head.

"No, sir," Giuseppe said.

"Good. And now, I think I shall go upstairs. I arose so early this morning, I feel the need for a nap. Try and keep quiet, whatever you do, and lock up the shop if you leave."

"We will," Frederick said.

Master Branch left them, and a pall of silence spread out from his wake that lasted several moments before the three of them shuffled through the front door. The noises on the street broke the silence between them, and Frederick was the first one to speak.

"I'm sorry," he said.

"We already forgave you," Hannah said.

"And that doesn't change just 'cause we got caught," Giuseppe said.

Frederick relaxed and smiled. "Thanks."

"We're going to help you find it," Hannah said. "So we can return it."

"It shouldn't be hard," Giuseppe said. "I mean, it's the middle of the day, and that thing doesn't exactly blend in."

"You're right," Frederick said. "Let's ask around if anyone's seen it."

Evening came, and they had not yet found even a trace of the clockwork man. The three of them stood perplexed on the sidewalk as Basket Street shopkeepers closed up their storefronts around them. The tantalizing smell of supper meat cooking over an open flame drifted around them. All afternoon Giuseppe had managed to avoid being seen by any of the buskers, but he knew the popular corners and had avoided them. Once or twice he had had to duck into an alley, or take Frederick and Hannah down a lesser-traveled byway, but so far he felt safe.

"It's like it just disappeared," Hannah said. "How could it?"

"It couldn't," Frederick said. "But it is a clever device. Apparently it doesn't want to be found."

"Wait. You mean it's hiding?" Giuseppe had assumed all day they were looking for a metal man running amok.

"I'm beginning to think so," Frederick said. "You two can go back to the shop. Or go home, if you like, Hannah. I'll keep looking."

"No," Hannah said. "We'll help you."

"Didn't you say you wanted to go up to Twine's mansion this evening?" Frederick asked.

Hannah shook her head. "Don't worry about that."

Giuseppe ran down all the places they had been, and all the places they had not. He was all for helping Frederick, but knowing now that this clockwork contraption might be deliberately lying low somewhere, just tick-tocking away, made the job of finding it seem impossible. And he was getting tired of the looks they received when they asked people in the different neighborhoods if they had seen a metal man with a bronze head running around.

"Well," Giuseppe said. "Where would a clockwork man go to hide?"

"I'm not sure," Frederick said. "But we haven't been down to the Quay yet."

"There's plenty of warehouses and buildings down there," Hannah said.

They turned south and headed down the street toward the River Delilah. Along the way Giuseppe watched the pedestrians, and passed a few open corners, spots he could have turned into money farms if he had the green violin. His old fiddle was back at Frederick's, down in the cellar where he had left it in the commotion.

"Giuseppe, I've been meaning to ask you something." Frederick's tone was softer. "That song you were playing the other night, up in Hannah's apartment."

"What about it?"

"I've heard it before. My mother used to sing it to me, except I can't remember the words."

"I don't know the words, either," Giuseppe said. "I heard it years ago when Stephano first brought me here."

"Where did you hear it?" Frederick asked.

"A lady was humming it out a hospital window."

Frederick stopped and grabbed Giuseppe by the arm. "What?" he asked. Hannah was looking at Giuseppe, too.

Giuseppe glanced back and forth between them. "What is it?"

"Which hospital?" Frederick asked.

"I don't know. The one on Orchard Street, maybe. Why?"

Frederick looked at Hannah.

"It could be," she said.

Giuseppe spread his hands out. "What could be?"

"My mother," Frederick said. He looked back up Basket Street, and seemed ready to take a step in that direction.

"Do you want to go now?" Hannah asked.

"No." Frederick turned south again. "No, we have to find the Magnus head first."

They continued down the street, and Giuseppe wondered what that meant, but then he remembered the conversation he had overheard when Frederick had asked Hannah to go to a hospital to find out about his mother.

Halfway to the Quay, dusk firmly settled, Giuseppe turned his collar down. The crowds on the street were thinning, and the shadows were blooming, and he felt more confident. But then he saw them.

Ezio and Paolo. Up ahead, they stalked the road toward him amid a throng of pedestrians. Giuseppe stopped, Paolo looked his way, and Giuseppe ducked out of the crowd against a nearby building. Frederick and Hannah stopped and looked at him.

"Keep walking," Giuseppe said.

"What?" Hannah asked.

"You're drawing attention, keep walking!"

The two moved on with puzzled expressions and backward glances. Giuseppe tried to be as flat as he could, and scanned for escape routes. The city blocks here were tightly clustered, barely inches between buildings, so no alleys. He could make a run back up Basket Street, but they would follow him. Had Paolo seen him?

Frederick and Hannah had stopped a few yards on, looking confused but unconcerned, like a couple of chickens pecking the dirt around the chopping block.

And then Paolo and Ezio appeared over their shoulders. They grinned at Giuseppe, and he ran. Frederick and Hannah called after him, but he kept running, and over his shoulder saw Paolo and Ezio closing fast.

Then, right in front of him, a farmer backed his cart of apples up to a grocer's stall, cutting him off. He skidded and tried to circle around, but slipped on the curb. Paolo and Ezio were on him like two wild dogs on a bone.

They beat him, a hail of fists, kicks to his side and stomach. Giuseppe tasted blood, gasped for air. Their fingers dug into his skin, and they twisted his arms back to the breaking point.

"You're not getting away this time," Paolo laughed.

Ezio hissed in his ear, "You're dead, you know."

Rough cord snagged Giuseppe's wrists as they tied his hands behind his back. Then Frederick and Hannah came running up. Frederick had picked up a length of wood somewhere, and he seemed ready to fight with it, but Hannah held him back. They looked helpless. Paolo and Ezio spun Giuseppe around, and marched him up the street.

Giuseppe heard Hannah cry, "Somebody, help!"

But he knew no one would.

No one ever did.

"So where've you been, Giu?" Paolo asked. "We've been looking for you for days now. Ever since you gave Stephano the slip."

Giuseppe said nothing. He spat blood on the cobblestones, and felt one of his eyes swelling. A few pedestrians offered looks of concern as he staggered past them, but no one said anything or asked any questions. Some looked away as soon as they saw him.

"I'd say my piece if I was you," Ezio said. "You can't talk with your throat cut."

Giuseppe had nothing to say because he felt nothing. A numbness spread over him with each step toward Crosby Street, as if his will were bleeding out, leaving a trail of it in the street.

A few blocks from Stephano's lair, Paolo asked, "What do you want to do with him?"

"We'll stick him in the rat cellar till Stephano gets back," Ezio said. "That way —"

There was a thud, and Ezio lurched forward with a grunt and fell to the ground. Giuseppe turned and saw Pietro standing behind him with a crowbar.

"Hey!" Paolo shouted.

Pietro swung the crowbar, and Paolo went down, clutching his knee and howling.

"Run!" Pietro shouted. The crowbar clanged on the street, and Pietro disappeared down a nearby alley.

Giuseppe bolted in the opposite direction just as Ezio struggled to his feet.

It was hard to run, one good eye and his hands tied behind his back. He bumped into corners and stumbled often. He would not escape hampered like this, and he knew it even as he ran. He had nowhere to go, no place to hide. Ezio chased him, screaming obscenities, and Giuseppe laughed at himself for even trying, but he ran just the same, just to keep from giving up. What was Pietro thinking? He had bought Giuseppe one last race through the city, but at what cost to himself? Paolo had probably already caught him.

Giuseppe rounded a corner wide and glimpsed the Old Rock Church. Yellow light from inside warmed the windows. Giuseppe sprinted for the churchyard, and dove among the tombstones, white in the blue dusk. Ezio charged in after him. He was breathing hard, moving among the graves.

"Where are you?" Ezio shouted.

Giuseppe hunkered down.

"I used to think you were a smart one, Giu. But you're dumb as a dead dog, ain't you?"

Giuseppe moved away from the voice, snakelike through the grass.

"Do you *want* me to hurt you?"

All Ezio had to do was take a few more steps and he would see Giuseppe there on the ground. Coming here was a mistake. There was only one gate, and Giuseppe was trapped. Unless he could make it around to the church doors. Would Ezio follow him into the chapel? Stephano might have hurt Reverend Grey, but Ezio would not dare. The old man was Giuseppe's last hope.

He struggled up to one knee and dashed around the side of the building, scraping his arm on the rough stone. A moment later he turned the corner on the front of the church. The wooden doors opened like arms, and Giuseppe sprinted right between them. He raced down the aisle between the pews up to the front of the chapel where an array of candles flickered as one.

"Hello?" he shouted.

Ezio burst into the church but stopped near the door. He looked around, panting. "Think you can hide in here?"

"Reverend Grey?" Giuseppe called.

"Hello?" came a reply.

Giuseppe turned as the reverend entered the chapel from a side room.

"Giuseppe!" The old man smiled. Then he noticed Ezio. "Giuseppe, is everything all right? My goodness, your eye! And you're tied up!"

"I'm sorry, Reverend. I didn't mean to come here."

The old man rushed over to him and worked at the cords behind his back. "I'm glad you did." Then he turned to Ezio. "You'd best get out of my church, young man."

Ezio shrugged and stood his ground, guarding the door.

The bindings fell free, and Giuseppe rubbed his wrists where the rope had scraped them raw. "Thank you."

The reverend's eyes flicked to Ezio. "Which one is this?"

"The worst," Giuseppe said.

The reverend scowled. "What would you like me to do?"

What did Giuseppe want him to do? Ezio would eventually have to leave, but he would just bring Stephano back, and no church or reverend could help Giuseppe then. He had been selfish and foolish to come back here.

"I'm sorry. It felt safe, but it isn't."

"What do you mean? What isn't safe?"

"I need to go."

"Wait," Reverend Grey said. "Giuseppe, I have to speak with you about something."

Ezio stepped forward, a lazy glide up the aisle. Giuseppe looked in his eyes. Something was different about them.

"I have to go, Reverend."

"No, that's what I'm trying to tell you —"

"Come on, Giu," Ezio said. "Sorry, Reverend. I just need to speak with Giuseppe outside."

"You'll do no such thing!" the reverend shouted. He stood up tall, defiance in his watery eyes. "Get out of my church!"

"Oh, I will, old man." Ezio pulled a knife from his pocket. A long, slender blade. "Come on, Giu."

Ezio's eyes looked flat, dulled, and cruel. There was less feeling in them than in the eyes of the cougar in McCauley Park. At that moment, Giuseppe knew that he would do it. Ezio would kill Reverend Grey.

The reverend glanced at the knife in Ezio's hand. "Giuseppe, you don't have to leave," he said, but there was doubt in his voice.

"I know," Giuseppe said. "Good-bye, Reverend."

Before he could reply, Giuseppe marched down the aisle.

Ezio met him halfway. "Do I need the rope?"

"No," Giuseppe said.

"Good, because I could always come back here if you somehow get loose again."

"I know."

They left the chapel, their shadows stretched ahead of them down the front walk. When they reached the street, the reverend appeared in the doorway, a narrow silhouette.

"Be strong, Giuseppe!" he called. "Be strong another day!"

Ezio chuckled.

Giuseppe flailed as he fell through the darkness, landing hard. Something popped in his ankle and pain sparks flared in his eyes against the black. A tumble over the floor ended in a pile of putrid rags, and he coughed and sputtered before crying out in pain. Even reaching down to cradle his foot brought a steel-jawed grimace.

"Giu?"

He strained to see in the darkness. "Who's there?"

"Pietro."

"Pietro." Giuseppe winced and shook his head. "That was really stupid, Pietro. And you went and got yourself caught."

Rats squeaked and scurried around and between them.

"I sorry, Giu."

Giuseppe felt his swell of anger and frustration collapse. "No. No, I'm sorry. Come over here."

He heard movement across the floor.

"Where?" Pietro asked.

"Over here." Giuseppe held out his hand, waved it like a flag. He grazed something in the air, and then felt Pietro grab hold of his fingers. "There you are."

Pietro settled down beside him. "I no like rats."

"They're not so bad. The stories aren't true."

"I no like rats."

They sat together, shoulder to shoulder. Giuseppe's ankle throbbed. "You were brave, Pietro."

"I happy you no dead."

"No. Who told you I was?"

"Stephano tell us you dead. He say he kill you."

"He didn't kill me," Giuseppe said. He looked up, the darkness above the same as the darkness to either side. "I know he made you tell. After you saw me, Stephano made you tell."

Pietro was quiet. "The day you mad at me, I no have money. Stephano make me to tell him. He say he think you hide extra money someplace."

"I did. I had a green —" Giuseppe stopped. "Never mind. That's gone. So's the boat ticket. It's all gone."

"Ticket?"

"Yes, ticket. There's a boat leaving for Italy in a couple of days. I was going . . . home." Giuseppe stopped. "Pietro, talk to me in Italian. Tell me about your home, and then I'll tell you about mine."

Pietro paused for a moment, and then began to speak.

He had come from a fishing village on the coast, and Stephano had not bought him as he had Giuseppe. He had stolen Pietro while he played in his yard, as the boy's mother hung laundry in back. It took only that one moment and a rag to gag him.

In spite of their meaning, the words fell on Giuseppe like a warm rain. He closed his eyes and tipped his head back and just soaked them into that part of him that could still remember what it was like to be home. His whole body responded to the rhythm of the words; the sounds seemed to settle in his bones, giving strength and a voice to his memories, as if he had to hear the language of his past to remember it.

"Me dispiace, Pietro." Giuseppe sighed. *"Lascia che ti racconti della mia casa."*

The words came haltingly at first. Giuseppe told Pietro of his father, a mountain shepherd. He described the sharp, earthy smell of matted wool shorn right from the sheep, and the smooth crumble of a fresh sheep's milk cheese in his mouth. He told of his mother and the blue handkerchief she always wore over her hair, the soft strength in her hands. He told of summer nights, when the open door let in a breeze, and his father played the fiddle while the family sang along.

After that, they both wept, and Giuseppe put his arm over Pietro's shoulder.

Pietro sniffed and asked what was going to happen to them.

"Non so," Giuseppe said. He did not know.

Pietro asked if Stephano was going to hurt them.

"Sì," Giuseppe said. Yes.

Pietro asked if Stephano was going to kill them.

"Non so," Giuseppe said.

CHAPTER 23

The Solving of Problems

FREDERICK AND HANNAH RUSHED UP AND DOWN BASKET STREET, calling for help. Curious pedestrians stared at them until Frederick made eye contact, and then looked away as if they had not heard him. Frederick and Hannah tried approaching a few men, but received tight-lipped dismissals in return. Some acknowledged Frederick and listened for a moment, but ended up shaking their heads and walking away.

In their search for help the two finally ventured down onto the Quay. Frederick had not been down there since the day he had sneaked into the coal yard weeks ago, and it had been much busier then.

Now, with the last glow of the sun an orange smudge over the river and the trees at the Quay's far end, the commotion of commerce appeared to be slowing, and more men and women were leaving than were entering. Only a scattering of barges and boats floated on the river and the livestock pens were empty.

To the east, close to where the river turned foul and met the bay, a new building struggled up from its foundations, half-constructed amid the tanneries and butchers. Scaffolds and supports bolstered incomplete walls, mortar still wet between the red bricks. Masons cleaned tools and hollered at one another, while a heavy crane lifted a load of bricks up to the top.

A policeman stood watching, hands behind his back. Hannah and Frederick hurried over to him.

"Excuse me, sir," Frederick said, out of breath. "We need your help."

"Yes?" The policeman looked them over. "What is it?"

"Our friend was kidnapped!" Hannah blurted out.

"Kidnapped?"

"Yes, sir," Frederick said. "Just now."

"Tell me what happened."

Hannah began. "We were walking down the road, and these two older boys snatched our friend and beat him and tied him up."

"What manner of boys were these?"

"Buskers," Frederick said. "They're going to hurt him."

"Street musicians?" The policeman put his hands in his pockets.

"Yes, sir," Hannah said.

"And your friend, is he a busker, also?"

"He was," Frederick said. "I think they've taken him to Crosby Street."

At the mention of the name, the policeman frowned and swallowed. "Crosby Street?"

"Yes, sir," Frederick said.

The policeman adjusted his cap. "This sounds like a matter between an employer and his employees."

"What?" Frederick was aghast. "His *employer*?"

"Yes," the policeman said. "Your friend's padrone is his employer and guardian. It's a legal arrangement, and I can't interfere."

Hannah stamped her foot. "But they're going to hurt him! Don't you care?"

The policeman leaned toward them and raised his voice. "Watch your tone there, lass. Do you have good evidence that his life is in danger?"

"Yes," Hannah said.

"Tangible evidence?"

Frederick and Hannah looked at each other. "No," Frederick said. "But we know it's true."

"Well, I can't lead a cavalry charge into Crosby Street on a whim. Not without good, sound evidence. Your friend and his padrone will have to work things out between them. Good evening to you." With that he tipped his cap, executed a marching turn, and walked away.

Hannah watched him with her mouth hanging open. Frederick's shoulders sagged in defeat. Who could they turn to if the police would not even get involved? There was nothing an old man like Master Branch could do. Frederick thought about Madame Pomeroy and that Russian, but would they help? Stephano probably had Giuseppe by now, and Frederick shuddered to think what could be happening to him.

"We have to do something," Frederick said, but he did not know what.

"Frederick?"

"Yes?"

"Look!" She pointed.

Frederick followed her gaze and saw a man standing down by the river where a large pipe ran from the water up to the new brick building. He had on a cloak, with the hood pulled up. It was hard to tell in the mud, but it looked like he was wearing metal boots.

"Could it be?" Hannah asked.

The man's chest and shoulders bulged oddly, and Frederick's heart began to thump. "I think it is." He knew how strong the clockwork man was, and he knew how badly it would go if the automaton attacked him, or worse, Hannah. But he also did not want to risk it escaping again.

He took a step toward the riverbank, and Hannah grabbed his arm. "Wait. What are you going to do?"

Frederick stopped. "I'm going to try and sneak around and turn it off."

Hannah looked skeptical. "How?"

"If I can get close enough, I can hit the button at the back of its head."

"Be careful, Frederick," Hannah said, but did not let go of his arm.

"I will." He stepped away from her, hunched over, and loped down to the river. The oily water foamed against the rocks and mud along the bank. The sour smells of acid and decay bit into his nose, and his feet slipped on unrecognizable, gelatinous lumps. The clockwork man had its back to him as he crept along the water's edge.

The heavy crane hoisted another load of bricks and lumber up into the air, and the clockwork man seemed to be watching it.

Frederick slowed his steps when he was a few yards away from the automaton. He reached out his hand and inched up behind the clockwork man, breathing as shallowly and quietly as he could. He took another step, and his foot sank in the mud, up to his ankle, with a loud gurgling sound.

The clockwork man spun around. Frederick saw the bronze arm flash and then his eyes filled with bursts of white and black. Then sky and the arm of the crane. He was on his back, the clockwork man leaning over him.

"No!" he heard Hannah screaming.

The clockwork man reached for him, and Frederick held his arms up feebly like a shield. But the metal hands grasped him gently and merely lifted him back to his feet. One of his socks felt cold and wet, and Frederick looked down. He had lost his shoe, the one stuck in the mud.

"Frederick!" Hannah ran up to his side.

"I'm fine," he said, and rubbed his chest.

The clockwork man stood there, watching them both.

Frederick hopped over, one-legged, to his lost shoe and tried to pull it out. The mud sucked on it and refused to let it go. Frederick almost lost his balance, but the clockwork man came over and lifted the shoe out, easy as plucking a dandelion. It presented the shoe, and Hannah helped Frederick keep his footing while he put it back on.

"You were sneaking," the clockwork man said in its bell voice.

Frederick and Hannah stared at it.

"You speak English?" Frederick said.

"I have learned it."

"How? When?"

"I listened. It is not an efficient language. It is more concerned with individual expression than with clarity and understanding."

Frederick was still a little stunned from the blow that had knocked him on his back, and ran his fingers through his hair. "Why did you run away?"

The automaton was quiet. "I do not understand your question."

Hannah tapped Frederick's arm. "You asked it *why*."

Frederick rephrased. "Did you have a reason for running away?"

"No," the clockwork man said. Then it turned back around and looked up at the crane. "Much time has passed since my last memory."

Frederick did not know how to respond to that. "You seem very interested in that building."

"I have never seen one like it before," the automaton said.

Frederick looked again. From this riverside view he was able to see into the building where that large pipe led from the River Delilah to a series of gigantic boilers. It appeared that water would be pumped from the river and then heated in the building. Aside from the pipe and boilers, the building did not seem remarkable to him. "What makes it unique?"

"The purpose for which it is built."

"What's its purpose?"

"It will supply Edison electricity."

"What's electricity?" Hannah asked.

"Uncertain. Possibly fuel. It shares properties with oil or coal, but it is invisible and flows along wires."

"You mean pipes?" Frederick asked.

"No. Wires." The clockwork man lifted its hand up before its eyes and inspected it, flexing its fingers. "There is something different."

"Your body is all new," Frederick said. "I built it."

"No. There is something else."

Hannah spoke up. "Will you come back with us? To the shop?"

The spinning eyes rested on her, then on Frederick. "There were three of you."

Hannah looked down, and Frederick cleared his throat. "Our friend was kidnapped."

"Is he in danger?"

"Yes."

The clockwork man began to shake. All the metal plates that made up its body rattled together.

"Are you all right?" Frederick asked.

"There is something different," it said. "Do you wish to aid your friend?"

Frederick nodded. "Yes, we do."

The intensity of trembling built so that Frederick worried about the mechanisms breaking. But the shaking climaxed when the clockwork man stomped one of its feet deep into the mud. It stared at it as if confused how it got there, and then it looked up. "I will assist you."

"You'll help us rescue our friend?" Hannah asked.

"Yes," the clockwork man said.

Frederick thought about the blow that had landed him on his back, the strength he had built into the heavy arms and legs. "We'll have to wait back at the shop until dark."

Frederick bunkered in the cellar with the clockwork man, in silence. Night had fallen thick and deep around the shop. Hannah had gone home to check on her father and let her mother know she was all right. The automaton idled, standing upright, eyes appearing fixed on nothing in particular.

"What are you thinking about?" Frederick asked, awed by the machine he could ask such a question of, and also afraid of the answer.

"I am cataloging."

"What do you mean?"

"When I observe something, I will either a) use it to affirm my existing knowledge, or b) attempt to incorporate any new information within my existing categories of recollection."

Frederick had to take a moment to think about what that meant. "So, you're trying to see how things fit with what you already know?"

"Yes."

"What happens if it doesn't fit?"

"I create a new category. I have created many new categories today. It has been difficult."

"Why — I mean, what causes you difficulty?"

"I have space for only a finite number of categories. Today, I have had to discard many obsolete categories in favor of more relevant ones."

Frederick could not imagine having to choose between the things he knew, and suddenly felt sorry for the clockwork man. Or more specifically, for the Magnus head. How much time had passed since it had last been in working order? How much had changed since then? Frederick likened it to falling asleep for years and years, only to awaken and find the world a different place, everything he had known dead and gone, replaced by things he could not understand.

"I'm sorry," Frederick said.

"You are in error. You are not the cause of the difficulty."

Frederick understood that he was not directly responsible. Albertus Magnus was the creator, and the limitations of the creator had become the limitations of his creation. But how could Magnus have prepared the clockwork head for a future he could never have anticipated? Perhaps the clockwork head was never intended to exist for so long.

"I am going upstairs," Frederick said.

The automaton did not respond, and Frederick left it to its clockwork business. He went upstairs to the shop, and then up to Master Branch's apartment. The old man sat staring at a mumbling fire, a book closed in his lap, a cup of coffee untouched by his side. Frederick sat down in the chair opposite him.

"I never heard you come in," Master Branch said.

"I thought you might be sleeping."

"I'd rather you woke me to let me know you were home safe. Where have you been all day?"

"Out with Giuseppe and Hannah."

"What were you doing?"

Frederick chewed on his lower lip. "Have you heard anything new from Mister Diamond?"

"No. Should I have?"

"No."

"I suppose he might simply be watching us." Master Branch took a sip of his coffee and frowned. "Cold."

"Would you like me to heat it?"

"What I would like is for you to be honest with me." Frederick heard pain in the old man's voice, and it shamed him. "What were you doing today?"

Frederick remained silent.

"Lad, I feel certain the time is swiftly approaching when you will have no choice but to confide in me whether you are ready or not. One way or another you will learn you can trust me." Master Branch rose and left his coffee on the side table beside his chair. He crossed to his bedroom and closed the door without saying good night.

Frederick returned to the cellar and found the clockwork man in the same attitude as he had left it. He sat down on the cellar stairs, elbows on his knees, clutching his head. It was all too much for him, an unbearable weight. Giuseppe kidnapped, the stolen bronze head, Hannah's treasure. And now he had hurt Master Branch, and had probably done so all along. And beneath all of that, thoughts of his mother surged like a cold, underground river.

"My cataloging is finished," the clockwork man said. "Can I assist you?"

"No." The pressure seemed to squeeze the air from Frederick's lungs. "I can't . . ." Frederick tugged on his hair. "I can't bear it."

"Let us analyze your problem."

"There're too many."

"Let us order your problems. Which is most concerning to you?"

"Giuseppe," Frederick said.

"Then let us assist Giuseppe. After that, we will address your next problem."

The clockwork man approached him, and Frederick looked up at the bronze face. It appeared blank, placid, and strong.

Frederick heard a rap on the shop door upstairs.

"Hannah," he said, and jumped up.

The clockwork man moved to follow him.

"Wait here," Frederick said, and rushed up to the shop. Hannah was pecking on the windowpane as Frederick unbolted the front door and opened it. She stepped through, ashen and wringing her hands.

"The police were there," she said.

"Where?"

"At my apartment! Miss Wool lied to me."

"Lied about what?"

Hannah proceeded to tell him all that had happened in Mister Stroop's suite, of the will and Hannah's deception, and Miss Wool's threat.

"You think she realized you made up the will?"

"She must have. Oh, Frederick, what am I going to do? They'll arrest me!"

"No, they won't," Frederick said. "We won't let that happen."

"How?"

"As soon as we've helped Giuseppe, the three of us will go up to Mister Twine's mansion, just as we planned. He can stop Miss Wool. We'll explain everything to him, and it will all work out. You'll see."

Hannah took a deep breath. "I hope you're right."

With Hannah there to sharpen his purpose, Frederick found he was able to ease out from under the weight bearing down on him to plan their next step. They went down to the cellar where the clockwork man waited, patient as a mantelpiece.

Frederick leaned forward, his hands on the worktable. "Crosby Street is the roughest neighborhood in the city. And from Giuseppe's description, Stephano's lair is at the back end. But I don't think it's safe for us to go into Crosby Street through the main entrance. We'll have to use an alley off the Cottonway."

They cloaked the clockwork man and ventured out into the street. For the length of their journey across the city, the automaton remained silent, almost grim. Frederick wondered along the way about clockwork emotion, and whether there could be such a thing. Could mankind's most ephemeral, most varied expressions be tamed within the predictable turning of gears? The regularity and constancy of clockwork seemed fundamentally at odds with human feeling. But in spite of that, there were fleeting moments when the clockwork man appeared to be expressing something like an emotion. Perhaps imitation had been built into the design.

They made good time to the Cottonway. Crosby Street butted up against it at a perpendicular, with buildings separating the two roads. They found an alley, a narrow break in the brick expanse. The sound of metal scraping followed them down its length as the clockwork man found it more difficult than Hannah and Frederick to squeeze through. They paused when they reached the end.

"What now?" Hannah asked.

"Let's watch," Frederick said.

Garbage piles and crates cluttered the street. From farther down the road they heard men shouting and women cackling. There were buildings on either side, with no way to tell which might be Stephano's lair. But within a few moments, a couple of boys approached a three-story house on the left. One of them, a very stout boy who looked to be Giuseppe's age, carried an accordion. As they reached the front door they slowed and even hesitated before going in, like they were afraid.

"That must be it," Frederick said.

"Giuseppe's in there?"

"He must be."

The clockwork man began to rattle again and Frederick turned around. The automaton stuck out its arms and strained against the buildings to either side like it was trying to keep them apart. "There is something different," it said.

"Are you all right?" Hannah asked.

"Uncertain. Allow me to go in to find your friend."

"By yourself?" Frederick asked.

The clockwork man's quaking worsened. "Yes. You will be safer here."

"But how will you —?"

The clockwork man marched toward them.

"Hey —" Frederick said. The automaton pushed them both out of the alley into Crosby Street.

"Wait here," it said.

"Hold on," Frederick said, but the clockwork man had already covered half the distance to the building in long, smooth strides.

"What's it going to do?" Hannah asked.

Frederick felt helpless. "I don't know. But we need to get off the street." He guided Hannah back into the alleyway, pushing her a little when she turned back to look.

By the time they were hidden, the automaton had reached the door, appearing from that distance as a large man wearing a cloak. It paused a moment, opened the door, and charged inside.

Within a moment cries of alarm issued from the building, mostly younger voices, boys. Then a clamor, splitting wood and angry shouts.

Hannah gripped Frederick's arm.

Frederick thought of the delicate gears in the Magnus head, and the clockwork of his own design. How easy it would be to damage it, in spite of the clockwork man's strength. Frederick thought about going in after the automaton to help it, and pulled against Hannah's hands.

"Don't you even think about going in there," she said.

Frederick clenched his fists, unblinking eyes drying out.

The commotion in Stephano's lair faded, as if receding into the building, but then rose to a crescendo. The front door burst open, and the clockwork man barreled out of the house carrying two figures, one under each arm. The hood of his cloak flapped behind him, sliced in half, his bronze head glinting in the night. He ran toward the alley.

Behind him, two older buskers leaped into the street, wielding clubs and knives.

"Run," Frederick said to Hannah, and gave her a push.

They fled back down the alley, the clockwork man's steps thundering behind them, along with the patter of smaller feet. Frederick chanced a look back and saw Giuseppe carrying a violin case, and another boy behind him, while the clockwork man brought up the rear. Behind the automaton, the two buskers closed the distance.

"I see you found your clockwork friend!" Giuseppe said behind him.

"We must go faster." The clockwork man's voice reverberated in the alley.

There was a shout from farther back, and then a sharp clang. Frederick flinched but kept running, listening for the heavy sound of metal boots.

"Faster," the clockwork man said.

They reached the end of the alley and poured onto the Cottonway, one after the other. But as Frederick turned around to look behind him for their pursuers, someone grabbed him.

"Aha! We've been following you thieves!" Mister Diamond breathed into Frederick's face. "Now where is the Magnus head?"

Frederick saw Mister Clod and Mister Slag sweeping their great ape arms toward Hannah and Giuseppe, easily catching them both. The little boy with Giuseppe looked paralyzed with fear, shaking in the middle of the street.

The two buskers chasing them tore out of the alley and launched themselves at the clockwork man, their clubs banging away on the Magnus head and the tin chest plate, oblivious to the three men from the museum.

"Help," the automaton said.

Mister Diamond looked up and shrieked. "What on earth? No!" He let go of Frederick and pointed at the clockwork man. "Clod! Slag! Save the Magnus head!"

The brutes took a moment to register the command before releasing the squirming Hannah and Giuseppe. Then they turned toward the buskers. Mister Clod snorted, and they descended like an avalanche.

One of the buskers saw and shouted a warning, but not in time. Before either of the boys could react, Mister Clod and Mister Slag fell on them, and in a flash each had one of the buskers up over their head, ready to snap them in two. The boys screamed.

Mister Diamond rushed toward his henchmen. "Don't kill them!"

"Come on," Hannah said. "While they're distracted."

The clockwork man stumbled toward Frederick, teetering, dents visible all over its body beneath the shredded cloak.

"Help me," Frederick said, and he and Giuseppe rushed to the automaton's sides.

Giuseppe guided them across the street to another alley. "This way. Pietro, come on!"

Hannah and the little boy followed Giuseppe and Frederick down a few sharp turns and byways, the sounds of the frightened buskers and the rumble of Diamond's thugs growing fainter.

The weight of the automaton dug into Frederick's shoulder. "Can we lose them?" Frederick asked.

Giuseppe spoke through clenched teeth. *"Non so,"* he said, which Frederick did not understand.

Their flight was dizzying and confounding to Frederick, down streets he had never seen, over forgotten courtyards with weeds sprouting between the cobblestones, through blind alleys where no gaslight or moonlight penetrated. It was like a different city, or a city behind the city Frederick knew. And then they turned a corner and he saw the sign to Mister Hamilton's tailor shop, which confused him until his disorientation settled like a spinning top come to rest, and he realized they were now on Sycamore Street. Farther on he saw Master Branch's shop.

They had made it.

"There is something . . . different," the clockwork man said.

"Let's get it inside," Frederick said.

They made more noise than he would have liked, bumping the door open and ringing the bell. But they managed to ease the clockwork man into the back room and down the cellar stairs. The automaton let them lay it down on the workbench, and Frederick felt suddenly like a doctor with a patient in critical condition.

They pulled the cloak open, revealing the extent of the damage.

"Oh, no." Hannah covered her mouth.

Giuseppe shook his head. Then he walked over to the little boy and put his arm around his shoulder. "You all right?"

"Yes," the boy named Pietro said, and pointed at the clockwork man. "What is that?"

Giuseppe looked at Frederick. "A friend."

Frederick surveyed the work done by club and knife, running his fingertips over the gouges and the dents in the metal. Most of the damage seemed centered on the chest and the Magnus head. One of the eyes had been smashed in, the other was spinning more slowly than before. Frederick's throat tightened as though someone had their hands at it, squeezing.

The destruction was beyond his ability to repair. He needed help. And Master Branch was the only one who could offer it. But asking for help would mean revealing everything to the old man. In trusting Master Branch, Frederick risked the loss of everything he had worked for. But if he did not go for help, the clockwork man would die.

Frederick stared at the chest plate. "I'm going for help."

"From who?" Giuseppe asked.

"Master Branch!" someone shouted upstairs. The voice of Mister Diamond.

Hannah and Giuseppe looked up at the ceiling, then at Frederick.

"Wait here," he said, and went for the stairs.

As Frederick emerged into the shop, Master Branch came down from his apartment, tying on his dressing gown. Mister Diamond stood in the open doorway to the shop, Mister Clod and Mister Slag completely blocking the view of the street behind him.

Master Branch gave Frederick a worried glance, and turned to Mister Diamond. "What can I do for you, sir, at such an ill-seasoned hour?"

"You can turn your apprentice over to me! I will see him to the proper authorities."

Frederick went cold from the inside out, ice in his stomach.

Master Branch swallowed. "On what charge?"

"Theft, Master Clockmaker. Theft of the Magnus head."

It was over. Frederick surrendered to the fact that he would be arrested. The future he had designed, the plans he had executed were slipping away like gears scattered from his workbench, down drains and under closed doors.

"Have we not been over this?" Master Branch swept his hand over the store. "You searched my shop yourself and found nothing."

Mister Diamond raised a hand and pointed at Frederick. "I just now saw him! He had the Magnus head on some monstrous body he's made. It is here!"

"I must insist that you calm yourself, sir." Master Branch eyed the behemoths brooding over Mister Diamond's shoulders. "Your guards are roaming far from home tonight."

"Extraordinary measures for extraordinary crimes."

"Well, I shall tell you now that no matter what you believe my apprentice to have done he shall not be leaving with you tonight, nor shall you be entering my shop."

"I demand —!"

"You are in a position to demand nothing, sir." Master Branch walked right up to the door to block Mister Diamond from entering. The old man looked so thin and frail, as if one blow from Mister Clod or Mister Slag would shatter him. But there was an authority in his voice, and a force of will emanating from him. Frederick walked up to his master's side and stood with him.

Mister Diamond twitched, and then his voice eased into a lilt. "Master Branch, I am certain that you would not risk the consequences to your guild by protecting a thief."

"Not at all," Master Branch said. "Just as I am certain you would not risk the reputation of the Archer Museum with an unlawful invasion of my property." He looked past Mister Diamond. "Or unlawful use of your servants."

Silence followed. The two men faced each other over the threshold, Mister Diamond's eyes raging against the unflappable smile Master Branch presented like a wall.

"This is not over," Mister Diamond finally said, and actually spat on the shop floor. He turned like a dust devil and churned down the street, Mister Clod and Mister Slag trailing behind.

Master Branch closed the shop door, locked it, and let out a long breath. He leaned his forehead against the door and began to tremble.

Frederick cleared his throat. "Thank you."

Master Branch did not look at him. "Do not thank me."

Frederick felt such affection for the old man in that moment. Master Branch had protected him. Frederick reached out and put a hand on the old man's back, felt the blades of his shoulders through his dressing gown. "Thank you," he said again, and a sob caught in his throat.

Master Branch turned to him.

"I have something I need to show you," Frederick said.

Master Branch merely nodded and followed Frederick into the back room and down into the cellar. The old man gripped the handrail and planted both feet on each step before descending to the next. He kept his eyes down until he reached the cellar floor.

Hannah, Giuseppe, and Pietro stood before the worktable, blocking the view.

"It's all right," Frederick said, and motioned them away.

His friends shuffled off, revealing the clockwork man. It had begun to twitch on the table, its remaining good eye fixed on the ceiling.

Master Branch inhaled a sharp breath. "Lad, what have you done?" He crossed the cellar floor and looked down on the table. His gaze fell over the clockwork body from the feet to the head. He bent closer to examine the bronze face and wire hair. "I did not think it was real."

"I only wanted to study it," Frederick said, his voice breaking. "I was going to take it back."

Master Branch placed a hand on the chest plate, the dented coal chute, as if feeling for a heartbeat. "But why?"

"I needed to make journeyman."

Master Branch nodded his head slowly. "I see." Then he paused, and sighed. "Frederick, you have more natural talent than any apprentice I have known. You could have trusted me."

And Frederick knew in that moment it was true. The old man had shown him that so many times. There in the cellar, the clockwork man dying beside him, Frederick realized he had wanted to trust Master Branch from the beginning, ever since the old man had rescued him from the orphanage. He had needed to more than he needed anything. But fear and anger as sharp and deep as a bramble wall had stopped him from reaching out, and had held the kind old man at a distance. Frederick's desire to become a journeyman clockmaker had only been a way to avoid that need, to hide behind ambition from his fear.

Tears broke from his eyes. "I'm sorry."

Master Branch softened, and his eyes glistened. He put his arm over Frederick's shoulder. "Tell me what has happened."

And Frederick told Master Branch everything. About the body he had made, and the museum, and bringing the Magnus head to life. About Giuseppe's capture and escape.

"I didn't know what to think," Giuseppe said. "One minute Pietro and I are sitting there in the rat cellar and the next thing we know the clockwork man comes crashing down. He grabs me up and I say, 'You got to take Pietro, too.' So he did. Then he jumps up out of the cellar like it's nothing, and then Ezio and Paolo started pounding on him. That's when I snatched my green violin back from Ezio."

"Such damage," Master Branch said.

"Can you fix it?" Hannah asked.

Master Branch turned to Frederick. "We will try."

Frederick looked at the clockwork man, and felt a swell of loyalty that lifted his chest. He nodded at Master Branch, and bent over the automaton. "We're going to turn you off to try and fix you," he said.

The eye kept spinning.

Frederick reached around to the button on the back of the head and pressed it. The forehead popped open, and the body slowed as if falling asleep. Frederick looked inside and felt a sickening despair settle in his gut. The damage looked horrendous, beyond repair. Gears bent, broken, jumbled. He could not imagine how the clockwork man had continued to operate at all.

"Oh, no," Master Branch said. "What a tragedy."

Frederick wiped at the tears blurring his vision. "I need my tools."

They labored until dawn crept down the cellar stairs from the shop above. Frederick and Master Branch had worked in concert over the Magnus head for hours, in perfect harmony. In the beginning it had been awkward, Frederick having to be the one to explain to his master what he had learned about the clockwork, and how it worked. But before long they had settled into a silent rhythm, and Frederick felt for the first time like a peer standing beside a fellow clockmaker, working together as equals.

Hannah, Giuseppe, and Pietro had all fallen asleep, leaning on one another against the wall. Frederick watched his friends, and their slow breathing relaxed him.

When Frederick and Master Branch replaced the last piece of clockwork in the Magnus head, Master Branch wiped his brow with his handkerchief. "Shall we move on to the body?"

"Let's see if the head is working properly," Frederick said. "Last time it was able to help me with the rest. Do you think we fixed it?"

Master Branch rubbed his hands in the handkerchief. "Let us find out."

Frederick pushed the forehead closed.

They had been unable to repair the ruined eye, but the other began to spin, flickering. There was a slight whirring inside, and the jaw slid open.

"Why?" the Magnus head asked.

Frederick almost laughed in relief. "I do not know."

The Magnus head paused. "I do not know, either."

Master Branch appeared awed. "Remarkable."

"There . . . is something different," the Magnus head said.

Its voice had awoken the three on the ground, and they stood up, blinking and stretching. Hannah walked over and leaned against Frederick, her hand on his arm. At her touch he felt cold and warm at the same time, anxious and enormously happy.

"There . . . is —" The clockwork voice halted, the eye skipped, and something in the jaw seemed to stick, hanging open.

"Frederick?" Hannah said.

Before Frederick could respond, something in the Magnus head clanged, and the jaw closed.

"Something's not right," Frederick said.

"Turn . . . me off," the Magnus head said.

"All right," Frederick said. "Master Branch and I will try again."

"No," the Magnus head said. "I am not . . . functional. Turn me off. Make it right."

But what if they could not make it right?

"There is something different," it said.

Frederick grew angry. "What is it? Why do you keep saying that?"

"I know why," Hannah said, a whisper at his side.

"You do?"

She nodded, and looked away from him. "I should have told you earlier." Hannah moved toward the clockwork man. She reached for the panel on the chest plate and opened it. "I'm sorry."

Frederick was confused. "Sorry for what?"

Hannah put her hand inside the chest and pulled out a lump of something. She held it out in her open palm, and Frederick saw that it was a chunk of dried clay, inscribed with letters he did not recognize.

"What is —?" he began, but a noise from the clockwork man stopped him.

The Magnus head shuddered, and the mouth opened wide. "Why?" it said, and the jaw closed. The spinning eye slowed, slowed, stopped. The clockwork fell silent.

"For its heart." Hannah began to cry. "I'm sorry."

Frederick touched the Magnus head, the bronze completely still beneath his fingertips. Dead. "What is that in your hand?" he asked, his voice so quiet he was not sure he had spoken aloud.

"It's a piece of a golem," Hannah said.

"A what?" Frederick asked.

"A golem is an artificial man," Master Branch said. "A protector made of clay."

Hannah still would not meet his eyes. "I took it from the museum. I didn't mean to. And then I put it in your clockwork man."

Frederick said nothing.

"The two were built with different purposes," Master Branch said. "The Magnus head to think and the golem to act. I would not have thought that a golem fragment could animate a clockwork."

"But it did," Frederick said.

"I'm sorry," Hannah said again.

Frederick studied her. Then he put his fingers under her chin and lifted her head so he could look into her green eyes. "Don't be. I think you made him something more than I ever could have."

CHAPTER 24

Mister Twine

HANNAH DID NOT KNOW WHAT TO SAY AS FREDERICK SLOWLY and methodically removed the Magnus head. Master Branch tried to assist him, but Frederick held an arm out, barring anyone else from approaching. He sniffed and worked with his tools, and Hannah wanted nothing more than to hug him. He had been so brave, and had sacrificed everything to save Giuseppe.

The two Italian boys waited at the edge of the room, as if they did not feel they were a part of what was happening in the cellar. But they were. They all were, and they had all witnessed the death of a noble machine. It was hard for Hannah not to blame herself for the death, as in some ways she was responsible for giving it life. Somehow, the fragment of golem had animated the body, but was never really part of it.

"There," Frederick said. He stepped away from the worktable. The Magnus head sat upright, as it had when Hannah had first seen it, looking just as lifeless. "I suppose I'll take it back to the museum now."

Giuseppe stepped forward. "Are you crazy?"

"You can't go back there," Hannah said, thinking of Mister Clod and Mister Slag.

"I have to," Frederick said.

"Your friends are right," Master Branch said. "I do not trust Reginald Diamond, and would not send you to his museum. I will return the bronze head."

Frederick shook his head. "But, sir —"

"I know you would do it if I let you, and that is enough. I will attempt to persuade Mister Diamond to accept the head and let the matter drop."

"Do you think he will?" Frederick asked.

Master Branch gave them all a sly smile. "I think so."

"Why would he do that?"

Master Branch picked up the Magnus head. "My guild would have a legitimate claim to a clockwork of such historic significance, and we have power and influence enough to cause Mister Diamond quite a bit of grief when we decide we want something. If he accepts my offer of the Magnus head, and agrees to forget about this whole incident, I will guarantee him that the guild will leave the head where it is, in the Archer Museum."

Hannah felt such relief she almost laughed.

"Thank you, sir," Frederick said.

Master Branch held the Magnus head to his chest. "It's quite heavy, isn't it?" The four youths moved aside to let the old man pass as he crossed to the cellar stairs. "I shall dress and go now," he said. "Sooner rather than later. Will you be all right?" He was looking at Frederick.

"We will," Frederick said. "Although I probably won't open the shop today."

Master Branch nodded. "I shall see you later."

The old man started up the stairs. Hannah and the two boys watched Frederick, who never took his eyes off the bronze head in his master's arms. Once Master Branch had left, he dropped his gaze to the floor.

Several moments passed in silence. Then Frederick shook his head and turned to Hannah. "Well. Shall we go?"

"Where?"

"Up to the Heights. To Mister Twine's mansion."

Hannah felt a flutter in her stomach. "Yes." She turned to Giuseppe. "But you are staying right here."

Giuseppe held up both hands. "No argument from me. Stephano's still out there."

At the mention of that name, Giuseppe's little friend flinched.

Hannah went to him and smoothed his hair. "It was nice to meet you, Pietro."

"Yes," he said. "You very nice to me."

Frederick waited at the foot of the staircase, and let Hannah go first. She heard Master Branch upstairs as they left the shop and went out into the street. She looked to the north, where gentle foothills rose up to a level bench of earth just above the city skyline. Just high enough for the mansions situated there to look down on the buildings below. Those great homes reminded Hannah of the castles in her fairy stories, with turrets and towers, high windows and lavish gardens, guarded by wrought iron gates and hedgerows. Frederick started up the street in their direction but Hannah hesitated.

This was it for her. Her last hope and only chance to save her family. Even if she got another job, she would never find one that would pay her as generously as Mister Twine had for her meager skills. Her family had far too little as it was. She returned again to the image she could not ignore, the image that had exhausted and occupied her for so long. Her family on the street, huddled in some building stoop, begging for food. Her father . . .

"What is it?" Frederick asked.

"What if he won't help me?"

"Then we'll figure something else out."

"What?"

"I don't know. Something. It's fine."

Hannah felt a jolt, like an explosion of swirling sparks from the collapse of burning logs. "But it's not fine."

Frederick acted as though he had not heard, just impatient and anxious to get moving. "Things will work out, Hannah."

That red-hot stove in her chest erupted. "I'm not fine!"

Her shout echoed through the street. A bonneted woman with a small child paused a moment and looked at Hannah out of the corner of her eyes before moving along. Frederick blinked at her.

"I am not fine," she said, a heat burning up her cheeks.

Frederick nodded. "All right. You're not fine." He led her off to the side of the street. "But who would be, Hannah? Why do you pretend you are?"

Something had given way inside her, the stove a flow of molten iron. Her blood had turned to hot ash and ember, her chest ablaze with pain, regret, and rage. Why did she pretend? Why did she lie to herself? She had given up so much, her school, her life. She had taken on such a heavy burden. So heavy she could not bear it any longer, could not stay upright. In that moment she hated her family. She hated her mother, so frail and helpless, always sad and overwhelmed. She hated her sisters for all their childish demands and their whining, their crying and fighting. And most of all, she hated her father. She hated him for simply lying there, for doing nothing, for letting her give up her schooling and slave away in the hotel he helped to build.

Hannah sobbed. She covered her face and fell into Frederick's arms. He stood rigid as a tree. She pounded his chest with her fist, and he hugged her for a long time. Her whole body heaved, her face wet and hot with tears.

"I hate them!" she cried. "It's not fair!"

"No, it isn't," Frederick said gently.

"I can't do it all!"

"No. You can't." After a long moment he said, "But you do what you can."

"And what if that isn't enough?"

Frederick held her shoulders and took a step back. He looked in her eyes. "Enough for what?"

"For my family."

"What more could they ask for than what you've given?"

She bit her lip. She sniffed. "I don't really hate them," she said.

Hannah loved her sisters, their laughter, and that no matter how hungry they were or how late it was when she came home, they always wanted Hannah to play with them. She loved her mother, her calm demeanor, her intelligence and compassion. And she loved her father. She loved him so much it hurt, like a knife made of sunlight in her chest.

Frederick was right. What more could anyone ask of her? Her tears subsided, and she found that they had extinguished the worst of the blaze inside, a charred and smoldering landscape left behind. She felt lifeless, burnt up. All she had been was gone. She had given everything.

"Are you ready now?" Frederick asked.

It took a moment for the question to reach her. "Ready for what?"

"To go see Mister Twine."

She wiped her stinging eyes and lifted them up to the Heights, resting like a crown above the city. A king's crown, regal, bejeweled, the prize of the treasury. And at the thought of treasure, something quivered inside her. She felt for it, and down among the black cinders she found a patch of green, a tender shoot with pale leaves, somehow spared. Hannah felt the beginnings of renewal.

"I'm ready to try," she said.

Frederick nodded. "All right."

She rubbed her cheeks and smoothed her skirts. "Let's go."

Mister Twine's mansion stood at the top of a series of landscaped terraces. A brick path rose level upon level from the street, bordered by rosebushes, like a long red tongue reaching down from the mansion's great double doors. Stately oak trees towered over the green lawn. Something about them seemed too perfect and unblemished, having been tamed by gardeners. Not like the trees in McCauley Park, which bore the scars of their long lives proudly.

Hannah turned around and looked down on the city. It smoked and shone, clamored and sang, looking and sounding familiar from this height, but also different. She usually thought of the city in its parts, its neighborhoods and quarters, but from up here it seemed to be one grand thing. The Quay and the docks were the arms, flexing and laboring along the river and the bay. The factories were the legs, pumping and grinding the city along. Gilbert Square lay at the heart, beating with people, sending them coursing down the streets to the city's far corners. And McCauley Park was the city's shadow, its other side, as necessary as the city itself.

"Shall we just knock on the front door?" Frederick asked.

Hannah shrugged. "I can't think of another way."

They climbed together, smelled the roses, and passed under the too-perfect shade of the trees. Hannah felt winded by the time they arrived at the doors, and took a moment to catch her breath before she reached for the heavy brass knocker. It hung from the mouth of a snarling lion, big as a giant's bracelet.

Hannah slammed it down one, twice, and flinched at the anvil sound that echoed around them. A moment passed with a ringing in her ears, something rattled in the latch, and the doors parted.

A young man stood before them, wearing a fine suit and a bland smile. If he felt surprise at seeing two children at his door, he did not show it. "Can I help you?"

Hannah scrambled for her wits and spoke. "We're here to see Mister Twine. Is he at home?"

The man nodded. "Mister Twine is in. But it is not his custom to receive visitors."

"Please, sir," Frederick said. "It's very, very important."

The man regarded them with his head tilted.

"Yes, sir, please," Hannah said. She heard the desperation in her own voice. "Mister Twine knew my father. He was a stonemason at the hotel."

The man sucked on one of his cheeks. "Well. Mister Twine did receive another woman from the hotel yesterday, and she came unannounced. Perhaps he'll see you."

Hannah's body went numb. "What woman?"

"The chief of maids, I believe. Miss Wool."

Frederick swallowed, and Hannah fell backward a step.

"Wait here," the man said, and shut the doors.

Frederick craned his neck and looked up at the face of the mansion. "What do you want to do?"

Run. Hannah wanted to turn around and run. But to where? "We try," she whispered.

They waited. A long time. Hannah stood frozen while Frederick paced around her, and a few timid birds chirped up in the trees.

The latch clicked and the doors reopened. "You are fortunate. Mister Twine will see you. Follow me."

He waited until they had entered into the mansion before closing the door behind them. They stood in dusty gloom, curtains drawn all around them. Hannah peered into the entryway, and her eyes adjusted, revealing walls paneled with dark wood from floor to ceiling, and a carpeted wooden staircase climbing up to the second floor. Tables flanked the stairway bearing empty vases, and massive portraits of unhappy-looking men and women weighed down one wall. Rafters spanned the vaulted ceiling overhead, fluttering with wisps of cobwebs.

"This way," the man said, and ushered them toward a series of doors.

Hannah and Frederick fell in behind him, their feet whispering over faded rugs. Everything in this mansion seemed so old, as though nothing had been replaced since the house was built. And yet Mister Twine left nothing alone for long in the hotel. Perhaps his home was the one place he demanded permanence.

The man opened a door and led them into a drawing room only marginally brighter than the entryway. "Mister Twine will be in shortly," he said, bowed his head, and left them.

Hannah turned to Frederick. "It's not too late. We could run."

Frederick smiled. "But we won't."

The room they stood in held several chairs in clustered gatherings, as though engaged in whispered conversations about one another. None of them looked comfortable for sitting. They were the kinds of chairs one stood next to with a hand on the back. The cold hearth hoarded what might have been last year's ashes for all the life that room held. A solitary clock ticked away on the mantel, and more portraits hung on the walls, their subjects' faces pinched in obvious and constant disapproval. Of everything.

A door on the far side opened, and Mister Twine stepped through. He looked as Hannah remembered him. Short, thin, bent, with white hair that retained just enough rust to suggest its former fiery red. Mister Twine moved toward them with a steady and purposeful gait, as though he practiced in a mirror to maximize efficiency.

"Hannah. I thought it might be you," he said. He did not extend a hand to shake, but motioned for them to sit in one of the uninviting chairs. "How is your father?"

Hannah sat, her back straight, her rump almost immediately uncomfortable. Frederick took a seat near her, and adjusted the legs of his trousers several times.

"He is doing quite we —" Hannah stopped herself. She heard Madame Pomeroy's voice in her head: *No more lies, Hannah.* She drew herself up. "Actually, sir, he is doing poorly. The doctor nearly had to amputate his leg."

Mister Twine stood across from them, his hand on the back of a nearby chair. "I am so sorry to hear that. But you say 'nearly' . . . I take it something or someone intervened?"

"Yes," Hannah said. "With medicine, and the help of friends."

"Friends are a precious commodity. At times I think perhaps I should acquire some." He stared off into a corner of the room.

Hannah cleared her throat. "Sir, if you will permit me, I must tell you about my situation."

Mister Twine's eyes glittered beneath his eyebrows. They were the eyes of a much younger man. "Before you go on, you should know that Miss Wool was here yesterday."

"I know," Hannah said.

"And yet you came," Mister Twine said.

Hannah stood up straighter. "I had to try."

"So you did. I take it the medicine was expensive?"

"It would have been."

"The diamond necklace was supposed to cover the cost, isn't that right?"

Hannah refused to look away. "That's right."

"A noble purpose by ignoble means." Mister Twine nodded his head. "I do understand something about that. You know why Miss Wool was here? You read the will as well?"

"I did."

"And in the process discovered secrets I'd managed to keep hidden for a very long time. But you are your father's daughter. I knew the risks when I took you on."

"And I appreciate the work you have given me, sir. You kept my family off the street."

"Perhaps I should have done more." Mister Twine gripped the chair. "But I refuse to give what has not been earned."

Hannah leaned forward. "Sir, since you know why I'm here, you probably know what I came to ask you."

"Yes. But you will do so on my terms. First, I am going to tell you a story, and then I will ask *you* some questions. After that, you may ask of me what you will."

Hannah felt impatient, but did not want to anger him. "I will listen."

Mister Twine nodded. "The history I am about to relate goes back a long way into the past. You know about our city's founders. Gilbert and McCauley were two sides of the same company, and they split the land in half, a seam right down the middle marking the boundary between civilization and the wild. Both the park and the city were born out of fear. Fear of what would happen if we conquered the land, and fear of what it would mean if we didn't.

"With the passing generations, McCauley's line ended while the Gilberts thrived. Their ambition and bravery dripped down through the years, from father to son, until collected and concentrated in two brothers. Anton and Archer Gilbert, as different as the wind and the mountain.

"Anton was a man after my own heart. He wanted to build. To shape. To enact. He created the Opera House and the hotel. He carved roads and brought industry into our city. His brother was of a different mind completely, and I daresay he was insane. Archer traveled the world, adventuring and plundering. He discovered new lands, new peoples, and explored lost cities, sending the fruits of his exploits back to his brother's city. The Archer Museum was built to house his massive collection of artifacts.

"The brothers fought continuously when they were together, so it was fortunate that Archer was seldom at home. But one day he returned and learned that the legacy McCauley had left behind to maintain the park was about to run out, and that Anton planned to strip the park bare and build over it to expand his vision for the city.

"Now, when Archer heard about this, he became outraged. You see, in all his travels through the crumbling ruins of fallen civilizations, he had picked up this notion that mankind is insignificant. That nothing we create will last. That we will all turn to dust. And it is only in nature that we find constancy and immortality. As I said, he was insane. But he had money. Archer spat in his brother's face, turned all of his wealth over to the legacy of McCauley Park, and wandered off into the woods to live the life of a hermit."

McCauley and Archer Gilbert. The land had enchanted them both. Well, Hannah had been inside the park, and she knew of its allure.

"And now," Mister Twine said. "We come to someone whose name you already know."

"Mister Stroop," Frederick said.

"Precisely. I remember the day he checked in to the hotel. If I had known then the trouble that man would cause for me, I would have turned him away. But I didn't and he stayed until the day he died. Hours he spent up there in that suite with his telescope, going slowly mad. I knew that Archer's legacy was running out, and I had my own plans for the park. But then Stroop called me to witness his new will. I had to stand there and watch as he signed away my ambitions, turning all his wealth over to McCauley's folly. Stroop entrusted me, as his executor, to see his wishes done."

"But you didn't," Frederick said. "Pullman said the legacy is running out."

Hannah narrowed her eyes at Mister Twine. "You stole his money?"

"Stole?" The old man's eyes flared, and his cheeks puffed up ruddy as a rooster's cowl. "Stole you say? How dare you! I am no thief! I have not touched a single cent of that money for my own use and I never planned to."

"But you kept it from going to the park," Hannah said.

"I prevented a terrible mistake," Mister Twine said. "When that legacy runs out I will be able to see Anton Gilbert's dreams fulfilled. My dreams. If the city does not grow, it will die, don't you see?" Then he turned to Hannah. "Unless . . ."

"Unless what?" Hannah asked.

"I am now going to ask you a question. If you want it, I will give you the money, all of Mister Stroop's treasure. In return, you will be required to keep silent and let the park pass into my hands."

"Or?" Frederick asked.

"Or, you leave the money with me, and I will honor Mister Stroop's will."

Frederick snorted.

"Why would you do that?" Hannah asked.

Mister Twine sighed. "Because it is the right thing, after all. I had planned on giving the treasure to a charity. But I would not object to your taking possession of it, which would relieve me of the need to exercise my own conscience, something I've successfully avoided for some time now. Do you understand the choice before you?"

Hannah nodded. But she did not want to make it. If she took the money, her family would be saved. They would have a home, a real home, and a doctor for her father all the time. They would have food, and clothes, and her mother would be able to laugh again. Hannah would be able to go back to school. Mister Stroop's treasure could be hers, for her family, but at what cost?

The park would be destroyed. No more trees, no more Mirabel, no more cabin by the pond for Alice. No more flowers, no more herbs for Alice to study to make her medicine, the medicine Hannah had given her father. Without the park, the doctor would have taken her father's leg. And without McCauley, there would have been no park. Without Archer Gilbert, there would have been no park. Without the legacy of either man, her father might have died.

The park was dark and dangerous, but also beautiful and life-giving. What would the city be without it, its green shadow, its other side? Both were necessary. Mister Stroop had seen that through his telescope. The park *was* his treasure. The park was a treasure that belonged to the whole city, a treasure of life. And Hannah had already found it.

"I want you to follow Mister Stroop's wishes," she said. "For the legacy of McCauley Park."

Mister Twine fixed her with a stare that she could only meet for a moment before looking away. He lowered his voice to a drone. "Very well."

"Hannah," Frederick said. "Are you sure about this?"

Hannah nodded once.

"What about your family?"

"I don't know," Hannah whispered. She had no plan, no idea what she would do. But perhaps if she pleaded, Mister Twine would give her old job back. "Sir?" she said. "Can I ask you something now?"

Mister Twine held up a finger, pointed at the ceiling. "There is something else you should know. Yesterday, I told Miss Wool the selfsame story that I have just told you, and presented her with the same choice." He brought his finger down. "I did not like her answer. So, I fired her."

Had Hannah heard that correctly? "You fired Miss Wool?"

"Yes. Miss Wool no longer works for the Gilbert Hotel."

It was as though someone had suddenly taken away a pain that Hannah had grimly accepted and grown used to. She shook her head, feeling lighter.

"I have a final question for you," Mister Twine said.

Hannah blinked and waited.

"Would you accept Miss Wool's position at the hotel?"

Again, she wondered if she had heard him correctly. "What?"

"It is true that you are quite young for the position, but also quite capable. And I see that you have integrity, a quality I prize in others."

Hannah stammered, searching for something gracious or thankful to say, but ended up breathing out a simple yes.

"Good. Be at my hotel office tomorrow morning at eight o'clock and we shall discuss your new responsibilities. As well as your raise."

"My raise?"

"Of course."

She felt Frederick take her hand and squeeze it. Tears clouded her eyes, but she welcomed them. "Thank you, Mister Twine."

He grinned. "I think I understand the desperate circumstances that led you to steal Madame Pomeroy's necklace. While it was certainly wrong of you, I have seen for myself the material your character is made of. We shall let the matter lie, and I shall see to the police."

"Thank you," Hannah said again. She rose to her feet.

"I don't mean to offend you," Mister Twine said. "But as the new chief of maids you will need to work on your appearance." He gestured toward her as though flicking dirt from something in front of him.

Hannah looked down at her shabby dress.

"Here." Mister Twine reached into his jacket pocket and pulled out a small leather folio. "Buy yourself some new dresses before tomorrow." He handed her a small wad of money. "You have earned this."

Hannah clutched the money to her breast. "I don't know what to say."

"In that case, you may go."

Hannah nodded and turned to leave, but remembered herself and dropped into the worst curtsy she had ever performed. Then she stumbled toward the door, and would have fallen had Frederick not been there to catch her. As she reached the far side of the room, she had a thought and turned back to Mister Twine.

"Sir?"

"Yes?"

"What about Mister Grumholdt?"

Mister Twine chuckled, a high huffing sound like a small bellows. "Every man needs a blunt instrument for the rough work, my dear. Something reliable in its own way. Don't worry about Hans. I only ask that the passageways remain a secret between us and your father. Agreed?"

"Of course, Mister Twine," Hannah said. "Have a good day, sir."

"You do the same. And give your family my regards."

"I will," Hannah said.

She and Frederick left the drawing room, then the dusty entryway, and descended the brick path outside. Hannah took one last look at the city from this height, the view of it that Mister Twine saw every day, before heading back down into the streets.

"I think I'd like to go see Madame Pomeroy," she said. "But before I do, I think it's your turn."

They waited in the lobby of the Orchard Street Hospital. The tang of antiseptic alcohol sharpened the air in Hannah's nose. But another odor brooded beneath it like a layer of dark silt along a river bottom. The iron smell of blood.

Frederick stared at his knees, which were bouncing like steam-driven pistons. Twice Hannah had tried to settle him with a gentle touch, but that had only calmed his agitation for a moment and she had given up.

"Where is this nurse?" he asked. "We've been waiting for —"

"It hasn't even been ten minutes," Hannah said. "She'll come."

But it felt like it had been longer to her as well. For a hospital, the lobby seemed quite lifeless. The only decoration was a rough-hewn cross, hanging on the wall opposite their chairs like a crack in the sterile whitewash.

Frederick's legs stopped. He leaned toward her. "I'm glad you're here with me."

"Me too," Hannah said. "I'm glad you came with me to Mister Twine's."

"Me too."

Hannah smoothed her hand over the wooden arm of the chair. "What's going to happen with your apprenticeship?"

"I don't know."

"Are you still going to try and build your own clockwork head?"

Frederick laughed. "No. Not even if I thought I could."

"I think you could."

Frederick gave a modest nod, acknowledging without agreeing. "Whatever I do, Master Branch will be there to help me."

"You're lucky to have him."

"Yes," he said. "I am."

At that moment a woman entered the lobby wearing a nurse's bonnet, and a bleached white apron over a sky blue dress. She was short, and walked with the waddle and bobbing head of a duck. She smiled and approached them. Frederick stood up to greet her, and she stopped.

"Why, you look just like her," she said, staring at him. "They told me Maggie's boy was here asking after her, and sure enough. Here you are."

"Are you the nurse that took care of my mother?" Frederick asked.

She nodded, and came the rest of the way till she stood in front of him with her hands folded in front of her apron. "For most of her time here. We became friends."

"She died here," Frederick said bluntly, but with a fragile certainty, as if he hoped to be told differently and knew he would not.

The nurse nodded. "Not long after she came. She was a wonderful woman, your mother. She used to go from bed to bed, comforting the other patients when she had the strength. She'd sit with them for hours and sing to them till there wasn't a dry eye on the ward. People used to stop in the street outside the window."

"I remember her voice," Frederick said.

"Lovely, wasn't it? Like the most beautiful songbird in McCauley Park."

Hannah felt like an intruder. She tried to ease herself away a bit and drew Frederick's eye.

"This is my friend Hannah," he said. "She's the one that got me thinking about my mother, and made me want to find out what happened to her."

Hannah curtsied. "Hello."

"Hello, dear."

"Do you know where she is buried?" Frederick asked. Tiny tears had lodged in the corners of his eyes, as if unwilling to fall.

"I think they laid her in the Old Rock Churchyard."

Hannah had been there. She might have seen her tombstone.

"Thank you very much for your time," Frederick said, and his voice caught. "I just had to know. For certain."

"Of course," the nurse said. "If I may add, she spoke of you often."

"She did?"

"Nearly every day. I take it you're not in the orphanage anymore."

"I'm an apprentice clockmaker."

"And he's brilliant at it," Hannah added.

"I don't doubt it," the nurse said. "You look well. Quite handsome. Your mother would be proud, I think it right to say." She appeared to hesitate. "I don't mean to add to your grief, but I think leaving you was the great sorrow of her life. Even more so than her husband's loss at sea."

Frederick stood for a moment, working his lips. Then the tears fell, one at a time, without leaving a trail. "Thank you again," he said.

"My pleasure. It was very nice to finally meet you, Frederick."

Hannah curtsied and Frederick led the way back out into the busy street. He wiped his eyes, and he was smiling. Truly smiling, wider than Hannah had ever seen, as though shutters had opened on the full light of the sun. He was staring at her, pedestrians brushing their elbows, horses and carriages trundling by.

"What is it?" Hannah asked.

Then he hugged her. A sudden, warm, gentle hug.

"Thank you," he said into her hair.

She put her hands around him and hugged him back.

CHAPTER 25

The Old Rock Church

GIUSEPPE HAD THE GREEN VIOLIN BACK. IT RESTED IN HIS LAP, smooth and warm. He and Pietro lounged in front of the fireplace on the top floor of the old clockmaker's shop. They had slept a bit down in the cellar, and upon waking found nothing to do down there and grew bored. The shop had proved more interesting, with things to look at but nothing they felt comfortable touching. Giuseppe viewed clocks with a wary eye now that he had seen Frederick's creation, as though every wristwatch, mantelpiece, and cuckoo were a secret, living thing, hiding silent thoughts and biding time rather than counting it.

After exploring the shop the only place left to them was Master Branch's living quarters, so they had prodded each other up the stairs and now sat with their feet kicked up, enjoying a fire from the comfort of the armchairs. Pietro sat so low in the cushions he bent at the neck. Giuseppe and he now spoke entirely in Italian when no one else was around.

"Do you think they'll mind if we're up here?" the little boy asked.

"Nah. Besides, they can't expect us to stay down there in the cellar all day. Like we're rats or something."

Pietro shuddered. "Don't talk about rats. I hate rats."

Giuseppe spit into the fire. "I hate Stephano."

They both fell silent.

"Where did you get the green violin?" Pietro asked.

"I found it floating in the harbor."

"Where do you think it came from?"

Giuseppe looked up at the ceiling. "I don't know. A place where they like to play music and change people's lives."

"I always wanted to hear you play it," Pietro said. "Ever since I saw you hide it."

Giuseppe rubbed his eyes. "Perhaps later."

The fire burned itself out and neither of them moved to toss more wood on. They sat there without speaking until the door to the shop opened downstairs.

"Giuseppe?" they heard Frederick call.

Giuseppe switched to English. "Up here." He did not rise from the chair.

Footsteps on the stairs, and then Frederick entered the room. There was something different about the way he looked. Perhaps it was in the way he moved. He stood taller and straighter, and his eyebrows were up instead of digging down into each other.

"How did it go?" Giuseppe asked. "Where's Hannah?"

"She went to tell her family the good news."

"What good news?"

"Mister Twine hired her back and gave her a promotion. He fired Miss Wool and gave Hannah her position."

"That is good news."

"Yes." Frederick sighed, and sat down at the kitchen table.

Master Branch returned shortly after that with meat pies he had bought on his way home from the museum. The four of them sat down for lunch and the old clockmaker told them that Mister Diamond had accepted his offer. No charges would be brought against Frederick, and the museum would keep the Magnus head. Master Branch spoke in heavy tones, as though mourning the loss of the clockwork head for his guild. Giuseppe expected Frederick to show similar feelings, but instead of grief the apprentice only expressed relief and gratitude to his master.

The pies were still warm, and the flaky crust crackled as Master Branch cut slices on everyone's plate. The dark gravy spilled out around chunks of meat, onion, and potato. Giuseppe could not remember eating so well. First the turtle stew and now this. Everyone but Master Branch had two or three pieces before the pies were gone.

After they had finished, the bell chimed on the door downstairs, and Hannah called up to them. Frederick hopped to his feet with a foolish grin and hustled down the stairs to meet her. Giuseppe smiled and noticed a similar expression cross Master Branch's face. Pietro licked the leftover gravy from his plate.

A few moments later, Frederick and Hannah came upstairs. Once they stepped into the room, Hannah walked right over to Giuseppe.

"I have something for you," she said.

Giuseppe sat up. "Oh?"

"Yes." She reached into a pocket in her dress. "I owe you something, Giuseppe. Without your music, my father would never have been able to lead me to the treasure. So here." She held out her hand.

Giuseppe lifted his, and she placed some money into it.

"What's this?" he asked.

"Mister Twine gave me some money for new clothes. I don't think he knows how much a new dress costs, because he gave me more than I will need. But he said I earned it. So did you."

Giuseppe tabbed through the limp bills. "There's fifty dollars here."

Hannah nodded. "Frederick tells me that's enough for a boat ticket."

"It is." Giuseppe got to his feet and tugged his cap from his head. His mouth hung open in shock. "I don't know what to say." He reached out and hugged her. "Thank you."

"No." She hugged him back. "Thank you."

He could scarce believe it. He had played and scrounged and saved for weeks, only to lose all his money to Stephano. And even though he had the green violin again, he had no idea how he would be able to play it on the streets, how he would be able to earn his way. But Hannah had given him a fortune, just like that, and suddenly he had all the money he needed to go home. Pietro stood up and peered into his palm. Giuseppe smiled at him, and then frowned. What would happen to the little boy now?

Frederick cleared his throat. "I think I'll head down to the docks. There's a ship leaving for Italy in a few days."

"You'll buy the ticket for me?" Giuseppe asked.

"It would be my pleasure," Frederick said. Giuseppe handed him the money, and Frederick shoved it in his pocket. "After all, I've been there once for you before. I'll be back soon."

Giuseppe did not know if Frederick was really gone as long as it seemed, or if his excitement only made it seem like ages and ages. He filled the waiting with idle conversation with Master Branch and Hannah, but his mind kept turning to thoughts of home. Images of hills and pastures, daydreams of hugging his brother and sister. During all of this, Pietro kept quiet. The little boy knew what was going on, but Giuseppe had no idea what to say to him about it. There was only enough money for one ticket.

Eventually Frederick did return, but he was no longer smiling. He clomped up the stairs, and his eyebrows had collapsed back into their normal argument.

"What is it?" Hannah asked first.

"He wouldn't sell me the ticket," Frederick said. "He knew."

"Knew what?" Giuseppe asked.

Frederick slumped into one of the kitchen chairs. "I tried to buy passage to Italy, and the ticket man just looked at me. 'One way?' he asked, and I said, 'Yes.' And then he frowned and got all suspicious. Then he said, 'Not many boys in this city wanting a one-way ticket to Italy, are there?' I said I didn't know about that. And then he said he had a message for a boy named Giuseppe."

"I don't understand," Hannah said.

A sense of defeat grabbed Giuseppe's stomach by the fist. "They're all in Stephano's pocket. Even the policemen down on the docks." He bled hope and turned cold. He was so close, and had lost it all again. "Stephano knew I might try and leave. What was the message?"

Frederick looked at the floor.

"What was it?" Giuseppe asked. Pietro had come over to his side.

"He said —" Frederick started. "He said that if you want your reverend to remain unharmed, you'll bring the green violin to the Old Rock Church."

"Reverend Grey?" Giuseppe's legs and arms went soft. "Ezio. Oh, no. I have to go. I have to give him the violin."

"No," Hannah said. "You can't go."

"We'll summon the police," Master Branch said. "That is what we'll do."

"That's too risky," Giuseppe said. "He could hurt the reverend."

"The police won't do a thing, anyway," Frederick said. "Hannah and I already tried that."

"I'm going," Giuseppe said.

"No, you're not," Hannah said. "Frederick, tell him."

"He doesn't just want the violin," Frederick said. "He wants you, and he's using your friend to get at you. But wouldn't Reverend Grey want you to stay safe?"

"Quite right," Master Branch said. "This ruffian, Stephano, would surely know better than to assault a clergyman. You and Pietro are welcome to stay as long as you need until it's safe for you."

But it never would be. Giuseppe knew that. Did he plan on hiding out in the old clockmaker's cellar for the rest of his life? He could not hide in McCauley Park with Alice, and he could not hide here. Not when a friend of his, someone who had only been kind to him, was in danger because of him. And Master Branch did not know Stephano. The padrone would assault a clergyman without any hesitation.

Giuseppe crossed to the window and looked out. He could almost feel Stephano's cold rage seeping through the streets like a fog from the sea. No busker would be playing any corner tonight. Stephano would have them all out hunting. Giuseppe had the green violin, but what good would it do him? He knew what it would mean if he turned himself in. The padrone would beat him, hurt him, break him. But perhaps Stephano would not actually kill him. Not if Giuseppe brought him the green violin and played it to fill the padrone's pocket. There would be no chance of escape after that, no voyage home, no family, but those were things he could not let himself think about. Money would keep Giuseppe alive, and the reverend unharmed, and that was what mattered in that moment. But he knew Frederick and Hannah would never see it that way.

"Thank you for the offer," Giuseppe said to Master Branch. He turned to Hannah and Frederick. "You're right. I'll stay put."

The two of them relaxed and nodded. They passed the rest of the afternoon and evening playing card games, and then Giuseppe played the green violin for them at Pietro's request. Master Branch applauded, Frederick smiled, and Hannah sighed, but to Giuseppe's ear the music lacked something. He kept thinking about Reverend Grey, and the green violin felt heavy as lead in his hands. Rather than taking flight, the music seemed to thud to the ground, dragged down by a weight. But Giuseppe obliged them and played several tunes before making a show of yawning. Then, later that night, after Hannah had left for home, and Master Branch had gone to bed early, and Frederick and Pietro had fallen asleep in the workroom behind the shop, Giuseppe got up to leave.

In the darkness, he felt for the green violin and slung it over his shoulder. On his way past Frederick's cot he stubbed his toe and let out a little yelp.

Frederick snored, but Pietro stirred. "Giu? What are you doing?"

"Nothing, go back to sleep."

He heard a rustling as Pietro got to his feet. "You're going to the church, aren't you?"

"No."

"Yes, you are."

"I have to."

Pietro grabbed his arm. "Don't leave."

Frederick mumbled something in his sleep and Giuseppe hissed. He grabbed Pietro and pulled him out of the workroom into the shop. "Pietro, I don't have a choice."

"But —" The little boy's voice broke off in a sob.

Giuseppe went to the shop door, climbed up on a shelf, and held on to the bell. "The key is in the door. Unlock it and open it for me."

Pietro did as he was told, and the door opened silently. Giuseppe hopped down. "Stay here. I think the clockmaker will look after you for a while. Hannah and Frederick will help you."

"I want to come with you," Pietro said. Tears brimmed in his eyes.

Giuseppe looked away, out the door into the night. "No."

"Yes!"

"No!" Giuseppe cocked his fist. "Now get away from me."

The little boy flinched and stepped back, eyes wide. His lip quivered. Giuseppe felt sick inside. "I'll be back," he said. "Lock up behind me." He shut the door, winced when the bell chimed, and waited until he heard the turn of the key. Then he headed down the street.

He did not bother to raise his collar or lower his hat. He was tired of being afraid. The streets were mostly deserted, and he walked with purpose and speed toward the Old Rock Church. Along the way he felt eyes on him now and again, watchers from the alleys and around the corners. The buskers were out in force, but he did not care or cast one look in their direction. But he wondered if Ferro or Alfeo were among them.

By now, Pietro had no doubt roused Frederick. They would want to help, to stop him, and might even be coming after him. Which meant that he had to move fast.

He soon arrived at the Old Rock Church. Despite the late hour, a faint light came from its stained-glass windows, and the chapel doors were open. Giuseppe did not sneak or wait to see if anyone was waiting nearby. He just marched straight into the street, up to the front doors, and walked right through.

"Reverend Grey?" he called.

The air inside the chapel smelled of old wood, with a hint of smoke and melted wax. The light in the stained-glass windows came from candles burning around the room in sconces. Apparently the reverend had never had gaslight brought into the church. The dim orange light melted from the walls over the pews and the floor.

"Reverend Grey?"

"Giuseppe?" The old man shuffled out of a side room. "Is that you?"

"It's me. Hello, Reverend."

"My goodness, it's a relief to see you." Reverend Grey walked over to him. He reached out one arm and pulled Giuseppe to him. "You worried me when you left the other night with that fellow."

"I'm fine. Are you all right?"

"Of course. Tired, I suppose. I just finished counseling a member of my congregation after a late night service." The old man went over to the nearest pew and sat down. "Come. There's something I want to tell you. I started to the other night."

Giuseppe went to sit down next to him. "I have to tell you something first."

"But I get the last word." Stephano stood at the rear of the chapel, flanked by Paolo and Ezio, both boys covered in bruises, poised like dogs waiting to be let off their chains. Stephano removed his hat and stroked the peacock feather, sending a little wisp of it fluttering to the floor. He set the hat down on a nearby pew, and gave a quick nod toward Paolo and Ezio. The two of them went back and closed the church doors, barring them with the heavy beam. Giuseppe rose to his feet. They were trapped.

"You must be Stephano," Reverend Grey said, and stood. "This is a house of God, sir. Depart at once."

"If this is God's house, who are you to kick me out?" Stephano walked up the aisle, his heavy boots sounding on the wood floor. "I'll leave when Almighty God drags Himself down here and tells me it's time to go."

"You blaspheme," Reverend Grey said.

"Constantly." Stephano stopped a few feet away. "I'm here for that lad."

"No. You will not take him." The reverend held out his arms, shielding Giuseppe behind him. "You have no claim on him."

"You're wrong there, priest. I have a contract signed by his uncle." Stephano looked at Giuseppe. "You're as predictable as the tides, boy. All we had to do was wait and watch, and sure enough, you showed up."

Giuseppe slipped the green violin from his back. He set it on the pew. "I got your message. You said you'd leave him alone."

Stephano slid his bottom jaw back and forth like he was grinding something up.

Reverend Grey stepped forward. "I have a copy of a new city law, sir," he said, and produced a piece of paper from his coat. "Signed by the city council and the mayor. The law no longer recognizes padrones as legitimate businessmen, and you no longer have any legal claim on the boys you have enslaved."

"What?" Stephano said.

"Your contract with his uncle is voided."

Stephano narrowed his eyes, the dark, weathered skin wrinkling up around them. He was silent for a long time. "And I just bet you had something to do with that."

"Yes. I did."

Thoughts swarmed through Giuseppe's mind like a flock of seagulls, none landing, all screaming. A new law passed, and the reverend had helped? Giuseppe was free? It was too much to take in. But if it was true, then Reverend Grey was dead. Whether Giuseppe had the green violin or not, the old man had just ripped away Stephano's means of wealth, his authority, and his power.

Rage rolled off the padrone like steam. "Tie him up," he said.

Ezio and Paolo leaped over the pews at Reverend Grey, while Stephano grabbed Giuseppe and squeezed his wrists so tight they started to pop.

"Take your hands off me!" the reverend shouted, thrashing. But Ezio and Paolo were younger and stronger, and had him bound to the pew within moments.

Stephano threw Giuseppe down beside the reverend. He pulled out his knife. "You've made a lot of trouble for me," he said to both or either of them. "And for that I'm going to bleed you right here, right now."

"You would not take an innocent life in a church," Reverend Grey said, horrified.

Stephano did something then that Giuseppe realized he had never seen. The padrone smiled, a hideous gap splitting his face, baring yellow teeth, bloodred gums, and a white tongue. "You don't know what I would do. What I'm going to do."

Reverend Grey paled. Even Paolo looked frightened, leaning away from Stephano. Ezio stood unshaken beside his master, and Giuseppe glared up at the padrone.

Stephano leaned over, his breath in Giuseppe's face. "You brought this on, boy. This man's death is your fault."

The reverend raised his voice. "Don't listen to him, Gi —"

Stephano snapped his hand and smacked the old man across the face. Reverend Grey whimpered a little, his head hanging to the side, and let blood drip from his mouth. The front doors of the church rattled, a parishioner trying to get in. Giuseppe thought about calling for help, but knew it would be pointless.

Stephano ignored the sound. "You're going to watch this old man die, Giuseppe. Right before I kill you. Before I kill all of you rats."

"You're a coward," Giuseppe said in Italian.

Those words seemed to stop Stephano, as though they were so far from what he had expected to hear they were incomprehensible. "What did you say?"

Giuseppe was not tied down, not by rope, not by fear. He stood up, and spoke with a loud voice in the language of his parents, his brother and sister. "You kidnap children because they're the only ones you can bully. You tie up an old reverend and think you're getting back at a city that hates you. You try and make everyone afraid of you because you think that makes you powerful." Giuseppe looked him up and down. "I say you're weak. I say you're a coward."

Stephano put the knife to Giuseppe's throat. Giuseppe did not flinch, or pull away, or take his eyes from Stephano.

"You die first," the padrone said.

In that moment one of the church windows exploded inward, and something very large and very dark crashed into the chapel. It flew through the air, and rolled across the floor in a shower of broken glass and flapping shadow. Then it rose up and Giuseppe saw that it was a man in dark robes, standing with his feet wide, fists at the ready. He was tall, with long black hair and eyes of blue ice.

"Let the boy go," he said in a Russian accent.

Wariness broke the resolve from Stephano's face. "Who're you?"

"Let the boy go. Now."

The tip of the knife shifted a little against Giuseppe's skin, pricking him, and he felt a hot trickle of blood.

Ezio and Paolo fixed their eyes on the stranger. Stephano glanced at them, communicating a silent order, and the three of them howled and charged at the Russian. The tall man dropped and rolled and came up swinging his fists in the midst of them. Paolo went down first, a blow to his gut, nose broken and gushing. Giuseppe watched in awe as the stranger moved between Ezio and Stephano, seeming to block, duck, and strike all with the same powerful movements.

"Who is he?" Reverend Grey asked.

"I don't know," Giuseppe said.

Stephano had his knife out. So did Ezio. The Russian fought silently, the only signs of stress a sheen of sweat across his brow, and the occasional grunt. The battle ranged across the chapel, over pews, up and down the aisle.

Stephano managed an elbow jab in the stranger's side, and in that moment Ezio's knife opened a red slash in the Russian's sleeve and arm. He feinted away from them, and Stephano and Ezio fell back. They circled, regrouping, planning their attack.

Paolo struggled across the floor toward the reverend, and Giuseppe ran and landed a kick to his head that laid him out flat and still.

The Russian stared, chest heaving, implacable, as Ezio and Stephano broke apart and took up positions on either side of him. They rushed him at the same time. The Russian braced and appeared ready for them, but at the last moment, Stephano dodged out of his attack and bolted toward Giuseppe.

The move seemed to catch the Russian off guard. When Ezio collided with him, they both went down in a tussle.

In the next moment Stephano was on Giuseppe, and had him around the neck from behind. Giuseppe thrashed and kicked but Stephano squeezed his throat and cut off his air. "No harder than crushing a rat," he said.

The world blurred, air came in gasps and gags.

"Giuseppe!" the reverend shouted, sounding distant and muffled.

Something flat and gray passed in front of Giuseppe's eyes, Stephano's knife. "You're dead," the padrone hissed, and Giuseppe felt the blade's edge begin to slice beneath his chin.

A deafening crack filled the chapel. The sound still echoed as Stephano's knife fell to the floor with a clatter. The padrone's grip on Giuseppe weakened, and then slipped away. Air rushed into Giuseppe's lungs, and something thudded on the ground behind him. He choked and held his throat and turned to see Stephano lying dead on the ground, a hole in his head.

The Russian knelt in the aisle, aiming a very strange-looking gun. Ezio lay next to him, unmoving and unconscious. A tendril of smoke issued from the weapon's barrel, and as the stranger got to his feet Giuseppe saw that the gun was shaped like a leaping tiger. The hind legs formed the handle, the tail made up the hammer, and the bullet left through the tiger's snarling mouth.

The Russian slipped the gun inside his long robes. "Are you injured?"

"I'm all right." Giuseppe felt the shallow cuts on his neck. "Who are you?"

"I am Yakov," the Russian said. "See to the priest." He turned and walked down the aisle to the front doors.

Giuseppe went to the reverend and worked at the knots binding him to the pew. Yakov lifted the bar from the doors and opened them wide. In rushed Pietro, Hannah, and Frederick. A large woman bustled in after them. When she saw Yakov, she sagged with visible relief.

Giuseppe's friends clambered down the aisle toward him.

"Are you all right?" Frederick asked.

"You're bleeding," Hannah said.

Giuseppe waved them off. "I'm fine."

Pietro had crouched down over Stephano's body, staring at it. Hannah noticed the dead padrone and gasped.

"Did Yakov . . . ?"

Giuseppe nodded. "He saved my life."

Hannah turned to look at the Russian, and then ran and embraced him. He appeared surprised and ruffled by the attention at first, but then smiled and cupped the back of her head with one of his large hands.

The strange woman surveyed the scene and nodded as if pronouncing it acceptable in some way. "Now you all know why they say I travel with a tiger."

Giuseppe did not know if she was talking about Yakov, or the gun he kept in his robes.

"My church," the reverend said, with despair in his voice. "My church." He held a handkerchief to his nose and broken lip, staring in disbelief. After a moment, he shook his head. "I suppose I should go fetch the police."

The large woman looked at Yakov. Yakov looked at the reverend.

"Wait a moment," the Russian said.

Reverend Grey blinked at Yakov, and stayed where he was.

The large woman turned to Hannah. "So this is Giuseppe?"

"Yes. Giuseppe, this is Madame Pomeroy."

Giuseppe bowed. "Pleased to meet you, ma'am."

"And a pleasure it is to meet you. Although that's a pleasure I might have missed if we'd come too late."

Giuseppe nodded. He figured Pietro must have woken Frederick. The two of them had gone for Hannah, and then to Madame Pomeroy and her Russian companion for help.

"I'm glad you came when you did, ma'am." And then his legs went out and Giuseppe slumped into a pew.

His body buzzed with shock, the way a pipe hums with the water raging through it. Everything had happened so fast. One minute Giuseppe was sure he was going to die, and in the next minute Stephano was shot dead. Giuseppe was free. He trembled and rubbed his forehead, eyes wide in disbelief. He was free.

His friends took up places next to him, hands on his back, his arms. He started shaking in earnest, and could not stop. He balled his quaking hands into fists. Tears fell in his lap. When had he started crying? His throat ached, racked with sobs.

"Shh," Hannah said, stroking the back of his neck, her fingers cool against his skin. "Shh. You're safe now."

He nodded and tried to calm himself, but his body was not finished. It felt out of his control, as though it had to take time to feel what there had been no time for while everything was happening. But eventually the tension in his body slackened, and the crying ebbed, and, like a receding wave, it left Giuseppe feeling raw, scraped clean. He teetered to his feet.

"There now," Madame Pomeroy said. "You've had quite an ordeal."

"I'm all right now," Giuseppe said.

Hannah still looked worried. "Are you sure?"

"Yes," he said.

Someone tugged at him, and he turned to see Pietro holding the green violin. "This yours," the little boy said, and presented it to him.

"What is that?" Madame Pomeroy asked.

"His green violin," Frederick said.

Madame Pomeroy touched the brooch at her neck. "Green, you say?"

Giuseppe felt a different kind of tears behind his eyes. He took the case from Pietro and held it for a moment before slinging it over his shoulder. He was free. He could buy a boat ticket. But what about Pietro? Where would any of the boys go? Even though Stephano had been a wicked, cruel master, he had provided a place for them to sleep at night. What would they eat? Who would protect them?

Paolo groaned and stirred. Yakov pulled a cord from within his robes, which he used to tie Paolo's hands behind his back. He did the same to Ezio, and then leaned in close to Madame Pomeroy.

"It is time," he said in a low voice.

Madame Pomeroy frowned and nodded. "Yes. So it is." She motioned for Hannah to come to her. "We must say good-bye, child."

Hannah went to her. "Good-bye?"

"Yes. I had planned to leave in a few days, but my enemies are closer than I'd supposed. My steamer leaves in the morning." Her lip quivered and she wiped under her eyes. "Oh, you see how I am? With all the good-byes I've said in my life, you would think I'd be used to them by now."

Giuseppe wondered where Madame Pomeroy's steamship was traveling.

Hannah reached into her dress pocket. "I want to give you something."

She held out the lump of clay. "Something you might like, because of what you always say about Yakov, and golems."

Madame Pomeroy stared at the object, at the markings inscribed over it. She reached out her hand to take it, but hesitated. "Goodness, child. Do you know what this is?"

"It's a piece of a golem."

Madame Pomeroy picked it out of Hannah's palm with her thumb and forefinger, as though afraid to smudge it with her fingerprints. "That is exactly what it is. How on earth did you ever come to possess such a thing?"

"I . . . took it. By accident."

"From where?" Madame Pomeroy asked.

"The Archer Museum."

"That is not where it belongs." Madame Pomeroy handed the fragment to Yakov, who slipped it inside his robes. "You know, when I took you on as my attendant, Yakov said you would one day offer me something of great worth. He saw it, the way he sees things, and I have learned to trust him. Thank you for the gift, child."

"You're welcome."

"And thank you for telling me the truth about your father and my necklace. You have no idea how much it means to me to understand why you did what you did. I sincerely hope your father's health continues to improve." And then she turned to Giuseppe. "You have a green violin, young man. Not too many of those out there in the wide, wide world."

Giuseppe adjusted the case on his back. "No. I don't suppose there are."

"Are all of you children walking around with legends in your pockets? Frederick?"

"Not anymore," Frederick said. Hannah and Giuseppe laughed.

"A green violin." Madame Pomeroy's voice became serious. "May I see it?"

Giuseppe felt reluctant, but slipped the case from his shoulder. He snapped the latches and pulled the instrument from the case. The wooden neck felt so right in his hand, like a living thing that knew him and welcomed his touch.

Madame Pomeroy sighed, and then in a hushed voice she said, "Giuseppe, would you allow me to buy that instrument from you?"

Giuseppe took a step away from her. Buy his green violin? What amount could he ask for? The instrument was priceless to him. But if he asked for enough, he would be able to buy a boat ticket for Pietro. "I don't know," he said.

"What plans do you have for it?" Madame Pomeroy asked with a determined curiosity.

Giuseppe looked at the ground at Madame Pomeroy's feet. "Play it for my family, I suppose. And for myself."

"Do you play well?"

"He has a gift, Madame," Hannah said. "It's like magic."

"I see." Madame Pomeroy laid a finger on her cheek, and held it there while she appeared to think something over. "Instead of playing for change on the street," she finally said, "how would you like to play for a king?"

"A king, ma'am?" Giuseppe said.

"Kings, actually. And queens. And emperors. And the finest musicians and composers in the world."

"I don't understand."

"I am leaving tonight on a journey across the ocean. Come with me, and play your instrument throughout the royal courts of the Old Country."

Giuseppe thought about it, but not for long. "There's only one place I want to go, ma'am, and that's home."

"Italy?" Madame Pomeroy asked.

"Yes, ma'am."

"That is where I had originally planned to go as well. But circumstances have demanded a more indirect route. Come with me, and in a short time you will see your Italy again. I promise you."

"No offense, ma'am, but I can buy my own ticket."

"Actually," the reverend said, "you can't, Giuseppe. A part of this new law means the city will be stepping in to handle the welfare of the buskers. I'm afraid no one will be permitted to leave the city until we have sorted things out. Eventually we may find a way to send the children home, but until then . . ."

"Could he leave with me?" Madame Pomeroy asked.

The reverend appeared to think about that. "If you'd be willing to sign as his guardian, I suppose he could."

"Then, we shall take care of that in the morning before my steamer leaves." She turned to Giuseppe. "If that is what you wish."

Giuseppe looked this strange woman over. Her eyes seemed to be hiding things, but not malicious things. Just secrets. But Hannah had trusted her, and something about Madame Pomeroy's manner told him that he could trust her, too. And Yakov had already risked his life to save Giuseppe's. With what the reverend had said, this might be his only chance.

But he stopped. "What about Pietro?"

Everyone in the room turned their eyes on the small boy standing in their shadows. He swallowed and inched closer to Giuseppe.

"I will look after him," Reverend Grey said. He went to Pietro and wrapped a sheltering arm around his little shoulder. "Personally."

"And Ferro and Alfeo?" Giuseppe asked.

"I will look after all of Stephano's boys until we can find them homes."

That was enough for Giuseppe. He met Madame Pomeroy's secretive eyes. "I'll come with you."

The next morning, Giuseppe stood with Pietro in the clockmaker's shop. He had come back for his old fiddle, while Hannah and Frederick had gone with Madame Pomeroy and Yakov to fetch her trunks from the hotel. Reverend Grey had gone for the police, and none of them wanted to be there when they arrived.

"You can't go," Pietro said in Italian.

"You'll be fine. The reverend is a good man. He'll protect you."

"I want to go with you."

"I wish you could." Giuseppe looked down at the old fiddle. It seemed unnecessary to hold on to it when he had the green violin, but it felt like a betrayal to leave it behind. Like abandoning an old friend. He needed to make sure it was cared for. "You take this," he said, and handed it to Pietro.

"But it is yours."

"I want you to play it."

Pietro accepted the instrument, breathing out slowly. "Thank you."

Giuseppe patted him on the back. "You head on down to the Old Rock Church now."

Pietro nodded, eyes on his shoes.

"Thank the reverend again for me."

"I will."

A sudden surge of affection swelled up inside Giuseppe's chest. "Come here," he said, and pulled the little boy into a tight hug. "Good-bye, Pietro."

"Good-bye."

Pietro pulled away and started for the front door, turned back to Giuseppe for a moment, and then ran out of the shop. Giuseppe smiled, took one last look around, and stepped into the street.

His walk to the docks felt strange. His steps were no different, the cobblestones the same underfoot as they had always been, the avenues and the storefronts and pedestrians all familiar. And yet his steps were not the same, because they were his last over each spot, each corner. He was already saying good-bye to the city; the closer he drew to the docks, the more of it lay behind him, left forever.

Each corner held a memory, or at times layers of memory like cross-blown winds, tugging him in different directions. The city had become his home. He had lived here longer than he had lived in Italy. But his brother and Marietta were not here, and though he would miss the city, he missed them more. So he tried not to let himself stop, and made the trip to the docks without indulging the past that pulled on him from all sides.

Gilbert Square bustled, alive and shining in the evening light. Giuseppe took it in and waved at the hotel, the Opera House with its giant clock, the Archer Museum, at all of it and none of it in particular. He waved to the city and said good-bye.

The city responded by carrying on the way it always did, traffic moving forward uninterrupted, without slowing, as if it were trying to demonstrate its permanence and show him that it would still be there if he ever wanted to return. That promise was the best and only thing he could ask of it.

He turned toward the docks and his footsteps soon thunked hollowly on the pier. The steamship waited at the far end, dignified and patient. Giuseppe marveled at its height and breadth as he drew near. White plumes of steam already rolled from the smokestacks, as though the ship were taking deep breaths to test its lungs before diving into the sea.

Giuseppe had no possessions but the clothes he wore and the green violin over his shoulder. He found his way to the gangplank, a steep incline rising from the dock to the deck of the ship, and waited at the foot of it. Farther down the pier, longshoremen loaded crates and trunks and chests up onto the ship. Fellow passengers milled around him, wealthy men and women who appeared relaxed about the sea voyage, able to travel as they pleased. They looked down at him as though he were a rat trying to stow away. Giuseppe felt small and alone in their presence, and anxious for Madame Pomeroy to arrive. He avoided their gazes and watched the gulls circle overhead.

Some moments later, Frederick and Hannah appeared on the docks and hurried toward him.

"This is good-bye," Hannah said, coming up to him, already starting to cry. "I can't believe it."

"I've been honored to call you my friend," Frederick said.

Giuseppe looked at them both. "The best of friends."

"We'll miss you," Hannah said.

Giuseppe would miss them as well, but in a different way than he would miss the city. A city could stay the same. The same buildings. The same streets. Not forever, but for a great long while. But Frederick and Hannah would never again be the people they were right now, stand-ing on the dock, wishing him farewell. Tomorrow they would wake up and be a little bit different and a little bit different the day after that, and in no time they might become people he did not recognize. Giuseppe knew it because they were already different from when he had first met them. He knew it because he was different from when they had first met him.

He cleared his throat. "So what are you going to do to make journey-man now, Freddy?"

Frederick looked at Hannah with a smile. "I have some ideas about that."

Giuseppe let that answer suffice. "Good luck in your new position, Hannah."

"Thank you."

"There you are!" someone called behind them. They turned and saw Madame Pomeroy and Yakov approaching from the shipping offices. "Our luggage has already been loaded. The legal papers are signed, and I just secured passage for Giuseppe. Everything is in order. Are we all ready?"

Giuseppe nodded.

A little sob escaped from Hannah.

"There, there," Madame Pomeroy said, and pulled Hannah into an embrace. "Take care of yourself, child. And you too, Frederick. I will commission a clockwork piece from you yet."

"Yes, Madame," Frederick said with a bow. "I look forward to it."

Madame Pomeroy blinked and wiped at her eyes with a handkerchief. She sniffed and turned to Yakov. "Shall we?"

He nodded, and she lifted her skirts and started up the gangplank. Then the Russian turned to Hannah.

"Like a princess," he said. Then he, too, stalked up the narrow walkway, his large frame straining the railing of rope to either side.

Giuseppe watched them go, and then turned to his friends. "Goodbye," he said.

Hannah rushed to him and held him tight. She said nothing, but trembled a little before letting him go and pulling away. Frederick and he shook hands, and then Giuseppe turned and took his own first steps upward.

Madame Pomeroy was waiting for him when he reached the top and stepped onto the deck. Hannah and Frederick waved to them from the pier. They kept waving while the longshoremen raced up and down the dock, hollering and letting loose the steamship's moorings, and were waving still when the engines engaged deep beneath Giuseppe's feet, like the earth rumbling awake. And all that time he waved back, until the ship had eased far enough into the heart of the bay that he lost sight of them.

"Giuseppe?" Madame Pomeroy called. "Come." She led him up to the bow of the ship, past women with parasols, past crew members, stacked deck chairs, and lifeboats. From that forward position Giuseppe watched the waves smacking the prow, their infinite ranks stretching to the edges of the world. "What do you think of this, my boy?" Madame Pomeroy asked.

"It feels a lot different from the last time I was on a ship."

"When was that?"

"When Stephano brought me over."

Yakov dropped his gaze to the deck.

Madame Pomeroy said, "I imagine it feels quite different."

A gust of fresh breeze off the sea caught Giuseppe, the most wild and free air he had ever tasted. The ocean glittered and rolled away from them beneath a sky even more deep and vast. Giuseppe wondered how long and far it was until he would see the first shy hump of land peak over the horizon. After that, how long until he saw the hills of his own country, and would he recognize them? Would he recognize his brother and sister after all these years? Perhaps not. Not at first. But he would know them. They were his family.

He shifted the green violin on his back. When he first found it, he did not think it would help him escape. He did not think it would play at all that day he pulled it from the harbor, but it had played, and it had helped him escape. But it had not freed him.

Giuseppe had done that himself, chasing a dream and a memory of home. There on that great ship, with the wind, and the sun, and the future open wide, he pulled out the green violin. Madame Pomeroy and Yakov watched him. An audience of passengers gathered.

And Giuseppe played.

EPILOGUE

Frederick followed the Old Fort Road out to where the city thinned, the buildings shrank to houses of brick and stone, and gardens began to fill in the spaces between them. The large box he carried had proved to be a heavier burden than he had anticipated, and he stopped often to adjust his grip on its sides.

He came to a modest cottage with cedar shingles and several lilac bushes blooming in the front yard. The open gate invited him through, and he set the box on the ground before knocking on the front door.

Hannah's sister greeted him. "Frederick!" she said with an open-mouthed smile.

"Hello," Frederick said. "Is Hannah at home?"

The girl nodded. "Please, come in."

Frederick picked up the box and stepped inside the cottage. The living room and kitchen smelled of cinnamon, something baking in the oven. Hannah's father sat up in the bed they kept out here for him, so he could be with the family during the day. Frederick bowed to him. Hannah sat at a table with her other sister, heads together over an open book and a slate.

She smiled and rose when she saw Frederick. "I'm helping her with her schoolwork."

"You are a good sister," Frederick said.

"I help where I can." Hannah glanced at the box. "What's that?"

"I'll show you. Clear the table?"

Hannah nodded, one eyebrow raised in curiosity, and she and her sisters moved the slate and closed the book. Frederick set the box down just as Hannah's mother walked in with a basket on her hip, full of produce from the garden.

"I thought I heard your voice, Frederick," she said. "To what do we owe this visit?"

"Hello, ma'am." Frederick bowed. "I was just coming to show Hannah my journeyman project."

Hannah gasped. "It's finished? When is your examination?"

"Master Branch presented me to the guild this morning."

"But you didn't tell me!"

"I didn't want to worry you. Besides, I wanted to be all done with it when I showed you what I made."

"Did you pass?" Hannah's mother asked.

"Of course he passed, Mama," Hannah said. "Didn't you?"

"I did."

"So you're a journeyman now?" Hannah's mother said.

"I am."

"You could have your own shop," Hannah said.

"I could," Frederick said. "But I don't think I will for some time yet. Master Branch will need me more and more. I think I'll stay and work with him, at least for a while."

Hannah clapped her hands. "Well, show us. Show us what you made."

Frederick took a deep breath and pulled the lid from the wooden box. He cleared away the straw packaging, and lifted out the automaton that he had been working on for the last several months.

The inspiration had come from that day when Master Branch had taken him through the guildhall's exhibition room, although he had not known it at the time. Back then, Frederick had not given much thought or attention to anything that did not seem helpful to his work on the clockwork man. But after the Magnus head had been safely returned to the museum, and Frederick had time to reflect, the answer was both simple and obvious.

He set the clockwork bird on the table. It perched on a metal branch among silver blossoms and copper leaves, modeled after a songbird he had spotted in a tree at the edge of McCauley Park. Each of its individual feathers bore the evidence of Frederick's painstaking work and attention to detail. As with the guild's clockwork rooster, it had jewels for eyes, and a delicate beak.

"Oh, Frederick," Hannah said. "It's beautiful."

"I've never in my life seen anything like it," Hannah's mother said. She stepped aside as though to make sure Hannah's father had a view of the table. "Look, dear. Have you ever seen anything so remarkable?"

Hannah's father smiled.

Frederick pulled several small cards from his pocket. "These are its secret," he said. "I got the idea from a book I read, and from my work on the looms at the orphanage." He walked around the clockwork bird and inserted one of the cards into a little gap in the feathers at the base of the neck. He pressed a button on the wooden base, and the bird began to sing.

The sound filled the cottage, lilting and clear. Hannah's sisters giggled and Hannah's mother shook her head in disbelief.

"It's magic," Hannah said.

"There's more," Frederick said. "Each of these cards has a different tune. I can make as many of them as I can think of. You just swap the cards out, and the bird will sing something different. Here, Hannah. You try." He handed her one of the cards.

She shook her head. "I wouldn't dare. I'd break it."

"Well, you'd better learn," Frederick said. "I made this bird for you."

Everyone in the room fell silent. The bird sang.

"For me?" Hannah whispered.

"Here," Frederick said, and pressed one of the cards into Hannah's hand. "Try this one."

Hannah took it, but seemed reluctant and unsure.

Frederick guided her to the table. "Turn it off first." He showed her the switch. "Now, reach in there and pull the old card out. That's it. Now, slide this one in."

Hannah pushed the new card in, and breathed out slowly as she took her hand away.

"There," Frederick said. "See how easy it is? Go ahead and press the button to start it."

Hannah put her finger to the switch.

And the bird began to whistle the song Giuseppe had played on his green violin. The song Frederick's mother used to sing to him, and to the patients at the hospital. That song brought the bird to life in a way that Frederick could not explain. All the cards were made the same way. Frederick knew that. There should have been nothing different about this particular song, but there was. Hannah walked over to him, took his arm, and kissed him on the cheek, leaving a little hot tear behind.

Across the room, from his bed, Hannah's father smiled. And began to tap his toe.

ACKNOWLEDGMENTS

This novel is the result of the instruction, inspiration, and support
I have received from many people.

Rick Wilber and Sheila Williams
gave me the early encouragement I needed when I first began to write stories.

Dr. Norm Jones taught me,
and deepened my love and appreciation of history.

Lin Oliver and Stephen Mooser
founded the Society of Children's Book Writers and Illustrators,
a tremendous resource and community to which I am proud to belong.

My dedicated critique group,
Walt, Leeann, Jane, Brittany, and Carolyn,
continues to provide me with valued insight and friendship.

Members of other critique groups,
Kimball, Randy, Carrie, Lorie, and A'ra,
Duane, Carol, and Elayne,
all provided input on the first chapters.

Fellow writers,
Rebecca Barnhouse, Julie Hughes, Elena Jube, DaNae Leu, and Kate Milford,
read this book as I was writing it and each helped make it better.

Dear friends who have cheered me on:
Bret & Jenny, Beth, Patty, and Gary,
along with many of my coworkers in the Davis School District.

Martine Leavitt taught me the importance of loving my characters,
and changed my life when she introduced me to my agent.

My agent, Stephen Fraser, is a true gentleman of the business.
He has nurtured me as a writer,
and he found this book the perfect home.

Lisa Sandell, my patient editor, has shown me
what a wonderful and collaborative process the making of a book can be.
Her keen eye and judgment sharpened and refined the shape of this story.

Elizabeth B. Parisi designed the amazing cover,
and the artist, Brian Despain, brought her vision to life.
I am grateful to them, and to the entire Scholastic team
who contributed to this book.

My nephews and nieces
and the students I work with
inspire me to always write the best book I can.
I hope that I can give to them
what other authors gave to me.

My brothers and sisters, by birth or marriage,
Amy & Mitch, Sarah & Tyler, and Josh
Orin & Jo, Tyson & Chelsea, Shantry & Shez, and Alton,
have all been very supportive of me.

My wife's mother, Jacqueline,
celebrated every success, big or small.
She believed in me from the beginning,
and never doubted, even when I did.

My parents, James and Jeanne,
filled our home with books and created a place for me to dream.
I write because, as a child, they read to me.

And most important of all,
Azure.
It was she who put my first laptop in my hands ten years ago
and encouraged me to start writing again.
Without her unconditional support and sacrifice,
I would not be the writer that I am.
She is my best friend, the love of my life, and in all things, my partner.

ABOUT THE AUTHOR

Matthew J. Kirby has been making up stories since he was quite small. He was less small when he decided that he wanted to be a writer, and quite a bit larger when he finally became one. His father was a doctor in the Navy, so his family moved frequently. Matthew went to three different elementary schools and three different high schools, and he has lived in Utah, Rhode Island, Maryland, California, and Hawaii, which means that while growing up he met many people, and had many wonderful experiences.

In college, Matthew studied history and psychology, and he decided that he wanted to work with children and write stories for them. So he became a school psychologist, a job he truly enjoys. But it was while working on his history degree that Matthew stumbled upon the true story of a boy the newspapers of 1873 called Joseph. Joseph had been taken from his home in Italy and brought to New York City as a slave to play music on the streets for money. One night, he escaped from his captor and fled to Central Park, where a kind old woman took care of him. Eventually Joseph's story became well-known, and he went to court to testify against his padrone, which led to changes in the law to protect other boys like him. Joseph's bravery and strength are what inspired Matthew to write *The Clockwork Three*, his first novel.

Matthew currently lives in Utah with his wife, where he still works with children and continues to write stories for them. You can visit him at his website: www.matthewjkirby.com.